The Shadows of Osworth

by

Blake Brennan

Printed in the United States of America

First Printing, 2016

Pazzle LLC
Hershey, PA 17033

Follow Blake on Facebook:
Blake Brennan

Follow Blake on Twitter:
@bbrennanwrites

Stay Connected with Blake on the Uncharted Page:
https://blakebrennan.unchartedpage.com/

I dedicate this book and all that come after to:

    1) my wife JB for putting up with my incessant ramblings and loving me still.

    2) my son RyRy— you are the greatest blessing and the strongest motivator I could ever have.

An Intruder

A dense fog rolled over the grounds just before nightfall, hovering like a low-hanging sheet that clung to the grass. The thickness of its cloak stifled the approaching car's ascent up the rambling, sylvan driveway that had been washed out by an earlier rainstorm. The headlights strained to cast light into the ghostly mist and Carl Fisher struggled to keep his car on the gravel road that weaved into the pine forest of his estate.

Traveling through the fog was made worse by the overgrowth of needled branches that invaded Carl's path to his home. He had intended to clear the driveway of the overgrowth on several occasions, but one thing or another seemed to find a way of distracting him. He regretted letting the trees grow out, on this night of all nights. Carl thought it eerie the way the branches extended their prickly arms into his path, as if they were trying to prevent him from venturing forward.

It was a bad night to be out. Carl knew it. It wasn't his intuition or experience that told him this— though both had sounded their alarms miles before. Instead, it was Lily's constant nagging about how he had yet to fix the road from the long, sodden spring. He had eyes after all and he was certainly aware that the roads had been washed out, especially this part of the driveway.

At the end of each spring, it was typical for him to spend a full weekend filling holes in his driveway with loose gravel and sand. He just had not gotten to it this year and tonight he didn't care. Home was where he wanted to be, embraced by his leather chair and a pipe to watch the day fade away.

The porch light came on as the car pulled into the clearing in front of their multi-story Brownstone. Their house had been built by a textile merchant named James Ryder at the turn of the twentieth century and it sat back on what became Ryder's Hill. Atop the hill, their house stood among the pines that masked the grounds from above. Their home was a tower perched on the outskirts of Concord and its lofty form caused many in the town to dub the residence "The Watchtower". Carl scoffed at this moniker; to him it was his home and nothing as grand as it suggested.

"At last, we are home, darling." Carl expressed, breathing a sigh of relief.

Although he would never admit it to anyone— not even Lily —his eyes had begun to fail him and driving at night was becoming too adventurous.

"Barely, Carl. Goodness! When are you going to fix the road? And did you see those trees? They need to be trimmed." Lily fretted in her usual way.

For as long as they had been married, going on thirty-five years, Lily had grown angry with Carl only a handful of times. It was not her way to get angry. But based on her tone, he knew if he didn't fix the driveway soon, the tally of his offenses would grow.

"I'll get to it, stop worrying about it. It's getting harder to take care of all this land. I think we should get ourselves a Mexican fella,

11

like the Kelvins have. Hank swears by his guy and his yard is always pristine. Even better is that it only costs him fifty bucks and a case of beer." Carl conceded, placing the car in park and terminating the ignition.

"You poor, sweet man, I believe Hank's guy is an illegal." Lily responded with a sudden change to her tone. She unfastened her seat belt, raising the strap across her hand-knitted ivory sweater and grabbing her indigo purse, before completing her thought. "We can find someone, if you need help."

They exited the car. The gravel beneath their feet was wet and slick and it made a grinding sound as they crossed over it. Carl held his wife's boney arm and guided her along the wooden railing that led up the granite steps to their home. Lily stopped and pulled back.

"Carl, the door. It's open!"

Lily turned to her husband before retreating several steps.

The maple door hung open on its golden hinges and disappeared into the darkness of the unlit house.

"Get to the car!" Carl ordered, guiding his wife down the stairs with haste.

"What are you going to do?" Lily begged as she shuffled across the gravel behind her husband's deceptive strength.

Carl did not answer. Unlocking the car, he pressed Lily into the driver's seat, shutting the door quietly behind her and then went to the passenger side. He leaned forward into the car, opened the glove compartment and pulled out a black tubular object. He tucked the object into his coat pocket and leaned further into the car to kiss his wife on the cheek.

"What is that Carl?" She asked, wondering.

"My gun."

"Carl, no. Sit down and we'll call the police."

"No. This is our house. You may call the police, if you wish. But I am ordering you to stay in this car. Keep it locked and do not move."

"Carl, please—"

"I love you darling," Carl interrupted, closing the door behind him.

Lily watched as her husband's slim figure vanished behind the smoky veil of fog, heading towards their house and whatever lay inside. Nervousness was her disposition and watching her husband disappear into uncertainty brought out the worst scenarios in her imagination. Her husband was going to be attacked and then killed, probably by some heinous, terrifying method that involved sharp blades. After this, the intruders would come outside, find her sitting alone in the car and do God-knows-what to her. This scenario replayed itself on an endless loop inside Lily's head.

Carl Fisher stepped inside his open front door without hesitation, staying close to the wall and holding his revolver against his right thigh. Scanning the front room— a hallway leading to three other rooms —he fumbled behind his back with his free hand, slapping for the light switch. The room lit up and at once he could tell the rust-colored Persian rug in the middle of the room had been disturbed. One of the rug's edges had rolled up onto itself and the tasseled fringe was chaotically distributed. Someone was here, this was enough proof for him. He raised his revolver to shoulder height and rested his index finger on the trigger.

The disorder in the rug implied someone had been moving left to right with a slight forward motion. Carl had little trouble deciphering things like this because of his days scouting in the 101st Airborne. In one hastened, hushed motion, Carl slid through the rightmost door that led to the living room, pursuing the evidence.

Carl moved with a purpose through the unlit room, knowing the precise placement of its fixtures. He made his way to the back of

13

the room, where an open doorway continued into his study. It had been two days since the maple door separating the two rooms was removed for repairs, but he relished this as a blessing because it allowed him to move through the darkness with stealth.

The study was quiet and felt untouched. There were no toppled chairs, strewn desk drawers or carelessly flung books. The books numbered in the thousands and sat like roosting birds on one-inch thick slabs of oak that circled the room. The room was empty.

In the far corner, beneath the door that lead to the dining room, a faint orange light leaked out. The light appeared to be the flicker of a candle, at least judging from the slight manner in which it swayed back and forth.

Inching forward, Carl held his gun at chest level, his arm bent at the elbow. He took a deep breath and pushed forward, hoping any surprise he held would not be washed away behind the trickle of sound. There was a *creak* in the door and Carl's heart sank.

He threw open the door, whipping his pistol outward in front of him with a tautness in his arm that was unmistakable, undeniable. His aging eyes saw a candle lit several yards in front of him, resting on the edge of a mantle. Across the room, in the corner, a pair of denim-clad legs bent outward from the rocking chair that his son had bought him upon his retirement. In the shadows, obscured, was an intruder rocking in runic silence. The chair rocked with a sedate rhythm, clicking against the hardwood floor with an uncomfortable tempo.

Click...Click...Click... That was the only sound.

For a long moment, Carl Fisher stood speechless with his pistol pointed at the intruder's chest. The indifference of the intruder was alarming. Could he not see me? Carl wondered. He just sat there, rocking in the chair. Not worried at all.

"What's your business here?" Carl demanded, moving closer to the corner.

"Put down the gun, Carl. You know it is useless. Besides you have beautiful furniture, you might damage it," a shrill, gruff voice taunted.

At once, the voice was recognized. How could that voice be forgotten? It was a painful, heart-wrenching squeal of a voice that offered nothing but horror.

"YOU!" Carl erupted and ripped two shots from his pistol.

Two quick sparks revealed a man with black shark-like eyes and a slack face with olive-gray complexion. His skin drooped like a potato sack dangling from a hairless skull that owned only a sadistic, man-eating grin. The two smoking fractures that had ruptured the silence fell in together, into one soft, muddled sound.

"Well done, sharpshooter. Got me square in the chest. Surely, if I had a heart you would have hit it," the man threw back an elated, snide chuckle.

"Why aren't you dead? Why?" Carl asked, moving to the far corner of the room, opposite the intruder who was still rocking in the chair.

"Carl, this is a nice chair. Did Benjamin get this for you?" the man asked and then continued with aplomb. "I wouldn't have any idea considering, you know, my absence. I hear he is studying law some place far away from here? You and Lily were always excellent planners."

"If only he could have gone farther away," Carl leered to no one in particular as he searched the angled joint of the two walls behind him with his free hand. Where was it? He asked himself, feeling around the empty space.

"You won't find it there, Carl. Do you think I'm that stupid? I was surprised to see that you remained so diligent after all these years," the man sneered.

He lifted a loaded fiberglass crossbow that had resided earlier in the corner that Carl Fisher now occupied.

15

The color rushed from Carl's face and he grew cold with the realization that he was unprotected. He laughed nervously; sweat dribbling down his wrinkled forehead and thick, salt-and-pepper eyebrows.

"I will be blunt with you Carl. You know what I want. You always have. Always a persistent and resourceful bunch, you people. I promise you that the time of my leniency has passed. You had a reprieve, but no more."

"I will never give you what you want, EVER!" Carl yelled, unwittingly taking a step toward the intruder.

"This game we've played is nearing an end, Carl. You and Malcolm have deluded yourselves into thinking you ever had control, thinking you can trap me or hoping that I will disappear. That will not happen. Even after seventeen years I returned. I can't be stopped and I will no longer wait. You have two options, as I hope you know. The question you have to ask is how many more people have to die before I get what I want?"

"That's not up for debate is it, Warren? Once you get what you want, we're all dead anyway," Carl sighed as sadness filled in, once more, that well-known void buried deep in his memory.

"Yes, I know. It is just a question of how you wish to die," the man laughed in an unsettling manner, halfway between maniacal and scorching rage.

"The suffering you have carried will never be enough to satisfy me. Only when someone finds a way to kill you will there be justice!"

Carl realized that his fingers were still wrapped around the perforated-steel handle of his pistol, four shots banked in its cylinder.

"Save it. You have three days. If what was taken from me is not returned by then, people will start dying and I will start with Lily."

"You know, I have another idea!" Carl suggested, smiling through a forced grin.

"And—"

The four remaining bullets jumped from the pistol's barrel and exploded across the room. Two bullets missed their target and sunk themselves into the wall behind the rocking intruder. The remaining two struck dead aim their target, the copper jackets tearing through the intruder's fingers and into the crossbow's curved fiberglass frame. It fell from his grasp onto the scratched surface of the wooden floor.

Without hesitation, Carl had the crossbow clenched firmly in his hands. The intruder flashed into the opening to the kitchen, charging for the backdoor and for the freedom of the woods on the other side. He moved with the speed of a sprinting colt down the hillside, as if he was a floating shadow.

Carl gave chase into the kitchen as quick as he could, but the intruder's movements were swifter and more accelerated than his own. There was little time left to act. Carl took aim at the backdoor as it opened— aiming for the door itself— and just as the intruder's hand was about to eclipse Carl's target, the crossbow's taut string went loose and it fired.

There was a whine as the bowstring tumbled and the arrow twisted through the air with a hiss. A resounding thud followed as the whetted steel tip bore an inch of its shaft into the wooden door, narrowly missing the eclipsing hand of the intruder, who disappeared outside into the blackness of the night. All that remained was the soft yellow moonlight projecting its eerie specter onto the curtain of fog that filled in the void where the intruder had decamped.

The adrenaline coursed through Carl's veins and he grew angry with his misfire. An inch lower and this all could have been over, he was certain of it. Then he thought of Lily, who sat outside unaware of what had just happened. He burst into an all-out sprint from his stance, moving through the house a man with panic pressing

17

against his lungs. Lily was alone and *Warren had returned*. Warren! The curse of his family! All that he had done— and could do —forced Carl's old body to move as if he were decades younger. Exiting his home, he moved towards Lily and towards the hope that she was alright.

Lily saw her husband dashing down the porch. He appeared shaken, exasperated by something still unknown. She went to open the door and as she did, a shadow slide by her into the clearing between Carl and herself. The motion light flared to life and there standing between them was her greatest nightmare that not even the heavy fog could obscure.

The car door flew open, but not behind her own force. Lily sat, paralyzed by fear, as cold shark-like eyes came at her with murderous pleasure.

"Hello, Lily! It's been a while." Warren indulged, tossing back a throaty crow. "My you've aged."

Carl rushed forward, his breath laboring from his hurriedness. He grabbed for the hairless orb bobbing inches away from his wife. It felt pleated in his hands like a rubbery fabric that had been stretched over a smooth ball of frosted iron. It felt nothing like a human skull. As his fingers dug into it, the most bizarre sensation fell over him as though he had been thrown into the frigid nadirs of space.

Warren tossed his head back with a jerk, sending Carl crumpling to the ground.

"Carl, you're starting to annoy me." Warren admitted, unaffected by Carl's attempt at harm. Warren turned towards the heap on the ground, his fingers bent like talons as if he was prepared to rip into him. "Any fight you have inside of you, keep it. I gave you three days and time is ticking."

Paying little attention to Warren's words, Carl rose to his knees and crawled to Lily, never looking away from the man coming at his wife. Carl found Lily sallow and shocked. But alive. She was alive and that was all that mattered. He clutched her in a loving embrace and shielded her from the sight of Warren and the painful memory that came from seeing the vile fervor of his man-eating smile. That smile hadn't changed. It existed just as it did that one fate-filled day so long ago; the day all their lives had been irreparably broken and dragged through a hell that could never have been imagined.

Lily forced out a shaky whisper, but it came out so weak and frail that Carl could not understand what she had said. He glanced down at her, taking his eyes off of Warren for a moment, but said nothing. He watched over her with a husband's care, blanketing her with his wide shoulders that made obvious his willingness to fight for her, to protect her from the monster that was in their presence. Carl raised his eyes back to Warren, but he was gone.

"He's gone. You don't need to be scared anymore," Carl assured his wife in a kind voice as he kneeled and pulled her sideways toward him; though he knew there was much to be scared of. He tried to convince himself that they would be okay as long as they fulfilled his demands... but such demands they were. How could anyone fill such demands?

"Carl, he came! After all this time, he is still out there. Please tell me he didn't come for him? Please!" Lily wept frantically as tears trembled down the weathered contours of her erudite face.

"I wish I could, darling. I wish I could!" Carl stuttered, pressing his wife's soft and graying head against his shoulder.

Lily pulled away from Carl with an intense burst of strength and in a quite scary, otherworldly voice that beamed of defiance, she roared through her tears, "he will not have my son"

Carl recoiled, surprised by the deceptive force that radiated from his normally sweet and reserved Lily. It was hard for him to see the jaded, young brown-haired girl who had thirty-eight years before

19

sacrificed the majority of her youth and rebuffed countless courtships from other men, to wait his return home from Vietnam. That woman did not reside inside Lily Fisher at this moment. Instead, Carl saw in his wife a fire that he had seen only once before— the day it all began.

"Warren will never have Benjamin, I promise you my love." Carl pledged to her and gave her a tender kiss on her forehead. In his head, Carl prayed that this was true.

The Impetus

Two Months Earlier

"Profitability is the essence of capitalism. Without it, who are we? China, that's who and the world does not look slanted to me," Alexander Fitzgerald III spoke through forceful gulps of his steaming latte, the tawny-colored overcoat he wore tossing behind him in the late-afternoon breeze. "It's the American way, Ben. To each their own. Survival of the fittest. Let the weak perish and the strong inherit the Earth."

He had a way when he spoke. The words cracked off his tongue like the lashing of a whip, snapping with conviction and vigor and even for me it was easy to see the potential lawyer in him. Sure, everything he was actually saying was complete and utter bullshit, but how he said it made it a special kind of bullshit. This type of bullshit was what a privileged person had deluded themselves into believing was reality and that was, as an act of great kindness, imparted on folks of lesser means like some kind of ancient riddle that had finally been decoded.

"Once more, Alex, you have failed to understand the basic concept of a utilitarian state. The best choice to be made is the one that gives the greatest benefit to the most people. Profit-maximizing firms care about shareholder equity and dividends, acquisitions and bonuses. They are soulless vultures that pull the guts from society one dollar at a time. They ask 'how much more of someone's paycheck can we siphon off? How many more minutes can we flash our shitty product in front of these pathetic mouth-breathers before they have dreams about it?' It is simple mathematics. The more a system is constrained, the greater the likelihood of system failure. Yea, it seems that capitalism is working, but I'm not impressed," I rebutted, raising my hands as if I was dumbfounded by his lack of understanding, which I was. The guy was smart, but stubbornly stupid all at the same time.

"This is America. We have the world's largest economy. The world's greatest education system. The world's most powerful military. All of this was founded on American principles and you, with your liberal ideals, want nothing more than to strip it away in favor of some welfare program. I am sorry, but I cannot tolerate such acts of treason." Alex slammed back, stopping his stride to look me square in the face, which exuded an astonishment and anguish, no doubt caused by my ideals. Apparently, I had offended him with my words against capitalism. I could only guess how much longer it would be before the "S"-word was used.

I stopped my departure from campus to meet his stare, which I could not do without laughing. On an organic, human level I felt that despite our disputes, we were the same in a way, naturally equal at the core, just a horse of a different color. I had thought us two young men forged by our parents' ideals with wishes of betterment and greatness for ourselves, but as I stared down at him, I was overcome by the inexplicable desire to poke him in his offensively large nose. The whole matter had become too humorous.

"Yes sir, I'm a modern day Benedict Arnold! Alex, you truly misunderstand me. There is a difference between loving your country and sitting back, watching her travel across a bridge set for demolition. America is growing old and its best days are behind it. Failing to accept this is why we have politicians. Don't you too fall for the myth of American exceptionalism. Look at the facts— the god-damn facts, man! Name one industry that America is considered the world leader? The ones that come to mind are fast food, prisons, technology and war. We feed you poison with a smile and steal our citizen's freedom while proclaiming to be the freest nation on the planet. We sell you devices that can track your every movement and remove any semblance of privacy or worse yet, we kill and indebt our children over fictitious fights for freedom while a select few become ungodly rich at their expense. Are you kidding me? These are not things to be proud of. The fools on the Hill spend their days foraging for votes, hollering from their pulpits about the virtue of their misled views. Yet, the whole time, they spend with such frivolity and lack of care that there is no focus or concerted effort to solve any real problems. Legislating has become a giant game of roulette where the House always wins." I paused, hyperventilating from my relentless negation and continued.

"Most people in this country leave college with a subpar education, little job prospects and enough debt to have been a mortgage. We are looking up at other countries in science and engineering. We offer no solutions to the raping of the environment that we facilitate more than almost all other countries. I argue for changes in our country because this empire has grown weak and bloated and is heading for a cliff. Still, you stand here, staring me down and beating the drum of yesteryear, completely dismissive of everything that is evolving before your own eyes."

My heart was a cannon in my chest and it was exploding with emotion. I should have stopped myself because I knew the silver-spooned trust baby would never make efforts to solve any real problem.

He refused to back down.

"You and your… what did you call it…utilitarian state? Just a fancy word for socialism, no doubt. "

There it was! The S-word. I laughed aloud as he kept mumbling until I caught up.

"What next, Ben? Hmmm? Would you like the government to tell us what to eat, or where to sleep. How about what cars to drive or where to work? How great it would be if we could wake up tomorrow and the rest of our lives were dictated to us, defined by the wishes of cronies and powermen who don't even know our names. They just know us by a number on a computer screen. Let's remove incentive and everything will be okay. These ideas are pure madness. It is craziness. The less government intrudes, the more society benefits," his voice hammered back, the veins in his neck pulsating with every emphatic cacophony.

"They already do tell us what to eat and where to sleep. Try sleeping in your car on Massachusetts Avenue and see if the cops don't tell you to move. Furthermore, we are not as free you may think and it is absurd to suggest the government can't be beneficial. Government can work, but only if we address the problems of today… not yesterday. We have no choice but to change. But the day we agree on this is the day—"

"Boys…goodness. You do know class ended fifteen minutes ago, right? I feel like I need to get a cattle prod or something," a sweet voice cut in from behind us and then added, "but if you guys really want to debate something, how about debating which one of you is going to buy me a drink?"

"Oh…hey Megan," I said, knowing the familiar kindness in her voice. I turned around and glanced down onto her soft, pretty face before retiring my gaze onto the neighborhood. "How are you?"

"Exhausted, stressed out and in serious need of something fruity and loaded with Tequila." She conceded in earnest as she caught up to Alex and me, her high-heels clacking against the pavement as she did. With her company the argument between Alex and I was over, forgotten by the lure of a beautiful woman. We all started walking together, heading towards the metro.

Megan had glistening auburn hair that fell a few inches below her ears and it was tossing in the light spring breeze. She was shorter than most twenty-something women; a fact embellished by the business-clad women exiting the surrounding office buildings, heading home or to wherever in search of a few magical hours to erase another day at the office. Each of these women towered above Megan's minute stature with considerable ease and resulted in an amusing image that popped into my head. In my mind was the image of Megan at some inevitable point in the future when she would be addressing a judge for the first time and would find herself standing too close to the bench that she disappeared beneath it. Of course, this hypothetical future judge would be some older, overweight Caucasian male suffering from nearsightedness and who, after realizing the pygmy-sized lawyer before him had vanished beneath his bench, would raise his plump hindquarters from his leather chair and whisper something wise and humorous to the fledgling lawyer. This image made me smile because it was so vivid and endearing in my thoughts.

"Why are you so stressed? It's not like this is Georgetown Law or anything." I asked, taking note of how amazing she looked in the short-sleeved lavender blouse and shin-high black skirt that massaged her body. I walked in awe as I watched her strut in two-inch high heels, baffled at how she didn't snap one of her sleek and athletic ankles. This was something that I never could wrap my head around. Why did women choose to wear such glorified stilts, risking fracture on every rogue crack or errant step? Sure, a woman with the proper assets could look amazing in them, but the risk seemed too great. Then again, I had never worn heels and maybe was exaggerating their difficulty.

"Professor Daric just assigned our property final and scheduled it for the exact same day as our torts exam. I mean what an asshole— Okay, that's the lack of alcohol talking. Forgive me!"

"That is unfortunate. Benjamin and I took Carson's property course. It was a take-home," Alex sympathized, though it sounded almost like he was holding back laughter. I guess it was the best he could do with his normal air of contention. "Then again, Dirac does have the reputation of being a major hard-ass," Alex added, before we stopped to wait for the crosswalk sign to flash 'WALK'.

We crossed New Jersey Avenue onto F Street.

"You know those Harvard types." I interjected with laughter.

Megan paused, thinking and then asked, "Alex, didn't you go to Harvard?"

"Yes Megan, Alex did go to Harvard. Us lesser mortals must remember this when we are in his presence!"

"Where was it that you went, Benjamin…FU?" Alex spoke, placing on abusively strong inflection on the "FU" portion of his remark.

I chuckled. "Fordham University, yep. Good ol' FU!"

Megan laughed.

"My good pal Ben was the big man on campus. Played football, graduated with honors in math. I mean when I first met the bastard I figured he majored in beer and babes!" Alex joked. "To my surprise, he actually had a brain."

I responded with a crooked grin and a not-so-subtle slap on the back.

"Is that true?" Megan asked.

"Well, I did play football on scholarship and yes I was a math major, but I can assure you that the beer and babes part is only half true!"

"Oh yea? Which half?" Megan giggled.

"Yea, Ben. Which half?" Alex piped in with a goading smile.

"The mathematician in me sees this as an unsolvable problem, so the lawyer in me pleads the fifth!" I replied in jest.

I saw in Alex's eyes a flare of disdain by my response.

"Well, why you were off trying to prove the Riemann hypothesis or whatever, I was doing something practical— earning my MBA —from Harvard." Alex boasted.

Megan looked at me, somewhat annoyed by Alex's comment. I shook my head knowingly and made an odd squinting gesture as if to say without saying it, 'yes, I know he's an asshole'. This type of result was a frequent end to many of Alexander Fitzgerald III's conversations and it was a phenomenon I had seen with great regularity since befriending him. The outcome was often the same: someone would say something, typically something innocuous and meant for amiable conversing, but then Alex would respond with some blunt, offensive statement that was filled with a brutality so forceful that the other person would freeze in slacked-jawed befuddlement.

I dubbed these ruthless gems— A-BOMBs —because that is what they were— weapons of mass discussion— and when used, they would hasten the end of any conversation. From what I could surmise in the short six months since having met him, Alex did not have any malicious intent in his criticisms. Instead, it seemed that he had never mastered that art of tact and the results were often incendiary assaults on a hapless, unsuspecting individual who had made the unfortunate decision of talking to him. Sometimes the event was stressful and cringe-worthy, as it was with Megan because the person on the receiving end just didn't deserve it. But in some rare instances, it was an absolute pleasure to watch Alex drop an A-BOMB on someone more annoying than himself and witness a scrunched-up face that held back the floodworks.

"Megan, don't let Alex get to you. His parents kept him locked in their vault with all that Harvard money. Just another asset, I guess." I quipped.

"I'm not bothered. I'm just not used to it yet. Alex is a hard-charging Type-A personality- he and everyone else here."

"But I am an exception, I went to Harvard!" Alex chimed in with a shallow laugh "Okay, that one was a joke."

Megan and I forced soft laughs. Even when it came out as unnatural, Megan's laugh was lyrical, smooth and infectious with repetitive waves of giddiness. I stared at her as the three of us moved into the shadows of the buildings on F-street.

"Fordham? That's a catholic university, right? Are you catholic, Benjamin?" Megan asked, sounding surprised.

"Well, I was when I was admitted, but it's complicated. I'm an atheist now."

There was a pause— that inevitable pause that someone of faith feels inclined to give a non-believer, as if they are praying for their absolution.

"How come?" She questioned, moving towards me and out of the way from an oncoming pedestrian. Her hair lifted into the air as she avoided the passerby and with it, a blissful aroma of strawberries and roses caressed my face. It was nice.

"My views evolved, but I wouldn't want to offend you with my opinions should you be a believer," I replied, looking away from her gaze as my stomach teetered with a growing sense of intrigue and desire.

"I do believe in God, but that does not mean that I am close-minded. I enjoy hearing other people's thoughts. It creates excitement and discussion. Besides, I love a good debate."

"Well, we can continue this discussion over a couple fruity, umbrella drinks—Margaritas maybe?"

"Ugh! Typical liberal, even your libations are spineless," Alex cracked in his usual offensive-yet-joking tone.

"Apologies friend, but whiskey is the drink of the corrupt and dishonest. I try to keep my intake to a minimal. No doubt it's the drink of D.C." I fired back, a crooked smirk rising on my face. Sometimes I wanted to punch him; other times he was a stand-up guy.

Megan looked at us both with a whimsical confusion and blurted out, "why are you two friends? You are always at each other about something. It is exhausting!"

Alex and I looked at her, then at each other and laughed.

"We may often disagree—" I started.

"—and we may think the other person's opinions are ridiculous—" Alex continued.

"—which they usually are!"

Alex paused, "but I think we respect each other as individuals, despite the differences in our values. If people can't debate matters that influence their existence, what is the point of anything?"

"Alex that was stated with an Ivy-league excellence and for once I agree with you."

"Gah! I am in need of a drink now more than ever. Ben, let's go," Megan agreed, though sounding more exhausted than interested in me. The three of us continued up F Street, darkness gaining on the departing daylight.

"It'll be fun! Spending Friday night with a gorgeous woman, discussing the merits of religion or whatever over a couple of drinks...well, let's just say that beats what I had planned. Sitting in my underwear with a bowl of Lo Mein, an open textbook and the Sox-Mariner's game on the TV is not nearly as fun." I replied in earnest.

There was a brief silence between the three of us. Then, to my embarrassment, it was broken.

"So, Ben you think I'm gorgeous?" Megan giggled, her jade eyes playing with me, my face flushing from my absentminded confession.

"Rutt-Roo!" Alex exclaimed in a mock Scooby-Doo voice, before turning his head away to snicker.

"Yes Megan, you're a gorgeous woman. As if you didn't already know this. Don't hold it against me." I stammered with a nervous twinge. Though my thoughts moved elsewhere to a place where I felt Megan's warm, silky lips against my own, her soft breasts pressed against my stomach, our bodies entangled in passion. I shook the thought from my head as if it were a wasp landing on my pale-white scalp. It was difficult to fight this lustful image, but after a few moments, it faded.

"Well, I usually need to work for it— show the right amount of skin, make eye contact for a second, then glance away, pretend to lack interest. You know, the Single Woman's Playbook! But hell, you went right at it. Blunt, to the point. I like that!" She smiled up at me.

I was quiet for a moment, not sure of what to say. I forced a smirk and then uttered like a muttonhead, "you can show me a boob if you want to!"

Moron, I thought to myself. I couldn't comprehend how those words fumbled past my lips, out my mouth and into the air as a liberated thought. It was as if there were two people inside of me, the nice guy and the Moron, each fighting for attention. The nice guy inside of me— the part of me who found my response inappropriate and offensive —cringed and wanted to kick the Moron in his testicles. The Moron, well, he was like most twenty-two year old males, a sex-craved mindless oaf fixated on seeing tits. I recovered and corrected my lewdness with an apology and an offer to take her to JayJay's.

JayJay's was a classic Irish pub built from oak timbers hand-cut in a Dublin lumberyard and fitted on-site six blocks from the Georgetown Law campus. To my surprise, Megan took little offense by my chauvinism and agreed to accompany me to JayJay's. It had been a while since I felt polarized by a woman like I was with her and in all honesty, it startled me. I was a grown man— well, as grown as a boy of twenty-two could be — and feeling this way was weird, like stumbling onto an abandoned sack of cash, overfilled with more money than one would ever need. You see the sack lying there, free from any obvious ownership and all you want to do is to snatch it up, clutch it close and run to a place only you know about. Yet, there is that lingering sense that keeps you from doing it. That sense that happiness is not that easy. That luck can't be that simple. A knowing sense that once you pick up this sack, reality solidifies into something material, something absolute that chases you like a tireless bloodhound. But sometimes, you know this and you decide to take the money anyway. You take it and run and never stop to listen to the footsteps chasing you. This was how Megan made me feel.

"So Alex," I whispered in his direction, "you know that threes a crowd, right? No need for a wingman. You get me?" The three of us had come to the last building on F Street, the

31

emerald and gold lettering of JayJay's electric sign was visible, jutting into the narrow alley that ran parallel to North Capital Street.

From where we stood, I saw what looked like a family of three enter the pub through the heavy oak front doors. The father, a broad man with thick arms ripping out from a black sleeveless shirt and a clean shine to his scalp, was carrying a young girl in the crux of his elbow. The girl was small, cute and maybe four or five years old. She was dressed in a pink windbreaker jacket and white tights and she had pig-tails that flopped back and forth as her father carried her into the pub. A rail-thin woman in faded jeans and stuffed into a tight pink T-shirt followed closely behind.

"Yes captain, I got you," he conceded to me in a whisper and then spoke aloud, "Megan. Benjamin. I wish to take no part in the revelry you two have consented to. I am sorry, but girly drinks and gushing on one another...well, that sounds insufferable. I'm going to call it an evening."

"Good night Alex," Megan said, lowering her head, a small knowing smile stretched across her cherry colored lips. She flashed a subtle flirty glance towards me.

"Night, Alex. Give me a call tomorrow... in the afternoon," I responded. I made sure to emphasize that last part, just in case the night turned out better than expected. Hopefully, it would!

"I will," he replied and then he turned up Massachusetts Street and disappeared into the rapidly obscuring veil of darkness. The back of his tawny-colored overcoat tossed behind him under the soft yellow glow cast by the streetlamps.

Head Over Heels

We entered JayJays through the front oak door and were greeted with an old-world image of brass-riveted leather-backed booths made from aged oak. The tabletops were weathered and the place smelled like the mix between a library and smoke shop.

A young colored girl, who looked eighteen or nineteen years old, welcomed us. Not old enough to be drinking legally, but despite this observation, she sipped from a pint glass filled with porter. She smiled and seated us in a booth right next to the bar. The menus she handed us had a thin layer of grease covering their plastic sleeves, which made me think about how poor a place like this might have been for a first date— if it was a date. Megan didn't seem to mind though. At the bar, a white-haired man stood in a sweat-stained light blue T-shirt and a raggedy white apron smeared brown from fryer grease. He poured pints of stout into grimy glasses and slid them down the crowded bar top. The scowl on his face was unfriendly, but wise. Men in leather jackets and ripped jeans lined the bar top, sitting on rickety stools. These men looked like strange henchmen just waiting for the misanthropic barkeep to bark out an order for them to stomp someone. They made me nervous. Their toothless smiles and cross-bone tattoos told me that they had a different way at looking at life and for my safety, it would be best to respect it from a distance.

"Ye guyz red-ee to orduh," a waiter as miserable in appearance as the barkeep asked us in a poor New York accent.

"You ready?" I asked looking across the small table to Megan.

"Honestly, I am not very hungry right now. How about a Bahama Mama and some water?"

"And yuze?"

"I'll have a Bahama Mama just like the pretty lady."

"You kidden me?" The waiter laughed in amazement, staring down at me. "Whateva!" He turned and left.

"Don't worry, I get that response often." I joked.

"I bet!" Megan laughed. "You don't look like the kind of guy that likes frilly drinks."

"I'm not really, I'm a beer drinker. But attach a pretty face to a frilly drink and I can be quite flexible."

Megan smiled and looked away for a moment.

"So what makes you decide to go on an impromptu date with someone that you have had like three conversations with?" I asked, hoping to gauge her level of interest in me. I figured that by her agreeing, there was some mutual attraction. Or was this not a date? I feared this could have been one of those dreaded social situations where one person— definitely me —thought it was a date and the other did not.

"The free alcohol." She replied deadpan.

"Ouch! So it wasn't my chiseled good-looks or my witty banter?" I smiled.

"They may have helped." She smiled. "But it was mainly the free booze."

"At least you said yes," I replied, knowing by the sparkle in her smile that she was enjoying herself. "What made you want to be a lawyer and put up with all this— well for the lack of a better word— bullshit?"

She hesitated. Her face innocent in beauty, morphed from jovial to focused and sincere. The narrowing gaze of her stunning eyes cast a new glow upon her. "My dad. He is the reason I put up with the frustration and stress of it. He passed away two years ago."

I wanted to hit rewind and stop myself from asking that question. Listening to other people talk about people they've lost, to hear them talk about death, made me feel trapped. Trapped in a way like nothing I could say would deflate the awkwardness or erase the pain in the other person.

"I'm so sorry to hear that. I can't imagine the pain that must have caused you," I replied, expressing the true heartbreak I felt for her. "How did it happen, if I may ask?"

She paused, looking into my eyes. A moment passed before she spoke.

"It was the April before my college graduation. I went home that year for Easter. Grant—my brother —had taken some time and came up from Nevada. It was nice, you know, having the whole family together. That hadn't happened for ages. We did as we always did, as if nothing had ever changed. We went to Easter Mass and in the afternoon, the rest of the family came over. I hadn't seen my Grandparents since that summer, so it was nice to have everyone over for dinner. It felt like I was a little girl again. But I should have sensed something was wrong. My dad was always happy-go-lucky... he never complained. He took each day as if it were to be cherished, a blessing from somewhere magical.

35

"Anyway, he was sitting alone in his study, smoking his tobacco pipe in this old recliner, Dad's chair— he always did that. Every night, like clockwork, he would sit in that raggedy old recliner and smoke his pipe. Anyway, I went to give him a hug and he said something to me that I will never forget. He said, 'Megan, I don't tell you enough how proud I am of you. Not because of all that you will accomplish or all the achievements you have earned, but because you lead with your mind and you follow your heart. Cherish this pursuit and sharpen it, never sacrifice who you are for another. I love you, Sweetheart.'. I went back to school the next morning and he died sitting in that same chair later that day. He told us that his cancer was in remission, but he knew the truth. So the final bit of fatherly advice my dad gave me is why I am here— something in my heart has guided me to this point. Call it fate, call it whatever, I just know this is where I am supposed to be."

I paused, stuck in both sorrow and amazement and then replied, "you are where you belong then. For what it's worth, I am sorry about your dad, but I am glad you are here. I must admit that my reasons for coming to law school are nowhere near as altruistic as your own. For starters, I thought becoming a lawyer would be more fun than other pursuits I had open to me. I played with the idea of getting my doctorate, but I wasn't too passionate about it. It would have taken longer than my patience would have allowed. I thought about working, but I wasn't ready. I guess I am still trying to figure out my life."

The ruby red liquid of our drinks sloshed against the walls of their glasses as the waiter placed them on the table. In the first few sips, the solemn atmosphere perpetuated by a single question lifted and what remained was the drunken cloud of revelry. Alcohol was funny that way. It was like liquid chattiness, a few sips and before you realized it, words flew from your mouth as if they were riding a rhythmic river— though the words that actually came out may not have sounded to others as they did to yourself.

The night marched on and I was learning more about Megan with each passing moment. I learned her last name, which for all of its importance is something that is often discarded when you first meet someone. Megan Ylva Nilson, that was her full name and she was of Scandinavian descent and for the life of me I could not pronounce her middle name. She told me of her great grandfather, Arvid, and how he immigrated to America at the age of twenty-two—the same age as me —from his native Norway with aspirations of being a fisherman in Gloucester. It turned out that life had other plans.

Instead of mastering the northern sea and pillaging it for its piscine plunder, Arvid met Megan's great grandmother Edda, a first-generation German-American, while at port in Norfolk, Virginia. Arvid then did what most love-bitten men do, he decided love conquered all and soon departed his bachelor lifestyle in New England for a chance at happiness. A year later, he and Edda wed and soon after that, they started the Nilson family that would one-day lead to the beautiful woman sitting across from me. Life was a giant Plinko game it seemed.

Her favorite color was purple and her one dream in life was to help at least one person live better because of her actions, which I thought was an awesome ambition for someone to have. She had an addictive laugh that was loud and infectious, but nerdy in a way. She was a year older than I was and had spent most of the year after her father's death sailing the Caribbean, hopping from island to island.

When I heard her say she spent almost a year sailing the Caribbean, I didn't believe her. I mean, she was tiny and while I knew nothing at all about sailing, I assured myself that someone of Megan's stature couldn't possibly perform the necessary tasks by herself. When I suggested as much, she put me in my place by recounting her nautical tales and beating me over the head with words that were clearly made-up and fictional. Words like *daggerboard, halyard, leeward*. I nodded politely and pretended to follow her gibberish. The one thing that I believed I comprehended and was confident that I could answer should Megan choose to quiz me later in the evening was that she had used a thirty-foot Cutter as her vessel.

Her passion for sailing was clear as I listened to her recollect. Of what I could surmise through all the nautical jargon was that when she was seven, her and her brother, Grant, had learned to sail off the coast of Virginia with their father and it had grown to an annual ritual— every third Sunday of every June— Father's Day. When they were both old enough, Megan and Grant spent the day crewing the ship and sailing their parents to nearby islands, like those off the Carolinas. At first, Megan and Grant required supervision from their Dad to get the ship seaworthy, but then after repeated effort, they become little sailors themselves. I found the whole thing exotic, exciting. The only water-going vessel I had ever steered was a boogie board at York Beach in Maine.

On hearing the breadth of her sailing experience, I realized I was being a chauvinist by thinking her incapable. Undoubtedly, she was far more capable than I had imagined, but I was still curious about the whole island hopping thing. Having been to Nassau once myself, I felt there had to be a great sense of danger in roaming the waters solo, especially for a young woman. Even I would have felt uncomfortable among the mob of moochers on the streets of Nassau. Megan, to my surprise, thought this concern to be sweet, but she assured me that she spent little time in port, preferring the solitude and chaos of the open sea.

At the end of the evening, after she had downed more alcohol than it seemed a tiny woman could possibly down, she started to teeter in her seat and giggle without a conscience, her body swaying like a buoy in open water. I knew at this point I had to get her home and I was fortunate that my sobriety was much less in question.

We left JayJay's at half-past eleven. The streets were quieter than they were when we had left Georgetown, but they were still alive. After all, it was Washington, D.C., nothing slept in this town.

Megan clung to me, wrapping her thin arms around my waist and rested her head against my shoulder. Together we stumbled our way down First Street towards Union Street. As we moved, I could feel her hand sliding smoothly down my stomach to the waistline of my pants. Her hand rested just beneath my navel, pressed against my abdomen as if I were pregnant and she was trying to feel the baby kick. The gesture seemed inspired by the alcohol, but I could not determine if it was from sexual arousal or a pending episode of narcolepsy. I knew where my mind was headed and I tried to force a detour by looking up into the night sky. My attraction to her was becoming unshakeable with each step we took. There was a tinge of pungent sweetness from the alcohol on her breath and I could not help but want a taste.

The sex-craving animal that was trapped inside my body, The Moron as I had grown to call him, had grown stiff with anticipation. The more she caressed my body, the more my throat grew heavy and my knees wobbled. But I respected her and I knew that my feelings for her were becoming greater than the lust that was beginning to fill my pants. So I forced myself to think of sad and terrible things like finding a fluffy puppy floating dead in a sewer. The image worked better than any cold shower could have, but the image caused me great sadness because I thought of Hamilton, my own puppy from back home, drowning in a sewer. He died years ago, but the image still tugged at my heartstrings. You never forgot your first pet.

We waited on the cement platform for the Red Line to arrive. Fifty or more people littered the same platform, many younger like Megan and I. It seemed a rite of passage for the twentysomethings of D.C to loiter and party on the weekends. From Monday morning to closing time on Friday, we were all business, working hard to make a successful life out of what opportunities we had been given. You could feel it in the air every weekday morning as you stepped off the Metro and onto the sidewalks. Thousands of professionals bounced from one building to the next, their expensive shoes clicking and clacking against the rough, gum-stained pavement as the sun reflected just a sliver of itself off the windows that towered to the sky. In a word, it was *power*. But that was during the workweek. Once the clock struck five on a Friday, pubs and bars were flooded with people wanting to drink away their stress, which has always been the wife of power.

Megan and I were leaning against a concrete barrier when one of the last scheduled Red lines pulled up. Moments prior, I had taken her phone and programmed my number in it. I didn't believe her current state afforded her the necessary dexterity to grip the phone and nimbly press-in the correct digits. This way I knew it was correct, but it also gave me a chance to steal a glimpse of the other numbers she had saved. She had an extensive phone book and many of the numbers belonged to people with guy names. I didn't like that. In fact, I felt the sudden urge to delete all of them, but then I realized that was both crazy and a tad bit unethical.

I guided Megan onto the grimy, sweat-stained Metro car and grimaced at how nearly any surface within the car was a potential source of typhoid or some other infectious, plead-for-death pathogen. I disliked using the Metro, but it was the best way to get around town. The city buses were so much worse, just a Petri dish on wheels. At least on the Metro you did not feel the need to wear a hazmat suit to ride; instead, you just clutched your backpack, tightened into a ball and leaned against the windows smudged by some alien substance that was both magically greasy and sticky. If I believed in God, public transportation would be what I prayed for protection from.

We sat nearest the sliding doors. Our stop was just a few minutes away. It wasn't all that surprising to me when I found that Megan lived off Dupont Circle, as I did. In fact, I already knew this information, but I didn't concede this fact. It was at the beginning of the school year, early October, when I found myself standing in line behind two young women wearing tight-fitting Georgetown Law sweatshirts, an observation I found pertinent at the time— well, part of me did— while at a coffee house just off the Dupont Circle Metro station. One of the girls was Megan and as I was heading to my apartment, I saw her enter an apartment building that was several blocks down from my own. Despite the small Norman Bates-like quality to this, it was a solely circumstantial series of events. It was, however, the moment I realized my attraction to her.

After twelve minutes of bobbing through dark tunnels, the squeal of the pneumatic brakes sounded and the automatic doors parted at our Dupont Circle stop. We exited, passed our fare cards through the electronic gates and slide by the receding barriers. We made our way to the escalators that would carry us to the street and started the excessive journey upwards. The first time I ever rode the Dupont Circle escalators, which stretched more than one hundred eighty feet in length, I was baffled at how long the ride took. One day I decided to time the ride up the escalator during an evening commute and found that it required five minutes, forty-three seconds to reach the top.

41

At the top of the escalator, downtown D.C was a few blocks away and we started toward it, heading towards P Street, passing blocks littered with stores, restaurants, and bars. One of the most energetic spots in the entire city, this was where the people who lived in D.C came for a night out. Within a few city blocks, anything a person could need was accessible. It was a much busier, crowded lifestyle than I had growing up and it took me a while to get used to the constant motion of big-world existence. Living in New York hastened my transition from country bumpkin to urban denizen. Now, I wouldn't trade the city for anything. I preferred people and life whirling around me at a chaotic clip. It was proof that one was alive. It made me feel as if I was part of something real.

"Here's my stoop," Megan stammered, holding my hand in hers. We walked up the small sidewalk to a secured entrance of a seven-story apartment building. Megan turned and faced me, wrapping her arms around my waist. "Do you want you come up?"

I stared down at her, into her beautiful face. Of course, I wanted to go up with her. It would have been the end game of any other evening. I mean, magical things happen when a woman asks you up to her apartment. But as she looked up at me with that playful smile, those seductive green eyes and her silky auburn hair draped across her soft, pierced ears, I was overcome by responsibility— by respect.

"Megan, I want nothing more than to come up with you, but I can't. Well, I can and I really want to, but I shouldn't. No, I won't. Tonight was such a great night and, maybe this is just me, but I want to have more great nights with you." I admitted.

The palms of her hand pushed against the small of my back and her face tilted sideways. She leaned forward, towards me. Her lips, so supple and warm, touched mine and together our lips danced with fervor. She tasted like sweet cherries. Excited, I pulled her closer. Her breasts brushed against my stomach. Her lips massaged me into a state of ecstasy. My arms clutched her, my hands caressed her firm ass—

Pulling her lips away, she looked up at me, her eyes wide with alarm, "Ben, my oh my. You have wandering hands! You're an animal!"

"Oh God, I am so sorry. I was trying to be—"

"You're sweet. I was just kidding. I had a great time tonight, too." She leaned forward and gave me a quick kiss on the cheek. She walked to the secured door and glanced back at me. "Call me tomorrow!"

She pressed something into the keypad on the wall beside the door and then opened it. As it closed she turned towards me and flashed a bright, clever smile that seemed to say 'Good luck sleeping tonight'. Then she was out of sight, down some side hallway, leaving me outside beneath the stars with just my racing heartbeat and my thoughts as companions.

For some amount of time, how much I couldn't comprehend, I walked alone down the street to my apartment, thinking... fantasizing. There were flashes of Megan in my mind where I embraced her in my arms and she was looking up at me with her effervescent stare, with those gorgeous green eyes. Her eyes were fiery jade lava and they burned me to my core. They melted away any lingering reluctance to my feelings, my hesitation to the emotions that were bubbling up inside of me. I knew at that moment, with only the stars illuminating the now quiet and desolate street, that there was something more to this bewitching encounter. Something from the events of the night seemed unscripted, but forced, in a way, by some invisible hand that pushed us together. I had been here before, where my feelings overtook me, but back then I had been burned by *that* word and for that reason, I didn't like using it. Still I knew how it felt and this was it. I was in love and Megan was the one.

A Failure to Act

Present Day

There was no denying the diagnosis. There was no reason to. Lily Fisher had always feared this day was coming, but as all dreaded things seem to, it approached with an unforgiving quickness. She knew she was not brave. Not like her husband. Carl was brave, she was not. Lily Fisher had always been a milquetoast. It was just a fact. But to her surprise, she feared nothing about this day.

As she sat swaying on her porch swing and looking out over the small city that had watched her grow from girl to woman, she was at peace. The sealed envelope in her hand held the letter that she hated to write. Its word carried the grievous truths of that day so long ago and released the horrific memories forever etched in her thoughts. Not one night since that fortuitous day had she not awoken to the cold sweat of fear. Every night since that day. That was every night except for the last. The last night was the first time that Lily Fisher did not wake with anxiety caused by the nocturnal rattle of a window-pane clattering against the house or a hooting shriek caused by a hunting owl in the not-too-far-off woods.

"No luck, honey." Carl's voice interrupted her thoughts.

"We figured as much. You can't blame him, Carl. Can you?"

"Can't say I do. I'll tell you though, his place is a fortress. I have never seen such a place. There are cameras on every corner, in every nook, every cranny, every crevice. Everywhere! He's got Dobermans running free all over his yard. Like a dozen of them. Don't think they've been fed in some time either. They are all feisty and pissed off. They damn near ripped me to shreds. Fortunately, I anticipated that kind of thing and bought several pounds of hamburger. That was nothing though. The craziest thing was that he has all the entrances to his house guarded by these freaky looking contraptions—almost like barbed harpoon guns nested into his walls. I don't know how they work, but they are quite intimidating. And I swear I saw a couple trip wires, too. God knows what they're hooked up to." Carl explained in bated breaths, illustrating with elaborate hand movements the things he had seen.

"Oh my. Did he at least come to the door when you were there?" Lily asked.

"No. I saw his face on a monitor though. In the lab, as usual. I talked to him though for about five minutes. He actually seemed excited about what I told him. I must admit, I am fearful of how lucid the man is."

"We can't possibly know what will happen. We can only hope that somehow we protect Benjamin. Malcolm will help us with this. You know that. Deep down, you know that. The man may be a fanatic, but Malcolm will do everything he can to protect Benjamin. He has to. For his own life, anyway!" Lily advised and rose from the swing, the envelope clutched firmly against her chest.

"He doesn't care about his own life one bit. I just hope you're right that he cares about Benjamin's." Carl confessed in earnest, guiding his wife into the house.

"Well then, should we get this show on the road?" Lily asked.

"We might as well. But first, one thing. Give me a moment." Carl said before vanishing out of sight down the hallway.

"I will be right down. I'm just going to put this in Benjamin's room," Lily offered as she moved upstairs to her son's bedroom.

Pushing open the door to her son's vacant room, Lily was greeted by the meek reminder of how life progresses forward, beating on at its own monotonous and persistent tempo. She moved about the room long since lived-in and sat down at the foot of the neatly made bed. She looked up at the walls, covered by tattered and sun-bleached posters of football players, dusty Heavy Metal memorabilia and glossy images of naked women. Oh, how she had disapproved of those. It still smelled like a teenage boy's room— the unique combination of stale sweat and cologne. That was the smell of Benjamin's room. It wasn't a great smell, but it was uniquely his. He hadn't been in this room for over a year. Yet, it smelled as if he had never left. He did leave for a reason. He was off trying to conquer mountains of his own.

Lily remembered the day Benjamin found out he had been accepted to Georgetown. He came running into the kitchen straight from the mailbox to tell her. He was so elated as he read her the first few lines of the letter that he momentarily lost his ability to form words, but the excitement in his voice was so tangible that words, even if they had been garbled by gaiety, were not important. Benjamin was articulate and concise in almost every sentence he spoke, but not that day and he didn't need to be. After he read the letter in its entirety, he threw his arms around her and hoisted her several feet off the ground.

That moment had been a mixed bag of emotions for her. Lily had longed to see more of her son while he had been in

New York for four years, but with his football games and the semi-frequent bus trips to the city, she saw enough of him that she didn't mind too much. Lily was also glad that New York was far enough away from the things he knew nothing about. He was protected, even if it was just for four years. Acceptance to Georgetown meant that Benjamin would not return home to live for the near future, probably forever. Lily had lost many hours of sleep thinking how to keep her beloved son from coming home, where the dangers to him were so exponentially greater than faraway places. But acceptance to Georgetown also meant that Benjamin would slowly evolve into a stranger, a fragment of his self lost to her memories.

They would talk on the phone as all separated families do. They would see each other a couple times a year, mostly for holidays, and also for the occasional vacation together. Maybe they would even keep in touch by email she remembered thinking. But eventually the calls would grow more sporadic, more infrequent, as Benjamin's life grew roots and blossomed into something of his own. She would love him just as much, but it would never be the same. Her son would always be her son, but he would never again be her baby boy.

Lily stood up and walked to the head of Benjamin's bed. She placed the sealed envelope in her hands against the ridge formed by the pillows. The contents of the letter would confuse him, but there was no other way. Benjamin was being hunted and there was no hiding now. They had been granted a reprieve— seventeen years —but never did they believe that it was over. Not with Warren and things he could do. Now, the reprieve was over and payment was due. Cold, merciless payment.

As she was about to exit the room, Lily looked down on the bedside stand and picked up a silver-framed photo. The photo had been taken the last summer Benjamin had been home and it showed him and his cousin Owen gripped in a playful tussle atop

Vermont's Mount Mansfield. A true *hurrah* moment captured in stillness. In the image, Benjamin's lengthy body clung onto Owen's back like a giant lemur, Ben's thick arms holding Owen's jet-black noggin in a headlock, his hand closed in a pre-noogie. Lily loved the picture because Benjamin was caught in that rare state of natural happiness, his smile beaming through the half-dour, half-smirk expression that normally dominated his face. You could see his dimples, too. My how she loved her son's dimples and his eyes…he had his father's eyes. Strong and assertive, those eyes. They were a deep brown, like the color of fresh brewed coffee. His hair was a fair yellow and rested atop his head as an untidy, bristled mane. This was her son and she loved him ever so much.

With a last look around, Lily exited the bedroom and pulled the door softly to a close, the faint click of the lock going into place confirmed it secure. It was all quiet in the house for a moment and then abruptly things changed. From downstairs, a faint and familiar music, restful in its tempo, began to fill the air. Lily started down the stairs and as she stepped off the last step, Carl greeted her with an outreached hand.

"My beautiful wife, would you give me this one last dance?" Carl asked, his glance mesmerized by Lily's ethereal glow.

"I would wish for nothing more!" She replied.

Placing her fragile hand in her husband's, Lily rested her head against his chest and together they danced. The song that filled the air was the song that had played when they first danced as Mister and Misses Fisher. Their feet moved gracefully in short circular steps, as Elvis's "Can't Help Falling in Love" crooned them into a dreamlike state. The marching of time, relentless in its stampede to the next perpetual state, made no ground in its charge while Carl and Lily held each other in their love. What they knew was coming, didn't matter in the slightest for those few minutes. All that mattered was each other and the entangled collection of memories that they had sculpted throughout their years together.

The music ended.

Their dreamlike state faded with the music and like a child who raises his head from a nap, slobber wetting his cheek, Lily and Carl resisted the need to let the feeling fade. It was now time.

With a lamenting sigh, Lily asked, "my mother once told me stars were the souls of the departed placed into the heavens to guide those left behind. Do you believe that?"

Carl thought for a second.

"In a way, I do. What does anyone have once their life has ended, but the hope that there is something more?" Carl spoke in earnest.

In stoic silence, Lily and Carl exited their home and got into their car. Neither said a word as they started down the driveway. They headed north to Osworth, the place where it all began; the place where it would all end.

Entangled

School was out and I had started working as an intern for a local law firm. The job was typical— research case precedence, complete general clerical work, assist lawyers with trial preparation, things that were far simpler than the whole pomp and circumstance that the image of law portrays. In fact, it made me question if I really should continue investing hundreds of thousands of dollars to become a lawyer at all. The logic and reason part of the career was what drew me to it, but I quickly realized that the profession was more about following procedure than cognitive capabilities. Read this. Do that this way. If this happens, blah, blah. The only real basis of creativity that seemed to exist in the profession was how one lawyer could use past cases to screw another lawyer or snare some less educated person into paying extortion in the form of a settlement.

What was the point of it all? That was what I seemed to ask myself every night when I left the cramped quarters of my office, if you could give a storage closet such a name. I was usually in a sour mood when I got home. That was until Megan came over and then I was refreshed, rejuvenated.

We had become inseparable since school ended. Everyone had set off for summer adventures leaving us alone to find comfort in each other's company. Most evenings Megan spent the night, which I liked and was starting to get accustomed to. But other nights she slept in her own apartment so that she could be early to her own internship at the office of a Virginia Senator. I was thankful to learn that it was a woman senator. I considered male politicians the kings of perversion— a fact that seemed to solidify itself as headline after headline came out telling of the exploits of some geriatric playboy politician and his weekly romp with a female staff member. These men were supposed to be men of honor, elected by the people, for the people and for the betterment of country. Instead, they were men of shame that wielded their power as a tool of seduction. These men did not inspire me and were just another reason I was beginning to loathe my decision of becoming a lawyer. It also made me more protective, perhaps even possessive, of Megan.

The summer season was flourishing and this lifted my spirits. The hot sun and fully-blossomed flowers made it harder to go to work. The steamy days meant other things as well, like bikinis and other fabric-deficient attire that women so willingly displayed. Megan and I had been seeing each other for about eight weeks and while I enjoyed the time with her, she had taken to punishing me for not going up to her apartment the night of our first date. Since then, Megan had slammed the brakes on physical encounters and kept me waiting...wanting. The physical attraction between us had become palpable and Megan kept this tension as high as possible.

To rid myself of my lustful thoughts, I decided that Megan and I needed to get away for the upcoming Fourth of July holiday. From my leather-bound chair, staring at my computer and thinking of the perfect place, I came to realize that what we needed was a few days of sun and fun. I had looked online for some possible places, like Ocean City or Virginia Beach. I thought either would do the trick. It just needed to be a place where the sand was loose and hot. It had to be a place where the salty sea air would swell in your nostrils as you slept and the mix of color from the sea-bound sunrise would shine through your balcony's glass doors, warm your cheeks with its light and lift you awake to thoughts of paradise. The best getaway spot would be the one that balanced romance, adventure and culture. Worries were not to be packed with the luggage and for the days we were gone, the only things that would matter would be deciding when to wake and where to eat.

I was debating the choices of destinations in my head as I sat at my desk. My computer screen showed an enlarged image of waves crashing against the shore with a couple, silhouetted, holding hands and strolling barefoot through cool, foamy water. Before I could chose between the two, my apartment door was thrown open and Megan was standing there in tears.

I rushed to her out of instinct. She stepped through my doorway and dropped the bags she was holding. She threw her arms around me as tears poured from her eyes.

"What happened? Are you hurt?" I asked.

I could see she was trying to speak, but her chin just shook. No words came out. Black mascara formed a wet streak down her cheek.

"Come. Sit down."

I guided her trembling body to my coffee-colored couch and aided her as she dropped onto one of the cushions.

"Are you hurt? What's wrong?" I clamored. My hands went numb, cold. My knees wobbled. I felt weak. I was scared. This wasn't like her— something had happened.

"Your…phone…I…took—" She burst into tears, her face falling into her palms.

"My phone? What about it?" I was confused.

She wept, filling the air with bellowing sobs.

She raised her head and looked at me, her eyes now small slits leaking tears. "I…took…it…by…ACCIDENT," she cut off, tossing her head back into her hands.

"Okay, no big deal. I don't care." I said with a mixture of confusion and relief. I didn't understand her reaction.

"No! Your phone. I had it and—" She cried again.

"Alright, calm down. Take a deep breath. Rest for a minute. Let me get you some water."

I walked to the kitchen, grabbed a glass, tossed two ice cubes in it and filled it with water from my fridge. I walked back into my living room and handed her the glass. She took it, placing it onto my glass coffee table next to a recent copy of *Scientific American*.

A bit calmer, Megan spoke through a shaky whimper. "Ben, I had your phone. I grabbed it by mistake this morning. I didn't know. It shouldn't have been me. I am so sorry."

"It's okay. Now tell me what happened? I'm not upset."

"He called, your Uncle Warren—"

I paused. Then asked, "Uncle Warren did you say?"

"Yes, he called."

"Babe, I don't have an uncle by that name."

"WHAT? What do you mean?"

"Exactly that. I don't have an Uncle Warren! Anyway, continue. What upset you?"

She looked puzzled, questioning whatever memory she had just formed. Her gaze was blank, emotionless. "Your phone rang and I answered it. The guy on the other end said he was your uncle and he was trying to get a hold of you. He said your name, Ben. He said 'I need to speak with Benjamin Fisher'."

I sat down, confused now more than ever. I didn't know any one named Warren. I tried to think if Megan had misheard the name. My only uncle was named Bob or Robert, though I called him Bobbo. I doubted she confused any of these with Warren.

"Anyway, what did the guy want?" I questioned.

"He said that your parents were dead!" Megan shrieked and burst into tears once more.

"WHAT? Let me see the phone."

She rummaged through her huge black and gold bag for a moment, tossing aside countless knickknacks and came out with my phone. She handed it to me. I accessed the call log and looked up the recent calls. At the top of the list was a number with no ID attached to it, but it started with the area code 603. That was definitely a New Hampshire area code. I called.

It rang five times and then just stopped. No voicemail, no operator, no message. It just ended. I tried once more, but got the same result. I then scrolled through my phonebook, descended to the Ms and highlighted MOM. I hesitated for a second, trepidation tiptoeing up my throat. I pressed CALL.

It rang twice and then someone picked up. There was silence, but I could tell there was someone there. I heard motion and random background noises. It sounded like a clicking noise and static.

"Mom, are you there? Hello?" I asked, waiting for a response.

Nothing. The phone cut out and the call was dropped.

"God damn it! These bloody things."

I redialed. It rang once and then there was an answer.

"Benjamin, is that you?" Asked my mother's calming voice. "Are you alright?"

"Mom I'm fine, but are you okay?"

"Oh yes dear, your father and I are just heading up north. Taking a nice drive up Route 16. Why do you ask?"

I told her what had happened and in my mother's typical fashion, she laughed it off, saying there are crazies in the world. Her and my father were fine, just enjoying some time together.

I was relieved.

"Alright guys, I will talk to you later!" I said, getting ready to hang-up before my Dad piped up.

"Son, I just wanted to tell you that your Mom and I love you more than anything. Remember that and please do me a favor?"

"Anything Dad."

"Keep fighting hard and never give up— no matter how tough things might get, okay?"

I found my father's words odd and out of context.

"I will of course, Dad. I learned how to persevere from the best!"

"I love you, Ben." My mom said, her voice fading away. She hung up the phone.

Looking at Megan, who was shaking with confusion and fear, I felt my heart warm. I couldn't imagine the kind of memories that brief phone call had brought back to her, images of her father and the hell she lived a few years ago. Whoever had called, had angered me. I couldn't imagine that another person found such a phone call amusing, but what was worse than trying to tell me that my parents were dead, was the viciousness that the lie had on the sweet woman sitting on my couch. She was visibly traumatized.

"Sweetheart, I am so sorry that you got that call. I don't know who would find that to be funny, but everything is fine. My parents are fine. The asshole who called was lying. Everything is fine!" I kept saying that.

Everything was fine, I was telling myself this just as much as I was telling Megan. I had heard my mother's voice, had heard her say everything was fine, but something deep down inside of me felt off. Things didn't feel right. The strangeness of the phone call Megan had received made it difficult to reason a purpose for it. What did this Warren character think he was going to accomplish? And how did he know my name? It made me uneasy.

I walked over to Megan, sat down next to her and wrapped my arms around her shoulders, pulling her in close to me. At once, she burst into tears and wept. For more than ten minutes I just held her and let her cry herself out.

"I'm hungry," she said in a matter-of-fact manner once the tears had stopped.

"Well, what do you want? We can go out or I can grill up some curried chicken thighs. That's all I have though. I have to run to the store tomorrow."

"I want to get out of here."

"Then we'll go out. Where do you want to go?"

"I'm in the mood for salmon. I don't care where. I just want to leave."

"Done."

I grabbed my apartment key and my wallet, slid them both into the pockets of my khaki shorts, and helped Megan off the couch. I had thought about bringing my cell phone, but, instead tossed it carelessly onto the table next to my couch. Together we walked out of my third floor apartment, locking the door behind us.

Bad News

We decided upon seafood. The temperature outside had cooled to something more mild and we both thought fresh salmon or oysters from the Chesapeake would be a refreshing end to a taxing day. We took a short ride on the Metro, up to 7th Street. It lasted about ten minutes and there was no wait for dinner, which was surprising considering the establishment.

Dinner was pleasant, but more than the quality of the food, it was an effective distraction from the day's earlier events. With each tiny forkful of cashew-encrusted salmon that Megan placed into her mouth, she became happier. She started to smile and laugh, eventually she just glowed as only she could. Her jade eyes sparkled and shined with a renewed vigor until happiness radiated through her endearing gaze.

I was slurping down the fourth of my oysters when I remembered my plans for the long weekend. I let the spiciness of the horseradish and the raw oyster sit on my tongue for a moment before sliding it intact down my throat. Oysters were one of my favorite foods, but because of their texture, they were not always as such. Years ago, when I was twelve, my father took me to a small oyster house in Bar Harbor, where we had been vacationing. He said to me, 'son, you're a man now, eat this'. He handed me a freshly shucked oyster. At first glimpse, I thought he was handing we some kind of sea rock and as I held it, I decided it wasn't edible. But my father assured me that it was. He laughed at my bemusement as I tried to determine how to eat the crazy little critter; at first, I had placed my lips against its half-dollar sized body and attempted to vacuum it into my mouth. This was wrong, my dad had said, and then he proceeded to show me the proper method for eating an oyster. I did as he did and detached the oyster from its shell, tossed it back like a shot glass and let the oyster slide into my mouth. At once, I spat it into a napkin, disgusted by how much it felt like a salty mouthful of snot. My dad, being a hard-nosed Vietnam vet, would have none of that and made me try it again. On my next attempt of putting that slimy little shellfish in my mouth, I tasted for the first time the oyster's subtle flavors. I sucked the briny juice from its serous body, savoring the slight sweetness of its grayish flesh and knew from then on that the oyster and I were to have many future encounters.

"So about this weekend, I was thinking we should get away."

"Yeah? Where did you have in mind?"

"Ocean City. I've never been, but I hear it is fun. What do you think?"

"You've never been to Ocean City? Wow! Oh right, you're a New Englander."

"You make it sound like I have leprosy.'Oh right, you're a New Englander'!"

"I didn't mean it that way. It just seems like everyone that lives down here, in the Mid-Atlantic area, has been to Ocean City. You know? I forget sometimes that you're not one of us," Megan giggled, taking a sip of drink.

"You do know the Civil War ended over a century ago? No need to hate the Yanks." I laughed.

"You know what I mean, smart ass. Where do Yanks go to the beach?"

"Different places, but for me, it was mostly beaches in Maine. Where I lived in New Hampshire, it was just as easy to drive to the Maine beaches as it was to drive to Portsmouth, Hampton or Rye. But my parents liked York beach the most, it had quant little restaurants and shops near the beach. An arcade too," I said, slurping back another oyster and repositioning myself in my seat. "My favorite place is this candy shop that's a block from the beach. They hand-make salt-water taffy— call 'em kisses. Best taffy ever. Oh, just thinking about their peanut butter taffy. Damn, so yummy!" Even though I was eating dinner, the thought of a sweet childhood treat made my mouth water.

"Best taffy ever? Hmmm. We'll have to see about that. On the boardwalk in Ocean City, they have these candy shops. I can't remember the name, but they have great taffy, too. And even better chocolate-covered strawberries."

"So is that a yes. We're going to go?"

"Yea, I think it's a great plan. Neither of us has to work and we both have three days off. Let's do it."

"Excellent! I was checking out some hotels there and in Virginia Beach earlier. I will give them a call when we get back. I'm hoping there will be some open rooms this close to the holiday."

"There will be. There may not be any on the beach, but who cares. We only need a room so we can sleep, it's not like we're going to be in there that much."

"Yeah, I don't much care about the hotel room either. As long as you're bringing your bikini and we got a bed, I'm happy."

"If I didn't know any better, I'd think Mister Benjamin believes he's got a chance to get lucky."

59

"Mister Benjamin is hoping."

"We'll see about that. I'm still mad at you for turning me down the last time. If you hadn't noticed."

"You're not the only one mad at me about that. My penis is pissed!"

She burst into laughter; her cheeks suddenly a rosy shade of pink. I chuckled aloud. We sat in trivial conversation for the rest of the meal, telling stories from our past, things we had regretted and things that made us proud. We spoke of our families and what they were like. We joked about things that had become an inside joke between us and we bickered with each other over our religious views.

One of things that I admired most in Megan was her conviction to her roots, her allegiance to her upbringing. She had grown up a devote catholic, spent her childhood going to Mass on most weekends and even participated in Confession a couple times. Now, as an adult, she held her faith, but had grown somewhat apathetic to the ritualized practices of the religion. This was fine with me. I was an atheist.

Often we quarreled about the interpretation of scripture and the prominence of the Papal doctrine. My dislike for religion had become clear after learning of the child molestation epidemic carried out by catholic priests all around the world and the glaring absence of prosecution. Any time the subject was approached, I would argue that such behavior from men of the cloth was as great a sin as any human could commit with the sole exception of murder. I truly believed their acts despicable, criminal in every way, but I knew that their titles ensured that shackles would never clasp their wrists. In my view, these holy men should pray that rapture never came because they would surely burn in hell, if a true-and-just God existed. I would prefer not to live quietly in a world that allows such behavior. Sure, I argued this point with an unrestrained attitude, but I always tried to be as polite as possible because I knew that I injected a lot of aggression into my arguments. More times than not, this aggression eroded the context of what I was saying. The fancy word for this aggression was *passion*. I laughed whenever someone called me passionate.

On three occasions in our burgeoning relationship, Megan and I had sat together on my couch in the early hours of the morning arguing about the existence of God. She would play the faith card, offering the inability of man to define life through science as evidence of a greater being. I would counter that while a precise definition of life could not be defined, it was without a doubt a symptom of biochemical structure, of molecular machinery and that one day soon mankind would be capable of producing life in a Petri dish. I generally went further and said this action was strong evidence against the existence of God. Megan would disagree and punch me in the shoulder. That was when it was time to end the conversation or risk it becoming a fight. It can be difficult to end such conversations and I have always had the urge to offer one more talking point. Typically, I would say that I didn't discount the existence of God, but that I rejected the idea of a God as propagated by religious texts, always finishing with my self-defined principle of the universe, which argued that if God did exist, it must be within the constraints defined by the observed world— by scientific fact. There were no fairy tales where magic and miracles existed in the face of tangible, measurable evidence. Life was a puzzle and all pieces had to fit, or so I wished to believe.

My hardheaded views on religion were the main reason we never discussed politics. Megan followed her parents political views and was a Republican. I was not a Republican. Not even close. But I also wasn't a Democrat. I hated such narrow classifications. If all the world were either black or white, I could understand the two sides. But the world wasn't black or white and its history would not be defined by a coin flip. The world was an infinite space, a spectrum of grays. Politicians never understood that and they continued to draw a dividing line. It was futile and ignorant and it bothered me.

To conclude our meal, we ordered dessert. A triple layer of Neapolitan Crème Brûlée arrived in front of us in a small, white dish. Megan wasted no time attacking it. Once the dish touched the tablecloth, Megan grabbed the nearest spoon and whacked the caramelized layer of speckled sugar with the curved side of her spoon, sending small shards of glasslike sugar piercing into the tri-colored custard below. A spoonful of the dessert quickly vanished from the disk, whisked upwards across her lips and devoured like a lover.

"Oh my goodness," she exclaimed in pure ecstasy. "Well this is another thing you're not getting any of."

I laughed. "That's alright. You had a rougher day than I did. Enjoy it."

She took another bite, looking at me with her mind at work. "I just can't comprehend what that was about. It seemed so pointless and mean. Do you think it was suppose to be a practical joke? It was not funny. "

"Probably. That's all I can think of—"

"Then that person is deranged."

"Yes, they are."

"But, Ben. He knew your name. How could that be?"

"I don't understand it either. Anyone who calls my phone pretending to be an Uncle that I don't have is probably not all there. Obviously, I would have known that the call was a fake. As for him knowing my name, it could be any one of a thousand reasons. I mean my phone number is still a New Hampshire number, perhaps the guy got it from an old, vengeful girlfriend or he found my name and number written in a bathroom stall next to 'Call For a Good Time'. It could be that my number was on some application I used before or in a database or something. I don't know exactly but let's stop worrying about it."

"You're right. It's over. We never have to worry about that happening again. Let's focus on our weekend together."

"Cheers to that!" I concurred, raising my glass of lager and mimicking a toast.

Dinner ended and we were both satiated, our stomachs holding the shape of small watermelons. We reversed our route and headed back to my apartment. Since we had started spending more time with one another, Megan and I always chose my apartment as the place we frequented because it was more spacious and accommodating than Megan's apartment. It also held a great view of the Dupont Circle neighborhood. Probably more than anything, Megan preferred my apartment because it had a washer and dryer right in the kitchen, a feature her apartment lacked.

We moved together up P Street, talking and laughing with each other, enjoying the summer splendor of sunny evenings— a far cry from the cold and early-to-dark days of winter. It filled me with joy to look down at my watch, see the hour hand at eight, the minute hand partway between the six and seven, and then look up into the melody of oranges and pinks in the evening sky. Comfort was the word for it— that feeling— much like hitting the snooze button and knowing you had nine minutes left of unadulterated sleep before waking up or hitting snooze once more.

We were walking back to my apartment when suddenly, my feet twisted over one another and I fumbled forward, stumbling violently to the ground. I threw my hands out in front of me to break my fall. The palms of my hands struck the stony cement with a *whack*, my knees following. My palms slashed against the rough cement, small stones embedding into my hands, cutting them. Blood trickled from the tiny holes that formed from my gravel-blotted palms. The skin on my knees sliced against the jagged surface of the ground, torn against its coarse plane, leaving just thin flaps of skin hanging from my boney kneecaps. Blood seeped from beneath the filleted strips of skin. I stumbled back to my feet, a broad throbbing spreading throughout my body.

Megan rushed towards me out of instinct, asking "are you alright?"

I was silent. My head throbbed. Something was wrong with me— inside of my head. I had felt nothing like it before. Then I felt a warm drip flow over my lips, into my mouth. It was salty and metallic on my tongue. My nose was bleeding. I dabbed my face with my fingers and stared at the bright red smear for a second. I hadn't had a nosebleed in years.

Then at once, the ground beneath me stretched away, running towards an absent space, somewhere distant. Everything around me hung in suspension. The world spun about my head, leaving just crimson shadows of reality and my heart sped up to an uncomfortable crescendo. Sweat poured from my forehead and my body convulsed. My limbs shook uncontrollably and tossed about to the beat of some odd rhythm. I was dazed. Then, with a sharp *thwack* the ground sprung towards me, the crimson haze departed and the world was as it was before it happened.

"What was that?" I asked myself.

I shuffled to a nearby bench and sat down. My skin assumed a clamminess. It was cool to the touch.

"Ben, are you alright? That was scary!"

Words escaped me. Nothing I thought of saying fulfilled how I felt. At last, I spat out, "that was the scariest thing that has ever happened to me. It was like I was suspended in space with everything still in reach, but still a distance from me somehow. I know that makes no sense."

Megan stroked my forehead. "Let's get you home, maybe dinner made you sick."

"Maybe."

I doubted it though.

We walked the rest of the way to my apartment. My heart had settled and my head had cleared. It was as if nothing had happened, but it had and I was worried, shaking and bleeding. The episode had been brief in time, lasting just a few seconds, but it endured unending in my mind. The feeling was like walking up stairs in the dark and over-counting the steps by one. You stride forward expecting to place your foot onto the flat surface of a step, but land instead, on a phantom space, leaving you to realize the step was never there before.

Dazed, I was unaware that Megan had taken my keys and unlocked the door to my apartment.

"Ben, I think you need to lie down. I'll tuck you into bed."

"No, I think I just need to relax. Put my feet up, maybe watch some TV."

"Honey, I don't think so. You fell and hurt yourself. Rest is the best medicine."

"I appreciate it, but I am feeling better. Just give me a moment to calm myself down. If I feel I'm getting worse, I let you play nurse."

"Funny! You know I am just trying to take care of you. It's your fault really."

"My fault? How is it my fault?"

"Well, if I wasn't getting attached to you, I wouldn't care."

"Awww. That's sweet. I am getting attached to you, too. The best thing I have—"

My cell phone rang.

"Hello?" I asked, trying to sound put together.

"You know, it's not nice to let other people answer you phone, Benjamin!" A raspy, gruff voice replied.

I looked at the number on the phone. The number was the same unidentifiable New Hampshire number as earlier in the afternoon. What nerve! I was ready to give this guy a piece of my mind.

"Who the fuck is this?! Do you think it is funny to call people and make shit up?"

"Oh, such language. Is that anyway to talk to your Uncle Warren?" The man spoke in a self-assured tone, almost goading in its coolness.

"Listen you batshit loon, you're no uncle of mine. Don't you ever call this number again. Ever! Do you understand me?" My blood was coursing through my veins at a rapid clip, the skin on my face growing hot to the touch.

"My, just listen to how feisty you've become. I am not sure your mother would have approved!"

"Seriously, man? What are you playing at?"

"Did your parents not tell you about me? What a shame. After all I did for them."

"Look fucker, when you called before, your sadistic antics upset my girlfriend. For that, I hope you choke and die. Goodbye—"

"Oh, I wouldn't hang up just yet, Benjamin. At least not until I have told you the terrible news. Your parents not telling you about me was a grave mistake. One they cannot correct anymore. Did they think they could just keep what they stole from me? Oh, no. Sadly, they had to pay!"

"Listen jerkoff, the last time you played that game, it didn't work. Why would it work now? You are a disturbed human being and I am done stroking your sick fantasies—"

"Sick? Maybe. Fantasy? No. Your parents died in a fiery accident while they were coming to pay me a visit. That is where they are now— dead on the side of Route 16. They died while you were sucking back oysters, thinking about fucking that pretty little whore of yours."

I was stunned. How did he know those things?

"I look forward to seeing you again, Benjamin. And when you come home, please bring Megan. She looks so delicious." The phone went silent.

Tick, Tock

The edge of the newspaper peeled away from Malcolm Campbell, who intently read the short blurb on the side column of the front page. He snapped the newspaper with a quick flick of his wrist and continued his directed scanning of the article. It read that another person had gone missing while hiking in the White Mountains, bringing the total to eleven people in the last two months.

"Fools. Damn fools." Malcolm muttered to himself with grumpiness as he sipped earl grey tea from his favorite mug. It was a black porcelain cup formed from the shape of two cats— one sitting tall with its front legs locked out forming the container for liquid, a second cat furled around the first forming the handle from its coiled tail. Together the cats symbolized both life and death in a paradoxical state of constant uncertainty.

It was Malcolm's Schrodinger's Cat mug and while it had weathered several chips and dings throughout its protracted history, it was still the consummate symbol of praise. Malcolm had received it from a student after being the youngest astrophysicist to earn tenure in Dartmouth College history. Seeing the mug's message— the duality of reality — so cheaply portrayed in a ceramic mug with "Made in China" stamped on the bottom always brought a smile to Malcolm's aged, cunning face because it reminded him of the dichotomy of human ideas.

The man who had gone missing, according to the excerpt in the paper, was named Albert Wickland and he, like the many before him, had been an avid outdoorsman, someone adept to the hazards of the wilderness. The writers of the article described Albert as a seasoned hiker who was renowned in his hometown of Meredith for the annual July clambake that he held on the shore of Lake Winnipesaukee. The clambakes helped to raise money for the children's hospital at Dartmouth. Short blurbs and statements by those who knew him best all said the same thing- 'there was no way Albert would have gotten lost while hiking on his own'.

Malcolm Campbell finished reading the excerpt, folded the paper half-wise and placed it neatly on a pile of fading newspapers next to his chair.

"People never learn." He said matter-of-factly as he walked to the spot on the table lit by an enormous heat lamp shaped like an eggplant. Beneath the circle of light was a mouse carcass with a half-moon incision cut around its underbelly, its furry white skin peeled back like the lid of an aluminum can. A network of pink and gray organs arranged according to some complex, indecipherable blueprint rested unaltered in the cavity of its tiny skeleton.

Malcolm grabbed the magnifying glass affixed to a swivel mount bolted to the table and swung it into position above the mouse carcass. The tiny organs grew beneath the conical-shaped lens of the magnifying glass. Malcolm picked up the scalpel that was laying next the mouse carcass and prodded gently through the network of organs.

69

"Stomach. Intestines. I don't need you," Malcolm said, detaching the stomach and intestines from the rest of mouse's organs. He discarded them into an empty beaker.

"There we are."

He continued cutting out organs, shedding the excess bits from his canvas so that he could continue his judicious pursuits. He sliced out the liver, segmented the Caudal Vena Cava in two, freed the kidneys from the renal artery and removed the rest of the circulatory system with surgical attention. He plucked the kidneys from the dorsal wall and then with a meticulous precision, he cut away the thymus and lymph nodes from the cardiovascular tissue of the mouse's heart. Finally, Malcolm detached the mouse heart from its nested position amid the lungs, hollowing out the tiny rodent and leaving just the lungs in its abdomen cavity.

Dissecting a once living creature was habit for Malcolm Campbell and he whizzed through the evisceration of the tiny rodent as if he were a gourmet whipping up a simple five-minute Ceviche. With two quick cuts by his scalpel, he liberated each of the lungs and placed them delicately beneath the magnifying glass. He cut small disk-like fragments from the tops of the lungs and set one of them aside.

He grabbed a rubber bulb and topped a glass pipette, then slipped its tip into a small beaker of solution. He compressed the bulb slightly and released it to draw the clear liquid into the pipette. Malcolm placed several drops from the filled pipette onto a short strip of indicator paper positioned on the table; upon contact, the paper absorbed the liquid and swelled in size, but as he expected, there was no change to the color of the paper.

"Alright, here we go," he said with a tinge of excitement in his voice. He emptied the remaining solution into one of the lungs. The pink, spongy mouse lung filled like a fleshy balloon. After a few seconds, Malcolm gently agitated the lung by moving it in

70

small circles with his fingers and then placed the lung upright against the wall of the Petri dish. Then he dipped the end of a second strip of indicator paper into the lung, making contact with the solution, and watching as the liquid climbed up the paper. He placed the paper on the table and waited.

Before his eyes, the paper changed colors from a purplish blue to a whitish red. Malcolm Campbell's body began to tingle from his elation. It had worked.

"My little friend, you have sacrificed your meaningless life for me, but still there is more for you to give," Malcolm expressed with zeal as he bent forward to look into its furry, white face. "I mean not to defile your sacrifice further, but you may hold the secret that I have long been searching for. So now I must cut out your brain! But, first— yes, I need a negative."

Against the near wall of the basement, there stood a set of metal racks holding three large cages. Two of the cages were filled with dozens of squirming mice, some white, some black and white, others a light brown. The mess of mice moved as a mass, crawling up and over each other, biting and nibbling at one another's feet and tails or on the thin shavings of wood lining their cage. They lived as rodents— as vermin —should, but the worst part was the pissing and shitting. All over the place, the vermin would piss and shit— on each other, in their food, out of the cage— it didn't matter. Malcolm hated the filthy creatures and to him they existed to serve only one purpose, the purpose he was forced to devout his life to.

It was chaos inside the cages. Malcolm enjoyed studying the way nature always seemed to provide the greatest battles. Watching dozens of stupid mice fighting each other for scraps of food was just the catalyst to observe primal behavior.

On several occasions, the battles had grown so fierce than Malcolm couldn't allow it to continue. In such instances, he would pluck from the cage a fallen warrior, replacing its half-eaten

71

corpse with something that couldn't be cannibalized. He had observed that when a nest of mice faced a food scarcity, the strongest of the mice would team together and kill the runts of the nest, then eat the meat from their kill. Seeing that for the first time brought Malcolm back to the first time he had independently verified the Casimir Effect.

A third cage, empty of inhabitants, was enclosed in a clear plastic structure at the end of the top rack. It had a set of rubber hoses running down from the back that disappeared into the wall. This was the cage where Malcolm could experiment on the vermin, routing specialized concoctions or chemically-laced aerosols up the rubber tubes and into the enfolded plastic structure. This encasement, constructed from a high strength, chemical-resistant polymer of Malcolm's own devising, also allowed him to euthanize the vermin for analysis. When it came time to put down one of his lab mice, Malcolm took a great deal of precautions to make their death as painless as possible. Treating vermin as vermin was one thing and letting the natural behavior of the mice run its course was all fine, but Malcolm did not believe in killing for the sake of killing and because of this view, he took to being as humane as possible when putting down a mouse for necropsy. He had found that the quickest, most efficient method that caused the least amount of panic and pain in the mice was to use his own blend of carbon dioxide and Sevoflurane.

Malcolm called this his Goodnight Gas and the eviscerated mouse that now lay on his table met its sudden death by inhaling it. Prior to death, the mouse had been subjected to a copious exposure of aerosolized Compound Zeta, another of Malcolm's own creations, to determine if the substance could penetrate the lungs and become sufficiently dissolved in the bloodstream. Getting the drug to enter the bloodstream was the crux of his research and it was not all that difficult. If Compound Zeta had entered the mouse's bloodstream through inhalation at a high enough dose, it should be capable of making its way across the blood-brain barrier. The success of passing the blood-brain barrier depended on Malcolm's ingenious design of the molecule and how it interacted with the endothelial cells at the interface. Once in the brain, the damage could be done. That is, if it all worked as designed. Malcolm was running out of patience. It had to work, had to. There had been too many years of tumultuous, drawn out failures.

Malcolm had been tinkering with synthesized antibodies and nanospheres for this purpose, but he had yet to find the right aggregation of substances that could break through the blood-brain barrier and deposit enough of Compound Zeta, the payload, into the recipients' brain tissue. If it failed to break the blood-brain barrier at high concentrations, Compound Zeta would be a failure. And if it failed, well, Malcolm couldn't bring himself to think of the consequences.

Malcolm needed a mouse that had not been exposed to Compound Zeta, but otherwise euthanized by Goodnight Gas, if he wished to continue with his analysis. He pulled a small white mouse from the first cage on the metal rack and placed it into the plastic chamber on the other end of the rack; he let the mouse scurry from his hand as it was writhing and twisting to get free. He closed the lid and fastened the top with a latch.

"Mouse, I assure you this will be quick and painless. You have only a little time remaining, so do whatever it is you enjoy, little mouse."

Malcolm turned on two valves, one hooked up to a large green canister holding compressed carbon dioxide, and the other connected to a far smaller canister housing Sevoflurane gas. Next, he applied a slight vacuum to the chamber so that the air inside would be sucked out and replaced by the Goodnight Gas. The mouse started scurrying about in its cage when the oxygen began to diminish.

It took a few minutes, but the mouse stopped running and sat in the corner of its cage, its red eyes dilating, its abdomen starting to compress and expand more rapidly. The mouse stretched out its legs and rested its furry face sideways against its front paws. Its eyelids shuttered and reopened several times, but the duration of each new blink became a fraction slower, until, mercifully, the reds of the mouse's eyes showed no longer.

Campbell waited ten minutes to ensure the mouse had departed before he harvested it from the cage. Once he was assured of the mouse's condition, he did as he had done to the first mouse on his examination table. He incised a flap about the size of a half-dollar in the freshly deceased mouse and removed its organs, but left behind the lungs. He wanted to ensure the mouse had no traces of nitric acid in its lungs, as the first mouse had. Nitric acid was produced as a byproduct of successful Compound Zeta uptake and was evidence that the agent had infiltrated the blood.

There was no nitric acid found in the lungs of the second mouse. Finding no trace amounts of nitric acid was what Malcolm had expected, for he took precautionary steps to avoid experimental contamination.

The cutting out of mice brains was not as nice and clean as dissecting the soft tissue of their underbellies. The most difficult step of extracting a mouse brain, of course, was getting it out of the head and more times than not, the best method was decapitation. It was a gruesome necessity, but a necessity nonetheless. After all, within the contents of their brains lied that answers to Malcolm's most daunting intellectual quest.

So he did the difficult deed to the two little mice that sacrificed their lives for his whims, sawing off their heads with a bone saw and drawing their skulls from their bodies as if plucking ripened fruit from the vine. Once their heads were off, liberated from the rest of the body, Malcolm peeled back the white fur from the mice heads after two quick slits with his scalpel. The cuts revealed red flesh hidden below that resembled licorice whips. With precise strokes, he whittled away the flesh, hewing to the bone and then finally, after even his iron stomach had turned sour from the gory massacre on his table, he had the mice brains in his hands, pried from their shells to a symphony of soft, sucking sounds. Deconstructing piece by piece the cleverly assembled ewer of a living organism, even if that organism had been a vermin, never failed to astonish Malcolm. He had learned years before that nature held secrets so astounding and so scary that they defied reason.

It was time. After all his hard work, after all those years, at last, the answer was in his hands. He could sense success. It had to work this time.

Malcolm exhaled audibly, pushing away his anxiety and excitement, and restored the stoic face of a hardened scientist. He pushed the sharp edge of the thin razorblade into the freshly-harvested mouse brain and sliced three nearly-transparent cross sections from several sections of the brain. The grayish-pink slices looked oddly like slivers of watermelon that had been left out in the sweltering sun for too long.

Campbell placed the slices onto individual glass slides, each labeled according to their origin by the use of a rather complicated 13-digit alphanumeric code that meant something only to Malcolm. Once this task was complete, Malcolm repeated it with the brain from the mouse infected with Compound Zeta. The whole process was a truly laborious and meticulous undertaking, but then again, the greatest of discoveries never grew from unattended soil. With each brain segmented, labeled and prepared, Malcolm was ready for his first look beneath the microscope.

It took him two hours to analyze and upload the scans of every slide to his computer. His eyesight had diminished over the last few years, likely the result of spending extended hours in the darkness of his basement laboratory, and this meant that he could not rely on his own interpretation of the scans by itself. Malcolm found it difficult at first because he was not a computer person, but he eventually succeeded at writing a computer algorithm to cross compare every scan from the treated mouse to that of the control mouse. Every conceivable combination of change in brain anatomy and any possible permutation of structural fluctuation between the two brains would be hashed out and reported on the computer screen.

He executed his program on the uploaded scans. A rotating hour glass popped up on the screen and the computer began ripping through the images. It was thinking.

Writing code and working with a computer was not something Malcolm gravitated towards, at least at first. Malcolm had always considered himself a "slate state" physicist because he enjoyed solving path integrals by hand on a chalkboard— the old-fashioned way — the way of Einstein and Schrodinger. This was his mantra, his belief. Great minds became great minds by working in a cloud of chalk dust and laboring through mathematical torture with crippling hand cramps threatening every next calculation. Yet, the massive computing power of circuit boards and semiconductors overwhelmed his traditional paradigms and he evolved into a modern day geek, turning to the yellow glow of a computer screen to sift through numeric chaos whenever it was advantageous.

The algorithm took only a few minutes to run and it could do far more in those few minutes than Malcolm could do in months with the same data. The rotating hour glass on the computer screen stopped rotating and the screen flashed for a second before displaying a large array of numbers and graphics. To most people, the output produced by the computer would have looked like the tenth circle of Hell with numbers to the seventh-decimal place streaming up and down the screen, but to Malcolm, he could see everything in those numbers.

There were some definite differences between the brains of the two mice after accounting for intra-species variability. The treated mouse had damage to its optic tract and fornix, which had impeded its cognitive function in the last days of its life. The damage was not so pronounced as to have been lethal, more causing disorientation or blindness in the mouse— this was of no help to Malcolm. The control mouse had a statistically larger amygdala than the treated mouse after adjustment of intra-species variability. This result interested Malcolm and made him recall a set of stimuli tests he had run on the treated mouse prior to euthanizing it.

In one of the tests, the mouse had to complete a ten-square foot maze that it had previously completed, but with one added difference— a motivator — an adolescent python set free within the maze to hunt the mouse. The python's mouth had been taped close so it couldn't actually eat the mouse, but it could still move freely throughout the maze. What Malcolm had wanted to see from this test, was how the mouse reacted to fear stimuli and what he witnessed was odd at the time. The mouse was weaving in and out of the maze, albeit at a slower pace than when it had first finished it, but when it took a wrong corner and came face to face with a predator, it did something a normal mouse would never have done— it scurried up and over the python to complete the maze. It showed no fear, not because it was fearless, but because the treatment of Compound Zeta had diminished its ability to process fear. In essence, Malcolm had made the mouse too stupid to be afraid of the python. The image of the shrunken amygdala on the computer screen was the proof.

Malcolm grew frustrated at what he saw. He leaned forward against the back of an aluminum chair, raising his glasses so that they rested on the gray frill atop his head and peered into the computer screen, examining every component with incessant scrutiny.

Nothing on the screen indicated Compound Zeta would be of any consequence in killing anything larger than a mouse. It lacked potency. It needed something more. This infuriated Malcolm.

He gripped the back of the aluminum chair, digging his fingertips into the unforgiving metal until they turned white. He hung his head and his eyes stared vacantly at the concrete floor. A frustrated, desperate scream jumped out of him and his body grew tense. Without hesitation, the chair was hoisted above his head and swung like an axe into the ground. It bounced off the floor with discord, a cacophony of metal scraping against rough concrete echoed in the chamber of his laboratory. The chair folded itself sideways against a plastic utility closet a few feet away.

Malcolm was quiet, deranged. He had failed again. How many times had he failed? Too many!

At the back of his laboratory there was a door. A cold and windowless door held closed by an antique latch half-rusted along its hinge. It looked like the door to a dungeon and anyone coming upon it would likely not wish to open it. But Malcolm did. He walked up to the door and opened it. It slid open with a screech.

Malcolm stopped just before it and stared inside, staring at the ground in front of him. To his side, attached to a nail in the wall, hung a wooden bat wrapped in barbed-wire. He pulled it from the wall and a heavy smile furled over his lips. He raised his face and his eyes were wild, bright with brutal thoughts. He stepped through the door.

Happiness Purged

A few moments had passed before I summoned the courage to dial the phone.

The call went to voicemail. I hung up and tried again...voicemail. I hesitated to call again, but I had to know. I needed the truth. I tried once more.

"Hello?" A stern voice replied.

"Who is this?" I asked through clenched teeth, knowing at once the voice to be unfamiliar, alien— the voice of bad news.

I stood and started pacing around my living room, my fingers tapping uncontrollably against my thigh.

"This is Officer Landry with the New Hampshire State Police. With whom am I speaking with?"

"This is Benjamin Fisher, the son of Lily Fisher. This is her phone number!"

I didn't know how else to respond, but I knew something bad had happened.

There was a rough scratching sound on the other line, like the sound of someone sliding their hand across the receiver to muffle what was being said. I heard a mumbling, but could not make out what was said.

"Mr. Fisher, where are you right now?"

"Washington, D.C."

"Well, son...I don't wish to be the one to tell you this, but...there has been an accident," he cleared his throat, his voice trailing off. "Your parents...uh... they were killed... Son, I am sorry!"

Sharp pains, like those from a flaming hot poker, shot through my stomach and down my spine. I was numb. Megan saw my face and raised her hand to her mouth. She sat down, wide-eyed.

"Are...you...sure? I mean...how do you know?" I questioned. I could not believe what he had said. This was surely a mistake. Maybe a case of mistaken identity? It had to be— something that could be easily explained. There was no way it couldn't be. No! I could not believe it otherwise.

"Son, we have made a tentative ID. It is based solely on the two drivers' licenses that were found in the wreckage and the registration of the car's tags. The two IDs were New Hampshire drivers' licenses. One was for a Carl Wilhelm Fisher and the other for a Lily Denise Fisher, both of 470 Ingram Street, Concord, NH. The car, a blue 2003 Toyota Avalon, had New Hampshire tags that were registered to Carl Wilhelm Fisher. A physical ID may still be required to verify their identities, but...it does appear that the victims were your parents. I am sorry, son." His voice was systematic and rough, almost robotic as he rehashed the identification of my parents' bodies.

"How?" I whimpered the muscles in my face growing tight and heavy. "How…did…they—?"

"We can't know for sure, it happened about an hour ago."

"Take a guess." I shouted through budding tears.

Officer Landry paused. The silence held an unwillingness to continue with the conversation, but then he added, "it looks like your father was driving, lost control of the car and it careened off the road, traveling at a high rate of speed. The car hit a rocky incline as it went off the road, which flipped the car. We think your parents lost consciousness after the initial collision. Gas must of leaked out or something and eventually caught fire. The car was engulfed in flames when the first responders arrived. It took a couple of minutes to put the fire out, by then it was too late. This is all preliminary mind you and we'll need to complete a further investigation."

"Do you believe that the crash was accidental?" I was about to burst into tears, but I needed more information. Officer Landry's systematic, robotic approach of retelling my parents last moments made it more difficult to maintain my composure. I wanted to crawl into a ball and cry.

"Once more, son, we know very little right now. But if I had to guess based on the collision damage and other factors, I would qualify this as an accident. There appears to be no other cars involved. There are no other tire marks or collision fragments other than from your parents' car. It is possible that a mechanical failure within the automobile or a medical episode led to the accident. This information will be established after further investigation."

I wanted to say something about the phone call I had received earlier, to tell him about Warren. But if it didn't make sense to me, it certainly wouldn't make sense to Officer Landry. I replied as calmly as I could muster, "thank you Officer for the information. What happens to my parents now?"

"The coroner has collected their bodies. Within the next forty-eight hours someone at the Medical Examiner's office will try to perform a more formal identification and there will be an autopsy. If any medical episode occurred, the autopsy results will show it. After this, their bodies will be released to a family member for burial."

"Who claims their bodies?" I choked out.

"Well, this is up to the family. Typically, the family contacts a funeral parlor that then works with the Office of the Medical Examiner to set up the necessary arrangements. Do you have anybody that you can call to do this, since you're not nearby?"

"I will take care of it."

"That should be fine. I can notify the M.E and provide your information as the primary contact," his gruffness waned and he spoke gently. "Son, this is an awful tragedy you have just been dealt. Losing your parents like this. I will do everything I can to make the process as quick and painless as possible. My condolences."

Tears swelled in my eyes and formed briny pools of sorrow that burned my eyes. The false mask of strength that I had assumed was slipping. With a heavy jaw, I lamented, "thank you, sir. I have to…go."

I dropped the phone and at once my composure burst like a dam. I was flooded with grief and sadness. I ran to the bathroom, fell to my knees and placed my head against my left forearm, which rested against the outer rim of the cold porcelain toilet bowl. My stomach compressed inward and the remnants of dinner moved upwards, burning the soft lining of my esophagus as it came. The contents of my stomach were like a chunky tomato soup, smelling sickly sweet and rancid as they cascaded from my mouth and splashed into the bowl. Sweat grew on my brow and tears poured freely from my eyes and down my cheeks before dripping into the bowl of pinkish liquid beneath my head.

They were gone. Just like that. My parents. Gone! Stolen from me. I felt like a giant claw had swooped down from the heavens— a death-bringing bird of prey— clutched a piece of me with its massive talon and ripped it from my body. All that remained was a hollow chasm that was once filled with memories of people no longer alive. I grabbed at my stomach, scratching at it, trying to feel—trying to feel something. I dug my fingers into my skin, into my flesh, and scraped at its smooth, peach-colored surface, slivers of my skin peeling from me. I did this again and again, scratching at my skin repeatedly.

How can I not feel? I could see the scratches, the small mounds of raised skin with speckles of red running up the center. Tiny mountain ranges of swollen skin with small lakes of blood at their summits. They traveled lengthwise up my body, growing deeper with each repeated scraping. Why couldn't I feel? I couldn't feel anything. Nothing! My body had grown cold and numb and I started to shiver, my stomach stirring for another vomit. I was intoxicated by grief, numb to all physical things. I could not feel.

I rested my head against my arm and let it hover above the toilet for an indistinguishable amount time. I spent each of the passing seconds allowing tears to roll down my face and the immense heaviness that had grown inside of me to hold in my chest. For the first time in my life, I felt lost and alone. I had always been a determined and decisive person, but now, I was Hansel lost in the forest. What just happened to my life? Somehow and for some reason, it was torn away from me.

My parents were dead. Dead! That word was so absolute, so complete...so final. Never again would I hug my mother and feel her endearing embrace. Never again would I watch another football game with my father and hear us yell in unison at the television because the Patriots made a poor play. Such a finality to everything. As a laid there, distraught, I was overcome by the brevity and conclusiveness of life. My last Christmas at home, was now my last Christmas at home...ever.

No more would I taste a slice of Mom's blueberry pie, which always came from the oven smelling of pastry heaven. Its golden crust flaking with the gentlest prod of a fork and its gooey purple filling, so rich like syrup, so comforting, would never again blend with a slightly-melted scoop of vanilla ice cream to make a dessert that was the exactness of a mother's love. Never again. There were no more lessons to be taught about how to be a man or about personal responsibility from my father, who wore the uniforms of a father, of a husband, of a provider with such consummate skill that I could not name one man nearly as capable. Lost were the days where a simple phone call to either of my parents would alleviate the stirrings of doubt that swirled in my thoughts because some new activity had roused my habitual lack of confidence. Gone were these days, all of them, never to exist anew. Now, there were just the memories...just memories.

Red-eyed and crying, Megan entered the doorway of the bathroom and leaned against its frame, looking fragile and weak. She said nothing, offering only her sleepy and teary-eyed gaze that did not look at me, but past me at some far-distant sight. The gaze that held the jovial spark of her fiery character had grown dark, extinguished, swapped with the frigid waters of fear and sympathy.

"*Babe...I...am...so...sorry this happened to you!*" She whimpered, still not looking at me. "*I am so sorry!*"

I said nothing. There was nothing to say. My parents were dead...why? I had just talked to them. Hours! The last time I would ever talk to them. Just hours ago! What wasted last words, calling them like that, asking them if they were okay. Words that could have been spent telling them how much I appreciated all they did for me or telling them once more that I loved them. That was something that I had stopped doing after I entered middle school—telling my parents that I loved them. I regretted that. A lot!

For the rest of my life, the final conversation with my parents would not be a thank you or a statement of gratitude. There would never be a conversation where I could tell them that I was getting married or that I was going to be a father. Whenever these times came, I would never be able to hear my son say "grandpa" or watch as my wife and mother plotted some family gathering at the dining room table. Memories of the past eternally etched in time, memories that have yet to be, forever erased by fortune. Instead, the last conversation was a question. A question of whether they were alright, a call to make sure they weren't…dead.

Then the truth struck me. They didn't just die. It was no accident. It was him— UNCLE WARREN.

He did this. He killed my parents. Murdered them!

He had said they died in a fiery crash on Route 16. That was exactly where my parents had been driving. That was exactly where their car was found. How did he know where they were? And more importantly, who was he? He knew my name and knew precisely where I was, what I was doing when my parents met their end. He knew about Megan too. He seemed to know everything. He was the reason my parents were dead. There were no other alternatives. I was growing more certain of it with every playback of Warren's villainous phone call. His nefarious words spoke the truth. He knew…but how? He did it. He murdered my parents.

This eureka moment renewed my energy and it made me feel again. It pushed away my sadness, however temporary it may have been. The scratches across my stomach that produced no pain as I tore into myself now stung with the prick of a thousand tiny needles. The skin beneath my collared white polo shirt had grown blotchy and red.

I raised myself from the base of the toilet and flushed away the vomit. My body was nervous and weak, twitching as if fueled by a half-dozen shots of espresso, but somehow I felt like a quiet clarity had come over me. It was as if a force inside me was telling me to move forward. Tears and pity did not answer my endless number of questions. Focus had edged through my catharsis and brought strength. I must not lie down and grieve. There was a reason for my parents' death and I was going to find it. I would not allow their death to have no meaning. I was going to find Warren. Thinking his name, embroiled me in fury.

Looking at Megan in the doorway, whose gaze was still not towards me, I barked, "I know you're sorry. I am sorry. I mean, Jesus Christ, my parents were just murdered. I can't just sit here and cry. I have to leave."

My face grew tense, the face of determination and anger. I stormed past Megan, brushing her aside and into the living room. I felt no compassion towards humanity at the moment. I wanted to hit something, rip at something. Destroy it utterly. For every time I thought the word 'murder', my blood pulsed and it grew inside of me...rage. It coursed through my veins, pulsated through my muscles and quaked through my body...rage. Never had I felt the sensation that was growing in me. At that moment, I knew what I would do if I ever found Warren. The actions I was prepared to take, both scared and exhilarated me. I felt like a ravenous animal prepared to maul.

I paced around my living room, stepping in tight circles around my coffee table as I stared at the floor. I needed to get a grip on my emotions.

I moved toward the couch and sat in quiet for almost fifteen minutes. Megan did not move from her spot against the doorframe of the bathroom. I realized in these moments of reflection that I was thinking things that made me a danger to myself…and to Megan. I wanted to harm something or someone. This feeling was alien to me and it scared me that I might harm the woman I loved. I took in several deep breaths and let in the fresh oxygen. A few deep breaths later, I had calmed myself down and reclaimed the clarity that I had temporarily lost.

I walked to Megan, who continued to just lean against the wall, lifeless. I turned her face towards me, slipped my arms beneath hers and clutched her close. Her face buried into my chest and her hair fell below my chin. I had lost my parents. I knew this and I was overwhelmed with sadness by it. But I had someone important to me that could help ease my pain. I could not shun the woman I had fallen for in the time of my greatest need.

That's not what a man would do…my dad would have said. A man would be both strong and caring. He would not bow to the pressure of conflict and he would not relinquish his responsibilities to the woman he loved. This was who I needed to be. I needed to be strong and I needed to be caring.

Placing my hand beneath her chin, I raised Megan's face so our gazes met. We were teary-eyed, shaken and distraught.

"Listen to me! I have no idea what is going to happen from here, but I have to leave. It may be for a few days, it may be for a few months. Regardless, I don't know what is going to happen between us. So I wanted to tell you that I love you."

Her eyes flashed new life at my words. Attempting a smile, she offered, "Ben, I want to come with you. You can't deal with this alone. It is too much! I am coming with you."

"Megan, you can't come with me," I rebuffed.

"Why?" She asked, taken aback.

"There are a few reasons. For one, my family and I need to grieve. Another is your responsibilities here. You have your internship."

"My internship won't care."

"That brings me to my third reason... Uncle Warren," Megan recoiled when I spoke his name. "I don't know who he is, but he seems to know who I am...and who you are. He killed my parents! I don't know how, but he did. I am not just going home to bury my parents—"

"Ben, don't say it. I know what you're going to say. Don't!"

"I have to. He killed my parents. He murdered them. What? Do you think I am going to let that go unpunished? I am sorry, but I can't have you tagging along for this. It's too dangerous."

"Tell the police. That's what you do. We go up together. Then, we go to the police and we tell them everything. They'll investigate and arrest him, if he had anything to do it!"

"He did!"

She did not understand my growing need for revenge.

"I agree with you. There's no question in my mind that he had something to do with it. But there are people better equipped to take care of him."

I held up my hands, palms facing Megan, as if I was surrendering to her and offered, "Fine, how about this? I leave on the earliest flight I can find and then you come up in a day or two. Alright?"

"Fine! You and your family need time together. I get that. But I know how hard it is to lose a parent unexpectedly. When my dad died, I wish I had somebody there for me that wasn't my family— someone just for me. A person I could talk to that didn't hurt as I did. I didn't have that person, Ben, but you do. You're looking at her," Megan said, leaning away from me to wipe a tear from her eye with the sleeve of her shirt.

I felt awful. The endless onslaught of emotion had beaten me down. Shifting my loosened embrace, I brought Megan towards me and kissed her forehead, letting my lips rest there for a moment.

"I appreciate you being there for me. I do. You have to understand though that I am entering into something that I am unprepared for. Nothing I have done in my life has prepared me for a time like this. I have to tell my grandmother that her daughter is dead. How could I possibly do that and introduce you to her at the same time?"

She paused, thinking and responded, "You're right! I just want to be there for you. That's it. So if you say that coming up a day or two later is what you prefer, that's what I'll do." She spoke as if she had been defeated, unwilling to argue any more. It was not a time to argue anyway, we both knew that.

"Thank you!" I replied.

"Ben, I can't tell you how much I wish I could take away your pain and make everything better. If I could turn back time, I would," Megan sympathized as she leaned forward and kissed my lips, our tears blending against our cheeks. She pulled from me and headed towards the door. I didn't want her to go, but knew she had to.

Glancing back at me, she reached for the doorknob and said, "you need to tend to your family now. I'll see you soon. I am so sorry Benjamin."

She was gone as the door rolled closed. I had never felt more alone.

Of Hills and Haunts

My flight touched down an hour before dawn to a torrent of rain. Sheets and buckets pelted the hull of the plane as it pulled into the airport terminal, beating the aluminum with a relentless barrage of water. I could hear the metal frame flexing and bending beneath the force of the shower as I sat with my head against the window. Soon loud cracks of lightning and furious roars of thunder joined the soggy onslaught.

I was quick to exit the plane after removing the tattered navy blue duffle bag from the overhead compartment. In my haste, I had thrown just a handful of clothes into the bag prior to heading to the airport. I had no idea if anything I had packed made a complete outfit.

I made my way through the near empty linoleum foyer to a rental car kiosk and I was greeted by a plump, balding man with a disingenuous smile. He was the only person working so early in the morning. I didn't care much to speak with him and yanked the keys from his sausage-like fingers once they were offered.

The automatic doors that gave entrance to the airport parted and I stepped out onto sodden asphalt. At once, I felt the torrid humidity that had spurred the thunderstorm. The muggy air was on me in an instant and I didn't much care for it. It felt more like the tropical coastline of Costa Rica than south-central New Hampshire. And the rain…was endless. It poured and poured and poured.

I kept under the covered sidewalk heading towards the rental car lot. The roof overhanging the sidewalk ended short of the lot. After a quick deliberation, I dove out into the surprisingly cool rain, holding my beaten duffle bag above my head for its meager protection. It didn't help. I was soaked.

The key I was given did not have automatic entry and I began to scan the entire parking lot for a blue Toyota. There were hundreds of cars, many blue and the parking lot was a giant rectangle, probably forty yards by sixty yards. I jogged up one row where there were several blue cars in a row. They were all Fords. I turned and spotted a pack of blue and red cars at the top of the rental lot. I started jogging towards them, into the slanted and relentless rain. My polo shirt clung to my torso, growing heavier with each sopping step that I took in my water-gorged shoes.

A blue Toyota came into view, but when I tried my key, it did not turn. Droplets of water dripped from the seams of my cargo shorts, down my legs and into my squishy shoes. I scanned the parking lot again, squinting through the sheets of rain. It was so loud— the sound of millions of tiny pellets falling from the sky. I could not see any more blue cars. I tried to find an attendant to help, but could not find anyone.

"Come on!" I shouted.

For the second time in twelve hours, I felt alone, helpless and close to tears. I dropped my duffel bag in a puddle at me feet and stood, unprotected, in the rain. I looked up into the darkened sky, hoping for a reprieve from what I concluded was a crime I had committed. It felt like all that was happening to me was a punishment for something I did. Was it because I did not believe in God?

Just then, a violent crackling erupted through the pounding rain— the lightning had returned— striking a tall pine tree at the edge of the airport runway. The lightning strike had to be no more than a hundred yards away. Then the thunder boomed, proclaiming its arrival and sending shockwaves down my spine. I had to get out of this storm.

I headed off towards the far distant side of the parking lot, my duffle bag in hand. It dawned on me that I should have paid attention to the rental car associate. He had told me where the bloody car was, but I had stopped listening.

A set of blue cars came into view. One of them was a Toyota, I could tell by its distinctive looping-T logo that reminded me of the Greek letter Theta. As I approached it, I stopped as the car's image crystallized through the downpour.

It was a blue Toyota Avalon.

It was not possible. The odds were so small...infinitesimal. This was the same car my parents had. Then I remembered somberly— it was the car they died in. It *was* my parent's car.

I did not want *this* car, but I was soaked and wanted refuge. I tried my key in the door. It turned and the door opened. This was my parent's car. The car they died in...the car they died in! I did not want this car. I wanted never to see another like it.

Suddenly, I felt like I was being watched from afar. Somewhere in the distance, a pair of eyes was watching me. I could feel the power of their stare. A shiver ran down my side.

As much as I did not want this car, I felt a surge of desire for a warm and safe place, even if it was *this* car. I tossed my duffle bag onto the passenger seat and dropped into the driver's seat, slamming the door closed and locking it at once. Locked in the car, out of the rain, I felt safe. The sense that I was being watched made me uncomfortable and the warm silence of sitting in an idled car, even this car, put me at ease.

I still had the sense that a distant pair of eyes was watching me. I flashed back to last night, when Warren had called and had said that he knew where I was when my parents died. I felt the same way then, but it felt heavier now, almost palpable. The feeling reminded me of when I was a child and I had to go upstairs to bed. I would walk alone down the dark hallway to my bedroom, tiptoeing as I went, ensuring to keep away from all shut doors because of the untold horrors that my childhood mind hid behind them. Then, inevitably, when I thought I heard a door creak ajar or thought I saw a shadowy specter creeping up from behind, I would tense up. With shivers shooting down my tiny body, I would shout out a belligerent expression to certify to the encroaching monsters that I was a courageous young lad and that I did not fear them. Of course, once I had established my bravery to all the wicked ghouls and demons that lurked behind closed doors, I ran feverishly down the hall to the safety of my Mickey Mouse comforter. Those fears of monsters and demons and ghosts were figments of an impressionable child's overbearing imagination. I think even as a child, a part of me knew there were no such things as monsters.

But what I was feeling now did not feel like the imagination of a scared child. As I sat drenched from head to toe, in the quiet warmth of a car that I didn't want to be in, I thought maybe monsters were real.

I took a moment to listen to the pounding rain. Sitting in silence, the rhythmic pelting over my head was soothing. After a few moments, I forced myself to relax. I made myself believe that some distant pair of eyes was not watching me and I was not being punished for anything that I did. The fear and guilt that I was feeling were symptoms of fatigue and grief. At least this was what I kept assuring myself.

I started the engine and put the heater on high. For all the humidity outside, I was freezing. I was too soaked to drive. Unzipping my duffle bag, I could tell most of the clothes were wet, but starkly drier than the ones I was wearing. I rummaged around and managed to pull together a pair of black crew-cut socks, boxers, silver-stripped mesh shorts, and a light green German beer t-shirt with a tear in the collar caused from by overzealous game of beer pong several years earlier.

Not worried about appearances, I stripped naked in the front seat of the rental car. The car was not large and I was not short, so I was forced to stretch and contort myself into positions that left my ass pressed against the driver's side window. Anyone within eyeshot would have been blinded had they caught a glimpse. All I could envision as I pulled up my boxers was a tap on the glass, followed by a Police officer's flashlight illuminating my nether regions as I struggled to maintain my balance on the car seat. None of this happened though and the new clothes helped to warm my frigid body parts. The car's heater had grown so hot that it began to feel like I was in a tanning bed. I did not mind though.

I pulled out of the lot and headed for Brown Avenue— headed for home. I realized with the thought that home did not mean the same thing that it meant before.

The rain had not stopped since my flight touched down and it showed no signs of yielding, but the lightning and thunder had stopped for a second time. It was difficult in the rain and limited daylight to read the traffic signs. I made a wrong turn down a one-way street in the labyrinth of interweaving roads near the airport when the road stretched away from me, as it did the night before. The world held in suspension and the crimson haze returned. The world felt different, away from me. My head ached, throbbed just as it had the night my parents died— last night — when I was walking home with Megan.

I swerved off the road, scraping the car against a guardrail. My head hurt so badly. The brakes squealed and the car stopped abruptly. My nose was bleeding. Things grew distant, hazed in crimson. The steering wheel was gripped in my hands, I could feel my fingers clutching it, but I saw it as something projected from me, almost like it was locked away in some box that I could not touch. The road was like this too. Everything was shrouded in crimson and locked away from me. The pain in my head... oh my head. It hurt worse than any pain I could remember.

I placed my forehead against the wheel and closed my eyes. The world around me was shaking, moving like an angry bull prepared to throw me from its back. I felt that the universe wanted to push me through its limits and spit me from its mouth, into the beyond. Then the world sprung back towards me and the crimson haze dissipated. My head stopped aching. My nose stopped bleeding. All was fine again.

This was the second time it had happened to me in less than a day. I had never experienced anything like it before and I wished never to experience it again. It was not something that felt normal to me and I could not think of anyone who would deem it 'normal'. I was sure such a feeling was a violation of physiological law and that the human body was not built to experience it.

With caution, I pulled back onto the correct road. I felt no residual effect of the incident other than the blood staining my face. I used my sodden clothes to rinse my face and then pushed the episode from my thoughts to focus on driving. After a couple back roads leading from the airport, I turned onto the main street heading into Manchester, the city of my teenage indiscretions.

Manchester in the misty sunlight of the early morning was exactly as I had remembered it: a hushed and slow moving city with a wry, charmingly sedate character. It was a sleepy hub of urban life and always had been, but when I called Concord home, it didn't feel that way. The largest city in New Hampshire, Manchester held the glamour and allure of a major metropolis for the small town folks north of Boston. In reality though, Manchester was typical for most small New England cities and different from the region's pinnacle city, something I did not learn until I moved away. As a teenager, I had always thought Manchester a city with near endless possibilities. They had the largest mall in New Hampshire, more than double the number of people than Concord and buildings that resembled skyscrapers. The city was my first musing into a world of amazing feats, demonstrating the capabilities of human beings.

On my fifteenth birthday, I visited the science center in Boston. Later, I went to Fordham in New York and then to D.C. It was apparent that the childhood magnetism Manchester held for me, being a place of wonderment, was diluted by city life. The skyscrapers I had seen in Manchester when I was young presented me with the gift of astonishment and instilled in me a keen admiration for history. However, the expanse of my imagination had been tethered by my inability to think more was possible— that larger cities swollen with more massive structures and a greater bounty of denizens could exist. Still, I felt comfort being back in her familiar embrace.

The rain finally subsided as I came to one of the dozens of Dunkin Donuts cast about the city. The familiar orange-and-pink signage of Dunkin Donuts was as much a New England staple as Clam Chowda and Fluffernutter sandwiches. After seeing it, I decided that a shot of caffeine would do me wonders. I pulled in and bought myself a hot French-vanilla coffee. Never had a cup of coffee tasted so good.

It was approaching the morning commute and the street was growing more congested. I passed a handful of cars on the left, quickly cutting back over to a chorus of honks and merged right onto 101, heading north to Concord. The only natural light that assisted my commute were the slivers of sunlight that slipped through the gray cloud-cover. I continued for several miles and took the ramp for I-93 North.

I was not certain where I was heading. I knew I didn't want go home, not yet anyway. I thought that I would go to my Uncle Robert and Aunt Jolie's house. They were as close to parents as I had now and they would help me through this. Maybe even tell my grandmother. I really couldn't bring myself to tell her that my mom had died.

Aunt Jolie was my mother's younger sister and like many of my mom's relatives, she lived most of her adult life within an hour of my grandmother. We were a true matriarchal family. After my Aunt married my Uncle Robert, who everyone called Bobby, they stayed close. I never called my Uncle Robert, Bobby, though. I couldn't say his name as a little kid. Instead I called him Bobbo, which was what I called him still. He and my Aunt Jolie lived across town from my parents, but they saw each other with such regularity that the distance didn't seem to matter. Twice a week, every week until I left for college, my parents and I ate dinner with Bobbo and Aunt Jolie and their two kids, Owen and Jessica. We alternated where we ate. The frequency of our gatherings ensured we were a close family.

Thirty minutes had passed until Concord came into view. The golden dome of the state house told me that I was home. Seeing the state capitol was surreal. It made me think of D.C where I could have just walked down First Street and gazed upon the nation's Capitol. Then I thought of yesterday when Megan and I walked the streets of D.C with thoughts of a weekend getaway. The sandy beaches of Ocean City seemed so insignificant now and so much further away. I took the Route-3 exit and headed south.

It was a few minutes later that I pulled into the gravel driveway of Bobbo and Aunt Jolie's house. Two cars were in the driveway. I suspected Jessica was still away at Boston College because I didn't see her pink beetle car with neon green polka dots painted on the roof. The paint job resembled a mushroom from the Super Mario Brother's video game. It was comically horrific.

I parked my car behind Bobbo's SUV and started for the front door. Their house was a blue Colonial with white trim. A white-railed porch ran along the front platform and down both sides and a sundeck occupied the open backyard. Two rocking chairs and a porch swing filled up one side of the porch. Taking it all in, the familiar surroundings and the smell of my Aunt's flower garden made me think, at least for a moment, that everything was going to be all right.

I stood on the granite steps and knocked on the glass window of their wooden door waiting for it to be answered.

Lies and Hidden Truths

I was nervous as I waited for someone to answer the door. They were not expecting me, but I knew they were home. Still, I probably should have called them at least to tell them the news and that I was coming up. However, I knew how it felt to be told that my parents were dead over the phone. It was a sledgehammer to the chest.

The door opened and Bobbo's broad boulder-like shoulders filled in the empty space.

"Benjamin? What the heck! I thought you were in D.C?" Bobbo asked.

His thick, silver hair was pulled back in a ponytail. His wide and hefty stature was intimidating at first glance, but his demeanor was everything but rugged or abrasive. Over time, especially as of late, wrinkles in his face softened this perceived ruggedness and made Bobbo seem almost like a gentle giant. His ears were large, not quite Dumbo large, but large enough that they resembled a pair of pectoral fins on a fish as they dangled from his head. His large ears helped to balance out his piercing, blue eyes, which gave him a foreboding appearance.

I shifted forward. "Bobbo, something happened to my parents!"

A look of concern grew across his face. "Come in."

I stepped inside and walked to the living room. Bobbo closed the door behind me.

"My gosh! Benjamin, what are you doing here?" Aunt Jolie gawked in her squeaky, faint voice from the entrance of the kitchen.

She had on a frilled blue-and-white apron with a picture of an embroidered pie in the center with the word HOMEMADE written beneath it in arching stitch. It seemed that she had been baking. From the smell, I thought maybe brownies and my stomach grumbled. Aunt Jolie's baking skills were exemplary and having seen Bobbo's waistline widen over the years, we began to joke that Aunt Jolie was trying to kill him with butter.

"I think you should sit down Aunt Jolie," I offered gently as Bobbo came into the room behind me, stroking his graying goatee as he had a tendency to do when he was anxious. "You too, Bobbo. Can you take a seat?"

Bobbo and Aunt Jolie looked at each other, the surprise of seeing me draining from their faces, replaced by a knowing look. Aunt Jolie came into the room, wiping flour from the front of her apron. They sat down together, knee to knee, onto a floral-printed couch, directly across from the burgundy recliner where I sat. I inched forward to the front of the chair, my elbows firmly on my thighs.

"What's going on Ben? You said something happened to your parents." Bobbo asked, grasping his wife's closest hand and placing it into one of his own massive mitts. He caressed them with fondness.

"Yes, I did. Last night I received a call from an Officer Landry from the New Hampshire state police," a lump grew in my throat as I retold the story. "…Um, well, anyway…Officer Landry said that mom and dad had been in an accident—"

"Oh my, are they okay?" Aunt Jolie asked in a hopeful tone that masked the inevitable truth that she knew. Bobbo pulled her close to him, sensing what I was about to say.

"No, they're not. My parents were killed last night." I cried aloud.

"What? No. I just saw Lily…yesterday. She can't be-"

She looked at my bloodshot eyes and my haggard appearance and could not escape the reality. Reality was a nail and my presence there, hundreds of miles from where I should have been, was the hammer. There was no mistake. My parents were gone.

At once, she balled. The sad sounds of Aunt Jolie's crying corrupted the air. She threw her face into Bobbo's massive shoulder and shook inexorably. Her cries began as muffled wanes that continued slowly into loud dissonances that pierced my ears. Bobbo offered no movement or emotion and I could not tell if he was in shock or if he was just trying to be a good husband.

Bobbo looked at me, still holding my traumatized Aunt Jolie against him and said, "You look awful, bud. When was the last time you ate something?"

I was taken aback by the calmness he possessed for the situation. He seemed unmoved, in a way, by what I just divulged to him. I was hungry though and dreadfully exhausted.

"Yesterday sometime. Though, I threw all that up," I admitted, me voice trailing away as I spotted a photo of my parents with Bobbo and Aunt Jolie from a Memorial Day cookout several years earlier sitting askew on a bookcase. The four of them looked jubilant; their smiles brandishing the pride of the good life they were living.

"Well, we have some coffee still in the pot and a couple chocolate-chip muffins that your Aunt made yesterday. Help yourself," offered Bobbo, he motioned me with his free arm to the kitchen with the authoritative gesture of a traffic cop.

I was starving. The whole trip was so abrupt, spurred by my parent's unexpected and taunted death that I had not even thought about food until seeing the familiar faces of home and letting down the barrier that obstructed my ability to feel. I went to the kitchen to rummage for food and to give Bobbo and Aunt Jolie a few moments to comprehend the gravity of my parent's death.

Two shelves, each about three feet in length, protruded from the wall leading into the kitchen and displayed blue-glazed ceramic pots. Each pot varied in size, some were the size of teapots, others were as small as pillboxes and each one had scribbled in black letters the name of a common spice or baking ingredient. Both shelves were sorted by size and importance of ingredient, forcing flour, sugar, and salt to the front position on the shelves; caraway seed and juniper were the laggards of the spice class, delegated to the lonely spots at the end of the bottom shelf. These two shelves were the personification of my neat and proper Aunt Jolie who, for as long as I could remember, was a tireless homemaker who always ensured her family's home was immaculate and welcoming.

Aunt Jolie's chocolate-chip muffins were delicious. At first sight, I unwrapped two of them from their foiled cages and stuffed both whole in my mouth. It was a rather amazing feat, shoving two full-sized muffins into one's mouth at once and even though I nearly choked on an unprocessed chocolate chip when I swallowed, I probably could have added a third. My first bite of food in half a day was one of the tastiest bites of food I had ever taken.

The sweet cakey texture of the breakfast treat lifted my spirits. Muffins were frostingless cupcakes and I chased it with a large mug of coffee, followed by a second. The additional injection of caffeine jettisoned my fatigue, making me feel as if I had just awoken from a twelve-hour siesta. Refreshed and ready to discuss the necessary matters with my Aunt and Uncle, I started back towards the living room, but stopped when I overheard whispering.

"—when he was here yesterday. I am certain of it. You hear it all the time, that people get a sense about it. They knew something was going to happen," Bobbo's voice whispered.

"I don't know, Robert. You really think Lily and Carl came over here yesterday to say goodbye? I don't believe it. If they knew, why would they have chosen to leave? Why not just stay home?" Aunt Jolie sighed. I could tell from the wavering tone of her voice that she was wiping tears from her eyes, probably still crying. I could not blame her. Aunt Jolie and my mother were inseparable, spending much of their free time baking or discussing a newly discovered book series.

"Maybe they just had a sense, not enough for them to change their plans. I mean, Lily came over to give you a card for the Fourth. Don't you find that a little peculiar?" Bobbo asked, his voice a notch above a whisper now.

"Why would that be odd? It's almost the Fourth!"

"Yes, but we were supposed to see them tomorrow night for steamers and lobsters, remember? Why would Carl and her come across town just to give us a useless card when we were going to see them tomorrow?"

"Robert, honey, I think you're grasping at straws. I think if they had any idea that they were going to get into an accident, they would have never left."

"Maybe," Bobbo replied, now not whispering at all. "Benjamin, you don't have to stand in the hallway. Come sit down."

I returned to my seat on the burgundy recliner nearest to the staircase that led upstairs and in front of the small corridor that gave entrance to the kitchen. Through a sheepish glare, I said "I didn't mean to eavesdrop on you guys."

"No worries." Bobbo said. "You've been dealt a very shitty hand. We're sorry for that, bud. We'll all get through this together."

"Thanks, Bobbo." I sat upright in the recliner, pushing myself backwards so I touched the back of the chair and continued, "I haven't told Gram yet. And honestly, I was hoping one of you could do it. I just don't think I can manage another emotional onslaught like that"

Aunt Jolie was quiet and misty-eyed.

Several seconds passed before Bobbo assured me, "don't worry about that. I get how hard that would be for you. We will make sure Maggie finds out. Before that though— if you don't mind — what exactly happened with your parents?"

I didn't care to answer, but I was going to have to sooner or later.

"The specifics are a little vague at the moment, but what I do know from speaking with Officer Landry is that they were in a rather bad accident. Bad enough to catch their car on fire apparently—"

"My God." Bobbo quaked.

"I can only hope if there is a God, he was with them at that moment." I muttered to myself, growing angry at Bobbo's declaration. To me the mere idea that a God could exist and allow such innocent people as my parents— his creations— to die in a heap of metal was too much. Allowing such savage butchery of one's own creation surely meant something about the existence of the almighty. I was sickened by the idea. Angered even.

I went on detailing what I knew of my parent's accident, "I don't really know how bad the accident was. The officer was still able to ID my parents by their driver's licenses— so, umm... that probably means the wreckage was somewhat salvageable. There is a lot more I don't know. For example, what caused the accident. Officer Landry said that he did not see any evidence of another car's involvement or the remains of an animal. He also didn't know if the accident was what killed them. I should find this out sometime today or tomorrow, after the autopsy."

"Where did it happen? Lily and Carl were over here yesterday morning and said they were heading up north, but they never said where." Bobbo offered, gesturing towards Aunt Jolie, who just stared at us with no interest of offering anything. He looked as if he wanted an affirmation to what he had just said. He didn't get one.

"Route 16," I declared, shrugging my shoulders. "Not sure where that is."

A stern, alarmed look came over Bobbo and Aunt Jolie, a look of concern.

"That's up in Osworth." Bobbo interjected, shifting uncomfortably in his seat. "Are you sure?"

"Positive," I said, raising my eyebrows and narrowing my gaze to be more observant of their strange behavior. "Why do you both look surprised?"

"Well, Benjamin it's not really that important right now. It's just an unfortunate coincidence, I'm sure," Aunt Jolie admitted. She was suddenly upright.

"What do you mean by an unfortunate coincidence?" I queried. Coincidence was something, along with God and randomness, which did not exist in my personal gospel.

"Ben, there is something that your parent's never told you. And frankly, right now, it's not important," Bobbo grumbled.

105

His consoling manner dissipated and he was defensive, his broad shoulders rigid as if he was preparing for an argument.

"Does this have to do with Uncle Warren?" I blurted out.

There was a look of befuddlement in their crooked glances.

"Who is Uncle Warren?" They asked in unison.

It seemed that everyone was just as stupid as I was on the subject of Uncle Warren. There was no way I was discussing the tribulations of Warren's phone call or his perceptible all-seeing power. It was too damn weird and I was starting to think that I misheard him. Or worse, that I imagined the whole thing. No one else had ever heard of him, not my parents, not Bobbo or Aunt Jolie. My sanity was being questioned by the one person who needed it most— me. Self-doubt was not what I needed right now.

"Right now, it's not important," I contended, standing from my chair to awaken my sleeping legs, looking up again at the photo of my parents on the bookshelf.

"You're lying, Ben. I can tell. You look away when you're lying. Who is Uncle Warren?" Bobbo asked.

"First, I want to know why my parent's death is an unfortunate coincidence?" I asked, raising my hands above my head and making quotation signs with my fingers when 'unfortunate coincidence' came marching out from my mouth.

Continuing, I justified "Look, I didn't fly up here to be jerked around. My parents were just killed and I haven't slept in over twenty hours. Life sucks right now and it won't get any better if you guys keep shit from me."

This was too much, the whole thing. I was annoyed by it all. The lack of sleep. The lack of food. The time consumed by travel. My family treating me like an illegal immigrant, not permitting me the right to know some secret that would, I was sure, end up being meaningless to their death. The whole damn thing exhausted me.

Bobbo stood up and began to meander across the room towards the bookshelf where he pulled down a brown-leather-bound picture album that was covered in a thick layer of dust.

"Two days, that was how close it was. Just two days," Bobbo said cryptically as he stepped in front of the window overlooking the backyard tomato garden. His back was to me and he began thumbing through the photo album in his hand, looking down at frozen moments in time. "Your aunt and I weren't living here at the time, we were both working in Providence. Still, it was a short drive up here, so we saw your parents enough. Back then, your mom and dad hung around with another couple...what was their name?"

"The Campbells. Malcolm and Macy," Aunt Jolie offered without hesitating, but looking away from me at the utterance of the names. Her body began to tremble slightly. I thought she was crying again.

"Yes, the Campbells, that's right. It was the sixth of August— just two days before you were born, Benjamin. Two days! Anyway, Carl wanted to take your very pregnant mother up north to settle her pre-labor jitters. The Campbells went too, as they spent most summers together back then. But there was another person that went with them." Bobbo paused and turned to face me.

He moved forward and extended the open photo album, placing his stubby finger on a photo of my mom, emitting a youth and exuberance I had never seen, with three other people scattered on the shore of some unknown beach. My mother was quite pregnant, as Bobbo had said, and it was difficult to fathom that in this snapshot of time, I had not yet taken my first breath. Now, years later and viewing this photo for the first time, both of my parents had taken their final breath. It was a cruel reality. A chill ran down my spine. I scanned the photo, scrutinizing the appearance of the other three people.

There was a young blond woman with a dimpled smile that stretched across her face. She was about the same age as my mother, her face reticent, distracted by something. It was a foretelling look, I thought. A fuzzy-haired man kneeled next to the woman, his right flank facing the camera. There was something collegial, almost academic about him. In the picture, he was extending his arms outward in an embrace towards a third person, a small child about a year old sat just outside of his outreached arms. Sitting playfully on a low-rising mound of sand, the tiny child sat, her little hands slapping at the ground with a child's focus.

There was something familiar in the features of the child, her lightly shaded brown hair reminded me of my own and her large eyes held a recognizable kindness. At first, I had assumed the child to be the fuzzy-haired man's based on the context of the photo, but then I saw the undeniable resemblance of my mother and I knew who I was staring at. I grew pale.

"It's your sister, Ben." Aunt Jolie offered heavily. She stood from the couch and walked over to me, placing her hand softly on my shoulder.

I was speechless. Not once in my life had anyone told me that I had a sister. I felt betrayed and lied to. I folded the photo album while standing, brushing aside my Aunt's hand and placing the photo album down onto the chair.

"Why the hell wasn't I ever told of this?" I barked. My life was starting to feel like it was never as I had thought it to be. There was an enigmatic figure in Uncle Warren that no one seemed to know, but who apparently knew me and had known my parents, even suggesting he had previously helped them with something. He was even responsible for their death. That alone was enough, but now I had a… sister?

Bobbo sighed, "we never told you because it was never our place to do so. I don't know why your parents didn't tell you about Grace. Perhaps they couldn't bear to remind themselves of that day's tragedy. Maybe it was frustration or maybe they just didn't want to talk about it. I don't know. Besides it doesn't really matter right now, does it? The real point is it happened in Osworth."

"What exactly happened to my ghost sister, hmm?" I taunted in anger, an expression of terse annoyance plastered across my face. The idea that I had been lied to for my entire life and then ambushed by this deeply held secret left me betrayed.

"Benjamin, she was your sister!" Aunt Jolie responded to my snide remark.

"Correction, she was my parent's first child and she, obviously, died prior to my birth. She was not my sister because I never knew she existed— everyone did a smashing job hiding that. Why now do you expect me to care about my parent's first child, this ghost sister of mine?"

"Bud, calm down!" Bobbo suggested calmly, waving his hands at me. "We don't expect you to bereave your sister, especially now that your parents have passed. All I am trying to tell you is that your parents died in Osworth, the exact same place where your sister drowned. That is the point of it all. It just seems rather peculiar. And it is—"

"Yes, it is odd but, I fail to see how this is anything more than a probabilistic quirk." I spoke bluntly. "It is sad that my sister died all that time ago, but that is a history older than me. The wreck that took my parents, on the other hand, is a fresh wound and deserves my fullest attention. Unless there is something tangible about this tragedy, I do not care about Grace."

In the kitchen, an electronic beep sounded and stopped my verbal lashing, at least for a moment. Aunt Jolie exited

109

the living room and went into the kitchen to attend to the beeping, hanging her head and shaking it softly.

"Christ, you can tell you're going to be a lawyer. But what I was trying to say, before you interrupted, is that your sister's drowning and your parent's car accident are just two incidents that have occurred in Osworth. There have been others in the area, especially over the past few months."

I found this a curious statement. "What kind of incidents?"

"Disappearances mostly. The tally over the last few months was eleven people missing and that is only the people declared missing. That is concerning in its own right, but that is not all. According to Owen's roommate Colin, who works for Fish and Game, they have been finding mutilated deer with giant holes cut through them. Big, fricken holes the size of dinner plates going straight through their bodies like they were drilled into or something. The kicker is that all of these things have happened within a five mile radius of Lake Osworth — the same lake where your sister drowned."

That was peculiar, I had to admit. It could not be a coincidence because those did not happen.

"Where is this place? Yesterday was the first I have ever heard of it."

"Osworth is a village about twenty miles south of North Conway, really out of the way of civilization. There are not many people there, maybe several hundred. Most of the area is pine forest in the mountains. A far cry from what you're used to these days, I'd guess. Still, the area gets the outdoorsy types. Hunters and hikers and the like. In fact, many of the disappearances are of hikers who just vanished. Not one body has been found. That is probably why the State hasn't shut down the area. In fact, the bumbling duffers that run this state have done very little. They did, though, put up signs warning potential hikers of the black bear population," Bobbo chuckled at this. "It is funny to think black bear have anything to do with these disappearances. I mean the last documented case of a fatal black bear attack in New Hampshire was before Washington was president. Before New Hampshire was officially a state. Whatever is happening up in Osworth, it has nothing to do with black bear."

"Do you think any of this has something to do with my parents? I mean when the universe percolates, I believe it is impossible to know the path of her chaos."

"What do you mean by that...when the universe percolates?" Bobbo asked, frowning.

I sighed and explained, "When something becomes volatile and unpredictable. When the universe is like this, it is a good way to end up in trouble or worse."

"I don't quite follow what you mean." Bobbo conceded.

"Well, in the case of Osworth, for years it sat as a small, obscure stretch of land that was quiet and essentially nonexistent, but in due course it became a hotbed of unspecified chaos— people disappearing, animals being mutilated, and my parents... you know. Nature is a ruthless tyrant and she wrecks havoc without warning, but there is always an explanation. It is just difficult to know before the chaos. And that chaos typically concentrates itself," I said, trying to express my views, but everything had caused a persistent torpor on my ability to think. "What I am really trying to say is that shit happens and it can lead to more shit happening. So maybe the disappearances and animal mutilations have something to do with my parents even though they would seem to be unrelated."

Bobbo raised his hand to his chin and his salt-and-pepper goatee. "Ben, you know I don't subscribe to conspiracy theories. While I do think weird things are happening up in Osworth, I can't see any relation to your parent's unfortunate death and everything else. It doesn't mean there isn't, but I struggle to see it." Bobbo sighed.

"Yea, you're probably right. I think right now I am just looking for some answers to why this happened and why—" I stopped in mid-sentence, suddenly thinking about Uncle Warren.

At times, his name was fleeting, hiding from my thoughts like some master hide-and- seek player. Part of me knew all the answers I sought resided in discovering Warren's identity and his relationship to my parents. To my mind, I had found a way to doubt myself about the nefarious doings of Uncle Warren. He held responsibility for my parents' deaths in some manner and I could not let myself forget that. My languid mind, though, could only think about my parents.

"Now, Benjamin. Who is Uncle Warren?" Bobbo queried, sitting once more on the edge of the couch. He sat in an awkward position, half kneeling, and half sitting. It was as if he anticipated having to run from the room screaming at an instant's notice and this made me laugh, but I didn't know why.

At this question, Aunt Jolie reemerged from the kitchen. It appeared eavesdropping was hereditary and she took up next to Bobbo on the couch. Together they forced their faces into stern, laconic expressions and from this I knew it was time to tell what I knew.

So I did, recounting the long-winded narrative of yesterday's events, mentioning all that I could remember despite the tax of emotion. First, I discussed the phone call and how it felt as if Warren had the power of prescience. I reiterated his cryptic confessions of having aided my parents. Then I sheepishly admitted how he had known that they died and was the source of the bad news. I even told of how it was as if he had witnessed their death or even partaken in it somehow.

I mentioned the way his shrill, gruff voice crept inside my ears and how it was as if he had crawled into the sanctuary of my thoughts. I told them about that way he had when he spoke. The cunning force it held— his voice. It incited fear and impelled loneliness. Through his words, Warren seemed able to capture all the happiness and hope inside of someone and tether them to an anchor that was then plunged into the muddy floor of some far-off, desolate quagmire. The person on the receiving end was left to wade in black ankle-high water with no knowledge of the nightmares that lurked beneath the murky ripples. Deserted and full of dread, cautious of each pending moment was the power Uncle Warren held with his voice.

"Jesum Crow, Benjamin!" Aunt Jolie gasped in her tiny voice and then apologized to me for her offensive language.

I laughed telling her I said much worse on a regular basis. Bobbo laughed, too. In my family the contrast between men and women was profound. Men swore like sailors and held their opinions with obdurate force; the women, my mother included, were nuns, never swearing a real swear— of the four letter variety— and they were magnanimous, passionate altruists wishing to see only the good in others.

"So you have never heard of him before? Either of you?" I asked, glancing from Bobbo's bushy-faced grimace to the heavy-hearted sulk painted across Aunt Jolie's gentle features. I knew the answer was a resounding no.

"We are sorry Ben, but neither of us have any idea who he is. Have you told the police?" Bobbo queried.

I shifted in my seat and contemplated my answer. Had they not just heard what I had told them?

"I fear that the police may not be a significant help in this matter," I suggested.

113

"Why? Couldn't they trace the phone number?" Bobbo countered.

"I am sure they can, but not sure they will. Still, my concern is more self-serving than that. I don't think much of what I just told you makes any sense, but it's all true. So how can I expect to persuade anyone if I myself question what happened?"

"It never hurts to ask," Aunt Jolie offered.

"And I will when I go to the morgue, but it is obvious that my parents have hidden things from me. Hiding the fact that I had a sister who died just days before I was born— fine, I can deal with that. I don't understand it, but I can deal with it. Yet, something feels terribly wrong about Uncle Warren. It is almost like my parent's deliberately withheld information from me...about me. Look, he claimed to have known me when I was little. He told me precisely what I was doing when my parents died. Precisely what I was doing! The police aren't going to provide me with the answers that I need. I have to find someone who will. Who would know something...anything at all?"

There was a long silence from the couch. They were hesitating.

"Bobbo, come on? Who is it?" I demanded.

"I will tell you, Benjamin, but you need to promise me something. Okay?" Bobbo faltered, his body wilting under its mollification.

"What is that?" I chirped.

"If you can find him, you do not meet this man alone! You take someone with you. Do you understand? You call me or ask Owen, but you do not confront this man alone," Bobbo warned, his eyes flaring, ballooning to the shape of oversized olives.

I was taken aback by his awe-inspiring massiveness. I shrunk back into my chair.

"Alright, I agree. Now who is this man?" I queried warily.

"Malcolm Campbell!"

A Crackle in the Brush

Derek Doherty climbed down from Mount Chocorua with nothing more than a Swiss Army knife in his pocket and a canteen of lukewarm water around his waist. Sweat trickled down his freckled, gingered brow and he stopped to take a second swig of water as he waited for his pudgy pal Jesse to stoop down off the slight ledge he was cowering on.

"What do you think this is? Everest! Just jump your fat ass down here!" Derek said, looking in the other direction.

With a loud thud, Jesse jumped from the ledge and landed in a small deciduous bush, his bloated belly jiggling like flan.

"I swear Doherty— you're trying to kill me. The next time we go out, we're going bowling." Jesse replied, opening another bag of M&Ms and deposited the hard-earned chocolaty goodness into his mouth, practically drinking its contents.

"Maybe if you weren't such a big lardo, you could handle a little hike," offered Derek, putting down his canteen."We head this way, towards that lake out there!"

"Already? We just got down climbing this mountain! Can't we have like five minutes?" Jesse pleaded, his navy blue shirt dripping with dirt and stench.

"I'll give you three. It's getting close to sunset and we need to find a place to setup camp." Derek compromised, pulling out his Swiss Army knife and extending the dull, chipped blade.

"What are you going to do with that?" Jesse asked, sitting down on a boulder half the size of own backside, feeling exhausted.

Derek searched the underbrush for a long, narrow stick. It had to be bendy and green, filled with chlorophyll. Those were the best. They were easier to cut and quicker to penetrate the water. After a few moments, he found one a few feet away.

"I'm going to catch me a delicious bass, that's what. That lake over there looks shallow and cool enough to hold a nice-sized dinner." Derek offered as he sat down beside his rotund friend and began to peel thin layers of wood from the stick in his hand. In little time, the stick was sharpened to a point.

"I don't care for fish! And aren't bass boney? I don't think you can eat them."

"I'm not fishing for you; you're on your own. It's time to go. I'll carry the pack for a while," Derek said, hoisting the overstuffed pack across his shoulder.

Jesse groaned. There were many things he'd rather be doing than this. There was a marathon of M*A*S*H on, after all, plus reruns of Battlestar Gallactica. Thank goodness for DVR. Besides, what did Derek care anyway if he stayed to camp for the night? Derek only hung out with him because their moms were best friends; by proxy, Derek had to be somewhat amicable towards Jesse. Friendships like his and Dereks' were more of a hostage crisis— for one of them at least — and unfortunately, for Jesse, he knew it was not him.

117

He had come to enjoy their infrequent rumblings about. It let him get out and away from his video games, even talking to the occasional girl. Killing Outland Orcs was important work, but even the greatest RPG warriors had to take a break when it came to girls. Even if he had never kissed one, just talking to a girl was thrilling— and terrifying. Girls were intimidating temptresses that smelled like vine-ripened fruit bathed in the warm summer's sun. Their hair was always so shiny, too. How did they get their hair so shiny?

What Jesse loved most about girls were all those curves and those luscious, supple mounds of flesh overstuffing their tight tube-tops. Tits were what Jesse loved best about girls, especially when a girl's nipples were hard when she was aroused. Jesse couldn't help but wonder what it would feel like to squeeze one. He had never had the chance, but he had, on occasion, squeezed his own prodigious flabby moobs. He was convinced that a girl's boob would be much better to squeeze than his own. For one, they probably weren't as hairy or as pimply as his. Try as he might, never could he make his own nipples as thick and swollen as the girls' nipples he had seen. That was one thing Jesse envied most about Derek was his ability to get the girl. Derek was smooth and cool. It probably didn't hurt that he spoke with a slight Irish accent.

Jesse had seen the impact such a brogue had on getting the girl— so much so that he had tried his own accent out on Hannah Swonster after school one day the previous year. She had been standing at her locker with two of her friends, getting excited about a party coming up— a party Jesse hadn't been invited to — when he approached her to start a conversation. Hannah Swonster was a flawless teenage beauty and popular, always having friends by her side. Hannah found it hilarious that someone so disgusting could think he had a chance with her— especially a person as fat as Jesse. She saw he was trying to talk to her and in an Irish accent no less.

118

Before he had even finished a sentence, she tossed him a one dollar bill and told him to go buy another Twinkie to stuff in his mouth so he would stop talking. The three girls had burst out laughing at this. Jesse had toddled off in embarrassment.

That was the first time a girl had laughed in his face. Sometimes he hated himself and that day he hated himself the most.

Later that night, when he had returned to an empty home, Jesse stole his dad's only bottle of Black Velvet and downed three shots. The shots made him brave, but didn't stop him from hating himself. Jesse hated himself so much that night that he wanted to end it all. He thought if he killed himself, it would teach Hannah a lesson.

"Come on, bro! The sun just went behind the treeline and I'm getting hungry. Let's go setup camp down there by the lake." Derek interrupted Jesse's painful recollection. They started down an earthy trail littered with decaying leaves and pine needles. The trail carved through thick, towering pines and snaked up a small incline before disappearing into the dense willowwacks common to the area. Only small slivers of rippling water could be seen from where the two of them stood. A small mountain stream was sourced at the lake, no more than ten miles away. The exclusive smell of New England wilderness was in the air. That balanced blend of smokiness and wood. It was a crisp and clean smell and Derek loved it.

It was the first time he had climbed Mount Chocorua. With its rocky, steep inclines and loose gravel giving way to poor footing, the mountain was a challenge to climb, but that was the lure of it. That and the supposed curse that people had been clamoring about. Jesse had told him about the disappearances happening around the mountain, in the village of Osworth. Derek didn't buy that anyone actually disappeared, some other rationale held the answers. He traveled down from Portland to check it out for himself, as was his way.

119

Osworth was such a small town that no one knew exactly where its limits were drawn, but one thing Derek knew was that the lake in the distance, the place to where he was heading, was surely Lake Osworth. To the south of the summit was Chocorua Lake, the place where he and Jesse had set out on their hike. They descended the mountain on the northwestern trail and the only lake there was Lake Osworth. According to numerous news reports, it was the proximate location of all the disappearances. Authorities had posted signs for people to stay away, but that wasn't Derek Doherty. Not at all! When it came to disobeying authority, Derek Doherty was a devoted practitioner and because of this, he had frequented many of Maine's finest county jails.

Derek had not told Jesse his true motive for hiking Mount Chocorua. He didn't dare. Jesse was a lummox incapable of putting on his big boy pants and investigating something as tantalizing and mysterious as the Osworth disappearances without fear of wetting himself. Derek knew this about Jesse, but for all his flaws, he also knew Jesse to be loyal. Derek was Jesse's only friend and even though Derek didn't like his mother pimping out his friendship on charity cases, it did have some benefits. Jesse was a love-struck puppy and would follow Derek anywhere, even to the point of no return.

"What lake is that you're heading to?" Jesse asked.

"I think that's Chocorua Lake down there," Derek lied.

"No, that's not Chocorua Lake. We started out at Chocorua Lake. It should be on the other side of the mountain," Jesse questioned, sounding somewhat alarmed.

"I don't know then. But hurry up! We have like forty-five minutes of daylight left." Derek offered as he moved up over the hill leading to the lake at a quickened pace, practically jogging. He sensed that Jesse was starting to piece together the

120

identity of the area and he knew the best way to keep the big lug's mind occupied was to force him to pant for air like some obese family pet.

Out of breath, Jesse replied through the hastening of his steps, "I'm coming as fast as I can. I'm not as athletic as you, man."

"You're right you're not as athletic as I am. But that's your choice, don't make me slow down because you can't keep up."

The shimmering reflection of the departing sun bounced off the glassy surface of the lake that began to reveal itself to Derek. Jesse had fallen twenty-yards behind and was looking at the ground, watching with intense caution every step he took. About seventy yards ahead of him, Derek spotted a clearing near the lakeshore that was well-suited for camp and moved to it.

The area was unconscious to the outside world, devoid of the chaos that seemed so abundant in these New England woods. An assortment of red oaks and paper birches leaned into the clearing to which Derek was to setup camp, offering a natural canopy in case of rain and a tether for their tent and tarp. The small thickets of grayish-barked shrubs that dotted the perimeter would provide some, mostly meager, protection from the nocturnal bumbling of hungry bears or the oafish scurrying of a startled bull moose. It felt to Derek like this small patch of forest in the White Mountains was one of those places with an unknown history; a place that simply existed since time began and matured to its present state without a witness to its growth.

"I know what lake this is… its Lake Osworth!" Jesse stammered uncontrollably as he came into the clearing behind Derek, who had begun to put up the two-person pop-up tent. Jesse paid no attention to Derek's labor as began to fidget nervously with a map.

"Derek, we have to leave. Now! This place is not safe. Remember all those people that vanished and the deer that were chewed to bits? It happened here."

Derek drove a thin metal stake into the ground and replied. "Listen up. It's at least a four hour hike back to the car. There is no way we can leave now."

"I can't stay here. I can't! We are both going to get killed, I just know it!" Jesse howled, turning around and heading back up the trail he had just come.

"Jesse, if you start back now, you're nothing more than a meal with legs for whatever is lurking in these woods." Derek laughed, playing to Jesse's fear. He knew that Jesse wouldn't dare head off on his own; he was too weak for such an act of gumption.

"Stop it!" Jesse stuttered, stopping before he continued down the darkling trail alone. He looked out into the twilight haze and the shifting shadows between the trees and knew he couldn't set off on his own.

"Don't cry you big cranberry. Everything is going to be fine. Consider this an opportunity to man up."

"What do you mean?"

"You're worried about this place because you believe there is some sort of bandersnatch or something out there in the woods waiting to eat you. Prove to yourself— for once — that you're not so weak." Derek invited meanly as he fed the last tent pole into its fabric lining and pushed it forward, watching as the tent gained structure.

"Do you promise everything is going to be alright?" Jesse whimpered as he stepped closer to the clearing. He hung his head with need of assuredness like a child needing proof no boogey man lived beneath his bed.

"Oh, everything will be fine. This place may have mysteries, but I have this—" Derek's voice trailed off as he unzipped a side pocket of his pack and pulled out a gun.

"What the hell man? Why do you have a gun?" Jesse asked, startled by the sudden look of craziness in his friend's eyes.

"Why do you think I invited you out here? I mean look at this place. Quiet, beautiful. No one around for miles."

"Derek put it away. You're scaring me."

"Put what away? This?"

Derek waved the gun in his hand, pointing it at Jesse. Jesse recoiled and cowered to the ground.

"FUCK! DON'T POINT THAT AT ME!"

"I could do it, you know? Shoot you right in the head! No one would ever know either. After all, people have been disappearing all around here. What's one more?"

Derek stomped towards him and placed the barrel of the gun against his chubby head.

"BANG!" Derek shouted, pretending to pull the trigger. "You're dead!"

Derek let out a disgusting, satisfied laugh.

Jesse felt the warmth of his piss flow down his leg, and then he felt queasy. Soon he fell unconscious to the sylvan dirt.

It was about an hour before he woke. He smelled of mud and urine. Not long after, he remembered what had happened and he was enraged. He pushed himself off the ground and rose to his feet. Jesse looked around the campsite for Derek, intent to cause him physical harm for his sadistic sense of humor, but all he saw was the gentle orange glow of dying embers in a makeshift fire pit nearby.

Jesse walked up to the tent and unzipped it. Derek wasn't inside. In fact, the tent was barren with no sign of someone's intent to sleep there. Jesse walked down to the lake, listening carefully for the subtle trickle of water sloshing ashore. Beneath the midsummer's moonless sky, the lake was a pit of darkness that stretched further than Jesse's eyes could see. It was eerily quiet and there was no sign of Derek. There was not a rustling of distant branches or a flapping of the wind across the glassy lake. There was just nothing.

"DEREK!" Jesse shouted aloud. "WHERE ARE YOU?"

He listened for a noise, any kind of response, but there was none.

He called to Derek five more times, each time with a greater sense of urgency and in an increasingly jarring manner. There was never any reply.

"OH SHIT, OH SHIT! WHAT DO I DO? WHAT DO I DO?" He muttered to himself, stopping where he stood, unwilling to move.

It was too dark and too far to head back to the car on the other side of the mountain. He would never make it. That much he knew.

"I could go out and look for him." He said. "Out there in the...woods...by myself!"

He shook his head. Nope, can't do it. Won't do it. Not after what he did to me, putting that gun to my head. Good riddance!

For a second, he smiled as the thought of Derek lost somewhere in the woods popped into his mind. Then he realized that maybe he wasn't lost at all. Lost implied searching for a place to settle. Instead, maybe he was dead. And that would mean... they weren't alone in these woods. It would mean that somewhere in the dark there was something possibly watching him, watching him with murderous eyes! This *WAS* the place where all those people had disappeared, vanished.

"FIRE! Yes, fire!"

In most of the movies he had seen, fire offered protection. So Jesse groped the ground on his hands and knees looking for loose twigs and when he had them, he tossed them onto the fading embers in the fire pit. It took several seconds before the short twigs smoldered and smoked and grew hot enough to catch a flame. After a snap and a crackle, flames grew in the basin of the pit. Jesse hurried to find more fuel to stoke the infant fire.

After tossing on two hefty logs that he had found near the lake, each at least a foot long, Jesse sat beside the fire, trying to take solace in the warmth it provided. He looked to the black all about. Only within the sphere of light that the fire conglobated were the shapes of the landscape made clear. Despite the darkness and isolation, Jesse felt somewhat safer. The warmth of a fire was always a blanket that soothed even the most startled and solitary souls.

He closed his eyes to wait for morning when a terrible crackling sound erupted from somewhere in the brush. It was a terrifying sound that came without warning. Then he heard what followed— it sounded like something being dragged in the distance —a sluggish and unusual sound.

"WHO'S THERE?" Jesse hollered uneasily. He jumped to his feet when there was no answer.

He listened. It was still there, the dragging sound. It was growing louder, closer. Something was here and it was heading towards him.

Jesse looked around frantically, spying every area for the source of the sound.

Suddenly, a small shadow came over the clearing, hovering from somewhere above— from the trees. Something was in the trees. The shadow started to grew larger. Without notice the shadow gave way and a body fell from the branches overhead, bouncing against the forest floor like an acorn discarded from an oak.

Jesse screamed.

The body had no face. A hole had been cut straight through the head. Jesse could see the ground through the skull. Part of the head had been carved out, bore out as if by a drill. Blood dripped from the part of the scalp that remained, into the hole where the face should have been.

It was Derek.

Jesse was frozen by fear as he stared into the cavity that used to hold Derek's face. He could see the white of his skull through the gigantic hole in his face and ground-up brain tissue dangling from jagged bone fragments.

The crackling came again, but Jesse did not wonder from where it came. In the empty space in front of him, a fleshy brown thing appeared. It took no familiar form, but moved like a serpent towards Derek's lifeless body, wriggling in a crooked, uneven manner towards his slouched feet. An opening grew at the top of the creature, stretching in size until its circumference was as wide as Derek's corpse. The creature waited for a moment before it continued and Jesse grew cold at the sight. The opening stretched into a mouth and lining the inside were rows of knifelike teeth that spiraled up the length of its body with no visible end. The teeth began to rotate and spin, clockwise in a rapid, frenzied corkscrew like a wood chipper.

In one smooth, vicious motion, the creature surged over Derek's body, sliding the rigid corpse into its mouth and up into the rotating spiral of teeth, grinding his dead flesh into a meaty heap of bones, hair and blood. It ate him, devoured him. Made him no more. Then the creature vanished right before Jesse's eyes. It simply disappeared. As quickly as it had come, it had vanished. There was no trace that the creature had ever been there and the only trace of Derek that remained was a reddish pulp that hung for a moment in the air where his body had been, drifting to the ground as the sole remnant of his life, of his existence.

126

Jesse ran. He booked it straight from the clearing, into the woods and towards the small hill that gave exit to this miserable place, his belly a bouncing ball of blubber as he went. His face was bone white, as white as the inside of Derek's skull. What was that thing? There was no way to answer it; the creature seemed bound by no earthly limitations. Quickly he was out of breath and forced to stop, his chest rising and falling in rapid succession.

A jarring crackle boomed like an exploded bomb right beside Jesse, disorientating him. He felt as it ripped into him, taking his insides away and then vanishing again into nothingness. His blood and remaining organs poured hotly from the cavity that had been carved into his stomach, emitting a sickly metallic odor. The gore from his insides fell out of him, splattering onto the ground with a dull sponginess. Jesse collapsed, the pain scorching through his midsection. Again the crackle came.

In the last seconds of his life, Jesse Mervine swore he heard the faintest of sounds— a circular grinding sound — like something was spinning.

Secret Jeopardy

What more of value is there in life but the hope for truth? That question raced around my mind as I headed to my parents' home, to my home, for a moment of much-needed sleep. Everything Bobbo and Aunt Jolie had divulged to me had unsettled my thoughts and left me, in all honesty, feeling betrayed.

Why hadn't my parents ever told me that I once had a sister? Deep down, even though I had told Bobbo and Aunt Jolie otherwise, I did regard the loss of my big sister as a true loss. How could I not? In the end, it was a true loss even if we had never met. She was the entity that came before me and if still alive today, she would bereave our parents' passing beside me and that thought made me envy this alternative reality. We would have been able to look back into the history of shared moments, of family moments, and together we would have extracted that inconsequential story from a vacation or holiday past that symbolized the absolute quirkiness of the Fisher family. We would have laughed together and boasted merrily in its remembrance.

I didn't have that though. What I had was another death to contemplate. Another thing to think about. It was all exhausting and I just did not have the energy to care.

The car ride home proved a therapeutic and occupying distraction. Without realizing it, I had found myself standing alone outside my childhood home in the middle of a gravel driveway atop a hill that overlooked Concord.

I looked out onto the city that had molded me. I saw in the distance the park where I played basketball as a teenager.

It was all too much. Everything, too much. I knelt down and cried.

The tears flowed from my eyes like brackish water from a spigot. Crying as I was would have typically made me feel embarrassed, but the comfort I found in my tears was almost like a mothers embrace.

I was alone and it felt as good a time as any to cry myself out. There was no one else nearby for at least a quarter of a mile, just me and a flock of purple finches chirping in a nearby tree. I was in a familiar place, a place of comfort and solitude. A fortress, of sorts.

Several minutes had passed before I felt like I had no more tears to shed. I wiped my eyes dry and that is when I saw him— a man standing in the woods behind my home. He was behind the cover of leaved branches, but I could see the black of his eyes. They were shark-like, vacant and dark. I had never seen someone with eyes like that before.

He seemed out of place, as if he didn't belong. I thought that maybe he was someone hiking the back trails behind our house. Those trails were not weathered by frequent use and didn't offer much in scenic value except for the trails near Penacook Lake. From time to time, a person bumbling about the trees would lumber onto our property asking for directions. Dad never trusted these

129

folks, always thinking of them as potential thieves or murderers scouring for their next victims. After the harrowing and bloody tale of the Dartmouth murders had come out, I understood my dad's concern about weird people in the woods.

"Can I help you?" I hollered towards the wood line and started moving towards the man.

He did not respond.

As I moved closer, I could see that his skin was slightly olive in color and somewhat slack, like the skin was loose on his face. He did not look healthy and this made me think that he was injured or hurt.

"Sir, are you alright? Do you need help?" I asked, stopping just beneath the sundeck at the back of the house.

Silence. The man just stood there, looking at me, unmoving and half obscured behind leaves and branches of the thick oak trees that filled the forest. He had not moved or blinked since I first saw him. Maybe he was dead. I mean, people, living ones anyway, didn't have eyes like that or a complexion like that.

"I am going to call and get you some help, alright? You stay right there."

I grabbed the phone from my pocket and began to dial for help, when I looked up and saw the man smiling back at me, an ear-to-ear grin plastered across his face.

All of a sudden, I felt like I wanted to be inside, away from the creepy man smiling at me from the tree line. I took a step backwards and glanced behind my shoulder at the utility door beneath the sundeck. If I ran, I could unlock it and get inside quickly— if in the event the man charged at me. The thought spun again and again through my head. Could I make it? Yes, I could.

I prepared myself to sprint— to run— fast. Before I did, I thought about the days in high school when I had tried out for track. Wait for the sound of the gun, then go. The gun. Wait for the sound of the gun. Pull the trigger, Ben. Do it, I kept saying this in my head. Shouting at myself! I just had to pull the trigger.

Was he still there, looking at me? I snuck a peek across my shoulder, back towards the tree line, trying to force myself to run, to get away from what felt ominous and when I turned back, he was gone. He had vanished.

This was enough for me to pull the trigger. I ran straight for the door, panic rushing through my chest. Where did he go? I didn't care. Get inside, Ben, get inside, I kept saying to myself. Everything would be fine inside, I assured myself. The keys were fumbling in my hands, their zigzagging metal shapes clanging together.

Jesus Christ, Ben! Get inside! I slide the house key into the lock and turned. The door opened and I scurried inside, slamming the door behind me, turning the deadbolt closed with a great sigh of relief.

Relief. That was what I felt when I heard the thick metal bolt slide into place, securing me from the outside. I turned and rested my back against the door, my breathing heavy, and a slight perspiration resting on my brow. Then a terrifying realization came to me— what if he was already in the house?

"Fuck!" I panted, wiping the sweat from my eyes with my right forearm.

I knew that the man in the woods was Uncle Warren. He looked as his voice sounded, brusque and capable of curdling the blood as it pumped through your heart. Something sinister and unforgiving rested in those vacant black eyes. He seemed a man hell-bent on something and I sensed from that maddening smile, he knew how to get it. Had he come to collect? I did not like the notion. I felt like I was being hunted.

My lungs were breathless and my chest recoiled as I took in the empty house. It was empty right? After a couple of forced, concentrated breaths, I persuaded myself into believing that my home— as silent and lifeless as it appeared — was a safe haven. There was no one there, but me... no one there, but me.

The silence in the house echoed an eerie presence. Somehow, as my heart rate approached normal, I felt at home. I felt safe between these walls. Still, I feared that my solace was temporary and I needed answers. The problem was the only question I felt needed answering was— who was Uncle Warren? The answer to that question was key to finding the truth about everything. I had never believed anything more than that.

I decided to arm myself with some type of protection. I knew my dad preferred to keep crossbows around the house. I didn't understand it given that he also had firearms in the house and was one hell of a shot in his day. I just never saw the benefit of crossbows over firearms.

Dad also kept a loaded shotgun upstairs behind his nightstand in a locked gun safe. That made more sense to me than the crossbows he always had lying around. Shotguns, after all, were designed to kill anything close to its barrel and were more of a certain shot.

I went upstairs through the utility room, which smelled of fresh paint and gasoline from the lawnmower. Based on the intensity of the gasoline odor, I figured that Mom had suggested Dad mow the lawn and that he had, probably shortly before they were killed.

The image played out in my head. I could see Mom suggesting this to Dad in her normal way, in that sweet, amicable voice, that held the power to feel not like suggestions at all, but orders from a high-ranking officer in some type of marriage militia. Imaging this made me smile and made me realize how inconsequential many things were.

The upstairs living room sat untouched, smelling of sage and elderberry— Mom's potpourri. It was a warm and comforting embrace that would never be the same. The sunlight from outside came through the beige curtains and caressed the floral upholstery of the couch where we used to sit together for movie night. The whole scene played out like a dream, as if all the things that had happened were images painted by the firing of my synapses. In reality, I was still in Washington, clutching Megan close to me, but the notion that it was all a dream, was itself the dream. Rather, a nightmare.

I sat in the middle of the couch and stared blankly at my reflection in the TV. The person who looked backed at me looked lost, confused and clueless about what to do next. I vaguely remembered that I wanted to find something to arm myself in case the man from the woods came back, but I was so sleepy.

For a few minutes, I imagined what life would have been like had my older sister never drowned. I thought about movie night then and recognized that four of us could not fit on this three-person sofa. Everything would have been different if Grace had never drowned, I convinced myself.

I walked up the creaky wooden stairs to my parents' room. The gun case was unlocked behind Dad's nightstand and the gun fully loaded inside. He must have forgotten to lock it, which seemed particularly odd considering how cautious he used to be when I had lived in the house.

Holding the gun in my hands and feeling its metal girth made me feel strong, almost empowered, as if the shotgun had extended my arms by ten feet and turned my fingers into eagle talons. The sensation was ethereal— holding those two steel cylinders loaded with explosives and ball bearings. With just the faintest and weakest of squeezes, I could end the life of something once living— cause and effect, that is what it was.

I moved down the hall to my room and found the door closed, unsurprisingly. I opened it, stirring up the smell of dust and old sweat.

A pair of fading and tattered posters of New England Patriot's cheerleaders still clung to the wall by loops of masking tape. Even now with my eyes flecked red from tears and a loaded 12-gauge in my hand, seeing the skimpy-cut silver and red bikinis of those young and beautiful women made me smile.

"Well, Ben. What now?" I found myself asking.

I placed the shotgun on the top of my dresser and collapsed onto the bed, falling into a sun-warmed spot on my comforter. I ran my fingers against the canvas and let my fingertips glide across the coarse contours of the fabric. This sent goose bumps up my forearms and down the side of my stomach. I extended my arms above my head and arched my back like a bridge, stretching out the tightened muscles in the middle of my back. It felt good to just stop and rest for a moment, to bathe in the sun's warmth as it glistened through the gently swaying trees outside. I closed my eyes and listened to the chirping composition of two songbirds outside my window. Their song was so simple...so peaceful...

... with a flap of their wings and an upsurge of wind, the two birds took flight, disappearing in the backdrop of blue sky. Benjamin Fisher opened his heavy eyes and blinked twice, then rubbed the goopy discharge from his eyelids. Somewhere down the hallway he could hear a muted rattling like that from a child's toy. He rose from his bed, lumpish in his legs and yawned.

"What is that?" Ben muttered groggily as he looked up and down the hallway. There was a loud instance of the sound again, a harsh rattle.

Ben then realized that he was no longer standing in his own home, but a house alien to him. The hallway was long, curved and damp. It was constructed out off stone and lit only by the

134

fire atop a set of torches lining the wall. The ground was slick and dirt-packed— muddy — as if it had just rained. Suddenly, a baby's laugh echoed from down the hallway.

Ben moved in the direction of the baby's laugh keeping along the cobbled wall of the hallway, which curved to the left and began sneaking away from the lit torches behind him, heading towards a dark and hollow alcove.

"Hello?" Ben hollered into the pitch-black recess as he slowed his pace to a tiptoe.

The undeniable chortle of infant laughter broke out somewhere in the darkness in front of him, coming in short spurts of uncontrolled amusement. The noise of the laughter made certain to Ben that a baby was hidden somewhere in the shadows.

Ben slipped his left leg into the patch of pitch-blackness and moved his foot in embellished circles, slapping at the ground to ensure that it was there. He placed his foot against solid terrain and pulled the rest of him into the shadows. At once, the world around him changed into something unwelcoming and ominous.

The child's laugh played over the silence again and as it did, a tiny sliver of light began to glow against the far wall from where Ben was standing. The light shined through a narrow gap in the wall and Ben crept closer to it, crouching to look inside. It was a keyhole.

But to what? There were no edges, no frames, no obvious seams in the stone that would forge a door. It was as if the hole had been drilled for a mythical key that would open the entire wall.

The light from the other side was blinding. But as Ben's eyes grew accustomed, he saw the outline of a chair break through the contrast of the room. It sat in the middle of the room, angled slightly to the right. Plopped on the arm of the chair was an infant with a hand securely placed around its back. The baby's face was turned away from Benjamin.

Ben tilted forward to peer through the keyhole, to try to see the person sitting in the chair, but the back of the chair obscured their identity. The sound of rattling came again, emanating from the chair and at once, the child laughed wildly and began to bounce with fervor.

"Do you find that funny baby? Do you?!" A voice said playfully from the chair.

The voice was his mothers. Ben knew it at first sound. She was the person sitting in the chair, even though he could not see her.

"Mom?" Ben whispered.

The baby laughed again.

"Benjamin, is that you?" called the voice from the chair. "Come in my son, come in!"

Benjamin Fisher pushed against the wall, but it didn't budge.

"Mom, the door won't open!" Ben said, continuing to push against the wall, trying to shake it open.

"Benjamin you must use the key. The key will open the door and then you can come see your sister. She is dying to meet you."

"My sister? I have a sister?" Ben asked, confused.

"Don't be foolish, my son. You knew you had a sister. Now come here and give you mother a kiss. I've missed you dearly."

Ben searched the ground and the wall for a key or something to open the door. His mother wanted to see him and his sister, his baby sister wanted to see him. Where was the key? They wanted to see him.

"There is no key!" Ben confessed with a sense of urgency.

There was a brief silence where Lily Fisher did not speak. When she spoke it was in a voice more hoarse and rough than normal, as if her voice had slipped into someone else's voice. "Use your finger, place it against the keyhole. This will unlock it!"

"My finger? Why my finger?" Ben asked.

"Darling son, you are the key! Open the door and come see you mother!" Lily said, now in her normal voice.

Hesitant, Ben slowly brought his right index finger to the keyhole and pressed against it. For a second nothing happened, but then a sharp prick ran through his finger. He recoiled at the pain and looked down at his finger to see it glistening in crimson.

"OW! Son of a bitch!" Ben yelled and placed his bleeding finger into his mouth.

The wall in front of him began to shake and rumble, then it began to slide apart, forming a seam straight through the keyhole and running perpendicular to the floor. As the wall slid apart, a foot of separation grew between the seam in the wall, which continued to expand and grow wider until there was no wall between Benjamin and his family. With his finger in his mouth, Ben looked up to see the chair still occupied by his mother and sister.

He moved towards them, saying, "Mom, it's Benjamin. My finger is bleeding. It hurts!"

The baby and his mother did not react at all to his advance. In fact, they did not even acknowledge his presence. It was as if he was a ghost to them. Then he realized that they had never looked at him when he was on the other side of the door. They had never moved from the chair, never glanced back to see him.

"Your voice changed!" Ben said aloud, suddenly realizing that his mother's voice had changed moments before, slipping into a voice not her own. He had heard that voice before, had recognized it and it had made his blood turn to ice.

137

The infant sitting on the arm of the chair stopped bouncing and grew still; its little body grew soft and began to shrink. Its cream-colored skin soured and began to rot into a greenish-gray leather that wilted from its bones. It no longer looked like a human baby. Rather, it resembled something long since dead, a mummified cadaver.

Ben tried to retreat back to the darkened recess of the hallway, but he was frozen by the rotting baby; the baby he had thought to be his sister. Suddenly, the baby's dried and mummified aspect faded, leaving only its skeleton, all hollow and still. Ben was speechless and in shock as he stared in horror at the bare bones on the tiny child, resting hollow and empty. Unable to peel his eyes away from the ghastly scene, Ben could not grasp what happened next as his sister's skeleton collapsed into hundreds of pieces and tumbled to the ground with a rattle.

"Come give your momma a kiss, Benjamin," Lily Fisher's voice started to call, but then slipped into something more gruff and chilling, "I said come give your momma a kiss!"

The chair was thrown backwards, falling onto its side and where it had stood was now a figure standing in denim overalls, its face still turned away. The figure whipped his head around and locked sights with Benjamin.

A murderous grin grew across the mouth of the olive-skinned man. His skin was icy, as if he had risen from the depths of the coldest ocean. His eyes were beady and of the deepest black. They haunted the soul of the person that scrutinized them.

The man charged Ben, who was paralyzed in place, and threw him hard to the ground. With an inhuman quickness, the man mounted Benjamin, pinning his arms to the ground. Ben tried to resist the attack, but the man was far too strong, despite looking at least a hundred years old.

"Who are you?" Ben screamed, trying to wriggle free from his attacker.

"I am the eater of men, the hunter of life, and the last living thing that you will ever see. I am your Uncle Warren!"

"Get the fuck off me!"

"It's time, Benjamin! Time to rid me from these chains. Time to free me from my cage."

Ben's throat tightened. "How exactly am I going to do this?"

"By watching me eat your flesh and drink your blood...

... For the next five minutes, I sat on the edge of my bed, gathering my thoughts and allowing the blood in my veins to settle. Never had a nightmare felt so real. I looked down at my right index finger and could swear I saw a tiny pin-prick. The whole thing had been surreal, as if I was watching my own nightmare unfold, but simultaneously partaking in it. I had both observed and lived my nightmare.

I felt groggy as I looked out my window. The sun had departed behind the forest and my bedroom had a certain yellow tint to it, like when you first light a gas lantern and watch as the propane-soaked mantle flickers to life. That is when I saw it, resting against one of my pillows at the top of my bed— a letter — sealed in an envelope with OUR SON hand-written on the front.

A Letter From The Grave

       I ran my finger along the edge of the envelope, contemplating its contents with steady unease. The envelope read OUR SON and I could not help but fear the words written inside. Did my parents write a letter to me before they died? The thought sent a shiver down my back. I was almost reluctant to open it, but I peeled back the envelope, taking out the several sheets of notepaper holding my mother's handwriting:

My Sweet Dear Benjamin,

       Having found this letter, you know that your father and I have died. You are probably a wreck and wondering why this has happened. Well, my beautiful baby boy, I am afraid that we have been keeping a secret from you. You should understand that this is what we thought was best. But if you are reading this letter, I am afraid we were mistaken. The reason we never told you was because you were too young, at least at first and then truthfully, we thought it had ended.

For seventeen years, it had ended. You were able to live out your life oblivious to the truth and we were able to breathe a little easier. But some things never die and that is why we are writing this letter. Ben, you must understand that you are in grave danger. This letter will give you the knowledge of what you're up against and where you can find answers, should you seek them. We pray that you do not. The best thing you can do is leave and never return.

There is something out there that looks like a man and we have come to call it, him, Warren. Since the day you were born, you have been in his crosshairs. He tried several times to steal you from us in the first years of your life and each time we were able to fend him off. With his last attempt, we thought we had found a way to end it. Your father had to do unimaginable things, but we thought we had ended it. Warren disappeared for seventeen years and it was only in the last few days that he resurfaced. He seems stronger this time.

From your first breath, your life has been both a miracle and a curse. Try as we might, we could never bring ourselves to tell you about the horror of the day you were born. Never in my life did a day fill me with such conflicting emotions. I guess I should start at the beginning.

It was August and your dad decided to whisk me and my pregnant woes away to the beach. We brought along two of our closest friends, Malcolm and Macy Campbell. We also brought your sister, Grace.

Forgive us, Benjamin, for never telling you about her. The pain of that day still resides in a hollow place in my heart. She was only fifteen months when they came. My first child, my sweet, beautiful child. Oh how I loved her. And I miss her so much. I do think I will see her soon though. I feel it in my heart.

142

The true nightmare of it is how it happened. Such things don't seem possible, but I saw them happen with my own eyes. The memory of it remains vivid.

It happened after lunch. I remember the sky growing dark, like the color of coal. There was a sense of urgency in the air, a raw feeling. I can't explain it any other way than that. We were on the shore of Lake Osworth in a section that we had stumbled upon by mistake. We were alone, not hurting anyone. Still, in this moment, and for whatever reason, you decided it was time to come into the world. I know you don't believe in God, Benjamin, but there was something inexplicable about your decision to be born at that moment. Then and there; something like fate was working that day, whether you want to believe it or not.

Panic set in at once. I knew I was in labor and we were in the middle of nowhere. You were coming regardless of where we were. Thankfully, Macy Campbell was there and able to deliver you. She wrapped you in a pink and blue beach towel and then handed you to me. You were screaming, but you looked up at me with those deep brown eyes. Your dad held your sister so that she could see you and for a moment, one happy instance, I swore you both smiled at each other. That was the happiest instance of my life, that one fraction of time where everything felt whole and complete. That's when they came.

From out of the woods, they pursued us. One man and one woman, both savage in appearance. Malcolm first heard the snapping of twigs and looked up to see them moving through the bushes. He knew something was wrong and then we all did, even I saw it unfold. They moved so quickly. I hesitate to think what could have happened if your father didn't leap to defend us all. He just seemed to know that they were there to do us harm. Your dad was a hero that day, using that knife he always carries to cut one of the attackers when they got too close to you. That's what they were after Benjamin... you!

Your dad's actions afforded us enough time to make for the car. He drew you into his arms and Macy grabbed Grace. I was much too weak to move, but Malcolm found strength enough to carry me. But the man and woman did not stop their pursuit of us, if anything, the man your father stabbed grew more focused to steal you from me. That's when it happened.

We were just feet from the car and seconds away from fleeing to safety, when the woman seemed to vanish behind us and reappear inches from our faces. Then the man did it too. Both of them stood in the way of our safety.

The man lunged for you with his gnarled fingers and your father stabbed him in the chest as he held you against him. The man fell to the ground, but the woman showed no concern for him at all. Instead, she lunged for you too. Macy, who was still holding Grace, stepped in front of the attack and then without warning the woman disappeared again. We thought we were safe for a moment, until Macy crumpled to the ground in a heap.

She died right there! Right there in front of us and with Grace in her arms. Malcolm went hysterical at the sight and when the woman reappeared he charged her. Your father and I stared down at Macy's body and back up at Malcolm's pain. We were in shock, so we didn't see the man rise up from the forest floor and pull the knife from his chest.

Your sister was sitting and crying next to Macy's body. The man went up to her and picked her up. I screamed and your father turned from watching Malcolm to look at the man holding your sister. Then the man spoke. I will never forget his voice as he said it.

"This child for that one" his voice rattled as he held Grace out to us, who was crying uncontrollably. He extended his gnarled finger at the soft pink-and-blue bundle in your father's arms. The woman appeared next to the man with a hideous grin snarled across her lips.

"What are you?" Your father asked with tears streaming down his cheek.

"Choose the child," the man yelled. He never took those shark-like eyes off you in your father's arms.

This was when Malcolm pushed me into the car and ordered your father to get in. Malcolm drove off, leaving your sister behind and abandoning his wife's body in the dirt. I will never forget the haunting words he spoke as we sped away:

"They're both dead! There is no choice to be made."

He was right too. Sadly, I would never hold my sweet baby Grace or kiss her soft, innocent head again. Once she disappeared in the distance, I never laid eyes on her again. I can just remember hearing her cry and being too weak and helpless to do something. To do anything!

Malcolm drove the hour back home without a word spoken between the three of us. The only sound to be heard was your crying.

None of us knew what to do. Macy was dead and Grace was gone. We couldn't explain what had happened, not to the authorities, not to our family. What we decided between us that night was probably much worse.

The three of us sat around our kitchen table arguing about what to do. We wanted to go back for Grace, but Malcolm was adamant that we could not. He had said that the best thing for us to do was to convince people that Grace had died. He was convinced it would be easy to fool people that Grace had drowned and that no suspicion would be drawn to us if we spoke of this conspiracy with conviction. Of course, your father and I did not listen to him. When Malcolm left, we placed you in your sister's crib and your father went back to Osworth.

He didn't see anything when he returned, not even Macy's body. It was six months before anything happened and when it did, we nearly lost you for a second time. We were not prepared for their attack. They came to our house, both of them. Somehow they knew where we lived. They were different though the second time. For one, they did not disappear and reappear as they had in Osworth. But still they seemed impervious to harm. The both of them made it into the house and to your room. We knew something was wrong when you started to cry and then abruptly stopped. Your father and I ran to your room and there they were, with you in their hands.

What ensued was a battle for you. I have never been a fighter, but I had to fight that night. They made it into the house through the window in your bedroom and when they saw us, they exited the house with you in possession. I remember screaming as I saw Warren jump from the roof and then watching as the woman tossed you from the roof to him below.

Your father did not hesitate. He was out on the roof almost as quickly as they were. He told me to get a gun and I did. But I had no idea how to use it. When I returned I saw your father running into the woods behind the house, giving chase to Warren and you. The woman never left the roof and instead came back into the house after me. Somehow, I got a shot off, but it didn't slow her down. Not at all. The woman chased me downstairs and attacked me in the kitchen. I thought I was going to die. Somehow, I was able to grab a kitchen knife and stab her in the neck. I remember fainting when the knife went in.

When I came to, your father was above me holding you in his arms, a look of terror on his face. I looked around, but did not see the woman anymore. Your dad was able to get you back when he met up with Warren in the woods and impaled him on a tree branch. When he returned to the house, he saw the woman pinned against the wall with the knife in her neck. There was no blood anywhere. When the woman saw you, she broke free and dashed out the door.

We learned from this encounter that these things did not want to be trapped. That night your father stood watch over you and the first chance he had, he acquired a set of crossbows. He figured they were the best weapon to protect you. Warren and the woman never got hurt, but they could be trapped.

This was useful information when they came for you again. It was almost a year later, but your father was ready for them. He had ensured that every path leading into our home had multiple layers of security. Their attempt to take you was stopped almost at once when your father trapped them against the house. We didn't know what to do with them after we had them caught. We knew we couldn't harm them, so you father decided upon something that I never thought he would be capable of.

With Warren and the women trapped, your father grabbed his chainsaw. The revving of its motor was a dreadful sound that informed me of your father's intentions. It was horrifying to watch, but the results were not as I had expected. There were no screams and their bodies held no blood or bone. To this day I still cannot fathom it. Your father buried the pieces and we waited to see if it was over. It wasn't.

By this point, Malcolm and us were estranged. We spoke only when it was necessary. He had become so obsessed with finding answers to these creatures. We just wanted it to end, for your sake. Malcolm though was losing his sanity. It was a surprise to us when shortly after we buried the bodies he called. He told us that he had captured the woman and he was holding her in a cage. We were in shock. It just did not seem possible. I watched as we buried their bodies. But sure enough we went to his house and we saw her standing behind iron bars, alive and annoyed.

Afterwards, we went and dug up the bodies. The pieces were still there as we had expected. We had no idea what any of it meant, but it did not mean that it was over. Three weeks after Malcolm captured the woman, Warren tried again to take you from us. That was the last time we saw Warren until a few days ago. It has been seventeen years since his last attempt. I wish I knew why he came back or even why he went away, but I don't.

What I do know is that your father and I love you very much. To answer a question I am sure you are wondering, we went up to Osworth in hopes of capturing Warren as Malcolm had captured the woman. We had conceded long ago that we could not stop these things. We could only hope to contain them, to trap them. But if your eyes are reading this now, I am sorry to say we lost in our attempt to capture Warren and there is only one thing I can say to you. Stay away from Osworth. Warren can hunt you, but he is controllable when he is not there. I repeat Benjamin, as your mother, please heed this warning. Do not go to...

The doorbell downstairs rang, startling me and I dropped the letter from my hand, letting its tinged, creased pages twist and flutter to the floorboards. I grabbed the shotgun by my side, took in a heavy breath and went to answer the door.

Decisions

Was it possible to love someone after just a few months? He had said the words, but had he meant them? More importantly, perhaps, was whether she loved him? These questions were the thoroughbreds racing in circles around Megan's vacant and fissured mind. She didn't have the answers, but there had to be something in her heart for Benjamin to lead her to this place, to his front door, all these miles from home. Megan swept her eyes skittishly across the features of the Fisher's Brownstone; the coarse contours of the layered slate tile, illuminated by the dimming sun, gave the illusion of a crooked gambrel roof.

She pressed the doorbell and then turned her back to the door to avert her gaze. Part of her didn't want to see him, or was nervous about seeing him, but then why make the trip at all, she wondered. It was a few moments before the door peeled open and Megan looked up at Benjamin's haggard, exhausted exterior. Sagging brown bags of skin clumped beneath his eyes, his thick brown curls were matted in sweat against his brow and his face was drawn taut by sadness. The two of them looked at one another, separated by a physical distance of only a few feet, but their spirits separated by eons.

"Hi," Megan mumbled in a near whisper, her face filled with spurious glee.

She inched closer to the door and caught Ben's gaze.

Ben took a double take.

"Oh, hey. How are you?" Benjamin asked as if he had been expecting her. The door turned and fell open. "Come in"

"Umm… okay. I hope it's alright that I came up a little earlier than first expected."

Megan walked inside. Ben held a shotgun in his hand as he walked over to the loveseat and lay down. He rested his head on one of the faded cushions of the loveseat and placed the shotgun on the floor next to him. He was bewildered and came across as almost crazy. He kept moving his head, bobbing it from side to side. Muddled, inarticulate sounds fell from his mouth.

Megan leaned over him and placed her ear close to the sound. She could barely make out the words—

"no choice" she thought he said. Was that it? "no choice". That didn't make any sense to her.

Megan listened harder, focusing on Benjamin's mumbling. What was he saying?

Again the words "no choice" came out.

Megan didn't understand.

"Ben, talk to me. I don't understand what you're saying. Please, let me help you," Megan pleaded, taking up a space beside him on the couch and resting her arm against his back.

There was no verbal response. Ben closed his eyes and slowed his breathing as if he was partaking in a stress-relieving exercise touted by head doctors. Megan felt her arm rise and fall on Benjamin's chest as he breathed in and out.

155

"I know you're hurting," Megan offered "and that's why I came. After last night, I couldn't stop thinking that if I were you, I would want someone else around. Someone who cared for you, someone to tell you that it is all going to be okay."

Ben's chest stopped undulating, but Megan could feel his heart still beating. When she looked up at him, he had his eyes open and he had a smile on his face— not the happy type of smile, but the helpless, thankful kind.

He knew from his Mom's letter that whatever was going to happen to him in the future, it was not going be good. He wanted to tell Megan about Grace and about the letter. Then there was all that crazy shit. He still didn't know what to make of that. His mind kept coming back to the letter and the things written in it— those impossible things. He wanted to tell Megan how his parents had lied to him about everything; well, at least it felt like everything. He wanted to tell her so much. But he was tired, so very tired and so he said nothing. He just smiled that helpless, thankful smile.

As if sensing that Ben wasn't in the mood to talk, Megan returned the smile. She placed her soft, warm hands gently against his cheeks and he turned his attention towards her. She leaned forward and kissed him.

"I love you too!"

She smiled again.

A memory at the back of Benjamin's mind seemed to bubble up to the surface through the tar pit of his emotions. A momentary instance of something lost now remembered. Forgotten in everything was that he had told Megan he loved her. He hadn't thought about it since last night when he said it and he wasn't even sure why he had said it in the first place. It was true of course. He loved her, but love was not an arrow quickly drawn from Cupid's quiver, it was something that evolved, cured and solidified into a tangible, palpable excitement that rested in the heart.

156

"Hey!" He said.

Without another word between them, Megan curled up behind him on the loveseat and they slept as if they were floating on the open waters just as Megan had done those months after her father had passed away. They slept peacefully and in the absence of dreams. They slept as if they were content, as if they were happy.

The Whipsaw

News of Lily and Carl Fishers' death spread up the worn and eroded streets of Concord, knocking on the doors of friends and families like a phantom whisper. All the people that heard the news that hazy Friday morning in July felt as if a piece of them had been ripped away, but to some, the news came as a deafening reminder of their own mortality.

Reverend Ernest Johnson had woken from meditation the morning of the news as blissful as he had any other day. From his chair swing overlooking the glassy stillness of Pleasant Lake, he sipped his morning chamomile, always with a squirt of honey and a fresh squeezing of lime. As he swung, he listened to the stoic, baronial caroling of the lake's inhabitant loons. For Reverend Ernest Johnson, formerly Nathan "Slinky" Johnson of the Bog Street Boys, life had not always been on the path to virtue.

Not overly smart, but being smart enough to know this, Nathan figured high school was a waste of time, he dropped out at the raw, impressionable age of 16. Nathan at this age lived with his mother, Kristen, whose penchant for selling and shooting up heroin had led her away for a handful of years in Nathan's early teens and ensured that the only work she would ever secure would be something akin to boxing knickknacks or gewgaws for an oriental shipping company.

One day while throwing rocks at squirrels behind the storage shed at Rollins Park, Nathan noticed three guys, all older than him and probably college kids, sneaking off into the woods. Curious, he followed them and crouched for cover behind a thick, thorny bush. Nathan watched as the three guys pulled an overstuffed backpack from a hollowed out hole beneath a boulder. One of them, a tall and tattooed, muscular guy, unzipped it and grabbed about a dozen small plastic bags. Nathan knew it was marijuana. He also knew he liked marijuana, thanks in part to the times when his mother's male friends came over with dime bags of it. They would let him smoke a couple bowls to get him high and so they could go have sex with his mom. Nathan waited for the three guys to leave and then stole the bag.

At first, he didn't have a clue about what to do with all that marijuana, but one day he asked the one person he knew would have an answer... his mom. When he did this, his mom swelled with pride, jubilantly squeezing him and lauding him as the "Man of the House". She even started calling him "The Provider", which was a major divergence from her normal apathy towards him. But take care of it she did. Two days after showing her his payload, Nathan was off doing drug runs of all kinds— cocaine, heroin, ecstasy, the whole lot — for the Bog Street Boys.

The Bog Street Boys weren't really a gang, even though they called themselves one. In reality, they were more like a collection of redneck entrepreneurs who happened to have a violent streak whenever one of their business propositions soured. Ruled by a mean and middle-aged leader of the drug trade, the Bog Street Boys believed that "breaking in" the newbies would eliminate those too weak for the business. Nathan knew that being too weak was not an option, even if he really was. When it was his turn to be "broken in", he offered no defense.

The beating was delivered by seven men, all older and stronger than he was. For an entire minute, sixty seconds of sheer hell, these grown men kicked him in the head, punched him in mouth, stepped on his fingers and kneed him in the ribs. When it was all over, Nathan stood in front of his attackers, his fellow Bog Street Boys, a blood-soaked and triumphant man. Not a boy! It was that day that launched Nathan's career in the drug dealing trade.

The day that ended his career was when his path crossed a couple in their late forties sitting on a bench outside of Memorial Field, watching their son run sprints. Nathan didn't give much thought to the couple, after all, he was there to collect a debt from a New Hampshire State University freshman, who had been known to play pick-up games of basketball at the Memorial Field hoops.

A minute after laying into the kid and tossing him to the ground, the middle-aged man leapt up from his seat and threw Nathan to the ground.

"What the fuck man?" Nathan remembered saying, lifting himself off the ground and brushing away the gravel.

"Whatever your grievance with this young man, this is not the avenue or the place to settle it, sir." The man had said, standing between Nathan and the guy he had been attacking.

"You fucking old people, get the hell out of my way," Nathan had ordered as he charged the man.

There wasn't much effort in how the man swept Nathan to the ground again, he just moved his feet like he was performing a dance step and let Nathan fall over his outstretched leg. Nathan was resilient though and bounced back onto his feet.

He had screamed as he charged again, "I will show you, you fucking old bastard."

The man then punched Nathan straight in the face and he fell to the ground, bouncing his head against the concrete. When he awoke, he was in the emergency room with stitches in his head and the man that had given him the stitches was sitting next to his bed.

Realizing Nathan was awake, the man leaned across his chair and looked up at Nathan saying, "I am sorry about what I did to you. It was never my intention to harm."

He stood up from his chair and reached into his pocket, pulling out a half-folded piece of paper.

"You may not want to hear it, but I'm going to offer you some advice. You don't know me, but I have killed people before. Not because I wanted to, but because I was asked to by my superiors. Killing another person, ending their life and making sure that their mother would never see them again is a burden that haunts me. No matter how hard you try, it can never be undone. The road you are heading down will lead you to hold the burden that I carry, or maybe it already has. Believing that you haven't yet taken the life of another, hear these words- don't let the hate in your heart poison your soul." The man had suggested, placing the half-folded piece of paper between Nathan's index and middle fingers.

As he was leaving, the man turned back and said matter-of-factly, "life is made up of choices and decisions, but asking for help can never hurt."

When he was gone, Nathan unfolded the piece of paper between his fingers and read the words "Concord Community Ministries" scrolled in looping letters across the top.

Reverend Ernest Johnson was reminded of his first meeting with Carl Fisher after scanning the local section of the Monitor and reading the headline **LOCAL COUPLE KILLED IN APPARAENT ROUTE-16 ACCIDENT.** He didn't know what drew his attention to the nondescript, ambiguous headline, but he

161

began scrutinizing the article's contents until his eyes came to the sentence. Buried about three paragraphs in were the sentences "Carl Fisher, 56, and his wife Lily, 54, were killed on impact. New Hampshire State Police are still investigating the cause."

Ernest Johnson read the lines again. "Carl Fisher, 56, and his wife Lily, 54, were killed on impact. New Hampshire State Police are still investigating the cause."

In that moment, the Reverend Ernest Johnson, no longer Nathan "Slinky" Johnson of the Bog Street Boys, bowed his head and prayed.

"Heavenly father, I ask of you, please watch over Carl and Lily Fisher and accept them into your loving arms. Embrace them with your warmth and light, bless them in your glory and heal the pain of those they have left behind. Watch over them, Lord, and assure them that they will be missed. Thank them for all that they did while here on your Earth and may they rest in peace. They were good people. Amen."

The Reverend reached into the front pocket of his flannel shirt and plucked from it a yellowing, tattered piece of cardstock, stained with the age of time. The words "Concord Community Ministries" were now just faintly legible and scrolled in looping letters across the top.

A male loon somewhere out on the lake emitted a long, mournful wail. The sound of the wild, the sound of a searching soul. From his chair swing, the Reverend leaned forward and tossed the card into the lake. It landed softly on the smooth, still surface of the water, sat atop it for a moment and then sank into the copper-colored void.

"Thank you, my friends!" The Reverend faded "Thank you!"

*　　　　*　　　　*　　　　*　　　　*

162

Owen hadn't seen Ben since he left for Georgetown, but he missed his friend something fierce. Ben and Owen were more than best friends. In blood, they were cousins, but in life they were brothers of the same generation, two boys growing into men in this jungle of a world. All through high school the two were inseparable; they did everything together— glued to the hip Owen's Aunt Lily had said. Most of the time it was football, with Benjamin playing middle backer and Owen playing defensive end, but it was more than that. They went double at prom, each escorting one of the Burton twins, who couldn't help themselves by wearing the exact same short, black dress. Although Ben and Owen never proved it, they swore that the Burton twins pulled the old switcheroo half way through prom. They often shared that laugh together when Ben found the time to Skype. That was hard, having his best friend go off to Fordham and then further south to Georgetown. In all honesty, Owen felt a bit betrayed.

Most of all though, Owen missed the summer afternoons they had spent together down at the Merrimack, behind the old dam, drinking stolen beer and chasing girls. Back then, that's what seemed to matter, the flirtatious grab of a beautiful, small-town girl who could instill a hopefulness by the simple way the light fell on her and the ideas she could paint when she talked. Back then, it was simple. Back then, it was the good years.

Those were the thoughts Owen pushed around his mind after Bobbo had called. Owen had been driving north on I-93, up from Manchester with his roommate Colin and Colin's girlfriend Collette, when his cell rang. It was an annoying ringtone, an electric guitar riff that was not mother approved, which alerted Owen that home was calling. It was particularly odd to hear his father's voice on the other end when he answered. He knew something had happened, he could hear the gloomy, choked-up sounds in Bobbo's voice and it was shortly after Owen learned of his Aunt Lily and Uncle Carls' passing.

Hearing the news forced Owen to pull off the highway. He took the State Liquor store exit and parked outside the bright red and white barn-like building. The giant barn-like structure reminded Owen of the trip he took with Ben to Hampton Beach one weekend when they were both seven years old. They were both riding in the back of Aunt Lily and Uncle Carl's car, wearing matching swim trunks with t-shirts depicting epic scenes of fighting reptiles. They were driving past the construction of the building he was now parked in front of, when Uncle Carl vocalized his disapproval about the state having a liquor store as an exit off the highway. He had called it 'one hell of a moral hazard'. It wasn't something Owen had ever thought about, until now.

Bobbo's phone call was brief, just a few short sentences. The call ended with Bobbo saying "Owen, come home. I love you". Those were not words he heard often from his brawny father and hearing them stated so freely, so unimpeded, pushed Owen to tears.

"What the hell is wrong man? Why are you crying?" Colin asked, staring in awe at his roommate, the usual stalwart of emotionless masculinity.

"My Aunt and Uncle died!" Owen choked out, trying to compose himself with quick, short breaths. He rubbed the tears from his eyes.

"Oh, my God!" Colin gasped, his thin, round face going slack from surprise. He too had known Lily and Carl Fisher through the occasional get together with Ben. They had always been gracious hosts and seemed to take an interest in his life.

"I'm so sorry," Collette consoled, her petite hand stroking Owen's right shoulder from the backseat. "What happened?"

"My dad said they were killed in a car accident last night."

"Wow! That was them? Peter— that crazy tree hugger at work — was up in Carroll County yesterday and sent out a dispatch last night saying the state police were called to a car accident off Route-16 that killed two people. My God, that was them? Terrible." Colin said with a startled rattle in his words.

"Ben's back in town!" Owen replied, before stiffly sniffling and restarting the engine. "Got in this morning. I think I'm going to stop by his house before heading to my parents. Do you guys mind?"

"No of course not," Collette agreed.

She was a quiet young woman with long, pale legs that looked like white stalks of asparagus. Her hair was dark blonde, almost brown. She had a terrible shyness about her, rarely speaking in crowds and at times, there was a nervousness about her, like she was uncomfortable in her own body. To people not named Colin, Owen described her as reserved and conservative with a touch of coiled aggression.

"I think he is going to need someone to lean on right now," Colin accepted.

Owen pulled back onto I-93 and drove the fifteen miles to Concord. The group in the car sat preoccupied, their thoughts elsewhere while a guitar solo from one of the Eighties hair bands rambled from the stereo. Twenty minutes passed before Owen pulled up to the Brownstone where he had shared so many memories with his cousin.

The sky above the Fisher's house was painted black with only a dabbling of stars to illuminate the swaying silhouettes of the forest. No lights were on inside, a fact that made Owen's heart skip a beat— of course no lights were on, they're never coming home, he thought. Then he saw it under the muffled glow of dim starlight and parked outside the house, a blue Toyota Avalon.

"What is their car doing here?" Owen blurted out, confused. "I guess that car must be Ben's," pointing to a German made red boxy car.

"Why aren't there any lights on?" Collette questioned as she walked through the dark, up the wooden steps to the front door.

"Be careful guys. It's probably hard to see, but there are a couple of steps." Owen cautioned, stepping across the gravel drive, swinging his arms out in front of him.

There was a loud thud somewhere in the blackness over the driveway.

"Sonofabitch!" Colin yelled. "What the hell—" He felt the ground around him and his fingers touched something made of canvas with patches of leather. "I think I just tripped over luggage. Jesus Christ its dark out here"

There was a pause.

"Yup, I'm bleeding!" Colin shrugged, pulling himself off the ground.

Collette pressed the doorbell; the others joining her at the door. A few seconds passed and then Owen knocked on the door. No one answered.

"Hmm, I think he's got to be here!" Owen wondered.

Collette went down the steps and around the side of the house.

Owen looked to Colin and asked, "Where does she think she is going?"

He could tell that Colin just shook his head unknowingly.

"She's going to hurt herself. It's too dark to see anything." Colin said with a kind of worried laugh.

The two of them followed her around the side of the house, but before they made the corner, Collette appeared.

"The house is completely dark. He's either not there or he's sleeping. In either case, we should let him be." Collette urged. Owen thought he heard panic in her voice for some reason.

"Everything alright, Collette?" He asked.

"I thought I heard something in the woods. Probably a squirrel or something. No big deal." She said.

"Well, let me first give him a call to let him know we stopped by."

Owen pressed 3 and speed dialed Ben's cell. There were four rings before the voicemail picked up.

"Ben, its Owen. I heard the news, man. I know you have to be devastated. I stopped by… your house… and well, I guess you weren't there. Dude, this sucks. Ahh.. I want to see you. Give me a call. I'm going to be at Bobbo's if you need me. If I don't hear from you, I'm going stop by and make sure you're alright. Umm..yea, call me." He closed his phone.

"If you guys want, you can drop me off at my parents and head to the apartment. I think I'm going to spend the night there— you know, in case Ben stops by." Owen faltered; he could feel the knots in his throat tightening.

Colin threw his left arm around his friend's shoulders and gave him a good-natured squeeze. "Absolutely."

The three of them returned to the car and drove down the twisting gravel driveway, away from the Fisher's place. It was a short drive across town to his parent's house and to the comfort of loved ones, but all Owen could think about was how different the house felt that he was pulling away from.

*　　　　*　　　　*　　　　*　　　　*

Malcolm Campbell had returned from the corner market with a paper bag filled with canned soup and baked beans plus a bag of dog chow. Those mutts of his were ferocious eaters—they'd eat him if he didn't keep their bowls full. Ravenous is how he wanted his dogs, he didn't give a shit about their company.

The streets near the market were empty, only a couple of cars parked on the curbside and one white, beaten-down cargo van parked at the back of the market, most likely for short pickups or drop-offs to shut-ins. The weather was tepid and breezy, more of an autumn day in how brisk the air felt— it didn't feel much like a midsummer's afternoon. As Malcolm walked home, clutching the paper bag like a toddler carrying her favorite stuffed animal, he could not help but notice how still the trees were and how immobile the sky had grown, just white cotton balls on a pristine blue backdrop.

Malcolm had seen things in his life that challenged his perception of reality, things both amazing and horrifying one in the same. Such events led him to realize that whenever the world grew this quiet, it was because it was plotting and planning some catastrophic tragedy. It was how Mother Nature prepared her anarchy and Malcolm Campbell knew no greater anarchy in nature than the true face of Warren.

The stillness in the air held a sense of looming conflict. It excited him, kind of aroused him in some sexual way. It had been twenty-two years lamenting the loss of his sweet, beautiful Macy and the social reclusion that Malcolm had imprisoned himself to as a result of it. Macy's death had turned Malcolm cold and wetted his thirst for revenge. The time was approaching where he thought he would have it.

It was three days ago when Carl Fisher had stopped to visit him and the same amount of time since Malcolm had learned of Carl and Lily's plan to get rid of Warren. Malcolm knew the plan Carl had divulged was destined for failure and Malcolm had warned him so, but he could see in the aged eyes of his frustrated friend that his words didn't matter. Carl had a plan, a fruitless plan to Malcolm, but a plan nonetheless. Malcolm had asked Carl to wait, telling him that he was getting close to stabilizing his Compound Zeta formulation. It was clear to him that when Carl left Malcolm's home that night, he was seeing the boy he met playing four-square in first grade for the last time.

Carl and Lily's death was a mere formality to Malcolm, not something he wanted to hear, but something he knew was coming. When it came across the police scanner that a blue Toyota had crashed on Route-16 in Osworth, killing two passengers, Malcolm could only shake his head in disappointment. He would mourn them, after all Carl and Lily were the only other human beings that knew the truth— not the whole iconoclastic truth as he had discovered— but they knew far more than the other blind pigeons of the world.

Deep down inside of him, though, he wasn't sad that Carl and Lily had died. It was a requirement for the next step on the path of vengeance. He would mourn them, he had to, because they were at one time his friends. More than this though, Carl and Lily were the only other people to know the truth about Macy's death- his refulgent, beautiful wife. Her disappearance twenty-two years ago had left him practically friendless, if not for the occasional comfort from Carl and Lily. When Macy was murdered, Malcolm was alienated and became a pariah in the community.

In the days after her death, Malcolm had reported Macy missing to the local authorities and even staged it to look like she had been kidnapped. It was practically a theatrical production, falsifying evidence and scheming a believable story. The years that followed this lie were the hardest for Malcolm. It was one thing to experience the stares from his neighbors and people he had thought were his friends, but undoubtedly they all came to the same conclusion— that Malcolm had killed his wife and covered it up. He knew that was what everyone believed and he could not terribly blame them— it did seem logical.

Over time, Malcolm thought the stigma would erode and that he could start meeting people again, but that was not the case. The stigma and stories about Malcolm killing Macy persisted, even escalating to the point where on the past Halloween night, a Trick-or-Treater dressed as Bo'jangles the skeleton, saw Malcolm raking leaves in his yard and said to his friend "that is the man that chopped up his wife and fed her to his dogs". Not taking too kindly to this, Malcolm had preceded to tell the child and his friend that his dogs were getting mighty hungry looking at them in their skeleton costumes.

Macy's death had been untimely, abrupt and it had happened in the most unconceivable way. It was just a day at the lake up in the mountains, something Carl and Lily had done with them dozens of times before. Never at Lake Osworth though, never there. But Macy's death, her murder, had done more than rip out Malcolm's heart— it carved out his humanity.

Nothing since her death had mattered to Malcolm— not living, not dying. For years, he had wondered about the events of that day, questioning how such things could have happened. He had been a professor of astrophysics at Dartmouth, where musing about the origins and innate complexity of nature were prerequisites for the position. Macy and Malcolm had spent many October nights looking into the night sky with awe and inspiration, asking each other how any one person could fathom it all. In the aftermath of Macy's death, Malcolm learned the answer to that question— no person could fathom it all. Mysteries would always exist. They would always drive the human mind.

But being unable to solve the mysteries drove Malcolm mad. He realized that he might never understand why Macy died or how it was even possible. That was until one night years after her death he found himself stumbling on the outskirts of Osworth, well passed two in the morning, drunker than he had ever been in his life. He had hoped to die that night, the same way as Macy.

Malcolm had been teetering through the woods, bouncing off the rough bark of pine trees and shouting merrily at the top of his lungs "for the monsters to come out". The monsters, as Malcolm had called them, did come. They came from the dark and moved into the glow cast by the moonlight reflecting off of Lake Osworth. The two who killed Macy and Grace came to him in the Osworth woods with smiles on their faces, as if they were meeting an old friend. Malcolm remembered that they looked as human as he did. They had arms and legs and a face with eyes, black and shark-like, but there was something odd in their human features, like they were upright in some Frankenstein way.

"One of you killed my Macy," Malcolm slurred. "Which one was it?"

"It was me!" The woman had said proudly. When she talked, her words came out with faint clicking noises as if she had never spoke before.

"Then it is *you* that must die!" Malcolm laughed, sloppily throwing a finger at her.

The monsters laughed too.

Malcolm pulled a handgun from his coat and shot her in the head. His drunken hands were calm and his shooting was confident as he squeezed the trigger. The woman fell to the ground, her face completely blown away. Malcolm pointed the gun at the man and shot him in the eye, he too fell to the ground.

Looking at the two monsters on the ground, Malcolm exploded in bewildered merriment.

"That was for Macy— you fucks," he slurred through a grin.

Malcolm sat on the ground next to the two monsters he thought he killed and pushed the tip of the gun beneath his chin. Malcolm looked up into the night sky and pulled back the hammer of the handgun. It clicked, the loudest sound Malcolm had ever heard. It was the last sound he thought he would ever hear until there was a crackle in the brush beside him, followed by another. He opened his eyes and looked to either side of him. They were gone. The two monsters had disappeared.

Malcolm was spooked. He darted to his feet and headed from the forest. As he retreated, the two appeared, just as they had when Macy was killed. They stood in front of him, their faces mutilated and disfigured from the bullets Malcolm had fired. How was such a thing possible? This was what Malcolm had been thinking when their two faces, dripping with flesh and hanging bits, began to creep upwards, stitching themselves back together. In short order, the two faces were whole and their sick, misshapen smiles returned.

"Malcolm, you cannot win," the man howled, leaning closer to Malcolm as if to show him the blacks in his eyes. "If you don't believe me, shoot us again."

Malcolm did. He fired the remaining three bullets at their skulls, two hitting the man and one splitting the woman's eyes. As they had before, they fell to the ground and laid still. Malcolm saw this and looked up at the starry night in deliberation.

Then it came to him— his idea. He moved down the disencumbered embankment to his truck, the drunken cloudiness that had led him to these Osworth woods receding into clarity. He pulled from it a tangled heap of thick steel chains. Malcolm dropped a hooked-end onto the hard, damp dirt and latched the other end onto the back of his relic pickup truck.

Malcolm Campbell threw himself into the driver seat, fired the engine and slammed the truck into reverse. His truck tore backwards with the driver-side door flapping back and forth, his tires tearing up the mossy earth as he accelerated up the disencumbered embankment. The truck came to a stop next to the two bodies, which had not yet vanished. Malcolm jumped down from his pickup and went to the back of the truck. Grabbing the free end, he began to wrap the chain around the woman's neck, securing the tension by fastening the hook inside one of the chain links.

Malcolm felt as if something was amiss. Why hadn't the bodies disappeared like before?

Malcolm hesitated, then pushed aside the momentary sense of foreboding. He returned to his truck and shifted into drive. He pressed the accelerator as far down as he could. The truck jerked to life and bolted forward, dragging the woman's body down the embankment and onto the dirt road that marked the exit.

As the woman's body bounced against the rocky, sylvan road, Malcolm concentrated on his rearview mirror and the faint, unmoving mass disappearing into the darkness as he pulled away. He watched, waiting for it— the body of the man —to vanish, but after not too long, the fuzzy mass Malcolm had been looking at was lost in a curtain of shadows.

Without warning, the man that Malcolm would come to know as Warren materialized in front of the rambling truck with a look a fierce anger. Warren stood in the headlights of the charging truck, threw his arms out in an aggravated, inviting show of aggression. Malcolm corrected his sinuous course and made straight for Warren.

As the truck closed in on Warren, he emitted a reverberating, concussive wail and threw his arms up in the air. He threw his head back and the truck ripped into him. For a second the truck had appeared to run through Warren, but as Malcolm continued onward, he could see that he had not struck him. Instead, Warren had vanished again. Malcolm did not care if Warren had vanished again or if he was playing hide-and-seek; all he wanted was to put the Osworth woods behind him and see how far he could get with the woman who had killed his wife dangling like a tin can from the back of his truck.

Malcolm had seen the sign for Route-16 in a cluster of drooping reeds on the side of the road, when a pair of hands jumped out from the empty space beside him. The hands lunged at his neck and clutched it, interlocking their cold, dead fingers around the nape of Malcolm's neck. The thumbs poked into his Adam's apple, squeezing it. The truck swerved and the woman attached to it swung to the left. Suddenly, Malcolm's throat was being squeezed, crushed by the ravaging hands that seemed to float in midair. Malcolm's eyes began to squint and the world in front of him, illuminated by his headlights, turned a shade of bright gray.

His truck swerved right onto Route-16 then fishtailed in the mud on the dirt road as it tried to straighten out. Taking his hands from the wheel, Malcolm pried at the choking hands, desperately trying to rip them off. Abruptly as they had appeared, the hands were gone. Malcolm could breathe again.

Malcolm cleared his throat with a mucous-filled rasp and considered what had just happened. Hands had been floating in the air and they had attacked him, choked him. But where did they come from? Then he realized that such a thing was not that bizarre, not here in the Osworth woods anyway. For a long moment, Malcolm was mesmerized by the hands that had attacked him until he looked up into his rearview mirror.

The woman he had shot between the eyes was still chained to the back of his truck. Malcolm had watched her body skid across the wet, blacktop of Route-16, as he headed back to Concord and to the vacant prison of his empty home. But before the Osworth woods were in his wake, Malcolm had seen the man appear in the road behind him, his eyes no longer black and shark-like. Instead, the

174

eyes that had gaped back at him where a cardinal red, bright and violent, and they held a caustic ire that sent a clear message to Malcolm. It had been a message of determination, of vengeance.

That was the image Malcolm recalled as he walked home from the corner store, thinking about his old friends Carl and Lily. Their deaths were only the beginning, he thought, seeing those cardinal red eyes stare back at him in his mind. Then Malcolm Campbell smiled.

Remains

The white linen sealed their bodies, holding in vestige the last remnants of their physical selves. When I first heard that my parents had been killed, there was a morose vacancy left inside of me like the feeling you get when you travel away from home and realize you forget your wallet on the kitchen table. It was a sense of panic, a selfish feeling. It was what *I* had lost. Seeing my parents' charred, blackened bodies laying on the morgue table, lifeless and rigid, cold and sterile, as if they were actors on a forensic television show was surreal and it brought home that I didn't just lose them, but they were taken from me. They were murdered; I knew it, even if the medical examiner or Officer Landry had yet to say it.

"Son, I know this is difficult, but can you physically identify these two individuals," Officer Landry offered in his militaristic voice, his heavy hand gripping my shoulder. He was the broad man his voice suggested, a Franz Josef mustache carving a hairy-W beneath his large, flat nose.

Megan squeezed my left hand as a show of support. Even though I wasn't looking at her, I could tell she was crying. I wanted to cry too. But I was sick of crying.

"Yes, they're my parents. Carl and Lily Fisher." I choked out.

"Alright son! I know that was hard. What happens next is Dr. Lider will provide proof of death so that you can make arrangements with a funeral home or burial service. However, this proof of death will not be their official death certificate as there have been some complications to the official cause of death. Dr. Lider is working—"

"Complications? What do you mean complications?" Megan interrupted.

"I can't answer that, unfortunately. You can ask Dr. Lider, but he may chose not to answer as well. This is an open case and there are sensitivities related to these types of investigations." Officer Landry voiced hesitantly, his broad, massive shoulders expanding in a somewhat defensive posture.

I sensed something was left unsaid.

"Can I speak with Dr. Lider then?" I asked.

Officer Landry exhaled vehemently before conceding, "Yes, one second." He left the side room where I had identified my parents through one-way glass.

Several minutes later, he returned with a bald man holding narrow facial features and large cheek bones. He was short, stout and possessed a keen, almost uncomfortable smile on his face.

"I am Doctor Henry Lider." The man said extending his hand to Megan, then myself. We each shook his outstretched hand. "I hear you have some questions?"

"Yes! I hear that there are issues with identifying my parents' cause of death. What seems to be the hold up?"

Dr. Henry Lider shared a brief, fleeting glance with Officer Landry, a glance of reluctance and bewilderment.

"Well, Benjamin is it?" Lider asked. I nodded and he continued, "What I do here, as head medical examiner, is attempt to

177

recreate the situation that led to someone's death using what information I have from the investigation and the information their body provides me through an autopsy."

I nodded, realizing this was his standard preamble. "I got it! I've seen CSI!"

Dr. Lider cleared his throat, "yes, of course. Now to your parents. Based on Officer Landry's report, your parent's automobile flipped over and caught fire. They were burned, but it was not fire that killed them. I know this because they had no smoke or carbon particulates in their lungs. That is, Benjamin, your parents died prior to the car catching fire—"

"They were in a car accident isn't that what killed them?" I asked, speaking the obvious.

"The accident itself was not enough to cause your parents death. There was no other car involved and no frontal or side impact. I mean by this that there were no significant trauma caused to them by the car accident—"

"But you said their car flipped over. Isn't that an impact?"

"Yes. However, the impact of the car flipping over was not significant enough to be fatal. Both your parents were wearing their seat belts and the roof did not collapse completely. Your father's left clavicle was fractured and your mother's right wrist, as she was in the passenger seat. These injuries are consistent with a car rolling over and considerable centripetal forces being generated, but these injuries were of no mortal consequence."

"So how did his parent's die? None of this seems terribly helpful!" Megan carped.

"And you are?" Dr. Lider asked.

"Oh, I'm Megan. I'm his girlfriend."

"I see. At present, I have not definitively found a cause of death… well not exactly."

178

"What does that mean?" I complained, staring at Dr. Lider who seemed to be perspiring.

"I have personally performed nearly one thousand autopsies in my tenor as head medical examiner and in every case, I have been confident in my recommendation as to COD. Your parents are both an exception."

"You have no idea as to why they died?" I pushed.

'Not exactly!" Officer Landry interjected, looking at the floor and breaking eye contact with Dr. Lider.

Dr. Lider cleared his throat again and made a mumbling sound. "What Officer Landry is eluding to is we know what killed your parents, but we can't explain it. Not even remotely."

"What killed my parents?" I urged.

"Their hearts were deformed." Dr. Lider revealed.

"Huh? I don't understand." Megan asked, a confused wrinkle spreading in her forehead.

"Your parents' hearts were…ah…compressed. Somehow, their hearts were physically crushed and it wasn't caused by an auto accident—"

"How do you know?"

"A car accident would have resulted in bruises or fractures around the area of impact. This would have occurred in their chest region most likely. Unfortunately, no such marks or abrasions were found. This means that something was able to cause traumatic stress to the organ while not impacting the surrounding tissue or anatomy. This is illogical. Nowhere in the annals of medicine has a case like this been recorded. I am truly at a loss." Lider confessed earnestly.

Something about the puzzlement in Lider's words seemed to make sense to me. The whole sorted episode— my parents death, how I found out, the lies about having a sister, the letter — all of it felt like it was converging to something…something

179

that made me uneasy, uncomfortable. I knew it all centered around Uncle Warren. He was a puppeteer, a shadow walker. My mother's letter had told of a man and woman coming for me when I was baby. I knew the man was Warren, but who was the woman? And why me? Why my parents? My life had suddenly become a treacherous game of hide and seek and I didn't know what happened when I got found.

"So you're saying that something or somebody, perhaps, was able to deform my parent's hearts. When you say deformed though, do mean that they were structurally changed or that they stopped beating because they was temporarily distorted?" I requested, not sure an answer would be provided.

"It was as if a person reached into their bodies, clutched their beating hearts and squeezed them like meaty orbs. I apologize for the graphic imagery, but I assure you it is like that. It is remarkably and completely not understood." Lider retorted, moving towards the door of the small room we were standing in.

"Well, it doesn't really matter does it?" I asked rhetorically. "My parents are dead regardless. So what do I need to do…ah… to lay them to rest?"

Lider handed me a manila folder he had been holding in a business-like manner. Just another day at the office for a man who deals with death every day.

"That is proof of death. It is enough right now to setup a service or whatever is needed to meet your parents' wishes. Within forty-eight hours, we will issue an official certificate of death with COD, but as we have just discussed, I may rule the death as 'accidental'."

"I appreciate your candor. I do hope though, that you can figure it out. Thank you for your time, "I said, extending my hand to comply with the niceties of the situation and to thank him for trying to uncover the cause of my parents' deaths.

He nodded to me and then to Megan. Before he exited he fired a scowling look at Landry, who just shrugged it off.

"Alright son, do you have everything you need?" Landry asked, making for the door.

"I think I do sir. Thank you."

"Once more, my condolences for your loss. I hope you can come to terms with it," Landry offered and then he left the room, leaving Megan and I alone.

Megan looked up at me with her fiery jade eyes and I saw in them the spark that had lured my interest those many months ago in that coffee shop off of Dupont Circle. I couldn't help but feel that my life had reached a crossroads there in the observation room of the morgue. My future was one path, standing in front me— a short, auburn-haired woman whose smile buckled my knees. She was the symbol of everything I wanted for myself— happiness, prosperity, a reason to wake in the morning. Then there was my past, which carved the other path in the crossroads. My past was lying on the examination table and its secrets nested inside the vacancy of my parent's bodies, like a cursed, parasitic snake coiled and ready to eat its way out. There was something hidden in these events, the feeling was in my gut. The letter about the day I was born, the lies about having a sister, my parent's death and it all revolved around Warren. I didn't know why, but I knew he was coming for me. Yesterday, he was the man in the woods watching me from the cover of foliage... I was convinced of it.

"I know what you're thinking, Benjamin. I think you should go tell Officer Landry right now. I am serious." Megan bossed, her arm involuntarily bending at her hip. That was one of her bossy mannerisms and I thought it was adorable.

"I can't tell him anything, because I don't know anything of substance. Besides—"

"Mister, I think you should tell him everything. Tell him about Uncle Warren, about the letter you were telling me about, the man in the woods yesterday. Everything."

"Megan, I can't," I conceded. "I promise—"

That feeling of the world moving away from me returned and the red haze shrouded my vision. I crouched onto my knees, my head pulsated. Blood rushed from my body and I felt cold and clammy like I was standing on the deck of a rocking ship. The vertigo was horrendous, tossing my internal sense back and forth. The motion pushed me towards vomiting and I fell onto my hands. I could feel Megan's hands on my back and she was speaking to me, I could hear her voice as if she was at one end of a tunnel, far away from me. Her words were mumbled as if she was speaking underwater.

The red haze began to spin and I could see the floor in front of me move away. I could see my hands hovering over the floor even though I could feel them against the cool, hard tile. I thought for a second, as the haze darkened to crimson, that I could reach through the floor to the other side, to cold, brown clay beneath the foundation.

The crimson darkened further to a blackened film across all that I saw and then the words came to me, as clear as a whisper from a lover.

"Soon Benjamin...Soon."

In my thoughts, I could hear my voice asking who was there.

A gruff, shrill laugh followed. "I am coming. Tick, Tock!"

The veil of black cascaded back to crimson then to red and finally back to clear. The world settled back into its rightful place. The vertigo and nausea dissipated. I lifted myself off the floor and brushed myself clean.

182

"What the hell is going on, Ben." Megan demanded, clutching my shoulders and looking up at me. "That is the second time that this has happened—"

"Third."

"Third? Oh my god, we need to get you to a doctor."

"No we don't. I know what's wrong."

"Then what is it?"

"It's him. I heard him in my head and he's coming for me."

"Who is coming for you?" Megan asked, confused at first, then a look of recollection dawned across her voice.

"Yes...Uncle Warren."

Lifted Up

"Tomorrow I will bury my parents," I said to my friends around the table, shooting back another shot of Kilkenny's Irish Nectar. It had been a few days since I saw them in the morgue and it was difficult to shake the imagery of them on the table.

"But not tonight. Tonight we drink to them." Owen granted, raising his glass into the middle of the table before downing its contents.

Megan, Colin and Collette followed our lead downing the amber whiskey.

"I say barkeep, another round for everyone," Owen laughed, picking up the bottle.

"Don't mind if I do," he then said in a different voice before pouring himself a glass and filling the remaining ones.

"Ay, now we're talking," Colin said, drinking up the whiskey once his glass was filled. "Come on Collette, drink up. We observe the five second rule here."

Timidly, Collette sipped on the liquid, making a pucker face.

I took the second shot and Owen filled it right back up again. I could see that look in his eyes that I used to see when we crashed college parties. It was a look of debauchery and carousal. Owen had the intent of drowning my sorrow in copious amounts of Irish whiskey and considering this was the eve of my parent's funeral, I was not going to argue.

"So Owen, I hear Ben was quite the ladies man in high school? Care to offer up anything juicy?" Megan asked, her soft cheeks flush with color and her eyes turning glassy.

Owen grinned mischievously. "But Megan I have only known you for like a day. Surely, you don't believe I would offer up some tasty morsel on my man's history after only two shots, do you? Ask me again after the fifth and I'll be sinking ships."

Noticing his glass was empty, Megan grabbed the bottle and poured Owen an abundant glassful. We all laughed. I emptied my glass and refilled it.

Colin, who was sitting to my left, leaned over to me.

"Dude, you did good for yourself," he whispered, tilting his head and raising his eyebrows towards Megan. His breath was hot and smelled of the whiskey.

I grinned merrily at him, my cheeks tingling and numb. My skin was red hot. My eyes caught Collette sitting next to Colin and she had a look of worry on her face.

"So how do you like Georgetown?" asked Owen.

"I hate it man. Seriously, it is horrible. The legal professional is filled with such sleazy people. For example, I interned at this firm, Smitson and Wales. My very first day there, I sat in on a meeting where the managing partners were giving their stump speeches to all the young bloods. You know, the 'why we're great' speech. One of the guys bragged about making millions of dollars suing a charity that failed to dispose of asbestos insulation it used in one of its shelters. I mean, being a lawyer nowadays is tantamount to being, I don't know, the anti-Robin Hood."

"Tell us how you really feel," Owen laughed. "What about you Megan?"

"I'm not nearly as cynical as Ben. Sure, seeing how a large law firm conducts business definitely knocks some of the idealistic wind out of you, but that doesn't mean a lawyer can't do good." Megan offered softly, pushing her auburn hair behind her ear.

I shot her a playful glance and like remembering something so obvious, I saw in her flirtatious smile back to me the pureness of her beauty.

"You know, I think Ben's right, lawyers are horrific human beings. Worst people ever. I wouldn't want to be one and neither should either of you," Collette blurted out earnestly.

Megan deflated, her face frowning. Those were the first words Collette had spoke all night and there was an arrogance about them. I didn't like her for saying that.

"No, Megan's right. Being a lawyer is a profession. It is the people that are the problem. The same could be said about biologists, cops, and teachers. Some people are just self-centric." I rebuked.

Collette's eyes flared wide and then went normal.

"Christ! You people need to drink up. Who fucking cares? Tonight is about remembering Carl and Lily Fisher, the best aunt and uncle I guy could have." Owen consoled, sipping a beer he had taken from the fridge.

"You know Owen," Colin interjected, "you really shouldn't mix beer and whiskey. It will upset you stomach. Make you puke."

Owen stared at him comically with his head tilted to the side. He then proceeded to chug down the full contents of the bottle in his hand and made an audible, taunting belch.

"Who the hell told you that?" Owen blurted. "This stomach is wicked strong, freakin' cast iron." He raised his white shirt to show his flat, toned abs and slapped it hard with an open hand.

"It's true man. Straight up. You can't start drinking hard stuff and then all willy nilly go to beer. Too much carbonation. Its science," Colin babbled, his face bobbing back and forth. I could tell from his glassy stare and the dumbfounded grin plastered across his face that Colin was two minutes away from collapsing into a drunken coma.

The night continued with revelry and pointless bacchanalia. It seemed like each of us was trying to bury something pejorative in the boozing and behind the deceitful face of happiness. For me, it was that I missed my parents. No amount of alcohol or companionship would bring them back. It was that and the horrible sense that something was looming, waiting, for my parents to be put in the ground. I think Megan had been thinking the same thing, but maybe this whole sorted ordeal made her think about her father. The rest of them, I had no clue what they were avoiding. Even if it was just for the night, I liked feeling numb, feeling nothing.

It was a bit passed four in the morning when silence ruled the house. Owen had collapsed on the couch, his curly, jet-black hair mangy and matted in sweat; he had somehow lost a shoe and his shirt in his mad rush to become the tavern fool. I had sort of forgotten how much fun he could be and I realized I missed that part of my life— the reckless abandonment of responsibility.

Colin, who I had recognized as a guy I had went to school with, but not much more, had migrated to the guest room with his girlfriend Collette. I found Colin a pretty decent guy and throughout the night, he passed on stories about the Osworth disappearances. As he worked for the NH Fish and Game, he had been acquainted with so-called "classified" information— of course, this information flowed out without a barrier halfway through the night. I think because he knew my parents had died in Osworth, the information would be somehow relevant. For the most part, it had been the same thing Bobbo had told me: mutilated deer with large holes gouged through them and hikers who vanished without a trace, including the most recent case of two kids named Jesse and Derek.

But one thing Colin mentioned seemed much more informative. Apparently, on several occasions, his coworkers had seen a man roaming the woods, only to vanish in front of them without a trace. In each instance, the man was the same, an olive-grey skinned man with solid, black eyes, that held a vacant stare and he was always dressed in denim overalls. When I heard this description, I knew it was the man from my nightmare and the same man that had been standing in the woods outside the house we were all sitting in. I knew it was Uncle Warren. Of course, Colin laughed off these accounts as a "good, old-fashioned ribbing" and gave it no merit, but my mother's letter made me think that it all might be true, even if it seemed to violate reality.

For a litany of reasons, one of them being what Colin had said, I found that I couldn't sleep and got out of bed around five-thirty. I walked down to the kitchen at the corner of the house and put on a pot of coffee. The house was dark and quiet, as were the outdoors.

I liked the quiet in the house. It was the first time since my parents had died when I did not feel alone. But at the same time I felt a sense of personal peace, a sense of solitude in the knowledge that I was the only one up and about.

I poured myself a cup of black coffee and went outside through the sliding glass door. The dawning sun was bleeding into the night sky, but I could still see the stars. I walked out to the deck and sat down on a wooden rocking chair that my parents had brought back from an Amish carpenter in Pennsylvania.

I sat in the chair, rocking back and forth, watching the day begin. The stars in the sky slowly faded to a tinted cyan blue and the silence that had been, was eroded by the chirping of birds and the scurrying of squirrels through dry leaves. It was the dawning of life once more. The morning was crisp and brisk, more autumn than a midsummer's morning. The day would be beautiful, I could sense it, but it would be a somber one too.

I began to daydream, thinking about the last few days— thinking about everything but my parent's death. I thought about Megan and the phone call that started it all. That moment was buried in D.C, back in another life and one that I didn't think I wanted anymore. Then I thought about my spells of displacement, how they came on without warning and dissipated just as quickly. The spells gave the perception that I was falling away from the world into something deeper, floating in a crimson haze as the world pulsated by me, as if a beating heart. Three times it had happened and each time had been more intense than the last.

It first struck me when I was walking back from dinner in D.C around the time my parents died. The second time had been right after I landed in Manchester, as I was driving home. The last time it happened, it made me wish my head had exploded in the observation room at the morgue. Whatever these spells were, I didn't feel like something was physically wrong with me.

My mind continued to drift, diving further into the events that unfolded since I'd arrived home. I thought about Bobbo and Aunt Julie, about the discovery of my sister and her death and the man in woods when I came home. Then there was the nightmare that I had about Uncle Warren and his cannibalistic urges. In the dream he grappled me to the ground and mounted me, his breath was warm and smelled of sour meat. It was a dream, but felt more real than anything I could imagine. And when I was startled awake, I

189

found the letter my mother had written to me before she died. These things were not random events; they were all connected.

The sliding glass door opened behind me and Collette walked out with a cup of tea in her hands, the steam drifting above it.

"Good morning," she accorded, staring off into the woods and warming her face in her tea. She walked to the railing overlooking the woods and leaned against them.

"It is a good morning," I partly agreed, looking up at her.

"Well, I'm sure you've had better mornings, but it is a beautiful day still."

"Yes it is. At least my parents will be buried under a golden sun. It warms the soil." I said.

"Warms the soil? They're dead! Why would they care?" Collette blurted out.

"I know it doesn't matter, but I'd like to think when they're lowered down it will be into a resting place that is warm and comfortable, like they're being tucked in to sleep." I said in a hush, suffocated voice.

"I guess if that helps you cope, whatever. At least you have Megan!"

"Yep!"

"How long have you two been together?" Collette inquired, her pale white face flashing towards me.

"Huh? Uhh... I don't know. Three months maybe." I said, inquiring about Collette.

"She most really love you to come all the way up here, leaving a great opportunity like she had."

I sat in silence for a second or two. "Megan does love me. Her comfort has helped me through this."

"So it is safe to say that you're going to have children together? Is she the future mother of your children Benjamin?

Hmm?" Collette interrogated, her eyes darting at me, cutting at me with neurotic accusation.

"Excuse me? How is this any of your business?" I demanded, my body swelling from the pulses of blood beginning to push through it caused by her audacity.

Just then the glass door slide open and Owen walked out with a massive glass of iced coffee.

"Damn! That shit hit me...HARD!" He spoke aloud to no one in particular. He sat in the wooden patio chair beside me and stared at the ground.

For a few minutes he simply stayed still, sipping his coffee. No one said a word.

"How you feelin'? You're hanging in there man, I'll tell you. You've always been one stubborn shit. How you aren't balling on the ground I will never know," Owen consoled in his way, resting his head against the back of the chair.

"My mind is thinking about too much. So, I don't have the capacity to be sad." I offered up, sipping the last lukewarm drop of coffee from my mug.

"Do you know what your parents were doing in Osworth anyway?" Owen asked bluntly. He was looking more awake with each sip of iced coffee; his pale, clammy appearance vanishing. "My memory is a bit hazy, but I remember what Colin said last night about the things going on up there. For a small, quiet place like the good ol' Granite State, the Osworth disappearances are a wicked big deal. I even heard the hot anchor— you know, the one smuggling watermelons in her blouse— on Channel 7 talking about it. And that's down in Boston. It usually takes a homicide to get a mention from those Chowda' heads."

"You know I have no clue what they were doing up there. Well, not exactly anyway. But I do know that they were hiding a bunch of stuff from me. So many things..." I said, my words fading

191

into thoughts about how much I wanted to divulge. It was Owen after all, but there was just so much to tell him and I had yet to wrap my own head around it.

"Like what? They weren't swingers were they?" Owen joked.

I laughed. "What? No, you fuck!"

"You never know. I could see Uncle Carl having yellow fever. All those years back in 'Nam and everything."

"Uhh, no. You're just as weird as always, man."

Owen shrugged and smiled.

"You wanna know one of the things I found out? Before I was born, I had a sister! Her name was Grace. Died the day I was born." I acknowledged, watching as two mourning doves flew by and perched themselves on a nearby branch. I caught Collette in the corner of my eye resting against a banister, quietly watching Owen and me.

"Are you serious? Or just joshing me?" Owen asked, looking confused.

"As serious as a shark attack," I said just as I used to whenever Owen and I discussed our adolescent quandaries, which mainly consisted of what movie we preferred or what famous actress we wanted to see naked.

A crooked, déjà vu smile rose on Owen's face. "How did she die... ah, your sister— Grace, is it?"

I nodded. "Well, that's the weird part. The day my mom died she wrote me a letter telling me about the day I was born and the day that Grace died. I was born in Osworth, Owen. My parents never told me this or anyone actually. Why?"

"Holy shit!" Owen swore. "And what happened to Grace?"

"A man and woman took her. They came out of the woods when I was born and tried to steal me. They got Grace instead." I told Owen, omitting the facts about the people vanishing and reappearing in thin air; I did not believe that myself.

"You're not fucking with me?" Owen asked in awe.

I shook my head.

Just then the door slid open and out walked Megan, Colin came out behind her in more of stumble than a walk. Megan held my mother's Best Brew mug filled with tea and Colin, of all things, had a beer in one hand, a bottle of aspirin in the other. He looked like hell.

"Good morning," Megan said half-groggy, half-somber.

Owen and Collette repaid the nicety. I met Megan and brought her in close to me, kissing her forehead. She rested her head against my chest and then kissed me on my stubbly chin. Seeing her today, standing in the warm sunlight, made my sentimental pessimism evaporate. I would get through the day.

"You know what would hit the spot— pancakes and sausage doused in maple syrup. Yummee!" Colin announced. "A day like this needs something uplifting anyhow."

Everyone grew quiet, looking at me as if they were all in agreement with Colin, but afraid to admit it.

"Damn straight. Pancakes and sausage it is." I said, walking into the house through the sliding glass door. Everyone hesitated at first, but then followed me inside.

Owen came up beside me.

"You gonna cook bro?" He asked, a look of surprise on his face.

"I can manage to wipe my own ass man. I mean I have lived on my own for a little while." I laughed, heading into the kitchen.

"Yea, but I thought that was a euphemism for dating some hot chick that could cook."

"Euphemism? Do you even know what that word means?" I asked, reaching above the granite stone aisle for two frying pans. I bent down and picked up a mixing bowl from the cupboard.

"Hey Megan?" Owen hollered into the living room.

Megan was sitting on the couch with her arms wrapped around her knees.

"Yes, Owen?" She asked, turning her attention away from Colin and Collette, who were both sitting in the chair beside her with Collette on Colin's lap.

"Do you cook? You know, for Ben?" He questioned.

"Nope, he's the chef. I offered, but he said there will be plenty of time for that when I'm barefoot and pregnant." Megan said in a monotonous, deadpan voice.

Owen looked at me as if he couldn't believe I said such a thing. I shrugged.

"Grab me like eight eggs and check the freezer for blueberries. Mom usually froze fresh ones from Maine, so there should be some." I ordered, whisking together some flour and salt with a bit of water.

Owen grabbed a dozen eggs and placed them on the shelf. He pulled out a plastic Ziploc bag of blueberries. They were a mound of frozen globules clumped together by furry ice crystals.

"I said like eight eggs, dude. Not a dozen." I joked.

"Well, I'm hungry and I know you're not putting eight eggs into that pancake batter. So just fry me up some eggs, Chef Boyardee. I am fricken' hungry and hung over." Owen replied, smirking. He started to walk towards the living room.

"Where do you think you're going? You forget the sausage, you bum." I teased.

"What? You didn't say I needed to get you sausage."

"I didn't think I had to, young man. You knew everyone wanted sausage. How many times do I need to tell you to

194

listen?" I kidded, pointing the whisk at him and peering at him with accusatory eyes. Batter dripped from the whisk. "And clean that up before you go watch TV!"

"You did that too well. I am a bit concerned, man. I am not sure you even need Megan to bear your child, you could probably do it yourself after a performance like that." Owen laughed, grabbing a package of sausage links from the bottom shelf of the refrigerator and tossing them on the granite shelf.

"Is that all there is?" I asked. "Twelve sausages for five people? That's like an unsolvable engineering problem!"

"Well, there are three men and two women. That makes a difference. So, the guys get two apiece and the ladies each get three. The ladies like the sausage," Owen said, a childish grin stretching across his face.

"Ha, ha! Not much has changed with you. The same damn scamp you've always been." I laughed aloud, wiping a tear from my eye. Lewd humor such as Owen's was a welcome reprieve for the day that lay ahead.

Owen left the kitchen and left me alone to cook. Working the frying pans was exactly what I needed. A smorgasbord of scrumptious food was being sculpted before me in a symphony of heat and pressure. The sausage links sizzled and crackled. The pancakes rose from the pan like spongy saucers. The fresh-cracked eggs grew soft and white, their yellow centers firming just enough as to wiggle when prodded by the edge of my spatula. As the smell wafted up into my nose, I was reminded of the Sunday mornings when it was Mom cooking at the stove and like my friends were now, Dad and I were waiting excitedly to devour the morsels.

I served breakfast to my friends at ten passed eight in the morning. We ate together and enjoyed each other's company for about an hour. We were all in festive moods, but none of us heard the car pull up the driveway.

Lowered Down

We were all startled by the knock at the door.

"Is it time already?" Owen questioned, stuffing another forkful of blueberry pancake into his mouth. He then tried to say something else, but his mouth was too full with the splattering of foods he had just shoved in there and it come out as "mhaam mmooe druby loolo."

Megan looked at him with a painful fascination. Colin and Collette paid Owen no attention as if his gluttonous shoveling of tasty morsels were an everyday occurrence. I was certain that it was.

"Sure, I'll do that." I said, nodding.

I ran to answer the door.

A man wearing a clergy jacket with a preacher's collar stood on the step.

He extended a feeble and frail hand and introduced himself, "good morning, son. I am Reverend Earnest Johnson."

I gripped his hand. "Oh, you're the pastor! Bobbo said he had asked you to do my parent's service. Come in, come in."

"Thank you, son."

"Ben, you can call me Ben. Are you hungry?" I asked warmly, letting the Reverend walk in front of me and then shutting the door.

"That's alright. I ate a bowl of melon and yogurt this morning. So how are you?" Earnest queried.

The classic black preacher attire Earnest wore, triggered something uncomfortable in me. I had grown to mistrust such uniforms of purity.

"I'm doing about as well as one can expect I guess," I replied before pausing. "So I have been told you knew my parents. How so?"

We walked into my father's study and sat in the two leather chairs that rested beneath the wide bay window that looked out onto the driveway. A loud crash came from above. Earnest looked startled.

"No worries. My cousin is loose upstairs. If left unattended the poor tike will rip the place apart." I said, smiling.

"Oh my. How old is he?" The Reverend questioned with curiosity as another loud crash rattled the floor. It sounded like someone was trying to put dishes away and was failing at it.

"He's twenty-two. A real mess, I'll tell you. So, how did you know my parents?" I inquired, squinting my eyes to take a better look at the man sitting next to me. There was something wrong about him, I could sense.

"I met your parents when your father punched me in the face and put me in the hospital for four days." Earnest snickered through a nasally wheeze and continued, "yeah, your dad way back when gave me one heck of a whooping. Can't say I didn't deserve it, either. I was a bad man back then." Earnest flashed a tender smile across his wrinkled, weathered face.

"Wait a sec! Are you saying my dad beat you up?" I asked, assured that he had made a mistake.

"Hard to believe is it? It shouldn't be. Your father was a prideful man, built on strength and courage. He saw me dishing out a beating on a college kid and he did the bold and difficult thing. He

197

stepped up and stopped me. How many people do you know who would have done the same thing?" Earnest posed, leaning forward in the chair, his cagey blue eyes were warm and comforting behind thin-wire spectacles.

I shook my head. I couldn't think of many people doing that. My Dad had his moments when he was a tough old coot, but I never saw him get physical. If anything, my father had been a gentle man, tender to almost everyone. I knew he was this way for all the killing he did in Vietnam. Murdering people beneath the banner of war haunted my father and every day since the bloodshed in the tall grass he tried to affirm meaning from the lives he took.

"Personally, your father saved my life. So did your mother. They were amazing people. If not for them, I would be in prison or dead. There is no hiding from that fact. It is the truth. I say this because you should grab that essence, pull it inside you and mourn. This is a terrible tragedy. Don't reside your emotions in anger and sadness. Sure, they exist, but remember your parents for the love they gave you. Hold it. Embrace it. Cherish it. The rest will fall away and you will be okay. You will be okay," Earnest spoke with a soft serenity as he stroked my shoulder.

"I know," I said.

Then, for whatever reason, I cried. I hated myself for doing it in front of someone I had just met. But I couldn't help it. At that moment, all I wanted to do was cry and scream. Cry and scream. That was all I wanted to do because my life made no sense to me.

My eyes burned from salty tears and my body shook. The Reverend placed his arm around me and patted my shoulder. I turned my head away from him, hiding my face.

"Son, it is okay to cry! It is alright." The Reverend comforted. "You've suffered a terrible loss and you're probably thinking to yourself, 'what will happen to me?'. You're a young man, too young to have to deal with all of this. But you still have people who care— family, friends. You'll get through this. I promise you."

I gathered myself and sat upright, wiping the tears from my eyes with the heel of palms. I was so tired of being lost in my own life.

"I'm good. Just a momentary crack. Nothing a bit of spackle and time can't fix." I offered through a smile, but I could tell my face was smeared with tears and sadness.

Today I needed to be like my father, brave and courageous. I could not let my parent's murder or all the questions from the last few days obscure the day's purpose, even though they lurked inside me like a ravenous, caged lion. There would be a time for answers and a time for vengeance.

The Reverend smiled perceptively and then looked at his watch.

"It is 9:15. Why don't you go relax for a bit. People will be arriving shortly for the memorial service. Your Uncle Warren should be here soon to setup," consoled Earnest, reaching into a haversack that I just noticed. He pulled out a worn, leather-bound Bible with a series of flags marking key passages and scripture.

My heart sank into my stomach.

"What did you say?" I asked nervously.

"I said you should go relax. Your Uncle Robert will be here soon to get everything together for the memorial service." Earnest reiterated.

"Oh, right. What time is the service? I know Bobbo told me, but I forgot." I asked.

"Whenever everyone is ready. Probably around eleven," Earnest suggested.

I thanked the Reverend and told him to make himself at home. As I walked upstairs, a quiet cackle crept out from beneath the closed study door. Did the Reverend close the door when I left?

199

The living room and kitchen were empty. The dishes had been cleaned and put away. The table had been cleared and the television showed only a black screen. All the doors to the rooms down the hallway were closed and I could hear water running from one of the bathrooms. I went into my room and flopped onto my bed.

The cool, soft sheets felt amazing. I rested there with my head in my pillow and listened to the sound of water running. Such a simple sound— the trickle of water, nothing more than droplets falling on tile— a soft patting sound.

The trickling water subsided and the subtle lull I had fallen into by listening to it ended as well. Still, I laid there on my bed like a zombie, not thinking about anything of importance. Not thinking at all, really.

The bathroom door opened and Megan emerged, wrapped in a white towel. Her hair was still wet, dripping a bit and she was combing it with feverish strokes of her brush. In the light from the bathroom, her body glistened in the steam, accentuating her curves. She was sexy! Damn, she was!

"Babe, you should hop in the shower. People will be here soon. I'll iron the suit I put out for you," Megan requested, walking to a chair in the corner of my room where her change of clothes sat.

"Um..huh? Right. Of course." I stammered, laughing awkwardly as my eyes were instantly drawn to her gorgeous features. At that moment, I hoped for a brief towel malfunction. Sadly, the towel wrapped around her glistening body held its form.

Megan glanced at me as she walked back into the bathroom and gave an amorous smile. She stood in front of the bathroom mirror and unwrapped the towel from around her body, letting it fall to the ground. She brandished her beautiful, naked body to me. A moment later, she turned on the blow dryer and shut the bathroom door.

"Damn it. That's not fair," I joked.

Twenty minutes later Megan appeared, donning a knee-length black dress.

"Come on, get in the shower!" Megan ordered. "I'll be back in three minutes and you'd best be in there getting clean. Make sure you shave too. You're starting to look grizzled"

Megan left my room, shutting the door behind her. I undressed and went into the bathroom. It smelled like cherry blossoms and jasmine. I thought about the smell and realized my bathroom probably never smelled so good.

I couldn't help but wonder what I was going to do with my life after today. It was a question I had to give serious thought to. I turned the water on, waited a few seconds for it to become hot and then stepped onto the tile and pulled close the curtain.

I lathered my chest and armpits with the stuff Megan had used; I wasn't keen on smelling like a woman, but push come to shove, I didn't care. It did feel good to get the drunken filth off of me. The door to the bathroom opened and someone walked in.

"I'm telling you babe, this cherry blossom and jasmine shower gel does wonders for my skin!" I chortled. "You should see what it does for my penis… simply amazing."

"Oh yes, let me see." A bestial and faux-feminine voice replied as the shower curtain tore open. Owen stood there with a shit-faced grin. "My god… it is sooo big."

Instinctively, I covered myself with my hands and arms.

"Dude, I knew it was you. I could hear your mouth-breathing," I lied, laughing and pulling down a clean towel from the rack on the wall. I turned off the water and stepped onto the bath mat.

"C'mon man! Cherry blossom?" Owen said with disapproval

"Yea, I know, I know."

"Lavender vanilla is where it's at," quipped Owen, amused with himself. "Just letting you know Mom and Bobbo are here— Gram, too. She's a mess. Anyway, just a head's up."

I nodded. "Thanks. Now, if you don't mind, I need to shave my legs."

Owen looked at me and shook his head. "I know that one's a joke— I've seen your legs. No need to shave those Teflon toothpicks."

He exited the bathroom and Megan returned in her black dress. She closed the door to my room.

"So, are you ready? A whole bunch of people just came up the driveway. I don't like funerals. Not at all." She replied, turning away from me.

Megan seemed distraught.

"What's up babe?" I asked, walking over to her with a towel wrapped around my waist.

"I have a bad feeling about this." She said, looking up at me with those jade eyes that had stolen my heart.

"About what? The memorial service? About how you look in that dress? If it's that, I'll tell you that you're rocking that black dress— in a mournful, sexy way of course," I confessed jokingly.

A smile snuck onto her smooth lips and cute dimples appeared in her cheeks. She hit my shoulder playfully.

"It's not the service. It's about this place, about being here. I didn't want to tell you this, but when I first got to your house the other day, I swore I saw someone in the woods. When I took a double check, there was no one there. And earlier this morning when you were out on the deck, I went to the kitchen and out the window I would've sworn I saw a person watching me from the woods. I just don't know what's going on, but I am scared." She conceded, hugging me.

"I am scared too. It is heavy around here and that's why I've been thinking about what to do after today. I think you and I should go back to D.C. I am not talking about in a couple of days either, I am talking about tomorrow. We'll sleep here tonight and then we'll head back tomorrow afternoon. What'd you say?"

She thought for a moment. "Are you sure you're okay with that?"

"I have thought about this to the point where I just need to make a decision. So much of my life has been a lie to this point. I believe that you're right, that someone's watching us. I don't know why, but let's not stay around for more trapdoors to open." I admitted in earnest, even though I was still convincing myself that running away was the preferred decision.

"Ben, think about it. If you need an extra day or two, we can do that too." Megan said.

"Thanks, babe." I replied, kissing her on the forehead. The warmth from her skin radiated against mine. "Alright, now get out of here so I can get un-naked— unless you object and wish me to stay this way."

I grabbed my towel, pretending to unwrap it and raised my eyebrows provocatively.

Megan laughed, "You've had your shot. Now, you'll just have to wait." As she was leaving the room, she looked back at me and said, "And do hurry up. I don't know anyone down there. I can only be cute and charming for so long."

My suit, pressed black cotton, hung from a wire coat hanger on the door knob of my closet, my slacks and belt overlaid

203

across the bottom wire. For the last year putting on such a uniform had been commonplace, given my choice of profession and all, but this task felt like so much more. I was putting on a suit to bury my parents and the act of putting it on felt like it marked the end of them. It was too official, too formal and I just didn't want to wear it. But I did. I put my suit on in the very room where my mother had taught me to get dressed as a child.

In my head, I heard Dad say, "Life marches on, Ben. She is not nostalgic and she has no memories. But hold her while you can, because she is amazing. True and pure."

I walked downstairs to a room filled with familiar faces and somber mourners. Almost at once, various members of my family— Bobbo, Aunt Jolie, my grandmother — found me and pulled me close for an embrace. My grandmother, a stout and sweet woman with a stern, chubby face, kissed my cheek. She had been weeping to the point where her wrinkled Scottish face had empurpled. It was an excruciating pain for me to see my grandmother deal with the loss of her daughter.

"I love you Gram." I said, hugging her and kissing her forehead.

"I love you too Grandson."

She flopped down on the couch in the living room and wiped her eyes with a bunched-up handkerchief she folded in her hand. She looked wretched and distraught. Bobbo and Aunt Jolie sat beside her, comforting her.

Born Jean Tolmach, the daughter of a whiskey merchant in the winter of 1934, my grandmother came to America on a cargo ship that departed Stonehaven, Scotland in January 1940, just three short months after the Nazi's bombed Scapa Flow. Gram had once told me that her father, my great grandfather, had sensed Europe teetering on the brink of collapse around that time and the bombing gave him reason to pack-up his family and leave dreary

Scotland. While she regretted never going back, Gram had always said she found a new home in Concord. To me, of course, whenever she said that, I would think how silly that was to say because Concord seemed so boring and Stonehaven, while probably just as boring, seemed like an exotic locale, a place beyond the horizon.

There were many people in attendance, some of whom I had never seen before, but the large majority were friends and neighbors that had frequented our Christmas Eve parties. Many of the familiar and even some of the unfamiliar faces came up to me to offer their condolences and to tell me how tragic my parents' death was. A few offered to assist me in whatever way they could, telling me not to hesitate asking for help. It was all overwhelming.

I made my way through the crowd of people in my living room and into the kitchen, where Megan had escaped. Owen and the Reverend were with her, chatting, when I came in.

"How are you holding up, son? There is a mighty crowd out there!" The Reverend said, placing his arm on my shoulder and stroking it gently with his thumb. "What a testament to your parents."

"It is. Most of them are familiar faces, some though I have never met before." I replied, leaning against the kitchen aisle.

"We can start in fifteen minutes if that is alright with you?" The Reverend asked.

"That would be fine."

"Good. I am going to go setup. I'll come back in five and call everyone outside." He stated, patting my shoulder once more. Before he left, he turned to Megan and Owen, "it was a pleasure meeting you both. I'll catch up again after the service."

"It was nice meeting you, too" Megan replied, smiling.

"Yeah, you're a pretty cool man of the cloth," Owen said, putting out a fist. The Reverend smiled and fist-bumped Owen's outstretched hand.

He exited and Megan looked up at me. I could tell she was close to tears, a real mess.

"Did you see that man with the long gray hair? He was looking for you, seemed rather adamant about speaking with you!" Megan asked, her voice catching.

I had to think. Did any of the people who I had spoken with fit this description? I shook my head, "don't think I did. Did he say who he was?"

Megan shook her head. "No! Before I could ask, your Uncle Warren started talking with him."

I looked at the two of them for a moment. Owen didn't react to the name Megan had used. Alright, I thought, am I unwittingly hearing the name Uncle Warren? Obviously, she was referring to my Uncle Bobbo, I just didn't hear that. Was I losing it? Reality was transitioning into the abstract.

"Can you point him out to me?" I asked Megan while moving to the kitchen door and holding it ajar.

Megan scanned the crowd, searching for the long gray-haired man. I did as well. I saw no one that met the description, just a lot of people wearing mourner's black.

"Sorry babe. I don't see him. Go ask your Uncle." She replied. "I'll go with you."

I nodded and walked over to my Uncle Bobbo, who was sitting on the arm of the sofa, talking to a gentleman in charcoal gray suit.

"Bobbo?"

He looked over to me.

"What's up, bud?" He asked, shaking the hand of the man he had been speaking with and who commenced conversing with a woman that I thought resembled my fourth-grade teacher, just aged a decade and plumped up a bit.

206

"I heard there was some guy looking for me. A gray-haired man?"

Bobbo rose from his seat and grasped my arm tightly, too tight to be honest and pulled me down the hallway. He guided me into a corner and turned me towards him. I felt for a moment like I was six years old again.

"Listen to me, Ben. Do you remember the conversation we had at the house? The one when you first got back?" Bobbo questioned, leaning into me and dropping his voice. His breath smelled of coffee.

"How could I forget it? You dropped a bit of a bombshell on me!" I replied.

"So you recall the individual I mentioned?"

I nodded. I did recall, as he worded it.

"I was going to wait until everyone left, but since you asked. The man looking for you was him…it was Malcolm Campbell. I told him he wasn't welcome here and escorted him out. But I know of the man, he will try to contact you again. Remember your promise to me! No good can come from meeting with him." Bobbo warned.

Malcolm Campbell, my parents once close, trusted friend and the man that was there in Osworth the day I was born— the day they came for me — was looking for me. He came into my home on this day of all days. For all the questions I had about my life, about the lies and hidden truths, I knew Malcolm Campbell was someone with answers.

"I did promise. Nothing changes that." I replied, knowing full well that if given the chance I would meet with Malcolm Campbell. My mother's letter told me he would have answers.

"I'm going to hold you to that." Bobbo said, slapping me on the back a bit harder than the situation suggested. He walked back to my grandmother and Aunt Jolie.

I looked at Megan and saw her perplexing look.

"What was that about?" She asked me.

"Long story. I'll tell you later." I replied. I slid my hand across her back, liking how her satin dress felt under it, and guided her across the room. That was when the Reverend came back upstairs.

He cleared his throat.

"Hello everyone. I am Reverend Johnson and in a few short minutes, we will be starting the service to honor Carl and Lily Fisher. If you would please accompany me to the backyard, we can start soon." He declared in his authoritative preacher voice.

The mass of people rose from their seats or departed from whatever corner of the living room they had declared their own and moved outside. I didn't know why, but from my distant view, the movement of all the people— some old, some young— moving together reminded me of a documentary I had seen on impala migration on the African savannah. Large herds of the African antelope would come to a river and search its banks for safe passage, but when the eventual crossing came, from beneath the surface of the calm river rose the reptilian nostrils of a crocodile. Much of the herd would make it through the river to the other side, but a few... well, they would not. That image then led to an uncomfortable feeling... what waited for me just beyond my sight?

Megan and I were the last two people to go outdoors. We joined the rest of the family at the front of a precession of aluminum chairs that had been placed in rows of twelve beneath the canopy of fully blossoming lilac trees that my mother had planted before I was born.

Not long after I sat down, a speaker about ten yards from me filled the air with music. It was a keyboardist playing Amazing Grace. I thought about how predictable and hackneyed the hymnal was to play at a memorial, but I still found it moving. It was sad music though, it was a song sung as a respite to life, an ode to those that were no more.

As the keyboardist played, Reverend Johnson appeared at the podium before a congregation of teary-eyed people. Beside him was an alter holding a picture of my parents in Bar Harbor that I had taken a few years back. It was a picture of my father holding my mother, his arms tightly gripping her, as waves crashed against the rock on which they sat. Their hair was tossed backwards by the maritime gusts that had surged that day, but Dad still had an ear-to-ear grin stretched across his face. It was a fulfilled smile, a smile broadened by loving another human being.

Megan reached for my hand and held it. She squeezed it tight for a moment and then released.

The Reverend stepped up to the microphone and began to speak.

"We are all here today to honor and remember the lives of Carl and Lily Fisher, two amazing people taken from us way too soon. But before we start, I would like to share a story with you. Listen to it… truly listen."

He cleared his throat, and continued "every year, for as long as I can remember, I have spent Christmas Eve at Saint Mary's of Nazareth children's hospital reading stories to the children there. These beautiful children, whose smiles warm the coldest of New England days, spend their holiday being pricked by needles, cut by scalpels and benumbed by innumerable drug therapies. They are battling all sorts of horrific things … cancer, respiratory illnesses, organ failures. Life has no greater tragedy than witnessing an innocent child fight for their young life."

Reverend Johnson paused for a moment of reflection, the white of his eyes flaring wide open.

"For the last three years, I have grown close to one child in particular, a boy named Elliot who has been handed a grave

209

fate. Sweet and small, Elliot is now six-years old and he has for the last three years been diagnosed with Ependymoma, a cancer of the brain. He has had five brain surgeries in this time period to remove or reduce the brain tumors. Five brain surgeries, that is a number so astounding to me. I personally cannot imagine the courage that Elliot must possess and to manage all of it with a child's glee... well, there are simply no words for it. Worse still is that one of the surgeries left Elliot blind! Truth be told, his prognosis is grim. Well, this past Christmas Eve while I was reading *'Twas the night before Christmas* to the children, Elliot, who had always listens intently to the words of the story, exclaimed that he heard sleigh bells. I put the book down and listened, so did all the children. It was as quiet as could be, but then we heard it. The ringing of sleigh bells.

At first, they were subtle and faint, but gradually they grew closer and before I knew it, there was a white-whiskered man enrobed in a red velvet suit and a woman dressed much the same. The two of them inundated the children with cookies and candy and all types of things that kids love and to each child they gave a present, made out specifically to them. I had no idea who the two Christmas masqueraders were at the time, but after they left, I saw Elliot's gift. It was a magnificent, bronze cross medal bearing an eagle and inscribed in a scroll beneath the eagle was something written in Braille. I asked Elliot what it had said and he replied— "For Valor". It was three weeks later that I realized where I had seen that medal before and that was when I drove to this address and hugged Carl and Lily Fisher.

See, the medal that was given to Elliot was the real deal. It had been given to Carl after he returned from Vietnam in 1972. About two weeks before Christmas Eve, I had told him of Elliot's story and that was all he needed. He took his very own medal —something he undoubtedly earned — inscribed the words "For Valor" in Braille and gave it to a child who he had never met before.

210

Think about that for a moment because those are the people we remember today."

A glimpse of my parents, smiling on the deck that overlooked the woods at the back of our house, rushed into my mind and for some reason, knowing that even though I did not believe in his existence, I bowed my head and prayed to God. With such a simple gesture as this, I felt the fear dim inside of me. My parents were home.

Whispers

I said my last goodbyes to my parents at their memorial service before friends and family. There is an immediate, suffocating frustration, a bastion of obtuseness, when speaking to your dead parents and not knowing if they ever hear what you say. It is a lot like slapping the wind.

When the service had ended, I felt a definitive end to my parents' lives. Before the service and the few days after their death, I still felt like there was an uncertainty about whether they had actually died, even after visiting the morgue. I guess it was the acknowledgement of their death by others that placed the last nail in the coffin of any hope I had that it was all a mistake, a nightmare. There was no mistake. Denying it would only cause me heartache. It was time to move on.

Most of the people in attendance had left, except for the Reverend, Bobbo and company. Owen had stayed as late as he could, but had to leave for work. Colin and Collette headed back to their apartment shortly after the service had ended and I for one was glad to see Collette go. There was something off about her, she had no courtesy in how she spoke to others. She had no tact in social situations to the point where, as she was leaving, she congratulated me on my inheriting the house. She reminded me of my friend Alexander from Georgetown, but without the loveable hubris. I couldn't put my finger on it, but Collette felt familiar, like looking at an old yearbook and spotting the childish features of a long-forgotten classmate.

"So Benjamin, what are your plans? Do you know?" My grandmother asked behind waning breath. She sat next to Bobbo and Aunt Julie on the couch in the family room, the Reverend sitting across from them in Dad's recliner. Megan and I had both pulled wooden chairs from the family room table and sat next to each other at an equal distance from both the Reverend and Gram. The whole ordeal felt like an inquisition.

"I have been thinking about it," I replied, reaching beside me to grasp Megan's outstretched hand, "and I don't think I can stay here. In fact, I am leaving in the morning."

There was silence as the four individuals in front of me shared glances.

"Ben, I understand the urge to move on, but do not bury this pain." Bobbo responded, his broad shoulders rising as he spoke.

"I appreciate the advice Bobbo. I truly do. But how will staying here, watching the layers of dust grow, do me any good? It is only going to remind me of how fragile life is— how quickly it can all be over. We just never know." I said.

The Reverend interjected, "Ben, I get it. Yet, if you wished to go back to D.C and leave things as they are, would that do you any good? Son, you are in an unenviable place in your life. No one can make the decisions for you."

"Agreed. I am going back to D.C. tomorrow. I have six weeks before school starts— even though, I am not sure if I will continue," my words drifted and I paused before continuing. "you know what I think I am going to do?"

No one replied.

"I'm going to Wyoming. That's what I am going to do." I blurted out all of a sudden.

"Wyoming?" Aunt Julie questioned. "For what reason?"

"No other reason than it is what I want to do, God damn it. Why do we need reasons? I mean Jesus Christ, look at us. We are human beings— the greatest race of species in the known universe. We can put people on the moon, build dams that alter how the Earth spins. Hell, we can split the atom and kill hoards of our own species. There are no limits to what we can devise... but, any misstep, a drive down the highway at the wrong time of day and BOOM! It is over. For all that we can conjure, we are all just one second away from being no more. So again, why do I need a reason to do anything? Because in the end, it does not matter." I scathed, finding myself standing upright with my finger thrusting forward in wild, animated gestures.

"Ben, honey! Whoa! Calm down," Megan consoled, stroking the back of my neck. "Come on, sit down. Everything is alright."

Megan's touch calmed me and the momentary rage rushed from my body. I made an audible exhale and sat back down. I felt out-of-control, as if I could snap at the slightest thing.

"Guys, I'm sorry. This is why I need to get away from here because this whole thing is killing me. I feel so helpless, I feel lied to and vulnerable. I just don't know what's going to happen next." I confessed.

It was at that moment that an image as crystalline and vivid as a live performance came into my mind. It was not as before when I had felt the floor moving away from me and my surrounding's turned a shade of crimson. This image was simple, but scarier. It was of Uncle Warren, with his shark-like black eyes and jagged smile watching me like a grandfather would watch his grandson. He sat in a rocking chair and rocked back and forth with the faintest of movements. The chair he was rocking in, that was my parents' chair... a chair that was in the house.

I jumped from my seat.

"Excuse me for a moment," I announced.

I ran downstairs to my father's study, trying not to offer any hint of concern as I departed down the steps. The study was dark from the curtains pulled closed. I tossed on the lights and looked around the furnace-colored study.

Where was it? I asked myself. Then I remembered— the dining room.

I went into the dining room and fumbled with the light switch on the wall. I snapped it on and light flooded the dimly-lit room. At once I saw it, the rocking chair I had made my parents for their twentieth anniversary. I grew cold as I watched the chair rock back, then forth, empty. The motion was a steady back and forth, until the chair rocked itself still.

In the kitchen I heard a jarring slam. My heart stopped. Had someone just entered my house?

I looked around the dining room for a weapon. There were only wooden chairs. I grabbed one by the back and hoisted it above my head in an awkward yank.

My arms began to shake and the chair wobbled, striking the wall as I crept into the kitchen. The kitchen was dim, only a fragment of daylight shone through the trees and onto the tile floor. I flicked on the light switch with my elbow, letting the chair rest atop my head to do so.

The kitchen was empty. I scanned the counter tops and aisle in the middle where I had cooked pancakes, but nothing was amiss. There were no jars or pans lying on the floor that might explain the sound I heard. If no one had entered the house and no

215

item had fallen from its roost, then what was the origin of the sound? It hit me. Someone had left the house.

"It's time to leave." I said to myself.

I marched upstairs, my heart trying to escape from the cage in my chest. My mind wanted to be any place other than here.

"Guys, I'm not feeling well. I think it's time for you guys to go." I barked, as I walked back into the room where everyone had remained seated. "We can pick this up in the morning."

"What's going on?" Bobbo asked, sitting up straight from his seat.

"Nothing, I swear. I am just an emotional wreck and would like to go to sleep," I lied, looking out the window overlooking the driveway.

My grandmother sighed, which probably meant I was about to get an old world lecture about something.

"Me too, grandson. And forget what all these people say. You do whatever the hell you need to and don't think twice about it," Grandma said in her sweet-and-stern, old lady way. "Now, come help Grandma up."

I did as she requested, aiding her to her feet where she reached up and gave me a wobbly hug.

"Please go get the car Robert," my grandmother asked Bobbo, who looked somewhat annoyed by his mother-in-law's order, but otherwise agreed.

My grandmother turned to the Reverend who was standing near the window, looking about aimlessly.

"Reverend, you gave a wonderful eulogy. My Lily was such a sweetheart and she could not have found a better husband than Carl. Thank you." Gram offered, clutching the Reverend's arm for support and wiping a budding tear from her venerable, tired eyes.

"We will miss them, but they're with God now. We have the difficult part," the Reverend smiled, leaning forward and folding his hand over my grandmother's.

My Aunt Jolie sat in indomitable silence, her legs crossed and her mouth a knot. She was not pleased with by my sudden request for her to leave and I frankly didn't care.

"Well, Benjamin, it was a pleasure meeting you, and you as well Megan. You two are a cute couple, take care of each other," the Reverend said, offering his hand and I took it. He pulled me in close and whispered into my ear, "Anytime you wish to talk you just stop by. Good luck to you."

I nodded gratefully and replied, "Thanks Reverend— for everything."

"Goodbye everyone. Julie, I will see you and Robert tomorrow."

With those words, the Reverend departed.

Aunt Julie guided her mother's arm and led her to the stairs. She turned to Megan, "it was nice to meet you. I'm sorry I wasn't better company."

"Oh, please don't worry about that. It was a pleasure to meet you too." Megan replied, smiling. "You too, Mrs. Learmonth."

"Oh deary, please call me Grandma. I see the way Benjamin looks at you — you really should get used to it." She suggested, turning to face the stairs and to take the first cautious steps.

Megan flashed me a look, her jade eyes glowing and a discerning smirk rising across her flushed pink cheeks.

"Benjamin, whatever you decide to do, please stop by the house tomorrow. Your Uncle and I would like to spend some time with you." Aunt Julie requested, moving down the steps behind Grandma.

"I'll stop by around lunch," I answered. "And Aunt Julie, Grandma— I love you both."

"We love you too, Grandson." My Grandma hollered up from the bottom of the steps in her shaky, sage voice.

They exited my house and the front door shut.

Moment

For about an hour after everyone left, Megan and I sat outside on the deck, discussing what we should do. My thoughts were uncertain and I wanted her opinion. Despite our attempt to be decisive, we failed to make a decision. In the end, we decided that we should arrive at a plan once level heads prevailed and with that thought, we walked hand-in-hand down the stairs of the deck.

It was night and a perfect temperature outside. Everything that the day had represented felt as if it had fallen away for a while when it was just Megan and me. I pulled Megan close to me and kissed her on the lips. I was lucky to have met someone as special as her and even though my loss was great, I knew I had gained something as well.

We went inside, preparing to end the night. I shut the front door, heard it click shut and then deadbolted it. I turned to Megan when I heard the deadbolt lock to say something, but she had disappeared.

"Hey babe, where'd you go," I asked in the direction of the hallway.

Only silence responded. I took a step towards my bedroom.

"I'm taking a shower, silly!" She replied, popping out of my room into the center of the hallway. "What does it look like?"

Megan stepped out of her heels, unzipped her dress and peeled it off. She was standing in the hallway wearing a black, lace bra and something that barely resembled underwear— black sheer underwear — that hugged her ass firmly. Then before my amazed eyes, she unsnapped her bra and slowly stripped off her panties, letting them fall to ground, before darting into the bedroom. It was the first time I had seen Megan entirely naked and it was wonderful.

I stood for a moment in awe, replaying the image in my head.

Water began to trickle from the showerhead and the plastic curtain slid open making the familiar rattling sound. There was a fleeting pause in the water hitting the linoleum and my thoughts went straight to Megan's tight, gorgeous body glistening in the moist air, the water rolling smoothly over her soft breasts. My cock went stiff at the thought.

Megan's body, the perfection of it, placed me in a trance and I found myself sleepwalking through the bedroom into the bathroom. I could smell strawberries and cream in the air, which was soothing and warm on my skin. A flutter of excitement moved through my body and I undressed myself. Eagerness shuddered through my stomach and into my testicles, which had become a firm, tight sack beneath my hard cock. I stepped into the shower.

"I think it's about time, don't you?" Megan allured, her wet hair set behind her ears.

I stared down into her luring, comely eyes, into that fiery jade lava that had melted me and for so many months teased me with this fantasy. My cock was a thick rod standing erect between us.

Megan stroked my face and pulled me close to her. Her lush red lips interlocked with mine and our tongues danced together. She wrapped her fingers around my cock and began to stroke it with soft jerks back and forth. I began to massage her shoulders and then I moved my hands down her body, caressing her silky, wet skin as the water beat down onto my back.

Megan's lips moved to my chest and then to my neck. Her mouth was warm and strong as she kissed me. She began to stroke my cock vigorously, pulling it towards her. I shivered with excitement.

"Take me," she whispered into my ear, before kissing my lips again.

In one motion, my hands moved beneath her butt and I raised her to my stomach, her legs wrapping around my waist. My left hand braced her back and held her close. I shut the water off and tore open the shower curtain with my free hand.

I laid Megan flat onto the bed and I kissed her lips and neck.

"Kiss me," she ordered, pulling my closer to her.

Her tongue fought with mine as we locked lips in an impassioned kiss.

"I want to taste you," I craved.

I kissed her neck. Her skin was warm and tasted of strawberries and cherries. My lips moved over her body and down to her supple breasts as my hands cupped them in a playful squeeze. Her nipples were aroused and my tongue teased them with a curled flick of the tip. Megan giggled in excitement.

I continued down her body, kissing just above her navel and then just below it. My lips massaged her skin and my hands caressed her curves. My lips danced above her waistline and onto her thighs, pressing against her sweet flesh. She gently pushed her pelvis towards me. My mouth moved inwards, embracing the warmth of her thighs. My hands touched her hips and my thumbs stroked the inside of her legs in a gentle rhythm.

Megan moaned with desire.

I pressed my lips against her clitoris and pleased her with my tongue. I moved my tongue in clockwise circles, stopping only occasionally to push my tongue into her and send shivers of pleasure up her body. Her hands clawed at the back of my head, pulling at me as her back arched forward and she wrapped her legs around my head in ecstasy.

"Oh yes, don't stop!" She shouted, her hips beginning to undulate forward and back in uncontrolled gyrations, pushing my tongue deeper inside her.

Her body grew rigid as I excited her more. She was close.

"I want you inside me," Megan burst out, unrestrained by passion.

I ran my lips up her stomach and across her breasts, pausing to lick one of her nipples, before continuing to her neck. My cock was hard enough to cut through diamond and it throbbed with wanting desire.

I mounted her and watched her eyes flutter as I entered her. I pushed gently and she took me. She grabbed at my back and pressed her hips towards me, I thrust deeper into her.

My body trembled and I began to roll my hips, sliding in and out of her. I made love to her slowly at first, until our bodies had become one lustrous machine, swaying in rhythm. We then moved faster, Megan's short, gasping breaths setting the cadence. My cock plunged into her with repeated thrusts and the tension in our bodies built.

My hands slid down her body as she grew tighter and I gripped her ass, my fingers clutching her smooth, tight cheeks. The heels of her feet rubbed against my lower back as she propelled herself towards me.

"COME IN ME," Megan shouted, her fingernails digging into me as she ran them up my back.

My cock plunged once more deep inside her, as deep as I could go. At once, I felt her body squeeze tight, gripping my cock, and then it relaxed. With her body, my muscles twitched, my veins pulsed and fireworks surged through my body. The tension that had been built up between us came flooding out of me in a glorious, euphoric avalanche.

Afterwards, Megan and I entangled our naked bodies beneath the covers and we drifted off into blissful worlds of our own creation. For me, the world I conjured in my dreams was a magical place where I could relive this moment and repeat it on an endless loop.

We had cuddled before. Megan would rest her head against my bare chest with her arm lying at a diagonal across my stomach, but this time was different. Before, it all felt novel and forbidden, like our relationship was only a tryout or some limited trial attempt at companionship. Tonight, it felt permanent, cemented by our throw of passion and by all that we had been through together. At that moment, it was difficult for me to imagine life being just a random string of events, some chaotic calamity of bombarding bodies moving through the medium of time. We belonged together and somehow through the gauntlet of our lives, we were meant to be curled up together in my bed.

Hours passed and darkness grew outside the house. I could see through the crack above my blinds the crystalline glow of a star eons away. The night's turn of events made me forget the urgency I had felt earlier to leave. The need to head back to D.C was not on my mind. All that I wanted was already in my arms, peacefully asleep... but something was off about the moment.

223

I slipped out from the covers, taking care to not wake Megan. I slipped on a pair of shorts that had been balled up on the floor from my first night back. I walked out into the living room. All of the lights were turned on. I then realized that my carnal appetite had thrown my sensibilities to the wind. Every light was left on and undoubtedly, I forgot to lock the door downstairs.

I started for the stairs so that I could check the front door, when the sudden desire to flee bubbled back to the top of my psyche. I walked to my parent's room and went into their closet. At the base, sitting on the floor was a black steel lockbox that was open. Inside, unsheathed, was an eight-inch steel-blade. It was an intimidating piece of weaponry and I picked it up, hoisting it in my hand.

I exuded a manliness when I held the blade in my hand; it was scary heavy. I could imagine my father sinking this knife into someone and then realized it would have been more than into someone, it would have been *through* the person given the blade length. Holding it washed away any sense of trepidation that had affixed itself to me.

I went downstairs to check the front door.

The entire downstairs was pitch black and I had to hold out my unarmed hand to feel my way through. I brushed the wall and raised my hand to the corner of a frame. I knew it was the mirror my mother had bought in a seaside shop in Bar Harbor.

As I moved through the hallway, holding the knife out in front of me I could see a light coming from the front porch. Our lights were motion lights, timing out on their own accord and flashing on only when their sensors activated. Why were they on? A knot grew in my stomach as I approached the door. It was not unheard of that a neighbor's cat or a deer would trespass in front of the lights, but remembering everything that had happened earlier, I was concerned.

224

I could see from down the hallway that there was an object attached to the front door. I hastened my gait, holding the knife in front of me like a fencer's epee. The object was an index card stuck in one of the window's corners.

The door was unlocked. I quickly opened it, snatched the index card and slammed it shut. I locked it in an instant.

Using the light from the front porch, I flipped over the index card. Handwritten in horribly illegible scroll was an invitation.

It read:

Ben,

Come to my home at 8145 Chesterfield Road. It is urgent we speak.

M.

At once, I knew who had written the letter and although I had never met him, I sensed he had the answers to my questions.

An Invitation

At first light, I woke. Megan stirred and looked over at me from the bed about ten minutes later, her hair a tangled mess, but her face pure and beautiful.

"Come back to bed!" She begged, as I rose out of bed and put pants on.

"If I come back to bed, sleep won't be what's on my mind." I replied, smiling.

She shot me a "ha-you wish" smirk and sat up in bed, her naked breasts exposed to me.

"How do you expect me not to come over there, flip you over and have another go when you tease me with those things?" I asked, half-serious, half in jest.

"Well, you could try. Maybe I would stop you, maybe I wouldn't." Megan replied, beaming bright through her bed-head.

Her flaunting ways were turning me on, but I knew the day was not for lovemaking— it was about getting answers. I knew wrestling in the sheets would not get me those.

"So babe, have a read." I responded, handing her the index card left on my front door.

Megan read it and then reread it.

"What is this?" She inquired, curling her knees to her chest.

"I found it attached to the front door late last night. I think it's from Malcolm Campbell. "

"He left it on your door last night? That's weird. So?"

"So what?"

"So when are we heading over there?" posed Megan, tossing the covers off her body and rising out of bed.

Once more, Megan was naked in front of me. I realized as I watched her move across the room that nothing held the power over a man's thoughts like the contours of a woman's naked body. It was a work of art, an elegant sculpture molded by primordial Mother Earth. My cock was hardening into an erection when I thought about last night and it twitched in my shorts.

"Um— over where?" I asked confused, then remembered, "The sooner the better".

"Let me hop in the shower— no joining me this time either mister, my little body wouldn't be able to take it." She laughed, starting the water and popping in once it was hot enough.

"Well, okay then. I'm going to make myself something to eat."

I wasn't hungry, but I had a sense that my day was going to be interesting if I did meet Malcolm Campbell. So I ate. I rummaged through the cupboards and came out with a box of Captain Crunch, those psychedelic-colored, crunchy, sugar spheres that tasted of berry-awesomeness. I poured a bowl and then topped it with some milk; after my first bite, I was transported to a summer day when I was eight, my Mom placing in front of me a bowl of bright colored things that looked like marbles. Back then, I had spooned them into my mouth as if I was a squirrel hoarding acorns. To this day, the crunchy sweetness of those unquestionably artificial berries is a taste that catapults me back into my youth. When I was finished, I slurped down the milk remaining in the bowl and thought how nice it would be if that were how milk came out of the udder.

It was about an hour later when we were ready to leave, but as we were leaving, I turned back and ran upstairs. Something, probably my subconscious, said that I should not leave unprotected. I grabbed my father's knife off my windowsill where I had left it after I returned to bed the night before.

"Ben, what the hell is that?" Megan asked astonished by the long steel blade I wielded in my hand.

"Just in case, babe. Remember what I told you about this guy, right?" I replied, sheathing the knife and placing it in the back of my jeans.

"Yes, I do. You said that everyone thinks he killed his wife... but you know that's not true." Megan retorted. "You read your mom's letter."

"I did, yes. But one thing I also know is that this guy has been suspected of killing his wife and probably doesn't have any friends. He has been cooped up in his house, doing God knows what— for I don't know how long. The man could be a real quack job— probably is. I know if I lost you, I would turn all types of batshit crazy." I confessed.

Megan came over to me and gave me one hell of a kiss.

"I love you," she said, wrapping her hand over mine and pressing them softly against her stomach. She kissed me again.

"I love you too!" I reciprocated, pulling her in for a bigger smooch. My hands developed a mind of their own and wandered down to her ass for an affectionate squeeze.

"When he was here for your parent's wake, he did look like a man on the edge. We both better be prepared." Megan replied, opening the front door and stepping out onto the porch into a muggy, sweltering summer day.

There were abundant sounds of insects emanating from the front yard— I had always disliked the sounds of grasshoppers in summer. As a kid, I had thought the sounds were a secret code between the grasshoppers and crickets where they were conspiring against humans. Those fantastic, whimsical delusions of youth had spurred me to set the maniacal insects on fire with a magnifying glass, destroying their coup for world dominance.

The drive through town, through the place where I had grown up and called home for most of my life, felt intangibly different, as if I was seeing Concord through a new set of eyes. I passed the once familiar places, the shopping centers where I had spent my teenage weekends and the homes of past classmates where we had snuck bong hits and shots of Canadian whiskey, which now were nothing more than ghostly reminders of life's ticking clock hands. As I drove by Memorial Field, the place where I had played football and the place where I had my first kiss, a bad feeling grew in the pit of stomach.

It was a few miles later when I parked my car next to Dregor's corner store at the intersection of Chesterfield and Baker. This area of town was a secluded Cul-de-sac of older homes nestled close together with miles of New Hampshire forest behind them. A great place for an ambush I thought to myself.

"Wow, its quiet out here. Kind of creepy," Megan said, stepping onto the sidewalk and looking around.

It was a gorgeous summer day and the kids were out of school, the air should have been filled with summertime merriment. But in this part of town, the streets were still. Not a car parked anywhere in sight. The only sniff of habitants were the dogs barking somewhere down Chesterfield. Even the corner store was closed.

"I don't get a good feeling about this babe," I voiced my concern, joining Megan on the sidewalk while looking at the sleepy, dormant neighborhood.

"You're just being a pussy," Megan laughed. "Man up."

I was momentarily angry, then I realized she was right. What the hell was I scared of?

"Thanks for the pick me up." I responded. "His house number is 8145 Chesterfield."

We started down Chesterfield, looking at the numbers on the mailboxes: 7106, 7122, 7138. The houses were ascending in number with the even numbered houses on the right and the odd numbered ones to the left. We crossed the street, still not a soul to be seen in the area.

"Look at these houses, Ben." Megan shuttered. "They're all abandoned. No one lives in them."

I hadn't been paying attention to the houses as we moved up the street, but Megan was correct. Many of the houses had shattered windows and brown, unkempt lawns. These were not the homes of kindly, do-good families. These were the homes of people who had lost their way. I was suddenly glad to have my father's knife.

We came to a break in the string of houses where a car garage stood. The garage doors were down, graffiti painted in colorful block letters.

"7673 Chesterfield." Megan sighed with her hands on her hips and panting in the heat. "Jesus, could you have parked any further away."

"Babe, you're sweating. I mean, sheets of sweat are pouring down your face." I laughed, even though I knew I shouldn't have. She just looked so adorable, all exhausted and angry with me.

"I'm sweating because my dumbass boyfriend thought it would be smart to take a two mile march down Hooverville in one-hundred degree weather. Hopefully someone will just kill me and eat my liver." She snapped.

I burst into an uncontrolled fit of laughter. My face grew tight and began to tingle as tears swelled in my eyes. My stomach muscles contracted as if I had been doing calisthenics.

"Damn, babe. You are funny. Overdramatic, but funny." I replied, wiping a tear from my eye as I continued to chuckle.

She ignored me as we moved up the street.

"Are you kidding me?" Megan cracked, stopping in front of a stripped down, weary old house with wrought-iron fences topped with spear-like ornaments. As I stopped to look at the house, I noticed barbed-wire woven through the fence and coiled around the base.

I looked at the number on the mailbox.

"Are you fucking serious?" I sighed. "Of course."

"8145 Chesterfield." Megan sulked. "Well done, Ben. Drag me out here so that I can take a tour of Charles Manson's playhouse. Look at this place."

She wasn't wrong. The house was a maze of potential dismemberment and maiming. Just beyond the wrought iron fence was a walkway leading to the front door and aligning it were stone statues holding genuine steel spears pointing inwards at the walkway. Alongside the statues on the front lawn were armed trip wires and several large ditches that appeared to drop off. The way the light hit the trip wires made it obvious that they were there. I followed the trip wires and saw that they disappeared behind a brush pile of oddly placed sandbags.

"Well, I guess I was right. The man is bonkers." I murmured, no longer laughing. If I wanted answers to any of my questions, I would have to enter this place... this pit.

231

"Dogs!" Megan yelled, her eyes forward and bewildered.

I followed her gaze and saw them, six, at least, vicious looking dogs. I couldn't really tell how many were inside the second fence just in front of the house because the dogs were running back and forth, jumping over each other. They were a mixed assortment of mean tempered dogs, each one either slobbering rabid foam from their open mouths or staring at us with a keen hunger. I could see at least two Pit Bulls and three Rottweilers; a Doberman Pincher lurked alongside the green and beige house, pawing at the ground. In the middle of them, was a gray, hulking behemoth of a dog that looked like a wolf, his eyes were a wild yellow and unwavering.

"OH MY GOD!" I exclaimed, not realizing I had verbalized my panic.

"Ben, let's go." Megan urged, starting back towards the car.

"I can't. I don't care how bad it looks."

"We walk through that gate, we may never come out. Nothing is worth the danger that exists beyond that gate." She cautioned, grabbing my hand to tug me away.

I sighed. In the realms of my brain where logic resided, I knew she was right. But standing in front of a house that I considered the fortress of a mad man, I thought of all the questions that had run through my mind. Who was Uncle Warren and what did he want with me? And why hadn't he tried to take it already? Then I thought of Grace— my sister — the concept was still surreal. What had happened the day she died?

"You know I can't just walk away. Not now. I have to at least knock on the door," I argued, my hands sweating from my nerves, the heat not aiding this fact.

Megan turned her head from me and I thought I heard a muffled expletive.

"Well, let's get on with it," she said, urging me through the gate and into the minefield.

I opened the gate and we started inside. At once, the dogs began to growl and huff at us. It was as if by stepping across the fence we had placed invisible steaks around our necks and the dogs suddenly realized how hungry they were. For the time, though, they could not reach us. Malcolm Campbell, for whatever reason, had segregated them from the front yard by a chain-link fence that blocked access to the front door. If we wanted to go knock on the front door, though, there was no other way but through the dogs.

As my foot pressed down on the first stepping-stone of the walkway, a slow gravelly sound emitted. From the corner of my eye I saw the two statues on either side of me begin to move. I raised my foot off the stone and watched as the stone statues began to retract their motion.

"This fucker is bloody mad," I said assuming my inner Brit out of awe. I looked back at Megan and stepped back from the walkway leading to the house.

She looked at me with a nervous stare. She was sweating worse than I was and I found it vaguely amusing given the situation.

I smiled at her and then continued, "Well, Mr. Campbell has engineered a lovely little Temple of Doom here. These statues in front of me are attached to a pressure sensor under the stepping-stones. When I apply a force, the arms of the statues draw back."

"So, what does that mean?" Megan asked, not fully following what I was saying.

"Do you see the spears?" I asked.

Megan nodded.

"I think if too much pressure is applied to the stepping stone, these spears are pitched forward, probably by some type of pulley and spring-loaded system. Rather fascinating, but definitely not very hospitable." I observed, turning to the open space of the front yard. Despite the threat of instant death looming in the yard, I was a small boy in a zoo fascinated by the sights around me.

"So, can we leave then?" Megan begged, reaching for my hand.

"I think we should go this way." I replied, ignoring her request and pulling her alongside me.

We went around the right side, moving behind the statues. This part of the front yard looked less hazardous. For one, I saw no obvious place where something sharp could be hiding, waiting to sink itself into our flesh. The only potential danger that I saw was a large, gapping hollow in the ground. It seemed simple enough to move around this and head to the front door.

"I think if we stay between that giant hole and the statues, we should be fine. Follow me," I ordered, pulling Megan close to me.

We walked parallel between the statues and the large hole in the ground, which must have been seven feet in diameter and almost a perfect circle.

"Just under 22 feet, that hole," I said. "That's like 264 inches."

"What the hell are you talking about?" Megan asked, scurrying alongside me.

We were halfway to front door and as we moved closer to the growling dogs, my heart thumped heavily.

"The circumference of the hole. I was just thinking about the circumference of the hole that's it. Math calms my nerves. I can understand it." I muttered, hurrying forward.

"You geek." Megan laughed.

Hearing her laugh was a welcome break to the tension in the air.

"Almost there," I said.

We stepped passed the last statue, about three feet before the front gate, when my foot stepped onto the ground and the earth beneath it vanished. As if a vacuum was underneath us, the grassy earth crumbled under our feet and everything was sucked downward.

Megan screamed as I sank into the disappearing ground and out of instinct, I pulled her towards me. At once, she began to sink lower too. Without warning, our bodies were separated and we were cascading downhill in an avalanche of dirt, heading into the center of the large hole in the ground. A few seconds later, there was a sudden drop and the ground became firm beneath me.

A second thud followed and I heard Megan groan.

The sides of my stomach throbbed. I stumbled to my feet, brushing the dirt off myself and taking in breaths as best I could. It hurt to breathe and I could taste mud and clay in my mouth.

"Megan, are you alright?" I yelled out, feeling around blindly.

My eyes were not adjusted to the darkness of the environment and I did not see Megan's fist sailing through the hazy light atop the hole. She hit me square in the chest, knocking the wind out of my lungs.

I coughed.

"You ASSHOLE!" She yelled, chasing me with slaps. All I could do was protect my vital spots and make my body a smaller target by shrinking into a standing fetal position.

"So now I know what an ostrich attack would feel like," I laughed, coughing.

I knew I should not have laughed. I mean the situation was not a good one, but I couldn't help it. After all, we had just fallen down a ridiculous hole in the middle of a lunatic's yard.

"Ben, how are we getting out of here? I don't like this AT ALL," Megan articulated with a fearful urgency.

I looked to the top of the hole; it was probably fourteen feet high. I then walked over to the spot where we had dropped. It was probably only ten feet at that point.

"It might be possible to climb back up. I think the soil is dense enough. We can probably get some decent footing by just, uh, punching into the ground I guess." I offered with reluctance.

As my eyes settled, I could see more clearly. The edge that we have fallen from was actually a chute of some kind. I looked around my feet and saw disintegrated two-by-fours.

"I think I know what happened! The guy had a—"

"Yea, I get it. He setup a faulty support so the ground would give way. This isn't Scooby Doo Ben. You need to ask what is going to happen when it's discovered we're in here. What's going to happen?" Megan interrupted, looking up at the sky and scheming an exit strategy.

Megan howled and fell to her knees, covering her head.

"What's wrong?" I asked, looking up to the top of the hole and there I saw it, a double-barrel shotgun aimed at Megan's head.

I froze.

"You should never have come here girl," a voice yelled from above.

First Impressions

"What's your reason?" The man demanded, pushing the barrel of the gun further into the hole, closer to Megan.

Megan shielded herself in her arms and began to cry.

"WHAT THE HELL IS WRONG WITH YOU?" I shouted, running to Megan and placing myself between her and the gun.

The man paused.

"Are you Benjamin Fisher?" He asked.

I nodded.

"And *the girl* is with me," I huffed.

"Hmm. Alright then," the man stated, disappearing from sight.

A few minutes passed and a rope ladder was tossed down to us.

"There you go," the man said, the shotgun he had held no longer visible. "Let the girl up. I promise no harm to her."

Megan was still cowering and crying. She was terrified. I crouched beside her, stroking the back of her neck.

"Babe, it's okay. I will not let him hurt you. I promise," I avowed, kissing her forehead.

She looked up at me and wiped her eyes with her dirt-smudged wrist.

Megan didn't speak, but I could see in her eyes that she believed me. I helped her to her feet and up the rope ladder. She stumbled at first, then regained her balance and started up the rope ladder, making it to the top in hasty fashion. Once Megan had reached the surface and made it out the top, I followed up the ladder, not wanting the two of them alone for any period of time.

When my feet touched down onto grassy earth, Malcolm Campbell was instantly there. Megan was standing as far away from him as she could, a distrustful grimace on her face.

"Benjamin, it is about time! Come in, come in. We must discuss many things," Malcolm urged in frantic, excited tones, wrapping one of his arms around my shoulder and leading me forward.

"What about the giant hole, man? Seriously! You could have hurt someone!" I admonished.

Malcolm stopped for a moment and looked at me with a deranged smile.

"That was the point my friend." He stated, before leading me to the gate with the dogs.

"Uh, right! Still, the gun. You did not need to point it at her," I argued, flashing a glance towards Megan who was reluctantly following us into the fenced in area with the dogs. So many dogs. I did not like it.

"She'd be dead if it was just her. Cannot take any chances, my friend. Not with them. You just can never tell." Campbell replied with a stern, confident smile. The sunlight forced a harsh outlined against Malcolm's wild, frilly silver hair and I realized that Campbell was a killer at heart, a man holding back a terrible rage.

The dogs charged us the instance the gate swung open. From their quickness and the ferocity in their eyes, I sensed that they were experienced maulers. At their approach, Campbell pulled out a remote and pressed a green button with some sort of squiggly line printed on it. At once, the dogs fell to the ground, whimpering.

"Quite whining Snap Jaw," Campbell said to the Rottweiler lying on the ground. "You'll be eating soon… I think."

The dog simply looked up at him and barked, as if to argue.

Megan pulled on the back of my shirt.

I looked back at her and saw that she had picked up the shotgun that Malcolm had discarded.

My eyes grew wide like saucers and I whispered to her, "What are you doing?"

"No worries, Ben. Your lady friend can keep the gun. I think before the day is over, she will need it." Malcolm suggested, putting his hand against an electronic scanner next to his door.

"Why will Megan need the gun?" I asked. "And, why do you have a biometric key to get into your house?"

"To make sure I am the only that one that can get in, obviously." He responded, opening the door. "One moment!"

He disappeared into the house. I heard the sound of electronic beeping, followed by a brief silence and then the sound of something mechanically engaging. Megan had come up next to me and grabbed my hand; she held the shotgun in her other hand, looking like some type of sexy post-Apocalyptic zombie hunter.

I laughed at the image.

"Who are you, Lara Croft?"

"Shut up! I don't like this at all. I want to go home." Megan hammered back at me. "This isn't a joke anymore."

Malcolm reemerged, holding the door open and inviting us in.

"What was that sound in the wall? Sounded like some kind of machine." I asked, stepping inside and pulling Megan across, into the house.

"Oh that," Malcolm laughed, "I have three crossbows that are always armed at every entrance. If someone enters and does not disengage them, they will be harpooned against the wall within twenty-five seconds. That's how I got this!"

He raised his shirt, revealing a quarter-sized scar that looked like a blister, pinkish and opaque on the surface, just above his right pelvis bone.

"Last time I'll forget the fifth number of the Boltzmann constant— that's my password 13806." He revealed, scanning his front yard several times before shutting the door and locking the series of five locks that ran down the side of the door.

I looked at Megan and she looked at me. We were both thinking the same thing. She was right; this was not a joke anymore. I reached back and checked the knife I had tucked into the back of my pants. It was still there. There was some comfort in that.

"Crossbows everywhere," I said, following Malcolm down the dimly lit hallway at the front of his house, it was stacked with milk crates and newspaper clippings. There were eight tarps that hung from the ceiling, forming a vast canopy that ran up and down the hallway and into adjoining rooms.

"Jesus Christ!" Megan said, vocalizing what I was thinking.

"Follow me to my laboratory."

Had creepier words ever been spoken? I asked myself.

At the end of the hallway, I could see a rusted and deformed basement door. The thing looked like something out of a horror film. This place, Malcolm's entire home, looked like something out of a horror film. Every room I passed was an eccentric arrangement of junk and oddities that formed an elaborate labyrinth.

"Why? I don't think that we need to go down into that torture— I mean — your lab!" Megan panicked.

She had begun to dig her fingernails into the skin of my arm like the talons of an eagle piercing the flesh of a trout.

"We must. There is simply too much to discuss. Too much to show you. It is the only chance we have against him." Malcolm warned.

"You are talking about Warren?" I asked.

Malcolm looked at me. The blacks of his eyes flashed that hidden rage I sensed was there. There was a desire for destruction, at hearing the name. He did not respond to my question, but flew open the rusted basement door and descended the damp, concrete steps into darkness.

I followed down the steps, into the darkness and into what was surely a dire place. I had to pull Megan along with me, fighting her instinct to flee from the house as fast as possible. She had started to tremble; I could hear the barrel of the shotgun rattling against her leg. In the dark, I grabbed her, embraced her in a hug and kissed her forehead.

"It will be alright. I promise," I assured her.

She squeezed my hand, but said nothing. Standing there, I could not imagine what twisted types of devices or pieces of equipment stood before us in the basement— in Malcolm Campbell's lab. I was certain that when the lights came on, I would not be looking at man cave with a billiard table and a bar.

The basement door slammed shut and Megan shrieked.

"Uh, Malcolm? Could you put on the lights please?" I urged nervously, wrapping an arm around Megan to calm her… and myself.

241

In the space in front of us, a strobe light began to flash, illuminating the room. For splits seconds at a time, I could see the shadows of cages holding mice with the pinks of their eyes a beacon in the distance, and an assembly of glassware extending outward and upward with differently tinted liquids dripping and boiling in them. I could hear a humming from around the corner and thought it sounded like a laboratory fume hood.

Then that feeling returned. That sense of the ground moving away from me, everything distant but still somehow within reach. The crimson haze followed the sensation and I fell to me knees again. I could feel Megan at my side, trying to help me up and somehow I could hear her panic. I looked forward; everything was clouded in the crimson haze. I felt as if I was about to vomit.

I staggered to my feet with the sensation that I was hovering above the ground, but feeling it still solid beneath me. Megan was begging me to stay on my knees, but I couldn't. I inched forward, moving forward into the narrow entry of the basement, moving towards the strobe light. I passed the mice cages and stepped on something that crunched under my foot. I looked to the ground and saw what appeared to be the skeletal remains of a mouse, simply fur and bone. The crimson haze had solidified and had inertia about it, unlike before when it went away as quickly as it came. Now, the feeling was not fragmenting with time, it was persistent and felt irreversible.

I went towards the strobe light at the back of the room, stepping into the main part of the room. I looked to the far right wall and there was a corridor leading away to yet another door. That's when the haze turned from crimson to a bloody black. My eyes focused and locked on to what hovered in the space above me. It was a monstrous thing; huge and quite scary... what the hell was it? My mouth fell open and then the haze shot away from me like a cannon and my knees gave way. I tumbled to the ground, still conscious, but my muscles unresponsive.

Then the strobe lights stopped and Megan was back at my side, helping me to my feet once again.

"Excellence, yes, yes! Excellent, most indeed... You saw it didn't you? I saw it in your face, you have seen it," Malcolm came rushing from the corner, tinted goggles suctioned against his eyeballs, but a most splendid smile on his face. "Sit my boy, sit."

Malcolm pulled a chair from his lab bench and assisted Megan in placing me onto it. My face was drenched in sweat and I was delirious. What had I just seen?

"What the hell was that thing?" I stammered, grabbing the glass of water from Malcolm's hand.

"Soon, but first, what did you see?" Malcolm begged, intrigued.

I sat upright in the chair and brushed the sweat from my eyes.

"Well, honestly I don't know. Although by now, I should be used to it. It just hits me, this feeling. The best way I can describe it is that it feels like I have fallen into a vacuum where everything grows away from me. But I can still touch the things that feel far away from me. I know that doesn't make much sense does it?" I rambled, staring at the far wall and the chamber of mice scampering across one another. There had to be dozens of them. Maybe hundreds.

"Now, tell me Benjamin, what was it that you saw?" Malcolm asked, his eyes narrowing to a point.

"I don't really know what it was, but it kind of looked like a mix between a dragon and a snake. It was neither, but it resembled them in some manner." I stated, trying to remember exactly what I had seen.

Megan looked at me, "is that what you think you saw? A dragon and a snake?"

I shrugged. I didn't really know.

"I will assure you young lady, that Benjamin did not see those things. What he saw is the greatest predator ever to be forged in this universe!" Malcolm stated with a sharp poke of his finger in the air.

Megan looked at him with a medley of fear, disdain and fascination.

"Let me ask you something, young lady. If I put a gun to your head—"

"You already did that, thank you very much. And my name is Megan. I mean if you're going to keep us in this death maze of yours, you can at least call us by our names." Megan fired back.

"Yes, yes. These trivial pursuits— names! When you're dead and worms have eaten your corpse, they don't shit out Megan or Benjamin or Macy— they shit out shit. Names are meaningless!" Campbell fumed, his hazels eyes brutal and uncompromising.

Megan fell silent and her face grew tight. Her lips began to quiver. I reached my hand out and stroked the back of her hand that was folded over her knee.

"I will not tolerate you disrespecting her. Please don't do it again!" I demanded, moving forward in my chair and matching the glance Malcolm was affording.

"You came here for answers and I am going to give them to you. But you need to grasp the severity of what I am going to tell you. You cannot be bogged down by... *your feelings*," Malcolm sneered and then paused, as he appeared to drift off in thought. "Answer me something?!?"

I nodded slightly.

"Suppose I gave you an egg, a plain chicken's egg freshly laid from a hen. Now presume further that your sweetheart has been tied, gagged and placed on the end of a plank hanging out over a steep drop-off. The only thing saving her from a most certain and painful death is a man of considerable size standing on the other end of the plank. Your task is simple. Remove the yolk from the egg without breaking the shell. If, at any point, you break the shell, the man raises his foot and your sweetheart falls to her death. If you take too long to complete your task, the man raises his foot and your sweetheart falls to her death. How do you save your sweetheart?"

"That is the most ridiculous thing I think I have ever heard!" I said, bursting into uncontrolled and nervous laughter.

"Regardless of how ridiculous it may sound, how would you save her? She's teetering. She's going over. Solve the problem!" Malcolm prodded.

I looked to Megan, who was still fighting back the urge to cry, and shrugged.

"And I can't go beat the hell out of this man?"

"Nope."

"Well, let me think about this for a moment." I said and began to think about it.

I strained my mind for a long while, thinking about a possible solution. I thought about using a nanoneedle, something so small as to fit through one of the eggshell's porous holes and extract the yolk with a syringe. I doubted that it was possible and it would definitely take too long. What a stupid question, I said in my head.

"It's not possible," I concluded, tossing up my hands in exhaustion.

"But it is, Benjamin. Your problem is that you don't see the solution because you don't know the truth." Malcolm claimed, a cheek-to-cheek grin stamped across his face.

245

"The truth about what?" I asked, curious at what Malcolm was getting at.

"The truth about Warren." Malcolm replied.

"You're right; I don't know anything about him except that he killed my parents and that he seems to know an awful lot about me!"

"Yes, he certainly killed Carl and Lily— just as he did your sister," Malcolm paused, his voice beginning to tremble, "and my Macy. Warren has taken much from me, but far more from you."

"Who is he? My mother wrote me a letter before she died telling me that the day I was born was the day he came for me. It was the same day that Grace and your wife were taken. But it wasn't just Uncle Warren, was it? There was a woman there, too." I recited what I remembered from the letter.

"Not who, Benjamin… what! I think you have known this since the beginning. Warren is not a human being. No, not at all. He is something else, something masquerading as a person. Listen to the things I am about to tell you and it will all become clear," Malcolm proclaimed.

Megan sat forward, lured in by Malcolm's words. I leaned in too and was reminded of story time when I was in Kindergarten.

He continued, "the world we inhabit is a spooky assembly of 'stuff'. Nothing is truly what it seems. Take for instance— us— people. Made up of trillions of cells— a monstrously large number — we are alive because tiny little molecular machines work together. But the number of cells in our body, that keep us alive, still pales in comparison to the number of molecules that make up those cells. And that number is dwarfed further by the number of atoms that make up the molecules that make up our cells. However, when you reach out and touch Megan, you feel her as a solid, indivisible body. Your mind is not thinking of her in terms of the number of atoms or molecules or cells. No, your mind produces some perception of her physical dimensions on a macroscale. Here is the fascinating thing though, if Megan were to be atomized and cooled to near absolute zero under a time-variant magnetic field, her entire body would collapse into a single point. She would not exist as a person, but a single quantum state of matter. Yet, your mind does not perceive this as a possibility, but it is true.

Consider further a different oddity of reality— a vacuum. By its very definition, a vacuum is void of matter. However, the creation of virtual particles can be observed in the absence of matter. This is the Casimir Effect and it is the creation of something from nothing. And it is very real. So those people, those ostentatious demagogues that claim our origins come from a God are mistaken. They are bombastic and blatant in their assault on science.

You see, when the universe erupted into existence fourteen billion years ago, it did not steamroll across the vastness with an evenly distributed force. It was very messy and chaotic. This is because when the universe was born, so was entropy...disorder. Chaos did not exist before the universe and neither did the dimensions of space. So, when that single point of zero dimension that would become the universe and everything in it exploded, it created matter, forces and dimensionality. This is why most of the universe is made up of stuff that we cannot directly see— dark matter and dark energy. You may think that what you see all around you is a fair representation of the universe. But you'd be wrong. What you see around you in our local galactic neighborhood is but a fraction of the universe, a pebble on Everest. The dark matter and dark energy that I just referred to makes up more than ninety-five percent of the universe. That means for every Benjamin that was created, there are nineteen other 'things' that are nothing like Benjamin. The great expanse that is space is mostly composed of stuff that you're not made out of, or that I am not made of, or her, or even a mountain, or a car are made of. In the grab-bag of space, atoms are the least likely thing to be picked."

"Okay, wait a minute! I am vaguely familiar with the concept of dark energy and dark matter. But what does any of this have to do with my parent's death or Warren or me for that matter?" I asked, my mind racing in circles. I shook my head in confusion and saw a similar expression on Megan's face.

Malcolm smiled knowingly and nodded.

"Yes, how does anything I just said translate into your parent's death? What does this have to do with Warren? You see Benjamin, when the universe expanded outward from that single point; it created the vastness of space and sprinkled it with chaos. This is why we have dark matter, dark energy, and multiple dimensions. This is why we can see something come from nothing, as in the case of virtual particles. It is all related to one thing… dimensionality.

When I asked earlier for you to provide a solution to the egg problem, the answer was simple. But in the perception of your mind, it was not possible. You see the world in only three dimensions when in reality it is made up of many more. So the solution to the egg problem is to simply extract the egg yolk from one of the other dimensions. Just reach in and grab it."

Megan laughed aloud, her body vibrating like an angry washing machine.

"I am sorry, but you are crazy," she blurted out, fighting back more laughter.

"Am I?" Malcolm replied, his hair tossing backward with his a sudden jerkiness towards her.

"Yes!" She said, not backing down.

"You say this, no doubt, because you do not see other dimensions when you look out onto the world. You believe that your eyes cannot deceive you or perhaps you are like some other people, supposed geniuses in the world of science, who believe that if other dimensions do exist, they must be a miniscule, nanometer-sized torus. Both these arguments are parasitic ignorance, hubris really. They persist because people are not as intelligent as they would like to believe. We have the great skill of assuming that nature creates to fulfill humanity's own purposes and that it is constrained to our own frailties. Benjamin, when you walked into the room and saw the strobe light flashing, what do you see?"

I had been quiet, struggling to understand Malcolm's claims before I answered.

"Um… I'm not really sure, to be honest. The room here turned black, maybe red, and I felt like everything was falling away from me. But then I saw something. A creature, I think, hovering above me. It was something I have never seen before—"

"— exactly! You are a very special person Benjamin. And that is why I asked you here. You have a gift! Something you probably never knew you possessed. You have had these spells where things become hazy and fall away from you before, yes?" Malcolm asked. He was like an antsy child awaiting his turn to open a Christmas present.

"I have. Several times before today. The first was back in D.C, just before I learned that my parents had been killed. The second was when I landed down in Manchester and then when I saw my parents at the morgue. What is it?"

"Now, during any of these instances, did you feel like someone was watching you?" Campbell prodded with a smirk.

"Oh, yes! When I landed in Manchester, I had the terrible sense that someone was watching me." I divulged.

"And in D.C, how exactly did you learn that your parents died?"

"He got a phone call from Uncle Warren. In fact he got two that day." Megan interrupted, drawn in by Campbell's line of questioning.

"Curious!" Malcolm replied. "When he spoke with you, did he seem to know things that should have been impossible for him to know?"

"He did. He even knew what I had for dinner the night my parents died. There was no rational reason for him to have known those things."

"Now, Megan, hearing this, do you still think I am crazy?"

Megan did not answer.

Malcolm continued, "I will tell you why he knew these things and why Ben has these spells of displacement. There exists on Earth a fourth spatial dimension, but it is a veiled dimension. A veiled dimension is exactly as it sounds. It is obscured by some physical entity, probably dark energy itself and human beings are oblivious to veiled dimensions. That is, every human except for one."

There was a long silence.

"Are you saying Ben can see another dimension?" Megan asked, her mouth hanging open and her face bewildered like she was watching an execution.

My mind was a whirling merry-go-round of thoughts and questions. Was he serious?

"Snapshots of it, at least. And that is why you saw the creature! You saw it— the one I captured. It was the one that killed my Macy and you saw her, Ben. You saw her true face. Do you understand what this means?" Malcolm shouted in excitement.

I was speechless and just shook my head.

"It means that you can kill them. You can kill the Beslemeks!"

Beslemeks

"Bes-el-what?" I heard myself asking. By this point, Malcolm had me so thoroughly questioning reality that I began to think I was walking up a staircase built by Escher himself.

"The thing you call Uncle Warren is not a person. It is a Beslemek! The universe's oldest and most vicious predator," Malcolm revealed as if this were common knowledge.

I saw Megan from the corner of my eye struggling to understand what Malcolm was talking about, as I was. Finally I just asked.

"What are Beslemeks? I have seen Uncle Warren from afar and he looked very much like a human being to me. I understand he is not, but he called me the night my parents died and talked to me like a person could."

"Perhaps the best way to express this is by analogy. Are either of you familiar with the Anglerfish?" Malcolm asked plainly, standing from his chair and grabbing a glass vial filled with a yellowish phlegm-like substance from the far side of the table before returning to his seat. He began to twiddle with the glass vial between his fingers, spinning it between his index and middle fingers.

"No." I replied.

Megan said yes. I wasn't surprised.

"Well, young lady please enlighten Benjamin about this marvelous creature."

Megan forced a smile, then looked at me with an abstruse, glum expression.

"They're a nasty, ugly fish— the Angler. My dad used to take Grant and me on submersible tours off the Outer Banks. The last time was before I left for school. We sat in these tubular submarines that sank a quarter-mile into near darkness. We would just float there in the ocean for a couple of hours. From our windows we saw all sorts of things, crabs on the sea ridge, sharks carving through the water and magnificent lights appearing in the distance. Bright neon lights! I thought these deep ocean lights were the most beautiful things I had ever seen. Dad moved us closer so that I could see where they were coming from. That's when I saw my first Anglerfish.

We were just gliding through the ocean when I saw a faint yellow light scribbling in the water. It came and went as if by magic, but it was fascinating. Grant and I moved to the window to see why this light's movements were so crazy. From the haze, we could barely see a tiny fish swimming at the side of the submersible. Then the yellow light appeared and we saw the little fish swimming towards it. In the light from the submersible, all three of us could see that the yellow light was attached to this dark brown balloon of a fish with long needle-like teeth. With a quick snap of its jaw, the Anglerfish swallowed the little fish and the yellow light went dark."

Megan spoke in a triumphant, melodious tone. A glint came to her eye and she laughed a bit, the kind of laugh that it is just for oneself— peaceful, personal.

"What a deft depiction of such a magnificent creature," Malcolm said through a broad smile. He was looking less insane than when we first met. "So, back to the Anglerfish."

"Yea, I am in dire need of some dots connected. What does the Anglerfish have to do with Beslemeks." I interrupted.

"The Anglerfish's mode of predation is rather ingenious, as Megan alluded to. In the depths of the ocean where there is little light, the Anglerfish illuminates the darkness by generating light from a barb hanging from its head. So if you are a fish just swimming along and suddenly you see a light in the middle of darkness, you're intrigued. You're thinking, 'Oh, my, how pretty. What is it? I dunno, but I think I'll take a look'. So you do. You investigate the light. But all the time you've spent looking at the light, you have not seen what's behind it and by the time you do, you're a meal. Bezlemeks are the Anglerfish of the universe."

Megan gasped in realization. "You're saying that Uncle Warren is the light coming from the barb. That means…"

"Yes! He is not a human being at all. He— it —is a decoy camouflaged as a person. But behind it all, lies the true face of the Beslemek. It hides in plain sight, it hides in the dimensions that can't be seen by nearly everyone. I have never seen the creature's true face, but I know it exists. Lily's letter said that the man and woman that attacked us just appeared out of nothing, right?"

I shook my head in agreement.

"It is easy to move in three dimensions if you can access a fourth. Simply lift yourself out of the cube and reinsert yourself." Malcolm finished.

"If I may ask… there is something about this whole, I dunno what to call it, conjecture, I guess. If Beslemeks really do exist—" Megan began to say.

"— They do! Still a nonbeliever I see." Malcolm rebuked.

"Maybe. It really is a lot of way-out-there stuff to digest. If Beslemeks do exist and they really are some horrifying creature hidden in another dimension, why is Uncle Warren free to move about? Ben says he saw him in the woods of his house... and thinks he was *in* his home last night. If the Beslemek is secluded to another dimension— I mean —you said yourself you have never seen it. I'm not convinced."

"Ah, yes. This is actually quite crucial to my whole theory. So Ben saw Warren outside of his home. Well, a few days before your parents died, Warren paid your parents a visit. How can such travel be possible if the creature is secluded to another dimension? The answer is the creature is not totally secluded to another dimension. Rather, part of the Beslemek, the large nasty bit of it, is restricted to a small section of woods in Osworth—"

I exhaled audibly, "all of those people that have gone missing in Osworth... the Beslemek?"

"Ha," Malcolm roared in an annoyed laugh, "these idiots that keep— they were a tasty snack for a pissed-off Warren. Oh, since he has returned he has been one angry animal."

For a fleeting moment, my heart slowed and I thought about being eaten alive. The thought of my flesh being peeled from my bones while I could still feel it, as if I were a roast chicken was too much to bear.

"Returned? What do you mean by that? Where did he go?" Megan asked.

Malcolm paused for a second, forming his response. "For the last seventeen years, there has not been a single incident in Osworth. No disappearances, no mutilation of animals, nothing. During this time, I returned to where Macy died many time, in hopes of finding Warren and capture him. For seventeen years, there was no sign of him. That was until a few months ago when

Osworth suddenly grew hot again. Warren had returned and he was not happy."

"It's because you have his mate, isn't it?" I asked.

Malcolm pursed his lips and nodded. "It is, at least that's part of it. I think there is more though. Warren made an attempt to rescue his mate before. He made attempts at getting you too. That all ended about seventeen years ago, for whatever reason."

"I remember my mother's letter. Do you think my father found a way to stop him?"

"Probably not. The last time he tried to take you was an October night when you were a kid. Your father called me after it happened. Warren tried to break into your house, but Carl was always ready for him. The first time Warren came for you really set your dad right. That night he dragged Warren from the house, tied him to a tree and set him on fire. Carl watched Warren burn to ashes. He just disintegrated. We thought that maybe it was the last of him because he disappeared for all those years."

I was horrified by this story.

"How is any of that possible?"

"He is a Beslemek. What you see and think is human, is fake. His human figure is equivalent to a fingernail or strain of hair on us. It can be destroyed without harming the vital parts. This is why when your father set him on fire, Warren turned to ash. What is more is that it will re-grow."

"But why did he disappear for so long?" I inquired. Malcolm had to have an idea as to why he simply vanished.

"I don't know the answer to that, but I imagine that venturing out of Osworth is quite taxing from an energy standpoint, even for a Beslemek. Warren's attempts at getting you and what's behind that door," Malcolm pointed to the wooden door behind me. "I can only assume that the last attempt was too much of an energy burden and he needed to recharge. This is purely a theory. But since he has returned, he has been consuming energy at a blistering pace, but he has not slowed down. He is not playing anymore."

"How do we kill it?" Megan interjected, "what do we need to do?"

"I have come to view the Beslemek as a two-part creature. The part that we are intended to see can kill, but we can see it and defend ourselves against it. The other part of the creature—I call it the gearhead —is the part that is only seen when it shows itself, unless you have the extra sight that Benjamin has. The gearhead can only show itself inside the woods of Osworth, where the dimension is open."

"So how do you think this relates to my vertigo?" I asked, thinking that I was beginning to understand it all.

"Vertigo it isn't, but you could classify it as such. You're the only person in the world who actually experiences it. I guess you can call it what you wish." Malcolm replied.

"Why can I see them though? Why me?" I questioned, shrugging.

"There's the question I've been waiting to hear. I will tell you why I think you can see other dimensions, but I have no way of knowing whether it is true or not. So you must weigh that fact, when I tell you." Malcolm warned, his face showing uncertainty in what he was about to say.

"Fair enough."

"Do you recall what I said happened to the universe the instant it came into existence?" Malcolm asked, still twiddling the glass vial of yellow liquid.

"In fact I do. You said something like the universe exploded outward from a single point in a lumpy mess, throwing about matter and dimensions. It was an uneven genesis because of entropy. Something to the effect," I recalled.

"He also said something about... black holes, I think. Never mind, I don't remember." Megan stammered, then hiding her face in her book-wise open hands.

"I never said anything about black holes, though they are captivating phenomena. In fact, they are how universes begin. Anyway, back to the point. Ben, you were close. When the universe came into existence, it spread the various dimensions across the vastness of space. But the thing about dimensions is that they are all independent of each other. There are barriers to moving freely between dimensions, a field that prevents orthogonal motion. A circle will never be a sphere, but a sphere can most certainly be a circle. All you have to do is project onto a plane of smaller dimension or take a cross section of it. In any seemingly random construction, there will always be some sort of unintended consequence." Malcolm was saying, speaking in a slow, purposeful voice.

"What unintended consequences?" I asked.

"Well, I believe there are points across the universe where the barrier between dimensions is missing. On Earth and the local space around it, there are no barriers to three-dimensional travel—"

"Gravity!" I blurted out, not understanding where the thought originated.

"Not precisely! Anyhow, there are limitations to four-dimensional travel in our local space— in our galactic neighborhood. I can move forward and back, up and down, left or right, but I cannot move in any direction outside of this cube. There are barriers preventing this extra travel. However, occasionally they are rips in the veil even in our local galactic neighborhood and I am convinced that one exists in the woods of Osworth."

"And that is why the Beslemek can move freely up there! I get it now." Megan said, her face lighting up.

I thought about what this meant for me.

"Why did they come for me when I was born?"

Malcolm broke into hysterical laughter.

"You stupid boy. Don't you understand? It was not because you were born, but the fact that you were born *there*. That is the reason they came for you. That is the reason they killed! We were not their prey that day. We— no, you— were a threat to them."

Malcolm's tone irked me.

"I must be a stupid boy because I don't get how a newborn can be a threat to anything, let alone inter-dimensional monsters." I barked.

Malcolm catapulted himself out of his seat to an inch from my face. His breathe was hot and smelled of sour hummus.

"You listen here! You see this stuff," Malcolm pushed the glass vial he had been holding into my face. "This shit has taken me twenty years to make and it is the only hope I have to kill the Beselmeks. Not capture. Not cage. But kill. And whether you want to or not, you will help me. There will be no arguing about it."

I pushed him off of me and stood up, my fist clenched.

"You want me to help? Then you will give me answers. You can start by telling me why a newborn baby was the target of a Beslemek attack?" I shouted, jabbing my finger into his boney chest.

Megan was standing next to me, her hand pressed firmly against my chest. I was certain she could feel my heart racing.

"Sit down and relax. I let my emotions get the best of me," Malcolm admitted before leaning against the side of his lab bench. He exhaled a forced breath. "I apologize."

I was pissed-off and I suddenly felt like a face-eating baboon. I took a long, deep breath. Then Megan and I sat back down.

"I have a theory as to why they came for you. The theory is this. As I have said Osworth has a special characteristic, a unique field that gives rise to higher order travel. This field is why the Beslemeks can descend from nowhere or just disappear outside of the cube. Anyway, I believe when you were born, you were exposed to this field and inherited the ability to see other dimensions. I think you were fundamentally altered."

"You're essentially saying that I am like a teenage mutant ninja turtle or some junk. I somehow touched the secret ooze and now I have the power to see another dimension!" I replied.

"Well, actually yes! This is why you have the ability to see the fourth dimension. When you took your first independent breath— the point when you are at first alive — a part of Osworth became part of you and it is still in you, in your blood."

"So what does he want with Ben?" Megan queried.

"Beslemeks have probably been around since before the dinosaurs. Yet, they have existed in near anonymity. Imagine if you have lived in the shadows forever and by some twist of fate, you were suddenly exposed. There is a person that can see behind the shadows, can see past the veil and see you truly as you are. Would you not want to eliminate such a threat, even as a newborn?" Malcolm lectured, raising one of his bushy grey haired eyebrows with a manner of mystique.

"I don't buy that's the reason Warren wants me here. I was a newborn baby, still wet from being pushed out into life. What are the chances that I would one day realize that I could see another dimension, travel to Osworth, stumble upon these creatures and then tell the world to arm themselves with crossbows and pitchforks. It doesn't make sense to me."

"Slim to none. But I think you're missing the point. The ability to see outside of the prison of three dimensions is not going to be just your ability. As I said, it is forever a part of you and it will be a skill passed on to anyone who shares your blood."

Megan looked at me with a dawning expression. I had realized it too.

"That's right. She," Malcolm pointed at Megan, "is the reason that he came for you twenty-two years ago. He knew that your blood would carry through time and the Beslemek's identity would be discovered eventually. They aimed to snuff out the flame before it ever grew. The veil is under siege the longer you— and now Megan —are alive. That is why your parents are dead," Malcolm snickered.

"But if what you say about the Beslmek is true— that it is stuck in Osworth. I see no problem then. I'll go back to D.C and buy myself a crossbow. If Warren comes looking for me, I'll shoot him. I think it is obvious the longer we stay here, the greater danger we're in. The energy he would need to expel to come after me would be massive." I exclaimed, a bead of sweat dripping from my brow. The room had sweltered into a Dutch oven.

"NO!" Malcolm howled, picking up a carpenter's knife that rested atop his lab bench. His mania had returned and I could see a disturbed realization in his eyes. He knew that my mind was made up and I wasn't going to help him.

It was then that an incessant clamoring from the dogs outside overtook the room. Something had excited them and the sounds they made were ungodly scary.

Malcolm stopped speaking, his eyes darting to a small window looking outside and I saw something in his eyes that scared me more than anything— fear. The dogs' barking roared and the walls around us began to vibrate.

"What the hell is going on," Megan yelled, moving to me and grabbing one of my hands.

Malcolm grabbed a crossbow from the corner and tossed it to me. I was startled by the action, but managed to catch it with the hand that Megan was not squeezing.

"What is this for?" I asked, examining the weapon in my hand. It was surprisingly light for its size.

I hardly heard Malcolm say, "Load it" over the escalating barking outside. I had never heard such a chorus of vicious barking before.

I pulled my hand away from Megan and stretched back the bowstring until I felt it lock into place. There were four arrows in the notched chamber below the stock. I slide one into the precut slot. The weapon was loaded.

Outside there came a set of loud cries, a mixture of pain-stricken yowls and yelps. The barking stopped and there was an eerie silence over the place. I listened for a moment, watching Malcolm as I did. He looked concerned, but his hardened eyes and their weathered sockets were reserved and anticipatory. There was a loud crash upstairs followed by a thwacking sound like that made from an arrow piercing wood.

I heard footsteps above, moving to the door above the lab. The steps were listless and methodical, as if their owner was not in any rush to find what— or who — he was looking for. There was an odd, minatory sound superimposed with the footsteps, a faint dragging sound like something heavy being pulled across an uneven floor. I heard the metal door above the laboratory toss open and then listened as the footsteps thudded down the steps, coming closer to us all.

Malcolm looked at Megan and me. A twisted, masochistic smile broadened across his face. He raised his left arm outright and a crossbow holding six arrows seemed to appear in front of him.

"Hide!"

Greetings

Instinctively, I pulled Megan towards me with my free hand. We moved behind the lab bench and crouched down next to a chamber of liquid nitrogen. I rested my crossbow against the table and aimed it at the door.

There was a blur of movement as the laboratory door shot open. What followed was a series of small eruptions and suddenly all the lights were out, casting total blackness throughout the room.

A heavy racket spilled out in the space before me and I heard Malcolm fire three shots from his crossbow. A shrill, inhuman wail boomed throughout the darkness as one of the arrows hit its target.

"Your blood will run, Campbell. I assure you of this," crowed a fourth person looming in the pitch blackness. At once, I

recognized the voice from the phone call that had started it all—
Uncle Warren was here.

I listened intently to his voice as it faded into silence
and I found myself recalling his gruff, shrill laugh as he mocked my
parents' deaths. Something stirred inside of me at the recollection,
something that had soured into an ethereal rage and detached from
me. Without owning the control of my body, I launched myself over
the table with the crossbow forced out in front of me, my finger
itching to pull the trigger. I charged towards the voice.

Something cold and spongy, like a half-frozen fish,
slapped into my right arm, before it moved away from me. A scuffle
broke out behind me and I heard the lab table scrape against the
cement floor. Glass fell to the ground and shattered. Then I head
Malcolm yell.

"BEN, SHOOT HIM!" Malcolm ordered, his voice
muffled and suffocated.

I threw up my arm and aimed the crossbow in the
general direction of the scuffle. A brief second passed where I
thought I could see in the dark and I pulled the trigger. The arrow
flew off the crossbow shaft into its uncertain flight. I listened and
heard it strike something, causing a soft sucking sound.

"You're just like your dead father. Thinking you can
stop me with a stick. You will watch this." Warren bellowed.

A hand struck me hard in the chest, forcing me
backwards onto the floor. A light in the basement flickered on,
blinding my eyes for the moment. I squinted my eyes upward, the
cool cement was hard against my back. I had hit my head against the
wall and my sight began to blur.

"Boy, it is time. No more stalling."

For the first time, I was seeing him up close and in
person. The skin on his face was slack and of an olive tint. It had a
used, slapped together feel as if his skin was a suit that he was

263

wearing. The arrow I had shot was protruding from him throat. He moved as if he did not notice it.

He smiled down at me with needle-like teeth— the most vile looking teeth I had ever seen — and I thought I saw a chunk of blood-red meat dangling from one of his incisors. His eyes were lumps of coal, soulless and ravenous, buried into the hollows of his frail-looking skull.

At Uncle Warren's feet were Malcolm and... my heart sank— Megan. They were both lying there still, Uncle Warren grasping their heads with a talon-like grip, raising them inches off the ground. Megan was in shock, her eyes, those gorgeous jade eyes, were smoky red and her face washed in tears of fear.

I wanted nothing more than to carve the smile from his face.

Malcolm was bleeding from the right side of his head and as I squinted, I realized that his right ear had been ripped from his head. His entire right side was soaked in dark crimson. I looked around the floor for his ear and then grasped the ghastly truth— Uncle Warren had eaten it. That was the blood-red stain I had seen in his sadistic smile. Despite the loss of his ear and the blood that had poured from him, Malcolm was alive.

"When are you going to finish it Warren?" Malcolm asked through a red smile. "You'll never get her back. She is dying."

Malcolm laughed.

Warren, pleased with Malcolm's defiance, raised him from the floor to his feet, holding him off the ground for a brief instant. Warren's other hand relaxed and Megan's head fell to the ground.

"Ben, I have been wanting to reacquaint myself with you for a very long time. I will tell you why. No games, no more playing. I have two requests of you," he sneered. "The first is rather simple. Behind that door," he raised his free hand and pointed to the old wooden door behind me, "is something that belongs to me. Malcolm stole it from me many years ago and tonight is the night I reclaim it."

I raised myself off the floor, onto my knee. "What do you want me to do?" I asked.

"I want you to bring me what's in that room. I think you know where I live. It's a special place, the place where you were born… and the place where your parents died. Such a pity!"

"Ben, whatever happens, you must not bring him what's in that room. She is almost dead for Christ sake. Let her die." Malcolm ordered, trying to pull away from Uncle Warren's deceptively strong grip. Malcolm was forced onto the ground and he moaned as his chest fell onto the concrete.

"It would be nice to eat you, Megan," Warren said through a smile, over articulating her name. He looked down at her and she shielded her face in her arms. "She looks just so… yummy. You return what belongs to me and I will return to you this delicious looking snack. If Malcolm has offered anything, I'm sure you know what I mean."

Hearing this sent a violent surge throughout my body. I was up and running full-throttle towards Warren, who simply reached out both of his hands and grabbed my throat. His grip was mighty and he began to crush my windpipe in his vice grip. I choked and gasped for air. I balled both hands into fists and punched him simultaneously in his head. As my knuckles struck the skull, I felt it give way and crack, but his grip was unforgiving, relentless.

I punched him again, but in the throat this time and followed quickly with thumbs to his eyes. I gouged his eyes, but my actions only hastened my suffocation. My life began to slip away as Uncle Warren tried to quell my existence.

Suddenly, he released me and I was on my back, on the cold, hard cement of Malcolm's basement. Then, I heard it, that mocking laughter, the gruff and frantic chortle that derided my parents' deaths.

"I won't take to killing you yet. I told you there were two things you were going to do for me. Now you know that there is little sense in fighting me." Warren said through that cunning, crafting smile, standing over my body. "And watch carefully what happens next."

Uncle Warren walked over to Megan and Malcolm's bodies, both of whom were laying there in a heap. With one arm, Warren pulled Malcolm to his feet. I could see that Malcolm was weary and weak. My heart skipped as I anticipated what was about to happen and for an instant before it was done, I followed Malcolm's gaze to his hand where he was tightly clutching the vial he had plucked from the table.

Then it happened. I watched as Uncle Warren stretched open his jaw and showcased his sharp row of needle-like teeth. In one blitzing moment, his mouth sank into Malcolm's neck and ripped a chunk of meaty flesh from it, splattering blood and tissue across the room. He dropped Malcolm's lifeless body like a crumpled tissue to the floor.

Malcolm was dead.

Warren spat out the chunk of Malcolm's neck that was in his mouth, sputtering "his flesh is so foul. It taste spoiled."

Megan raised her head from her arms and saw at once Malcolm's bloody corpse, half missing it's throat. She screamed in terror.

"Don't worry, Megan. I'm not going to do that to you," Uncle Warren laughed. "I have something so much better planned."

He paused and looked down at her, then spoke to me without looking at me. "Night's approaching. Don't make me wait."

With those final words, Warren grabbed Megan by her hair and dragged her upstairs, out from Malcolm's basement laboratory. Megan screamed and pleaded for me to help. But when I went to her, the room turned crimson and moved away from me. The ground shook with a ferocious quake again. My vertigo had returned. My knees gave way and I tumbled flat to the floor.

A thousand blades pierced my brain. Oh, it hurt so bad…but Megan, my beautiful Megan. I raised my head and tried to pull myself to her. I scrutinized in pain and helpless as the love of my life vanished up the stairs, dragged away from me by something that was not of my world. The room around me dimmed and my eyes closed. Everything else disappeared from importance.

Shadows and Streetlights

I woke at first without recollection. The horror, at least for a few minutes, was lost. My memories had been lassoed and corralled, stolen by a stealthy bandit that swept through and snatched them away from me. It was not until my arm ran through the blood on the floor that it all came flooding back.

A crimson mirror painted the concrete around Malcolm's corpse. I looked down at him, at the giant chunk of neck meat and tendons lying like a sponge beside his body. I could see my reflection in his blood. He had been a man tortured by his past and the loss of his love. He had been crazy, driven into madness, but he did not deserve such an ending to his life. He was the only person alive who knew that Uncle Warren was a Beslemek. More importantly, he was the only person who had an idea of how to kill him.

Warren had taken Megan and I had no plan of getting her back. The more I thought of it, the more I felt like there was no chance in hell that I could save her …none. She was going to die; I knew it in my gut. Every part of me just knew it. Like my parents, like Malcolm, Megan was going to die and Uncle Warren was going to kill her.

The thought of losing her, of never holding her again brought me to my knees. What was I going to do? I stared up at the lights in the ceiling, helpless and hoping for some guidance.

"I don't believe in you. To me you simply don't exist," I found myself speaking aloud. "But as I look around, I see that I don't understand everything that I thought I did. So maybe you are real. Maybe I am wrong. I hope I am because I could really use your help right about now. I love her and I need her back."

I dropped my head to stare into the crimson blood puddle again.

"Everyone is gone," I heard myself saying in an ethereal voice.

I stood up and felt a sharp prodding in my back. I reached back and my hand grabbed the handle of my Dad's knife. I had forgotten that I had it and the realization of having it in my possession empowered me for some reason. Maybe I wasn't alone.

My foot knocked something as I rose from my knees. It was the glass vial that Malcolm had been holding in his hand the moment before he was killed. I turned the vial in my hand and saw in handwritten scrawl the words *Compound Zeta- Test238_0715384*

Test 238! What did that mean? It didn't really matter. Malcolm wanted me to have the vial, I was fairly certain of this. Just before Warren ripped out his neck, Malcolm made sure that I saw it.

There was a black cabinet set back in the corner of the laboratory with papers and notebooks strewn about. I rifled through the loose pages on top of the cabinet, many of them were covered with inarticulate squiggles and a few mathematical equations that I vaguely understood. In the bottom drawer were sets of dust-covered notebooks labeled with a range of numbers. I found the notebook labeled **211-240** and leafed through it until I came to 238. Test 238!

On the pages beneath the header, Malcolm scribbled the salient detail of Test 238. His penmanship was atrocious and was represented by short, dashing scrawl that hardly resembled the doings of a human being. His vowels were squiggles squashed into a disparate mess of equally illegible consonances, numbers, equations and chemical structures that morphed collectively into an inconsequential glob of ink.

I sifted through the documents at a scabrous pace, often having to stop reading because I could not understand the hieroglyphics on the page and had to trek backwards to an earlier reference just to verify that I had not become completely lost. Reading Malcolm's lab notebook was like navigating a maze blindfolded and with the walls allowed to move. Only one passage struck me as important, it helped that is was also the only passage I could fully decipher:

TEST SUBJECT A7L9G SUCCUMBED WITHIN MINUTES OF EXPOSURE TO THE COMPOUND WHEN ADMINISTERED INTO THE EPIDURAL SPACE OF THE C-5 AND C-6 CERVICAL VERTEBRAE. MORTALITY OF SUBJECT A7L9G WAS VERIFIED BY ABSENCE OF PULSE AND NON-REACTION OF PUPILS TO LIGHT STIMULI. THE EVENT WAS PRECEDED BY NOTICEABLE DIFFICULTY IN RESPIRATORY ACTION AND A VIOLENT CONVULSION THAT WAS PRECIPITATED AFTER SUBJECT EXPERIENCED SYNCOPE. CAUSE OF DEATH HAS NOT BEEN DETERMINED, BUT EARLY SUGGESTIONS ARE SUDDEN ONSET ENCEPHALOMALACIA AS A RESULT OF THE COMPOUND. VERIFICATION IS REQUIRED WITH ADDITIONAL TESTING.

I searched through the remaining notebooks, but found no reference of further tests being performed. The date atop Test 238 was recent, having been reported the last few months. From everything I could gather, Test 238 had been a success. It appeared that Malcolm had tested the lethality of a novel compound on mice by varying routes of administration. Based on the summary of Test 238, death came quickly to the mouse when the compound was injected into the spine just below its brain. Other routes of administration did not appear to be as successful, at least there was no other mention of mice succumbing to the compound, from the bits I could riddle out.

Before Warren killed him, Malcolm had held the vial of liquid as if it were his own flesh-and-blood child. After reading the summary of Test238, I knew what Malcolm wanted me to do with it—jam it into Uncle Warren's head and hope it killed him. I wanted nothing more than to do this. He had my Megan and only in my worst nightmares could I think about the horrors she was facing.

Still, something felt off. It bothered me that I could not find proof that he verified the compound's lethality. How could a man of numbers and nature, someone as staunch a scientist as Malcolm, who had devoted his life to finding a way to kill the Beslemeks, not verify the thing that could prove he found what he was searching for? Not verifying the results was tantamount to flipping a coin once and saying that it will always lands on heads.

My thoughts were interrupted by a voice from behind me.

"The Door, Benjamin." The voice echoed from somewhere in the shadows.

"Hello?"

Again the voice spoke. "The Door, Benjamin."

"Who's there? Show yourself!"

I focused on the patch of blackness leading out the basement doorway. I knew I heard someone.

"Come out, whoever you are! Show me your face."

There was no response.

A chill ran down my spine as I felt a hand grab my shoulder. The hand spun me around as if I was standing on a

271

turntable. I stopped when I was facing the far wall of the basement laboratory.

In a fortuitous moment, my eyes caught a glimpse of the old wooden door in the corner of the room to my right. The door was antiquated, dry and warped. It was fastened to the beam by ornate rusted hinges, made of cast iron that curved to a point as if they were arrows. Two components stuck out against the hoary farmhouse décor: a polished silver cam latch and corroded iron crossbar with new brackets.

It was clear from the look of the door that Malcolm did not want people seeing what was inside, but then I realized it might be the opposite— maybe he wanted to keep something from getting out. Whatever it was, I sensed answers would be found on the other side of the door.

The room beyond the door was a prison with an iron cell that ran lengthwise along the wall. There were no windows in the room and I could see from the only light in the room, a dim heat lamp casting a reddish glow that the cell was made for tight quarters. It was no longer than six feet wide and was no more than four foot deep. The concrete floor was cold, unforgiving, even on a sweltering hot day like this.

"Holy hell," I heard myself saying as I saw the body lying in a heap in the center of the cell.

It was a woman with an olive-tinged complexion and slack face that resembled a burlap sack with a yellow wig. Her eyes were closed and she did not move. She looked dead and her body mangled. She had no legs, just stumps where knees used to be and her fingers were bent at harsh angles, clearly broken and dislodged. Her face had been crushed in forming a bowling-bowl sized hollow that left the structure of facial bones shockingly misaligned. It was difficult to look at.

It was clear to me, even before I found his torture chest, that Malcolm had mutilated this... *thing*... in front of me. I wanted to, well, part of me anyhow, wanted to grieve for what looked like a terribly disfigured woman that could not possible be alive. But then I remembered, or tried to believe, that she was not a human. She was something else. Something that did not bleed. At the site where her legs once were there was no blood or loose, dangling flesh from the hacking that was done. There was nothing like the crimson lake of blood that pooled beneath Malcolm's corpse in the other room. This human looking thing was not as she appeared; she was a Beslemek.

"Get up," I ordered, stepping up to the iron bars. "I am taking you home."

The Beslemek lay motionless in the center of the cell, twisted in a wad of human-looking parts.

"I'm not asking a second time."

As I spoke, I fastened my sights onto a rack nailed into the stone wall past the door. Hanging from the various hooks was an armory of weapons. Swords, baseball bats wrapped in barbed wire, a chainsaw and a flail all fulfilled the malevolent bounty of Malcolm's battering bulwarks. It was unfathomable to see the armament and to consider what Malcolm had done to the creature in the cage.

Probably for years, since he captured it, he tortured it, hammering its flesh with his weapons and mutilating it with his blades. I suspected that he had even injected it with some of the death serums he conjured up, hoping one day the creature would simply die. There was no proving of such a charge, not even in the pages of his lab book. I also imagined that he thought of Macy while he did it and for that, I could not blame his evil tactics. But for Malcolm, all the brutality neither killed the Beslemek nor brought back his wife. I think I would have gone mad too facing such insurmountable feats.

I picked up the flail from the assortment of weapons. It was much heavier than I imagined and I shuddered to think what devastation its business end would deliver when it made contact at full force. The creature's crushed face...

I looked to the cage and there standing on no legs was the creature, the Beslemek, her face disgustingly shaped like a crescent moon. She appeared to hover, having no feet, ankles or shins. She smiled at me with a wretched, excited smile. A snarl more than anything. She was awake and ready to go home.

"LET ME OUT," she howled in a sour voice, rattling the cage door with her hands and crooked fingers.

I went to her and stared into her cold black eyes, the eyes of a shark, the eyes of a predator. I saw in them the same undertone of savagery and indifference that I had seen in Warren's eyes. The creature lunged towards me, her arms stretched outwards through the gap in the iron bars, but her reach was just short of reaching me. I stepped backwards.

"HE WILL KILL HER," the Beslemek crowed, a twisted smile rising on her crushed skull. She rattled the cage, shaking the bars with a violent rage and I watched as the hinges holding the cage together began to loosen.

At that moment, I understood that I could not succeed on my own. I needed assistance to get Megan back.

I called Owen, knowing he was the only one crazy enough to not ask questions. He picked up.

"What up, cuz?"

"I need your help and I need you to not ask questions." I stated bluntly.

"You kill someone?"

I paused at the question. "No, I didn't kill anyone. But people are dead and..."

"Shit! Alright, what do you need me to do?"

"Megan has been taken and is being held hostage. Owen, she could die tonight."

"Fa-uck!" He swore in disbelief. "I'll be there. No rules tonight, whatever you need."

"I need you to come to 8145 Chesterfield Road," I paused for a moment, trying to compute the logistics of how this was going to work. "And Owen, bring your pickup truck."

"Done. I'll be there in twenty."

The phone went silent.

I turned to the Beslemek and looked into the feral anxiousness beaming from her crushed-in face. Its expression reminded me of the foretelling gleam in a chess grandmaster's eyes just before moving his queen into position and proclaiming 'checkmate'.

Brothers in Arms

"What the fuck is that?" Owen protested, grabbing the knee stubs that extended out from the bottom of the tied-off blanket.

"No questions remember? Hurry up! Let's get it in the truck. I don't want anyone to see her." I rebutted, brushing away the obvious appearance of a felony as if it was my everyday job.

"SHIT! SHIT!" Owen jumped up and moved frantically in chaotic paths.

He was muttering to himself something about prison and having a tight white ass. I did not care about the appearance of unlawfulness.

"Keep her straight. We need her whole body to slide in there," I stepped up onto the back of the tailgate and pulled the Beslemek up into the cab. "Alright, just roll her in."

Owen stared at me. I could tell he was having an issue with this. "Who are you?"

"I will explain, but we have to move."

"No, dude. I can't do this." Owen confessed, his hands still firmly around the stubs of the creature.

I jumped out of the pickup to help Owen when the body in the blanket moved.

"— OH SHIT!" Owen jumped as it began to twitch and writhe. "It is still alive. Ben, it's not too late. We can fix this. Dude, we can make this right. Come on!"

"YOU RIDICULUS THING!" I roared out of frustration and jumped back into the bed of the pickup truck. Without hesitating and without fear, I grabbed my dad's knife from the back of my waistband and sunk its tip into the twitching mass twisted in the blanket. Like a mad man, I stabbed again and again, repeatedly burying the blade until it went no further. I heard myself howl like an animal.

I felt Owen's arms wrap around my neck and pull me backwards, out of the pickup truck onto the asphalt. He pushed his knees into my forearms, pinning me to the ground. With his hands, he wrestled the knife from me.

He did not say a word. He simply stared down at me with a shocked, vacant gaze, his eyes hollow, emotionless.

"Get off of me." I demanded, thrashing my shoulders to loosen his hold on me. When I could not get him to relinquish his hold, I thrust back my hips and kicked him in the back. He fell off me and I rolled to my feet. I reached down and picked up the knife.

"Owen, you do not understand. Look at the knife!"

I waved the blade in front of him, showing him all the angles.

"Don't you see?" I asked.

Behind me, tires squealed and a car came to a screeching halt. The cop car wailed a high-pitch siren that flashed pulses of bright blue and red light. The driver side door came open and an officer drew his gun on me.

"Drop the knife and get on your knees," the cop ordered.

I raised my hands and let the knife go slack in my fingers; the blade orientated itself towards the ground. I looked down at Owen, who sat on the asphalt with his arms back and his legs bent out in front of him. I could tell that he was confused and puzzled about the scene unfolding in front of him.

"I said drop the knife and get on your knees!"

"Megan," I whispered to myself.

I dropped the knife and watched in slow motion as it fell to the ground, bounced off its handle and then came to rest in the center of the street. I saw in the reflection of its blade, the sun behind a large oak tree swaying in a light breeze. I fell to my knees and placed my hands behind my head, never looking away from the reflection in the knife.

"Interlock your fingers behind your head and lie flat on your stomach."

The asphalt was warm against my cheek as I placed my head against the ground. I heard the footsteps approaching me when a voice spoke to me, inside my head.

"Benjamin, you must not rest. You must not surrender." The voice said. It was a familiar voice, the voice of my father. It was strong and stern and I thought of him. *Unrelenting.* In a word, that was my father.

I felt the officer's hand grab my wrists and move them to the small of my back. A cold, steel handcuff clicked around my left wrist and then again around my right, restraining my hands behind my back. The cop lifted me to my knees, then to my feet and began to march me towards his cruiser.

I looked up again at the sun behind the oak tree and watched the branches sway from side to side. It was a beautiful image, somewhat different from the image in the reflection of the knife.

The cop was making a mistake of guiding me to his cruiser while walking behind me with his legs offset to mine. I hesitated for a moment, realizing there was no going back from what I was about to do. Then I acted.

I stopped suddenly and raised the heel of my right foot straight into the officer's testicles, then stomped the instep of his left foot with the edge of my heel. I placed my foot just to the outside of his and bent down slightly. The kick to the groin caused the officer to crouch over and as he came down, I launched my right shoulder into his jaw. His head whipped backwards and as momentum carried him away from me, I transferred my weight onto my left leg and kicked him in the solar plexus. He fell to the ground in one fluid motion and once on his back, I kicked him in the side of the head.

He was unresponsive on the asphalt, blood dripping from his face. I sat on the ground beside him and brought my hands under my feet so that they were in front of me. I found the keys to the handcuffs and unlocked them from my wrist. I grabbed the officer's firearm, a 9 mm, and handcuffed him as he had me.

I went to the cruiser, which was idling in park, and killed the engine. I took the keys from the ignition, disconnected the transmitter from the police dash and ripped it from its framing. I threw the keys and transmitter into a nearby sewer and picked up my father's knife.

"Give me the keys!" I ordered Owen, who had not moved an inch since I threw him off me.

He did not respond. I was bewildered and not going to be stopped.

279

I went over to him and attempted to pull him up. He withdrew from my aid, his hollow gaze directed towards the fallen police officer.

"I did what I had to. Simple as that. Megan needs me and there is no time to wait. If you come with me I will explain everything- I promise."

Owen did not reply.

"We don't have time to dick around, man. Look at me. Dude, look at me." I urged, tapping the side of his face to force him to make eye contact with me.

"You killed someone right in front of me and then you assaulted a cop. You're not in your right mind, Ben. You need to turn yourself in." Owen decided, pulling himself of the ground and brushing dirt from his legs.

"You saw the knife. If I killed someone, as you say, where was the blood? There was absolutely no blood anywhere."

A look of consternation grew on his face. "Fuck," he paused, thinking. "You're right. What the hell does that mean?"

"If you come with me, I will explain everything, but I can't stay here. Megan needs me and this cop is going to come to. I don't wish to assault him a second time." I confessed.

Owen was reluctant; I could see it in his body language— his shoulders were angled away from me, his body was rigid, and his face showed confliction.

"You either come with me or not, but I need your keys. I am not asking."

"I don't understand. Why wouldn't there be blood on the knife?" Owen asked to no one in particular.

"Come with me and I will tell you everything. You will not believe it, but please trust me. You are the only the family I have." I implored, hoping to convince him to look past the obvious and suspected events he had laid witness to.

"You are my brother. You have always been. I don't understand yet, but I trust you— I love you bro. Let's do whatever crazy thing we need to do to get your girl back."

Owen tossed me the keys to his pickup and we both got in, with me in the driver seat eager to leave, to find Megan. Owen was next to me as uneager as one could possibly be.

"So where are we going?" Owen squeezed out as I locked the doors and turned over the engine. His pickup revved angrily and I slammed on the accelerator and peeled out, driving to meet the Devil.

"You know the disappearances happening in Osworth? I know what is doing it. It's the same thing that killed my parents. They're called Beslemeks, they look like us, but they are not like us. For one, they do not bleed," I declared, slowing to yield through the STOP sign at the corner Baker and Clinton.

"That doesn't make sense man. I want to believe you, but this is crazy."

I checked the rear-view mirror, as I turn left onto Greenwich.

"Take a look in the back."

Owen looked over his shoulder into the bed of his pickup.

"HOLY FUCK," he yelled. "It's so disfigured. How is it still alive?"

The creature had escaped from the blanket and sitting there with its caved-in face. It had freshly made stab wounds in its head and it watched us with a grin. It did not try to move or run from the pickup bed, it just watched us with the placid enjoyment of an elderly person watching kids play on a jungle gym.

I took a sharp curve and watched as the creature fell to the side, before sitting back up and continuing to stare us down.

"Do you believe me now?"

281

He nodded. "Yup, so where are we going?" Owen asked, clutching the handle above the passenger side door with two hands as I took another sharp corner.

"Osworth!" I said. "That's where this all began. That's where it will end."

"But do you even know where you're going? Or how to get there?"

"I have an idea of how to get there. Once we get there, I figured she'll come in handy."

"We need Colin!" Owen stated. "The kid has spent weeks up there over the last few months. He'll know where to go."

I thought about this and knew Owen was correct.

"I'm not sure. There is some serious shit that's gonna go down." I admitted, knowing that the chances of survival were probably twice as high having Colin with us.

"That sonofabitch is an adrenaline junkie. He'll be all about this."

"Call him, then. We don't have time to waste."

Forty-five seconds later, I pulled a U-turn against oncoming traffic, hollering at the top of my lungs like some type of battle cry and drove out to find Colin. My mind went to yesterday morning, at the breakfast table, where Megan and I sat laughing amongst our friends and dreaming about our futures. I had never thought that just twenty-four hours later that our futures would be so uncertain.

To Osworth

By luck, we found Colin in Concord visiting a friend off Maple Street.

"I can't be a part of this!" Colin asserted, rubbing his eyes in disbelief. "Just look at what you two have done. I should call the cops."

"Look man, this may look bad. I get that. But you've got to trust us. There is some crazy, weird shit going down right now and we need your help." Owen pleaded, shaking his prayer-wise hands like a street beggar.

"Trust you? How can I trust you? First, I hardly know this guy," pointing his head in my direction, "and there is a body— a fucking body —in the bed of your truck. Now you're trying to tell me that we need to go to Osworth because Megan has been taken by some out-of-this world creature. The same creature, mind you, that you're claiming is the cause of all the disappearances up in the mountains. As far as I know, this could be Megan," he jabbed his finger at the covered mass in the back of the trunk.

I was devastated by the insinuation knowing in my heart that I loved Megan more than anything and knowing further that her life hung in the balance of getting Colin to help me— to believe me.

"Here, I'll show you. This is not Megan. It's not a person at all. I assure you." I replied, stepping up into the bed of the pickup truck, bracing myself against the side as the truck dipped under my weight. I knelt down next to the wrapped body that rested motionless on the floor of the truck bed. Owing to the distraction it presented to passersby, we forced the beneath the blankets. It was odd as the creature was still as minutes earlier it had been thrashing about. It was almost like it was playing dead. I began to pull back the blanket when Collette stopped me.

"Babe," she said, turning to Colin, "you have known Owen since you both were in high school. He has never done something as terrible as what you are suggesting. Neither would his cousin. Trust your friend."

Colin looked her over, saw the sincerity in her face and the effulgent glow he had come to love in her. He whispered, "How do you explain this? It looks really bad."

Collette placed her hands against Colin's cheeks with the tender softness of a lover and conceded, "I can't. That's what trust is!"

In that moment, I observed a heady exuberance behind Collette's emotionless face, sort of a hidden excitement that rested just beneath the surface. I sensed she had convinced Colin to help us.

Colin exhaled a forced sigh as if the request to help us had transformed into a menial task akin to taking out the trash. "Fine!"

"Then we have no time to kill—" I urged, then realizing my gaffe. "Not the best choice of words. Anyhow, we should move!"

Owen nodded in agreement and jumped into the driver's seat. He buckled the seat belt and nervously slapped the roof of his truck waiting for us to pile in.

Colin slid into the backseat of the extended cab and waited for Collette to join him.

"One moment!" Collette paused, her voice elevated. "I will be right back."

She vanished into the apartment complex as I secured myself into the passenger seat. A handful of minutes later she returned carrying a small satchel slung over her shoulder.

"What's in the bag?" Colin murmured, trying not to be overheard.

Collette smiled. "Insurance! Now, drive Owen, drive!"

I looked at them with distrust. Insurance? What the hell did that mean?

She tapped Owen on the shoulder and closed her door. As if Owen had been a marionette whose strings were wrapped around Collette's crooked fingers, the truck took off on her command.

Under Colin's direction, we departed Concord with the sinking sun a burning ember at our backs. We entered the on-ramp and merged on to I-93 North, the same road I followed home a few days before to lay down my slain parents. The northbound lane was quieter than the lanes that headed out of the city and I wondered if I would ever leave this place again.

The conversation amongst our assembly was scarce, limited to the misguided attempts to lighten the dense disquiet that was a stranglehold on our alleged friendship and to the secretive whispers between Colin and Collette that, from the capture of stray words, appeared to be the formation of a plan should something go awry. I cared little about their opinions or conspiring; my only concern was that they help me find Megan and regardless of their wishes, they were going to help me.

Twenty-five minutes at felonious speeds and break-neck maneuvering in and out of cars was all it took to reach New Hampton. I had never been to New Hampton, but I felt at once that it was the epicenter of the New Hampshire lifestyle. It was a small New England village bound together by the quintessential charm of a Granite Stater with their wholesome, family-oriented heritage. I sensed it was a town built on neighborliness and devotion for others, but with a veiled suspicion about outsiders.

I rested my head against the glass of the passenger side window and glanced out at the quant village wondering what life was like in a place like this. There were no massive shopping centers, no commuter rail, no monuments erected to the heavens. I knew there were fewer people here than in Georgetown and there was little more than thick New England forest to keep them company.

As Owen sped through New Hampton, charging towards a confrontation I was not prepared for, I thought how liberating life could be in a place like this. I began to wonder what it would be like to grow old in such a place. I would wake every morning with the sunlight falling on my beloved Megan's soft, wrinkled face, with both of us having entered our golden years. We would each open our eyes and without saying a word, gaze at each other for the longest of moments, smiling and blessed. The sun would warm our sheets through the aged window of our lake house;

the dawn-reflecting surface of the lake outside would ripple softly in the early morning breeze...

...Suddenly, I was running...hard. I was sprinting through thick pine trees and over small hills. Smoke swelled up from below me, blocking my vision. My heart beat violently, threatening to shoot from my chest like a ball from a cannon. Laughter erupted all around me. It was the mocking snicker of children and it was coming from all directions.

I was being chased. But I could not see my assailant.

My legs carried me into a clearing with small bushes to one side and a bare dirt path heading straight across a meadow. As I ran through it, my eyes moved up into the sky and I saw not a moon looking back at me, but the face of a baby with a lifeless, vacant stare laughing at me. There was something familiar in its face, something wrong.

I could not outrun the laughter, it surrounded me, smothered me, but I couldn't stop. My legs were burning, weakening as I fled. My ankles ached and my thighs burned from exhaustion. Then at the far side of the clearing, I saw her. Megan.

"Oh, thank God," I heard myself shout. "We need to get out of here."

Megan was still, her gaze directed at me, but unflinching. I could see just her outline beneath the shadows of the trees on the other side of the clearing. Why wasn't she running to me?

As her figure solidified, I slowed my sprint and stopped cold at the edge of the field where the moonlight beams illuminated the expanse. I fell to the ground in horror.

She was dead.

Her eyes, those beautiful eyes of jade, had been ripped from her head leaving bloody strains of frayed nerves hanging from the sockets and her chest had been ripped open, leaving behind a large diameter hole.

'NOOOOOOOO!" I howled, my body convulsing in rage and grief.

"Come now, Benjamin! It is time." A gruff voice boomed, cutting through the childlike laughter, which stopped at once.

"I don't know what you want from me?! I DON'T KNOW!"

There was an unexpected movement behind Megan's body and then I saw it, rising above her body, some alien monster that had vague familiarity to the beast I had seen in Malcolm's laboratory. Its massive body had no clear and obvious set of eyes, but it somehow was looking at me, in my direction, as if it sensed my presence. It knew me, but nothing about the thing looked familiar to me. It was the most hideous and intimidating creature I had ever seen. I could only call it by the name I knew it as…Beslemek.

My body was immobilized by its stature and I was helpless, as it moved to the edge of the clearing, no more than a foot from me. Its body throbbed and wretched and there was a measurable inkling lurking in my belly telling me that it was about to attack me.

You mustn't go into the woods.

The words materialized into thoughts as if they were gifted to me from somewhere away from here. *You mustn't go into the woods.* The words came again, clear as day.

"It is time Benjamin. I have waited much too long to wait any further. Resign yourself to death and come to me." The Beslemek uttered in an assured, slow cadence, speaking from some organ buried inside its body, not visible to me.

Once more, the words scrolled across my thoughts as if a ticker tape: *You mustn't go into the woods.*

"I cannot. I WILL NOT. You have taken the love of my life from me. You have lost any collateral you held over me. So I will not heed your demands, I do not need to. Not now, not ever. I know you cannot claim me if I do not enter the woods, so I will hold myself here, just inches from your reach, until I wither and die." I goaded, understanding what my intuition meant.

There was a brief pause and the creature receded into the woods, disappearing from my view. All that remained was Megan's corpse, propped against a tree as the lifeless shell of the woman I loved. Her empty eye sockets watching over me...

"Ben, Ben!"

My body was jostled and I was thrown back into Owen's truck from whatever forsaken backwoods place of my mind I had just been residing. My eyes were heavy and my heart was reverberating beneath my chest. It was nothing more than a nightmare— a too real nightmare — but that was all.

"Whew! I just had the worst nightmare of my life."

"Well, get ready to experience it in real life. We'll be in Osworth in five minutes." Owen warned, sounding very unsure of himself.

"Where do we need to go?" Colin asked tersely.

There were no other cars on the road and the sun had fully set, dipping behind the mountainous horizon while I was asleep. A sign on the road told me we were heading north on I-16, but all I could see from the headlights were trees and darkness, no way of knowing whether we were heading north or not. It seemed surreal how dark this place had become after the sun had set.

"There's no moon tonight! How can that be? There's supposed to be a moon tonight!" I pondered, remembering the dream I had just endured.

"What are you talking about?" Collette interjected. "Why are you suddenly concerned with the phases of the moon? You should really be concerned with what is about to go down."

She was right. But the fact that my nightmare had played out beneath the moonlight, which did not exist tonight, put me in state of total unease.

"Uh, right. Um, we need to get to Lake Osworth. That's where we need to go!" I directed.

"How do you know?" Colin questioned. "Some crazy shit has been happening there. I'm not sure that is where we want to end up."

"I know for certain that is where we need to go!"

"How?" asked Collette with more than a tinge of skepticism.

"Well, it is where I was born... and the place where my sister was killed. It is where Malcolm Campbell captured the thing in the back. It is also where my parents were heading when they were killed. I have never been more confident in my life about anything. This is where we are supposed to be."

Colin and Collette shared another clandestine gaze and a whisper, Colin sighed audibly.

"When you enter Osworth, you will come to four-way intersection. We need to go straight. It will still be Route-16 heading towards North Conway. You follow this for about a mile until you pass a gas station on your right. If you were to continue straight, you would end up in the village of Chocorua, but you will want to take a left on Jameson Road. I will guide you the rest the way once we're on it." Colin instructed, leaning forward into the partition between us, his arms hugging the back of our seats

Owen turned to him, his eyes narrowed. "Are there no signs?"

Colin coughed out a laugh and shook his head. "No! Lake Osworth is about as out of the way as you can get. It is buried by woods, with no clear entrance or egress points. You'll need to park between trees. It is a beautiful lake, but you'll need to work for it. Alright, we are coming into Osworth now."

Owen pulled up to a wooden sign hanging from a tree branch over the road. The words hand-carved into it aspired to welcome visitors:

Welcome to Osworth

The Heartland of the North

"Oh, isn't this cozy. 'The Heartland of the North'. What bullshit is that? Ain't no one ever heard of this God forsaken place." Owen offered as the truck came to a stop at a four-way before continuing straight.

Being here in a place filled with blackness unnerved me. This place had been the crux of my life, yet I had no memory of it, no recollection of any of the events that apparently had sent into motion this very drive more than two decades before. I was someone who had returned to a lost land, untouched by the ticking clock, preserved by the sands of time. After years abroad I had stumbled back onto a place which was forgotten memory.

"Take this left. There?!"

"Yup, got it."

The pickup pulled onto a dim, pebbled road that descended down a hill into the thick pine forest of the White Mountains. There had been only one building that I had seen since crossing the town border — only one sign of civilization — an old gas station with something pretending to be a garage leaning against it and seeming to crumble under the pressure of being looked at. The fluorescent lights affixed to the faded walls beamed down onto oil-stained concrete and a rusted-out pickup truck resting on cinder blocks sat at the side of the building. I half expected the owner of such a place to have the face of a stroke victim, distorted and paralyzed, and a smile coated in leathery yellow teeth stained by chewing tobacco. It did not seem to be a habitable venue.

The four of us were jostled as the pebbled path transitioned to arid brown dirt. The dirt road was a compressed and hard surface, but smooth as if it were brick. The street narrowed as the trees on the edges grew inward, choking the navigational width of the road. Houses, small ranch ones with tin roofs set to steep angles, began to pop up on either side of us, most of them set back off the road. Their interiors were either dark or dimly lit.

"You'll want to take a left in about half a mile. There should be an old brown church with a weird looking chimney in the back— on your right I think. The road's just after."

Owen nodded.

"So Ben, I am curious how you think this thing will play out? What's gonna happen?" Collette quizzed me.

As shameful as it was, I had thought very little about how this was going to work. I still had so many questions about everything. I just didn't understand how reality could be so different than how I came to understand it, how I thought everyone understood it. More importantly, I had no real reason to believe any

292

of us would come out of this alive. I wasn't going to say that aloud, but I sensed it was the truth.

"Before the night is over, everything that we have come to believe as true will fragment. You may think that I came here only for Megan, but that's not true." I offered in a trance-like voice, staring unblinkingly out the window.

"What the hell does that mean?" Colin whipped with a hardened concern.

I tapped my finger against the glass that my head was resting on.

"We all will find out together." I confessed.

Owen shot me a demanding look, his mouth fused shut, only a hint of the standard clowning grin stitched on his face. He knew that we would never forget this night.

A church appeared ahead of us. It was set back in the dark with only a single light glowing beneath a wooden crucifix that towered above the congregation and disappeared into coniferous foliage. I stared up at its grandiose doors, which seemed to be made of unyielding wood, probably hickory or oak, and all held tightly together with ornate iron fittings. The craftsmanship in the door was exquisite as deep hues of brown and black blended with hints of earthy reds, all swirling together into some kind of magnificent painting drawn by Mother Nature. I thought about the safety and refuge that resided behind those sturdy doors.

Then Owen turned left and the church light above the doors quietly faded into the depths of the blackened night.

For a few passing seconds, no one in the car spoke, but I could sense that Colin was growing hostile. He had not spoken a word, but instead began to rustle audibly in the back seat, thumping the door with his elbow and making known his mood with forced guttural sounds.

What happened next felt like an inevitability.

293

"STOP THE CAR!" Colin erupted, throwing open his door before Owen had any chance to brake. Colin tilted over the edge as if he was preparing to jump, but Collette had just as quickly lassoed her arm around his neck, pulling him away from certain pain... or worse.

I had it with their attitudes.

"WHAT THE HELL IS YOUR PROBLEM?" I exploded, sensing the coming surge from within me, but trying to keep the fiery floodwaters that boiled in my gut at bay.

Colin focused his cold and rigid body at me. His shoulder turned ever so slightly towards me as if he was going to punch me. I instinctively threw up my hands to guard my face, but then I lunged towards Colin with my own fist cocked when my body jerked towards Owen, his arm pulling my shoulder. His face was grave and stern.

Collette consoled Colin by patting his chest and stroking her hand through his hair.

"How can you blame him for losing it? You drag us up here with a mutilated body in your trunk and a lunatic explanation about how it got there. The fact we came along at all was an act of good faith, but honestly Ben, I think there are some secrets being held back. You've been saying some cryptic things. He has every right to want to get out of here. Hell, I want to get out of here." Collette attacked, her gaze was a hammer as she looked at me.

Owen began to pull over to the side of the road.

"What are you doing man? You need to keep driving!" I ordered, waving my hand onward. "We're good here."

"Ben, no I don't." Owen stated bluntly before pausing as if to think. "First off, I have not the slightest idea where in this shit-stain town I am going. Second, do you have any idea how we're going to get Megan back? I mean I saw you put a blade through the

294

head of that thing back there and, somehow, it still moved. I don't know if Beslemeks are real or not, but I do know human beings do not survive a knife being put through their head repeatedly. Whatever it turns out to be, you're my boy. We're blood! But we need a plan. I don't want to die here in this monkey anus."

There was a silence in the truck for a moment until someone's laughter radiated into the silence. It was a maniacal changeless laugh that grew into a crescendo that pierced my ears. The unrelenting source was Collette and her howl lured Colin's hate-filled gaze away from me, even if for just a brief reprieve.

"What's so funny?" Owen asked, his head cocked sideways.

Collette shook her head, shaking off Owen's question. Her golden hair partially covered her face, which was a ruby red tomato beneath her locks.

"A hell of a time to get the giggles!" Colin stated with a similarly confused look upon his face.

"Never mind me, let's keep going. We're all probably going to die anyway. Ah, let's see what happens." She said matter-of-factly, waving Owen forward. "Tell him where to go."

Colin hesitated. He watched her to see if she was sincere and then he flashed his cold eyes back towards me. It was then that I realized that I trusted neither of them.

"Well, let's get on it with it!" I said to him. Hell, I wanted to punch him in his teeth.

"Yo, you crazy assholes. We have no plan. I am not moving this car an inch until we have a plan." Owen protested as he looked around where he obviously saw the lesser primates in all of us.

"We have what he wants. He is not going to harm us," I began thinking aloud.

"And when we give her to him... or when he just takes her?" Colin stabbed. "What then, hmm?!"

I stepped down from the truck and walked towards the back. I must have startled Colin because he recoiled, thinking perhaps I was coming for him. He was lucky I was not. Instead, I was in search of a plan... a surprise or something. An advantage. Owen was right, we were as good as dead.

Their eyes were on me as I rummaged through the pickup bed. I turned over empty beer bottles and beef jerky wrappers that littered the back and were like packing peanuts for the body at the center.

"You're a damn slob dude," I yelled to Owen as I tossed aside the rubbish.

I rested my arm against the rail of the truck, scanning for options in the mess where there appeared to be none. There were a couple of golf balls rolling around and a Wiffle bat hidden beneath the trash, which I pushed away. In the corner there was a coiled rope that looked like one we had used to ascend Mount Lincoln two years before on a damp September morning. I stared at the rope for a long second. I had an idea, but not a good one.

The Veil

"Hit the lights!"

Owen shut the headlights off as the truck eased to a stop behind a leaning jack pine. The bog we had pulled into was cast in the coopery glow of the northern night sky. All the open space held a kind of agrarian light that made the outline of objects clear. Colin had urged us not to go directly to Lake Osworth because he thought we needed distance between us for my plan to work. He was right.

"Owen you're going to go with Colin. Collette you're going to come with me—"

"Hold up! No she's not!" Colin barked, his face holding only distrust and disdain.

"You're wrong, she is going with me and you are going with Owen. I don't trust you two together to see this through. This way, you'll both be motivated to see that this ends well for everyone." I made clear, opening the passenger side door and stepping down. "Come on."

I went to the back of the truck as the other doors crept ajar and the rest of the group edged down from their seats. The peat of the bog was soft, having little integrity to keep us from sinking several inches when we moved over it. This observation concerned me a great deal, because I did not think I could run for my life on such a surface. Though running for my life, might not be a possibility considering what would be chasing me.

"Where is the lake from here?" Owen asked, looking out into the wild.

"Just on the other side of that pine ridge over there. Probably three-quarters of a mile. The lake's southern shore will be a stone's throw from there." Colin directed with pointed hand gestures.

"Is that too far? I mean if we need to high-tail it out of there?"Owen pushed.

No one answered for a few moments, probably because we were all thinking the same thing— that it was pretty far.

"It's just far enough. Far enough to give us the advantage and close enough if we end up running for our lives," I stated as confidently as I could without it being obvious that I was lying.

"Alright, before we do this... um, let's make sure we're good." I cleared my throat and tried to focus. "Collette and I will take the body—"

"How the hell are we going to carry a body all the way over there? Even if we could, there is no chance we are going to be quiet doing it. Anything waiting for us over there is going to hear us coming," argued Collette.

She was right.

"You're right. Okay... okay, ah fuck it! I say we forget trying to spread out and just gun this thing up there," I slapped the side of the truck. "He knows we're coming, probably knows where we are right now. We know what needs to get done and we have a plan once we're in the thick of it. Let's just do this."

Even as I was saying it, I knew improvising on the fly was a death sentence for someone. I liked none of my options.

Colin projected from somewhere in the dark, "if we drive there, we put all of us at risk because we will all be together. We also put the truck in jeopardy. What the hell are we going to do if the truck gets screwed up? We are in the middle of nowhere!"

Just then, off in the direction we were to be heading, a jet of flame shot up over the trees and smoke began to swell from the pine ridge.

"What just happened?" Owen yelled, his frame a dark shadow embroiled by the flames pouring into the sky in front of us.

As it had before, the ground beneath my feet stretched away from me, running towards an absent space, somewhere distant. Everything around me hung in suspension. The world spun about my head, leaving a crimson haze. My legs shook uncontrollably and gave way, sending me to the spongy wet floor of the bog. Stabbing, pulsing pains pierced my skull and I began to taste the salty warmth of my own blood dripping into my mouth.

Uncle Warren's voice— gruff and callous —was all I heard as it thundered in my head.

"Benjamin, welcome to my home. You have come far. Now come just a little further. I have shown you the way. Go into the smoke and there you will find the answers to all of your questions."

His words held a luring comfort, a sense of warmth that I didn't want to accept, but their pull was strong. I felt in his words the embrace of my mother as I was boarding the school bus and my father's hand tousling my hair after playing catch on a Sunday afternoon. His words were hollow but they still tugged at me and drove me towards the flames pouring above the pines.

Reality snapped back into focus.

"We go into the fire!" I exclaimed, getting into the driver's seat of the truck and firing the engine with the keys Owen had left in the ignition.

Owen jumped in beside me, his eyes wide and wily.

"Fuck man, this shit just got real. Let's go get your woman!"

I half expected him to yell "Yeehaw" and slap me on the back.

"You two coming?" I asked, looking at Colin and Collette, who were both captivated by the flames boiling out from the forest. "I know where I am going. I don't need you two to come."

Colin gave me a passing glance as if all the things he had charged me with had been absolved.

"No way," Colin stated, his eyes fixated on the waves of orange and yellow beginning to spread across the pines. "There is an evil burning inside there."

"We'll help," Collette said, tugging on Colin's arm. "Both of us!"

Colin did not protest, but simply nodded. For all his harsh words and hesitancy, the sight of the fire and the guiding words of Collette steered him into risking his life to get Megan back.

"We have to stay near the lake. There is less to burn there," Colin said, grabbing Collette by the waist and hoisting her into the back of the truck before joining her.

I forced the truck into reverse and accelerated backwards towards the road. The soft ground of the bog was flung forward and the truck slid from side to side at the start, but I corrected its position. Once I felt firm ground beneath the tires, I put the truck into drive and compelled us forward into the angry fire bursting into the black sky.

Colin gave me terse directions in short, tense sentences that pushed us further into the smoke. My stomach turned sour as the smoke became a thick, dense fog that surrounded us and began to seep into the truck cabin. I started to cough followed by Owen and the others.

"Damn it, I can't breathe," Owen coughed, pulling his shirt over his face.

Collette started screaming about her eyes burning and Colin started to gag. I didn't care, I knew the lake was in front of us. If I could just get us close enough.

The smoke was suffocating. I sped up over a small embankment between two small birch trees and the truck left the ground for a moment. We landed and were propelled around a cluster of evergreen trees into a small clearing where the smoke seemed to thin out.

I didn't see the lake until we began to accelerate down a narrow decline and by the time I applied the brakes, the loose sand of the beach sank beneath the tires. We lurched and wobbled towards the water. I jerked the wheel to correct our lean and the front of the truck whipped out of the water while the rear end sank deeper into the water. The action seemed to create a back current pulling the truck into the lake.

I pressed on the accelerator and heard the tires whirl. We did not move. The truck floated there in the water of Lake Osworth until the engine died.

"We need to get out of here— NOW!" I yelled, fumbling with the lock on the door.

The truck drifted backwards in the water until it fell to the bottom of the lake. We were fully submerged when water began to seep through the cracks around the door and the truck's ventilation system. It started as a trickle but hastened to a gush. The pressure building against the windows was incredible; I could hear the glass creaking behind the pending ambush of the uncountable gallons trying to force their way through.

I finally found the lock after a frantic search, but the door would not budge as I pushed against it. Owen was trying to force the door open by pushing off the dashboard with his legs and thrusting backwards against the door. That did not work either. As I was ramming my shoulder against the door for a second time, I caught a glimpse of Colin and Collette kicking at the back window trying to break the seal of our aquatic tomb. None of us were successful.

My hands felt the floor in desperate pursuit of something to break the glass. My fingers ran through carpet hairs, but came up empty. I then remembered that I had my father's knife and even in the panic of the moment, I shook my head in disgust. How could I have forgotten something so obvious? The butt of the handle of my Dad's knife was raised to a point.

I pressed the hilt into the palm of my left hand and looked at Owen, who was driving his shoulder into the unyielding door like a battering ram. Owen saw the knife in my hand and gave me the unspoken permission to break his window with a whimsical, frantic smile that he forced across his face.

With a quick stabbing motion, I turned my face away and drove the bottom of the knife into the glass. At once, the glass imploded and a thousand shards came screaming at me, chased by a torrent of cold mountain water. It did not take long before the cabin was full and there were bodies floating about, clamoring to escape.

I was the first to get out. I pulled myself through the window, pumping my feet and paddling my arms like a frog the way my mother taught me when I was a boy. When I was out of the car, I swam until my lungs clutched and screamed for air. The water stifled me and was a shade of translucent gray that whispered only secrets of death. I forced myself out of the water, by crawling through shallower water to shore, delirious as to my exact location.

I collapsed to catch my breath on the same sand on which I was born and its coarse texture rubbed against my cheek. My lungs sucked down on air until they stopped burning. There was a sound of something splashing in the water behind me and I rolled onto my back to see who it was.

"Yes, sir. That'll get your motor running!" He gasped as he spat water from his mouth. His hands were on his hips and the look on his face was one of pure disconcertion. The last few minutes came without warning.

"Where's Colin? Collette?" Owen asked, scanning the water around him and the site of his sunken truck.

Not a second later, Colin stumbled from the lake with Collette in his arms.

"She's not breathing!" He yelled, running from the water and laying Collette onto the sand. Her lips were blue and her face was pale and her body limp.

Colin tilted her head back, pinched her nose and breathed into her mouth with desperate intention. He gave three breathes and then compressed her sternum in forceful downward thrusts that made her soaked, frail body crest and trough. Colin's movement was piston-like, up and down with focused, surgical precision. He transitioned from pumping to mouth-to-mouth and then back again in a tireless effort. Minutes had gone by. Owen and I shared a fearful glance. She was dead. We both thought it, our faces told our thoughts.

I walked over to Colin and placed my hand softly on his shoulder. "I think she's gone!" I heard myself say as I gently squeezed his arm. I realized this was the worst thing I could ever say to someone trying to revive his love. It was giving him permission to quit on her. But Colin did not quit.

He ignored my words and continued, pressing in for one more mouth-to-mouth to foment Collette to life. His lips extended around hers and I watched as he exhaled. Collette's body convulsed and, miraculously, awakened. Her body sat up almost on instinct and coughed for a minute, water running from her mouth. She stopped coughing and looked up at Colin.

The next words heard were not from Collette.

"Ben! Help Me! Please!"

Megan's pleas came from behind the curtain of flames engulfing the forest above the beach. A shutter of elation ran through me as I ran toward the fire.

"Megan, I'm here! Where are you?" I yelled, scanning the orange blaze.

"I'm over here!" Her voice came through the crackling fire as a limp echo just as a large flaming pine tree tumbled to the ground, throwing up a mist of sparks and dust. I turned away to shield my face as the flames roared.

"Megan?" I shouted, trying to listen for her tender voice over the crashing conflagration. I heard nothing. "Megan?" I retried.

I waited for a response, but one did not come. I turned to Owen for help, but he only returned my look of helplessness.

"Over there!" Colin spat in a half-startled voice.

He was pointing to a bracken of broken bushes that had collapsed into ash from being set ablaze. Standing behind the broken fragment of char was Megan, her body a visible shamble. She was terrified. Blood was smeared across her forehead.

"Ben," she whimpered, slanting her head and holding open her arms. She wanted me to go to her, to hold her, to save her.

I was uncertain. I wanted nothing more than to go to her, but I knew I had entered the lion's den and he was near. I knew he was lurking just out of sight, though if all that Malcolm had said was accurate none of it would have mattered. I asked myself that if Beslemeks were real and if Uncle Warren was one, why was he hiding? He could kill all of us without any issue. All he would simply have to do was come across the veil as Malcolm had called it.

Despite my concern, I ran to her. After all, reason cannot outlast love. My body was trembling as I got closer and I could see more clearly her distraught-soaked beauty.

I ran through the bracken and at once threw my arms around her.

"I'm here! I'm here!"

I pulled her close into me and kissed her head as if I had not touched her in a lifetime. I didn't care what was about to come. I only cared that I had my Megan back. I had never wanted to hold someone forever until I wrapped my arms around her and replayed in my memories the moment when we first shared a kiss. That night was magical and orchestrated by an invisible attraction that pushed us together. I did not know it then, but the attraction that pushed us together was love— true love...

"True love. That is what this is all about!" I muttered, slowly rising to my feet as the truth of why I was here began to sink in.

"What did you say?" Colin asked as he and Collette watched me from a few feet away. Owen was sitting on the sand, mesmerized by something in the distance.

"BEN, BEHIND YOU!" Owen shouted, jumping to his feet and sprinting towards us with hands balled into tight fists.

A surge of fire behind us illuminated a silhouette moving in the flames. A figure was heading towards us. Before my eyes, Uncle Warren appeared from the flame unscathed and stood over us with a gotcha smirk.

"You are filled with true stupidity Benjamin Fisher. If you at all understood the ramifications of you being here, you would have never come!" He let out a laugh and shook his head.

I stood up, placing myself between Megan and Warren.

"We have brought her back. That was the deal. Megan for her!"

"You have complied with the first part of our deal, yes. Yet, you failed to ask about the second part of our deal— not that it really is a deal. Everything I need is now right here. After twenty-two years, everything has fallen into perfect alignment. Do you want the answer to the question racing through your head right now?" Uncle Warren queried.

"And what question is that?" I asked, fearing his response.

"Why you and your friends are still alive!"

He knew what I was thinking. I looked around at everyone else. There were looks of sheer dread on Colin and Owens' faces, but Collette's face held no such trepidation. That was odd.

"You need not worry, son."

The gruff and shrill voice that I had come to know as belonging to Uncle Warren began to morph into a familiar voice. A voice I thought I would never hear again. Then before my eyes, Uncle Warren's frame and features began to mold themselves into a new shape, into a new person. After a few moments, I was staring at my father with every feature exact, down to the strains of hair and wrinkles on his face.

"Oh my God!" I gasped.

"You see, I am going to kill you all, but opportunities like this are so rare. You see Benjamin, you are special. You are different from any other of your species. How you wonder? Before you die tonight and liberate me and my kind, you shall learn why you are here," Uncle Warren stated, appearing as my father.

He continued, "We were created long ago as nature's greatest hunter and we were given the gift of refuge to shield our true

306

identity. Since the formation of life, we have been trapped in a world different from your own. We can interact with your world, but we cannot fully access it—"

"You mean you can't kill us wherever you wish. You are trapped for a reason. Trapped here. Your species is too weak to flourish and you are not without limitations!" I contended while trying to catch the attention of the others.

"You are insufferable. Your father was just like you. Both of you not knowing when you've lost," Uncle Warren sneered, stepping toward me. "You are about to die. All of you, even the small one that grows inside her. Do you wish to jump right to it? Do you really want the killing to begin?"

His words took me by surprise. I looked down at Megan and for a moment, we shared an intimate, knowing glance. Choices. We had very few.

"By all means, continue. Tell me everything," I shot back. My eyes met Owen's and he nodded. Time was a scarce resource.

"Do you think that I do not know that you all are planning to scurry off like rodents? Rest assured, you all can run. A challenge is what I have craved for quite some time," my father's doppelganger seethed before his body morphed again, into my mother.

"My baby boy, come to Momma. Give me a kiss!" My mother screeched in her voice, her tongue writhing from her mouth like an uncontrolled fleshy snake.

An evil laugh cut through the night and Uncle Warren formed out of the morphing flesh of my mother's figure. It was not her, I kept telling myself.

"Why the hell am I here?" I yelled.

I was done being toyed with.

"My you are no fun, but fine, if you must really know. You know the significance of this place— of Osworth. It is one of a few places that allows us to move from the higher world to your lower world. I am one of a superior being that views humans like all other animals. You are food!. They were meant to be eaten. Until you came along. Right over there," Uncle Warren pointed to a small patch of beach a few yards away, just above the lake. "That is where you were born. Do you know the significance of that? Of your birth here?"

"Other than you killing my sister right there and the two-decade long nightmare that you caused my parents, I do not. Enlighten me, asshole." I barked, feeling by body tense with nerves and rage. This thing killed my family.

"How many times has it happened? You know, when the world seems to stretch away from you. How many times has your world been altered?" Uncle Warren smirked.

Megan looked up at me with fearful eyes. She knew what he meant. How many times had it been? Too many.

"Awww, she knows. The reason that you experience these episodes is because you were born here. You represent the only living thing to have ever been born here. When you took your first breath, a part of this place became part of you. By being born here, you became the only thing that can see beyond your own world and into mine. You bleed, you breathe, and you can move freely as you wish. You see, you are the only thing in history to be able to move freely between the higher world and the lower. Don't you get it? You can see behind the veil and you can hunt my species. You have the ability to enter my world, but you don't yet know how to access it. My species cannot do this... yet. That is why you are here. Your blood and your flesh, can remove the barrier that restrains us. By eating you, you become part of us and with that, we can hunt anywhere. There will be no more safe havens to hide. We will be released from our shackles and the universe will be ours." Uncle Warren roared.

"The hubris you maintain will be the death of your species. You think that your only limitation is your inability to access my world anywhere you wish, but it's not. Your arrogance will be your downfall. I may die tonight. We may all die tonight, but one thing I will guarantee is that before I go, I will kill you first. It's going to happen," I spat with defiance, my blood coursing through my veins and all I heard was the rapid beat of my heart.

I inhaled a breath of thick smoke from the burning timberland surrounding us. I had become so focused on Uncle Warren that the environment and the danger it held had been shut out from my thoughts. There was fire everywhere.

"Strong words. I am excited. You're excited. Your friends don't look so excited, though. That is unfortunate. But in all this excitement, did you forget something?"

There was a sudden appearance of another thing to the right of Uncle Warren. It resembled an aged woman with a wicked scowl that stretched across her slack leathery skin. Unlike the creature I had taken from Malcolm's torture chamber, the creature I was staring at was now whole. There were no more missing limbs and her face was no longer caved in. My nightmare had crumpled into a black hole of despair, where not even hope could escape. How had I forgotten about her? The odds were not ever in my favor.

"Why have you waited so long to get to this point? It makes no sense. Why have you waited?" I pressed.

Uncle Warren looked at me with curiosity.

I continued, "It seems pretty clear that we cannot win. We could never win. Not my parents, not Malcolm, not us now. Yet, still you waited for this moment. Why?"

"Despite your inabilities to kill us, you have always been able to trap us. When Malcolm captured her," Uncle Warren was referring to the now whole creature beside him, "he proved that much. We are not invulnerable. So I needed an insurance policy—"

He paused and I looked around at everyone else. They were unblinking as they watched Uncle Warren. Colin and Owen were behind me rigid and still; Megan was fused to my side by my relentless grip on her. Where was Collette?

"And that was?" I asked, fearing the answer.

"YOUR SISTER!!"

I heard two gunshots behind me and when I turned, both Owen and Colin were on the ground, blood gushing from their stomachs. My eyes rose to the shooter and staring back at me was Collette with a revolver pointed at Owen. I suddenly knew why she had looked so familiar…

The Tears of Fate

"A family reunion!" Uncle Warren squealed with malevolence. "Well Ben, say hello."

I was dumbfounded. What the hell just happened?

"You shot us! You fucking shot us!" Colin forced out through gritted teeth as he tried to pull himself up an overturned tree that was burning at its tip.

"Shhh, you're bleeding. You mustn't die yet. Mother does not want dead meat." Collette said through a broad smile, walking closer to Colin and Owen with the revolver in her hand.

"What are you talking about? Collette, stop it! Please!" Colin begged as his lover stalked him.

"Don't call me that! My name is Grace! I was once Ben's sister. But no more. Not since, I was left here to die. Now be quiet! Mother needs to eat. She is so hungry. It has been much too long since she ate!"

The words had no sooner faded into the backdrop of time when a massive flesh-colored creature appeared at Colin's feet, writhing towards him in a sinuous pattern. As the creature came, my vision projected from me and the world I perceived was different in every direction. Somehow, I could see out of my body as if stairs had appeared in front of me that could take me out of the space that I resided in, but without physically moving from where I stood. I could see the fourth dimension without that feeling— the feeling that the world was falling away from me. At once, I could see everything around me with much greater clarity and in an entirely new light. Everything in my purview held an extra attribute to it.

I could see into my friends' bodies, and felt that if I reached out, I could touch their hearts, their lungs, their brains. The fire that was burning around us vanished in the fourth dimension, not even a plume of smoke made it across the clear and present barrier—the veil.

It was then that I saw the two creatures on the sides of me and their intimidating statures befit only one name.... Beslemek. The eater of men, the eater of life. Their bodies were tubular and wrapped in a coarse flesh that resembled the skin of a reptile. Their extended tubular shapes merged into something that looked like a bursting burlap sack twice the size of an elephant and seeped with a sticky brown mucous. I imagined that this was the creature's torso. About a third the way down its torso, there was a barbed appendage that protruded into the lower dimensions. Dangling from this appendage was something of human form. I knew it was not a real person, but it resembled one in so many ways. On the one side of me, the barbed appendage looked like Uncle Warren. It was now clear that he, rather it, was only a decoy and the true terror existed in the fourth dimension. Malcolm had told me this— repeatedly —but seeing their huge mass and smelling the foul, rotten odor that came from the mucous oozing from their bodies brought it home.

"We waited this long so that we could train your sister. It took some time, but I got her to see us as her true parents. Once she saw me as her father, I held no fear that I would be captured. I had no fear that you would run from my grasp because you can't hide from her. She is not limited like we are. Grace has shown herself invaluable as of late. Like right now, she has brought food for us to eat," Uncle Warren revealed, his human figure staring at me from the lower dimension and what I could only surmise was the face of the creature, which held no apparent eyes or mechanism for sight was facing me.

I took an inventory of the carnage and the dire state we were in.

Owen was on the ground unmoving, but alive. I could see his heart beating with my new sight. Colin was alive, but his pulse was slowing amid considerable blood loss. Megan had not relented in her grip of me; I pulled her tighter.

"Eat!" Uncle Warren barked out.

We all watched in horror as the creature at Colin's feet revealed a gigantic mouth with hundreds of jagged teeth rotating in a spiral. I thought of a wood-chipper and as much as I wanted to, I could not turn away.

"NO! PLEASE GOD NO!" Colin screamed, trying to escape up the charred remains of the crashed tree behind him.

In one rapid movement, the creature snapped forward taking Colin's feet into its mouth and in an instant of bone-chilling screams Colin was sucked into the creature. He was gone. I watched my friend die. I witnessed as he disappeared while screaming for help. It left nothing. All that remained of him was a red mist that hung in the air like a fog, before falling to the earth like a red rain.

I could not believe what I had just seen. I turned to Megan and watched as her face grew ghostly white and she slumped to the ground, unconscious.

"Eat more!" Grace urged.

"Yes, EAT!" Uncle Warren ordered.

My heart sank. I knew what they meant— Owen. I could not let him die.

"NO! Take me instead!" I yelled.

"Not yet. First him, then her and then you!" Grace declared.

"Fine, but wait just a second," I stalled. "Is it true that you're my sister?"

"No. I am not your sister. She died the day you were born. The day I was born. I was left here to die, but I found life. I have waited ages to see you die in these woods as I was left to." Grace seethed.

"Grace, Stop! You are my sister. My blood. Mom and dad loved you. Years after you were gone, they cried and mourned you. I remember seeing Mom cry for what I thought was no reason. When I asked her, she just said she missed someone. She missed you. And every February 18th, Dad took Mom and I out for cake and ice cream. Always. I never understood why until now. That was the day you were born. He wanted us to celebrate your birthday," I pleaded with her, hoping she held some power over the Beslemeks. I hoped she held even the tiniest bit of my parents left in her heart.

She paused, looking at me. For a fleeting instant, I saw my sister in her eyes. I saw the woman who grieved and was hurt and wanted to be comforted. Had she ever known comfort since that fateful day?

What I thought I had seen in her eyes faded away and her eyes again grew callous and cold, like those of a shark, of a predator.

"February 18th is my birthday?"

I heard Grace say this as the Beslemek that ate Colin raised itself from the lower dimensions and reinserted itself beyond the veil. I watched the creature move to where Owen was lying motionless on the ground and I grew frantic. He was my best friend. I had to save him.

I found myself sprinting towards him, my legs like wheels driving themselves. The events that came next came in rapid succession and it started when my hand slid to my lower back to grasp the handle of the knife that was there. The Beslemek reentered the lower dimension at Owen's feet and I watched as it opened its mouth again, revealing rows of sharp teeth. It lurched towards him and as it did, I leapt at its mouth, sinking the blade— my father's blade— into its flesh. I ripped the knife down the creature's body until it came out, its skin peeled away and the Beslemek made a high-pitched hiss.

It stopped short and turned towards me, as if trying to stare at me with its eyeless face. I gave it no time before I sank the blade into its body a second time and then a third. The Beslemek began to tremble as thick bile began to seep from its wounds. I was hurting it. I ripped the blade from its flesh and began to hack at it in short, vicious strikes that made the blade repeatedly disappear to the hilt. My hands were covered in a slick fluid that smelled of rotting onions. The creature stumbled and fell to the ground. It was hurt.

Suddenly, Uncle Warren appeared next me in his truest form— the monster. There were rows of razors whirling about that screamed towards me. He moved with the purpose of vengeance.

He snapped at me with his mouth and when it was inches away from tearing a hole in me, I dove out of the way, pulling the knife from the other Beslemek. I grabbed Owen by one of his ankles and dragged him over to Megan, who remained unconscious on the earthy floor.

From the short distance away, I watched as Uncle Warren reemerged as the being that had killed my parents. I watched Uncle Warren approach his wounded mate and look over the damage.

"Do you know how I killed your parents?" Uncle Warren seethed, before proceeding. "I reached into their bodies while they drove and just stopped their hearts. That's all it took, a little squeeze and your bitch of a mother was dead. I took extra pleasure in ending that pathetic thing you called a father. What a disgusting mess they were. So you know, I'm going to take pleasure in eating these bonebags that you call friends. You will watch and then I'm going to drain you of your blood."

Uncle Warren vanished again behind the veil and charged towards me at an uncompromising pace. He was coming for Owen and Megan.

I slapped Owen on the cheek, "hey ass clown wake up. We've got to go. Megan, honey, wake up." I shook her, trying to rustle her awake.

Megan stirred and looked up at me, dazed and delirious. I smiled at her in a panicked, deluded way that tried not to show how scared I was.

"We've got to move!" I forced out, pulling her up and simultaneously kicking Owen. "Owen, you bastard, wake the fuck up. Come on, man!"

I turned around and walked into a revolver aimed at me. Grace, my sister, pressed it into my chest. She was rattled and conflicted; I could see it in her eyes— my Mom's eyes. Megan stood behind me, not sure of what to do.

"Wake Owen, whatever it takes," I told her while not turning away from Grace. "You don't have to do this. You don't.

You can live a normal life. I'll help you. Let's just leave. All of us. Together."

Uncle Warren reappeared at Megan's feet and at once, he rushed towards her in an angry torrent of whirling teeth. I lunged at him with my blade outstretched, trying to cut and kill him. The Beslemek turned directions when I lunged and it snapped at me, striking me in the arm with its body. I was knocked backwards as if a large, angry man had punched me. It rammed me in the chest with its head and I fell to the ground. I knew at that moment, it did not want me dead, at least not yet. It was trying to wear me down, weaken me.

The creature disappeared again and Uncle Warren emerged over me. His hands clutched my throat and I fought to get them off. But I could not overpower him. His grip was relentless and as I began to lose consciousness, I caught a glimpse of the night sky flecked with thousands of far-off lanterns and I thought about how long it took for their shining light to traverse the heavens. And then I thought about my parents. I wondered if they were traversing the endless space above and if they were watching me die. The heavens, what a creation.

As I began to fade, I thought of Megan and Owen.

"NO," I yelled, burying the knife into Uncle Warren's side, but his grip only grew stronger and he leaned into me.

"Soon your blood will run through me and I will be free from this prison. You should know that the first people I am going to eat are the ones that you hold dearest. Well, the ones that are left. I am going to rid you from history, you little mistake," Uncle Warren roared with triumph.

A shot screeched from above me and suddenly Uncle Warren's grip loosened enough for me to break free. I yanked the knife from his side and scurried to my feet. It was to my shock that I saw Megan holding the gun and Grace was on the ground, clutching her arm.

"Hey, you! Yeah, you!" Megan shouted at Uncle Warren. "Watch this!"

She marched over to the Beslemek on the ground, which had begun to twist in a show of apparent strength. She fired two shots into its body, below where I had attacked it. The creature howled out in pain and fell back to the ground where it stopped moving.

There was a silence that held in the air for a moment before it was broken again by Megan.

"Ben, I love you and I'm sorry for this. I really am! But it is the only way we have a chance. We must remove the uncertainty." She choked out through tears streaming down her dirt-smeared face.

She raised the revolver and with the last bullet banked in the chamber, Megan shot Grace in the head, killing my sister.

"Now let's kill this thing!" Megan howled through a quivering lip and tears. Her body convulsed and she vomited through a cacophony of unhealthy sounds.

I stared in awe at the body of a sister that seventy-two hours before did not exist. It was an unbelievable lie that had been hidden from me since the day I was born. The ground on which I sat was the very ground where I took my first breath and as I sat looking into my sister's eyes, lifeless and gone— my mother's eyes— I didn't know how to feel. She was my sister in blood and I saw glimpses of my family in her, but her life had been stolen from her. She was not my sister in heart. It had been twenty-two years since she was first thought dead, appearing to die on the same heap of earth where her life would actually end. Her life was never her own. How much of my family had to die for me?

I rolled onto my side and then onto my knee, my eyes stalked Uncle Warren as I waited for him to rise up. This had to end.

Uncle Warren lay face down; the gnarled flesh of the top of his head was all that I could see. Then, out of the silence of his still frame came a roar that started as a rumble and escalated into a seething boom that shook the ground. Uncle Warren raised himself from the dirt and began to walk towards me with a deliberate pace. His steps were not hastened or extended, but forward in as straight a line as there could ever be and I was in his path.

"They're dead!" I yelled through an angry, jaw-clenched grin. "Life's a bitch. Welcome to the club!"

His hands came at me like talons, ripping at my face and stomach. The strikes were surgical and vicious, striking my face and body and causing me to bleed. Blood began to run over my mouth and down my chest. Uncle Warren did not stop once I was bleeding and I could do nothing to stop him. My attempts to defend myself were futile; the knife I held failed to slow his assault.

My mind was racing to find a solution as with each strike I moved closer to death. Then it hit me— the vial from Malcolm's basement. That's what I needed.

"It's time!" Uncle Warren declared, stopping his attack and then retreating a few feet away from me.

I fell to a knee, my hands rising to my face. It all happened so quickly. Too quickly! I never had a chance. My hands were coated in crimson and my body hurt. My face had been ripped apart. I could feel the lacerations and cuts across my face and abdomen. To Megan I thought that I probably wore a mask of blood.

"Gonna be straight with you asshole. I'm hurting!" I coughed out, as I wiped blood from my face. I suddenly found myself giggling, as if staring death in the face was a comical experience. I staggered to my feet while reaching for the vial in my back pocket... empty. I began to panic. Where was it?

Warren was silent and then vanished behind the veil. When he crossed, I could see across the veil again and I knew it was only a matter of seconds before he would be back in his true form.

Megan ran towards me and threw her arms around my waist. Her grip was strong, unyielding and with it, I was back in D.C, kissing her beneath a brilliant star-filled sky. For a few transitory moments, our bodies were pressed together and I lost myself in the fiery jade of her eyes. The eyes that had captured my heart. Was this the last time that I would look into them? I caressed her body and then my hand stopped at her stomach. I pressed against her softly.

"You think it's true?" I asked, wondering about the suggestion Warren had made earlier.

"I do!" Megan cried, tears rolling down her face.

I kissed her forehead and pressed her head against my chest.

"Christ!" Owen hollered, his eyes open and suddenly aware of the gunshot he was wearing. He pulled himself up, scanning the scene. "Oh shit! What the hell went down here?"

Even in perilous moments, Owen could make me laugh.

"Glad you could join us. Now, you two need to get the hell out of here. We have no time!" I ordered, guiding Megan over to Owen. "Help Owen get to the road. I will be right behind. Promise!"

"No!" Owen and Megan shouted back in unison.

"Yes! This isn't a debate. I think I know how to kill Uncle Warren. He might be able to do a lot of things, but he can't be in two places at once. You both need to leave. It's the only way. Go!"

They did not budge.

Uncle Warren came back across the veil and charged me as a muddied, serpentine creature dripping of a vile slime. His mouth showcased jagged rows of teeth that spiraled towards us with lethal intent.

"Run!" I screamed.

I grabbed Megan by the hand and we took off. I caught Owen trying to follow, but he was unable to run. He hobbled a few yards and then fell to the ground. Warren was giving chase and closing in on him.

I turned back, leaving Megan alone. I made it to Owen just as Warren lunged for him. Warren's mouth whirled by us a half-second after I pulled Owen out of the way. Somehow, despite the blood running from my body, I felt strong. I threw Owen over my shoulder and ran to where I left Megan. I heard the crushing of dried leaves and the snapping of branches behind me; Warren was in pursuit.

My body rushed with adrenaline as I hurdled fallen logs and maneuvered uneven terrain, trying to flee the Beslemek at my heels. I saw Megan and yelled for her to run. She did. We ran for what felt like minutes, watching for any sign of a road or a way out of the hellhole of Osworth.

We ran until I could not run anymore. We stopped to catch our breath, but knew we had to keep moving. Uncle Warren was behind us somewhere, or in front of us, we didn't know. Running from a creature that could move in and out of our dimension was like a goldfish trying to escape the paw of a hungry cat. The adrenaline that had been coursing through my body had faded twenty yards back and my body was trembling in a way it hadn't before. I had lost a lot of blood and I did not have the strength to carry Owen any longer. I dropped him on the ground and collapsed, placing my head against the ground. My vision was fading out of focus.

I could smell the stale earth from the decaying leaves beneath my cheek. They felt dry and rough, but a comfortable place to rest my head. My eyelids grew heavy. My breathing slowed. A few minutes of rest were all I needed.

As my eyes closed, a hand shook me awake with a violent jolt.

"Not happening. You're not going to sleep. Get up, Ben! Get up," Owen demanded, jostling my body back and forth across the hard forest floor.

I turned towards him and looked up into his face. Megan was standing above him with concern stitched across hers. My head jogged a little bit as I tried to wake myself. The trees above me were no longer in flames and no longer resembled trees, but instead were smoldering spears standing crooked in the ground. The smoke that they emitted rose upwards and gradually vanished into the backdrop of the tiny lanterns in the clear black sky. I couldn't let myself die. The Beslemeks had taken so much from me, but I couldn't let them take anymore. Somewhere in the reservoir of my mind, I found the last drops of strength and I sat up, breathing in the mountain air that filled this place.

"Let's go." I forced out while struggling to my feet.

My foot stepped on a small, glass cylinder holding a brown-yellow liquid. I recognized it as the vial from Malcolm's laboratory and the one for which I had been searching. I picked it up. I strained to think how it might of ended up here, but I found no explanation and I really didn't need one. So many of life's turns had been against me, maybe this was one that was for me.

We were off again, trekking through the forest and searching for a way out of this terrible nightmare. But it was too quiet, the panting of labored breaths and rustling leaves were the only soundtrack playing. The quiet was unsettling and just as the thought crossed my mind, a sound I was becoming acquainted with filled the absence. Warren slithered from the empty space in front of us, his writhing tubular frame descending towards us without compromise. I had no opportunity to jump out of the way, but somehow, thankfully, I had the wherewithal to push Megan and Owen from his whirling jaws.

Warren's body whipped me in the chest and I was flipped into the air, landing on top of him. My hands clutched the mucous-coated, foul-smelling folds of flesh that rippled beneath me as the Beslemek bucked and jerked trying to throw me off. It was not a place I wanted to be.

A voice bellowed from inside the Beslemek, loud and audible, "After all these years, the time to be free is here!"

Warren made a sudden lunge and a crackling sound shook my body as a shockwave overtook my body and rocked me backwards. With the sound, the three-dimensional world that surrounded me broke down into pieces of diminishing material like the fading light of dying fireworks and what filled the void was a world expanded in directions that my mind strained to comprehend. Though my body did not feel much different, I knew Warren had crossed the veil and taken me with him. I had been taken out of my world and placed into one I could hardly fathom. Reality stretched forth and sideways, in and out. From here, I could see Megan and Owen frantically investigating where I had disappeared to and I could hear them screaming for me.

Warren bucked hard and twisted abruptly, throwing me from him and onto the ground. But I was not thrown to the forest floor as I had expected, but instead I was dumped into a puddle of water a few inches deep and several feet wide. The water had collected in a shallow hole that was carved into a sand dune. Wherever I was, it was not Osworth anymore.

The landscape had changed drastically. Osworth had been a mountainous terrain— leaf-covered earth hidden beneath towering pines and crooked birch trees that surrounded a glasslike lake that reflected off-distant peaks. The place I ended up was somewhere I had never seen before. The land was an outstretched checkerboard of dark shaded puddles like the one I was lying in and dry, burnt patches of sand beneath a scorching light that seared my skin when I placed my hands beneath it.

Moments before I was thrown from Warren's back, I could see Osworth and Megan and Owen, but now I could see as I always had. I could see the ground beneath my feet. I looked up into the sky expecting a roaring sun but found a patchwork sky filled with alternating depths of shade and brilliant orbs of bold light. The sky held a thousand suns.

I pulled myself up and looked around for Warren. Off in the distance, there was a silhouette, moving towards me. The figure was not of material substance, but instead a dark void that seemed to float above the ground. Staring into its body, I realized I was staring into a secret of the universe. It stopped and in my mind, I heard it speak.

"They come for you now Benjamin Fisher. This is the end. Use your father's blade, coat it with the substance of the vial. The one you thought had been killed will come first, behind you. Be swift with the swing. Strike the head just behind the mouth. Then turn to your left and sink the blade as far as it will go. That will end the second- the one you call Warren. Follow these instructions exactly. It happens now."

The voided figure was gone and as I digested the words, the patch of sand behind me began to rattle. From the grains of loose sand, a familiar brown, tubular body rose up and I was staring, again, at rows of razor sharp teeth that were spinning.

I hesitated, but then did as the voided figure had instructed. I pulled the knife from my waist and with my free hand, pulled the vial from my pocket and unscrewed the cap with two fingers. I flipped the vial over and ran it along the length of the blade, then coated both sides using the palm of my hand. At once, an itching, burning pain injected itself into my hand and began to spread up my arm.

The Beslemek lunged at me and I pivoted myself enough for it to miss me. I swung the blade and struck it in the head just behind the mouth. As I felt the full force of the sharpened blade sink into the Beslemek, the sky of a thousand suns began to dim into pure darkness. A shrill screech cut through the black and I knew for certain that this time the Beslemek was dead. I felt its body, even the subtlest of vibrations, cease movement and it collapsed to the ground.

I could not see in the dark, so I trusted the words of the figure and my own sense to protect me against what I believed was a coming attack. I turned to my left, squeezing my father's blade in anticipation of ending this nightmare. A sound, so faint, was born in the dark. It came out like the soft ripple of a plastic bag in the wind. I lunged forward, throwing my weight into the source, but struck only air. I stabbed at random, swinging my arm in wild arcs trying to strike something.

A puff of humid aid condensed on the back of my neck and I knew Warren was behind me. A surge of pain exploded down my arm as something cut into me, tearing a piece of me from my arm. I spun around and threw the blade into the creature, striking its body somewhere that I hoped could kill it. The blade moved without resistance and my hand became coated in a hot, thick liquid. Warren was bleeding.

Warren thrashed, but I kept a firm grip on the handle and carved deeper into him. Everything that had been taken from me, every person that had perished, every lie reinforced since the day I was born, all of it was the result of this man— no, this thing.

As I felt Warren beginning to die, I thought of my parents and of how they only wanted to protect me. I thought about Grace and how her life was taken from her long before she died. I thought of Megan, the love of my life and how she now carried a life inside of her. A life I helped make, but a life I feared I would never be a part of. The realization that I might never see my own child started to grow inside my chest like an inflating balloon filled with hatred and rage.

"YOU NEVER DIE!" I screamed, tearing the blade from the creature and gripping it as hard as I could in both hands.

A labored, defiant laugh boomed back at me in the dark, "and never will. I have what I need."

A fleeting speculation halted my next action. Was it true, did Warren have what he needed? I thought of the sharp pain that ripped into my arm and recognized that he may have had what he needed.

In a moment of crystalline lucidity, standing there in the blackness, I could see. Warren was hovering beneath me, lethargic and wounded, his head bobbing back and forth in signs of diminishing life. The time had come to end it.

"Congratulations, now, it's my turn!" I howled, slamming the knife into the skull of the Beslemek and feeling the blade's tip power through the bone beneath. When the knife would go no farther, I twisted the blade and listened. There was a faint murmur, that dimmed and faded into a hush of pure silence and again the world was black to my eyes. At last, Warren was dead!

Legacy

Four years later

"I don't care Owen! I know the facts," Megan asserted as she switched the phone to her other hand and then remembering to keep her voice down. She stepped outside onto her patio and slid the glass door shut.

"I wasn't suggesting that you didn't. I am just saying that we can't keep doing this. He's gone," stated the voice on the other end with no hint of jest in his voice.

"That is unproven and until it is, I do not care what it takes. We will find him and bring him home. If he is gone, we will find his body and bury it. That is the least we can do."

There was a pause followed by a muffled sigh, "this weekend then?"

"Yes! Your parents will watch Carl Benjamin?"

"Of course, Bobbo loves that little booger. Alright, I have to go. I just hope that for once we find more than shadows in Osworth— something, anything."

Megan broke into laughter.

"What?" Owen asked. "What's so funny?"

"Nothing. I just think it's ironic that ever since that night when we were nearly killed like a dozen times, we have been complaining that nothing has happened. My how the times have changed."

"Yea, I sure miss having bullets pulled from my body and running for my life, trying to dodge interdimensional dragon-creatures. Not something I ever want to do again, but anyway I gotta run. Give CB some uncle love for me." Owen requested.

"You know you're not his actual uncle, right? You're his cousin." Megan reminded him.

"Ben was my brother, regardless of what my family tree says. That makes me an uncle to his son."

Megan smiled, "that's the truth. Owen, and one more thing before you go. Can you take a look at Carl Benjamin's baby monitor when you get a chance? I swear I keep hearing someone talking on it. My guess is that it's feedback."

"Hmm, interesting. Sure, I'll take a look when I get a chance. Bye kid," Owen hung up.

Megan walked back inside and was greeted by tiny shouts for "Mommy".

"I'm coming honey," Megan replied, while jogging up the stairs to her son's room.

She opened the door and danced into the room the way moms do, with overly animated gestures and the singing of silly songs. Greeting her from his crib was a fluffy-haired little boy with big, brown eyes and a mischievous, playful smile.

"Hee momma," the little boy squeaked as he began to jump up and down in his crib, his tiny hands gripping the railing like he was prepared to catapult himself from his bed and run down the hall a toddler possessed by wild imagination and untamed energy.

"How's Mommy's little man today?" Megan asked, reaching down into the crib and plucking her son from his bed. "Did you sleep well?"

She kissed him on the cheek and placed him on her hip as he wrapped his legs around her stomach.

"Is lov yu Momma!"

Megan let out a laugh and rubbed her nose against her son's, "I love you too sweetheart. Do you want to go watch TV while I get your breakfast?"

"Yes, Captin Crun?" Carl Benjamin asked, his small body tensing up under the excitement.

"Of course. Mommy is going to let you walk, ok?"

Megan put her son on the ground and he ran to the edge of the steps and then cautiously down them. It was amazing to watch the systematic approach her son had when it came to his morning routine. He would walk over to her chair, to the oak side table, grab the TV remote off it and then grab his favorite plush toy— Herman the hedgehog. Together Herman and Carl Benjamin would scale the heights of the couch and in always the same sequence. At first, Herman would fly to the top of the couch under Carl Benjamin's deceptive throwing power. Carl Benjamin would then follow up the great summit of Mount Couch using an unnerving cliffhanger approach where one of his legs would be resting on the cushions and the other wildly kicking in the air. His leg thrashing was never enough and the only way he was ever able to overcome the threshold was to claw his way up the cushion with his little matchstick fingers. Once Mount Couch was conquered, to the victors went the spoils. For Carl Benjamin and Herman the stuffed hedgehog, this was control over the TV before the warden of the house came in and took control. It was a ritual that Megan loved to see unfold given all she had lost since Ben had disappeared across the veil.

"Here you go sweetheart," Megan's voice radiated with love as she handed her son a blue bowl filled with cereal.

"Thant yo Momma."

"So CB, Mommy wants to tell you something. Can you listen to Mommy for a minute?" Megan asked, her tone growing more serious.

She knelt down in front of her son, whose eyes were affixed to the television and a group of dancing bears singing about popcorn rain. Megan guided her son's attention to her smiling face with the soft touch of her hand on his cheek. Looking back at her were those big brown eyes, the ones that she had fallen in love with back when the world seemed so simple.

"Tomorrow we are going to go see your Great Aunt Julie and Uncle Bobbo. Mommy told you before that she wants to find your Daddy, right?"

Carl Benjamin shook his head yes.

'Well, I need to keep looking for him and I need to go into the woods to do so. While I do that, you are going to stay with Julie and Bobbo. Do you understand?"

The toddler looked into his Mommy's eyes with confusion.

"No woods Mommy. Daddy not in woods."

Megan tilted her head in doubt to what she just heard.

"What did you just say C.B?"

"Daddy not in woods, Mommy."

"Hmm, then where is he?"

"Um… he's in farway place. I see him. He talks to me."

Megan stood up, a charge of fear running down her back.

"He talks to you? What does he say?"

330

"Ah, I dono. Sometimes he scared and ask for help, Mommy."

"C.B, why is Daddy scared?"

Carl Benjamin's gaze was redrawn to the television where the dancing bears were at it again.

"C.B, why is Daddy scared?" Megan implored, refocusing the toddler's attention.

The toddler smiled up at his mother, before shaking his head, "Daddy not alone. Daddy no come home."

Epilogue: Primordial

I see the creatures that scurry into the shadows; I see the beasts that burrow into our nightmares. They are the things that burn our hopes with flames fueled by our own despair. They are the things that turn all that we hold dear to ash and sinter. They are the flames that burn too hot...

Up Next in The Osworth Traveler Series:

The Origins of Osworth (Book 2)

One cannot hope to defeat life, for life holds the great equalizer— death.